D0429261

CALGARY PUBLIC LIBRARY

OCT   2017

THE ANTHILL MURDERS

Also by Hans Olav Lahlum

Hans Olav Lahlum

THE ANTHILL MURDERS

Translated from the Norwegian by
Kari Dickson

MANTLE

First published 2017 by Mantle
an imprint of Pan Macmillan
20 New Wharf Road, London N1 9RR
Associated companies throughout the world
www.panmacmillan.com

ISBN 978-1-5098-0952-3

Copyright © Hans Olav Lahlum 2014, 2017
English translation copyright © Kari Dickson 2017

Originally published in Norwegian in 2014 as *Maurtuemordene*
by Cappelen Damm, Oslo.

This translation has been published with the financial support of NORLA.

The right of Hans Olav Lahlum to be identified as the
author of this work has been asserted by him in accordance
with the Copyright, Designs and Patents Act 1988.

All rights reserved. No part of this publication may be reproduced,
stored in a retrieval system, or transmitted, in any form, or by any means
(electronic, mechanical, photocopying, recording or otherwise)
without the prior written permission of the publisher.

Pan Macmillan does not have any control over, or any responsibility for,
any author or third-party websites referred to in or on this book.

1 3 5 7 9 8 6 4 2

A CIP catalogue record for this book is available from the British Library.

Typeset by Ellipsis, Glasgow
Printed and bound by CPI Group (UK) Ltd, Croydon, CR0 4YY

This book is sold subject to the condition that it shall not, by way of
trade or otherwise, be lent, hired out, or otherwise circulated without
the publisher's prior consent in any form of binding or cover other than
that in which it is published and without a similar condition including
this condition being imposed on the subsequent purchaser.

Visit **www.panmacmillan.com** to read more about all our books
and to buy them. You will also find features, author interviews and
news of any author events, and you can sign up for e-newsletters
so that you're always first to hear about our new releases.

To

JONAS LIE

(1833–1908)

DAY ONE

A Very Unlikely Murder Victim

I

I have imagined standing here waiting every night for several weeks now. But today, Monday, 24 April 1972, I am actually here, for the first time.

My watch says ten to eleven. The evening is dark and wet. But the rain only adds to my excitement. When I left the house, I still had my doubts as to whether I could do this. Then, the moment I was finally standing here alone in the wind and rain, any doubts were blown from my mind. A neater formulation than I realized at first. I chuckle to myself. I've always known that I'm sharper than most people think.

There is even less traffic on the road at this time of night than I expected. I've been standing here waiting for nearly ten minutes now without seeing a soul, and only two cars have passed. No one will see us when the moment comes. And the rain will wash away any evidence I might leave behind by the roadside.

My body is quivering with anticipation. I, who normally feel a little sluggish even in the morning, feel more awake than ever, even though it's late. I would have done it tonight even if I knew that I couldn't get away with it tomorrow. It feels more and more like a duty, a kind of instinct that's always been there. Or even a divine task that I have to perform *before I can return to daily life. I just have to be strong. And afterwards, I need to be quick and clear-headed to avoid getting caught.*

I can't see anyone yet in the dark, but I can hear her footsteps. Ever since I was a lad, I've had exceptional hearing and a knack of remembering different people's footsteps. When I was two, I could identify my grandparents on the street from the balcony of their second-floor flat. And I recognize her footsteps instantly. They belong to the young woman I'm waiting for. She's beautiful, but cold. A woman of hot promises, with a heart of ice. The kind of girl who apparently forgets to do up the top buttons on her blouse, who likes men to notice, but has no intention of letting them see more.

I'm standing here waiting to kill one of those women who love only themselves. That's why I don't think she deserves to live. I'm perfectly aware that it's actually not about her – it's purely about me and my own self-interest. In that sense, I discovered myself a long time ago. And now it remains to be seen if anyone else will.

I have several times, most recently on Friday, heard her say that she nearly always walks this way between a quarter to eleven and five to eleven on a Monday. She's obviously a little late this evening. People are so unreliable these days, particularly young women. It's three minutes to eleven now and, hearing the sound of her quick steps drawing nearer, I finally see her emerge from the dark, about twenty yards away.

Her steps slow down – because she's seen me standing here, and I've put out my hand to stop her.

Already, a few weeks ago, I'd worked out what will happen. First she'll stop for a moment. Then she'll feel uneasy and wonder what's going on. Then she'll recognize me. And she'll relax a little, perhaps even deign to say something vacuous and patronizing. My guess is that she'll show no imagination whatsoever and simply ask why I'm standing here. Then the reality and horror of the situation will dawn on her –

when she is close enough to see a different expression in my eyes. She will quickly understand why I'm standing here. But by then it will be too late.

She's taller than me. I often feel that she looks down at me whenever we meet. But I'm far stronger and much better prepared. I will put my hands round her soft, white neck long before she manages to scream or put up a fight. And then all I need to do is squeeze. Squeeze and squeeze, as hard and as fast as I can, until she's lying dead at my feet. And afterwards, I will walk calmly away and hide myself among the masses in the city.

She stops. I take two steps towards her and look up, so she can see my face.

'Oh, it's you. What are you doing here so late in the evening?' she says.

Her voice is less patronizing and more anxious than I'd expected. I feel a whisper of sympathy – the last traces of doubt. We look at each other for a moment. But it's too late – both for her and for me. I see that she understands as soon as I reach my hands out towards her.

She doesn't scream. Just stands there without making a sound, petrified, while my hands tighten round her throat and squeeze harder and harder. For a few seconds I feel her warm breath on my face. Then it stops without warning. Suddenly she collapses, a little sooner than anticipated.

II

'Agnes Halvorsen,' I said.

Neither of the other two said a word in response. It was five to midnight, the air was heavy with rain and the atmosphere by the roadside in Hovseter was bleak.

The constable to my right glanced briefly at the student

card in my hand and nodded. It said: HALVORSEN, AGNES, in capital letters. The photograph was of the woman who was now lying lifeless between us. Her tongue, which could not be seen in the photograph, was slightly blue and sticking out of her mouth. But the shoulder-length blonde hair and blue eyes were the same, and the necklace was the same – as was the small mole high up on her right cheek.

Agnes Halvorsen was lying on her back by the edge of the road, staring at us with wide eyes. She had nothing on her head and was wearing a long green raincoat. A silver cross lay in the hollow of her throat and a bit lower down, a white blouse could be glimpsed. A calf-length black skirt was visible under the green coat. The deceased had been a tall and presumably very beautiful young woman. I felt that there was something wrong with her clothes but, annoyingly, I could not put my finger on what it was.

According to her student card, Agnes Halvorsen was in her second year at the Norwegian School of Theology and would have turned twenty-two in a month. Just over an hour ago she had been at her best friend's house, drinking tea and chatting about their studies and life, as they did nearly every Monday. Then just over half an hour ago, her friend had found her dead. The friend lived about eighty yards back down the road – and it was no more than fifty or sixty yards in the other direction to the deceased's home. The friend had found her lying here in the dark and the bruising on her neck seemed to indicate that she had been strangled.

That was all that I knew so far about Agnes Halvorsen's life and far too early death.

'I was supposed to move away from home in March. And Agnes would be alive now if I had. But it wasn't my fault. There were no rooms available in the student halls until May,' said the dark-haired young woman standing to my left. She had given her name as Nora Jensen, but for the time being, I simply thought of her as the best friend. She seemed to be a good best friend, and was genuinely upset.

I thought to myself that it would be hard for the young Nora to live with the now fatal implications of her postponed move. Out loud, I said that she could not possibly have guessed that this would happen and that she must not blame herself in any way. She swallowed and nodded, but said nothing.

Her silence felt increasingly awkward. I followed up by asking if she had last seen Agnes Halvorsen alive at ten to eleven.

The best friend nodded gratefully and rushed to answer.

'Yes, it was just like I said. We normally finish off around half past ten, but were having such a nice time tonight that we sat and chatted until ten to eleven. Agnes never worried about walking alone late at night. She knew that I was more nervous about it, so she always phoned as soon as she got home. She was fit and walked fast, so it usually didn't take more than a couple of minutes. You can imagine how anxious I was by five past and then ten past eleven, when she still hadn't called.'

I could well imagine – and almost felt the friend's fear rising as soon as there was silence. So I asked her to tell me again how she found the body.

'I called the parsonage twice at twelve minutes past eleven, but there was no reply. Her brother moved out last year, and her parents were away for a few days, so I got really worried when Agnes didn't answer the phone herself. After the second try, I threw on my coat and ran out. I found her a few minutes later. She was lying here lifeless with her tongue sticking out, her eyes staring straight at me. I was overcome by fear for my own life, so I'm ashamed to say I turned on my heel and ran home as though the devil was after me. As soon as I was safely indoors, I called the police.'

She had already told exactly the same story once before, but it was still convincing. The friend had sounded both out of breath and frightened when she called the main police station just before half past eleven, but had been remarkably clear about what she had seen and where.

I said to the friend that she had dealt with the tragedy very well and that no one could have done better. But then I asked her to think carefully again all the same, to be absolutely sure that she had not seen or heard anyone else outside before she found the body.

She shook her head.

'I've been running through what happened as I've been standing here. I was scared when I ran out and terrified when I ran home again . . . but I didn't see or hear anyone else.'

It still sounded very convincing. Regardless of whether Agnes Halvorsen's murderer had been standing here waiting or walking in the opposite direction, he would hardly have hung around after the murder. All things taken into account, it seemed that the murderer had killed her right here where I was standing, just before eleven o'clock. And that he then had been smart enough or lucky enough to get away before the friend turned up fifteen minutes later.

I heard myself asking whether she had noticed if Agnes had been anxious or uneasy about anything. Had she known if Agnes was worried about a present or previous boyfriend, or an unwanted admirer?

'No, no, I wouldn't have let her walk home alone if she was.

Agnes didn't have a boyfriend, and as far as I know, never has had one. She had a strict upbringing and was rather proper that way. She was just normal this evening. Looking forward to tomorrow and a bit worried about the exams next week.'

Her voice started to break when she said this. Then once again, there was silence. I wondered if Agnes Halvorsen had seen her attacker's face in the dark – and, if so, had she recognized him? It would certainly make the case less difficult to solve, though no case was ever easy. The rain had become heavier and there was no reason to believe that the perpetrator had been helpful enough to leave behind any evidence.

Agnes Halvorsen's handbag was lying on the ground beside her. I was holding her purse in my hand. Apart from the student card and a monthly travel pass for Oslo Transport, it contained two fifty-kroner notes, three ten-kroner notes and two one-krone coins. This was slightly more cash than one might expect a young woman to carry with her, but by no means a surprising amount.

There was nothing to indicate that Agnes Halvorsen had had financial worries. And there was no reason to believe that robbery had been a motive.

Other than her purse, the handbag contained nothing more than two lipsticks, a handkerchief and a key ring with two unmarked keys on it. And a small scrap of paper, about an inch long and slightly less wide. I looked at it, puzzled. It was a drawing, and judging by the sharp edges, it had been cut out of a book.

'Do you know if she usually carried this with her?' I asked, showing the piece of paper to her friend.

She looked it for a few seconds, then quickly shook her head.

'No, I've never seen it before, and I find it hard to believe that she'd keep it in her bag. Agnes was a very tidy person and always threw away any bits of papers or notes that she no longer needed. She didn't have any younger brothers or sisters, so she didn't read children's books. And she wasn't particularly interested in animals, certainly not insects. No, it doesn't seem very likely that she'd carry it around with her.'

I stood there and studied the small drawing of a brown ant, with the odd certainty that this apparently insignificant find could be very important to the investigation. Either, for some unknown reason, the twenty-one-year-old Agnes Halvorsen had suddenly started to carry around a picture of an ant cut out from a children's book, or the murderer, for reasons that were even more unclear, had left it in her handbag.

As we stood there, it suddenly dawned on me what was wrong with her clothing. Beneath the raincoat, her blouse had been buttoned up wrongly. And that did not tally with the impression I had of the deceased so far. I promptly asked her friend if her blouse had been buttoned up wrongly an hour earlier.

Nora Jensen gasped and swayed for a moment, but managed to stay on her feet and her voice was controlled when she spoke.

'No, I am almost a hundred per cent certain that it wasn't. Agnes said she couldn't breathe properly if her blouse was buttoned all the way up in warm rooms, so she often left the top buttons undone. I've never known her to button her blouse up wrongly, and I'm pretty sure that it wasn't like that this evening. We were sitting opposite each other, so I would have noticed and said something.'

All three of us looked down at the dead woman and the buttoning on her blouse. Her best friend sobbed quietly.

The constable rather unexpectedly came to my aid. He remarked that there was no sign of a struggle and that she still had her skirt on, so the detail with the blouse probably meant nothing.

I said that I agreed. Nora Jensen said nothing, but she breathed more easily on hearing this. The late Agnes Halvorsen's wrongly buttoned blouse was nonetheless a new puzzle within the greater mystery, and it bothered me.

III

By half past midnight, the crime scene had been cordoned off and the ambulance and the forensics team had arrived. I left the constable on duty, and took the best friend home. She thanked me politely, and looked around twice before letting herself into the house. The door handle moved three times after she had gone in; she clearly wanted to make sure that the door was locked. I guessed that Nora Jensen had always been Agnes Halvorsen's slightly shorter and more nervous best friend, but tonight she had shown that she possessed both fortitude and initiative, all the same.

After she had disappeared into the house, I paused for a few minutes, then walked back past the scene of the crime to the parsonage where Agnes Halvorsen had lived.

No one answered the door when I rang the bell, but the outside light was on. The parsonage in Hovseter was a big, brown, elegant wooden house, and the garden was exceptionally well tended and lush for the time of year. According to the nameplate by the doorbell, Valdemar, Henriette, Helmer and Agnes Halvorsen lived there. Only that was no longer true. I felt rather uncomfortable standing there looking at the nameplate.

And I felt no less uncomfortable when I let myself in with the dead woman's keys. I told myself it was my duty to check that there were no fresh clues in the deceased's home. The large key turned smoothly in the lock.

The house was almost irritatingly tidy and orderly. The parents had obviously hung any outer garments they were not using in the wardrobe before they left. A yellow summer jacket was the only thing hanging in the hall. And I guessed it belonged to Agnes Halvorsen herself. But there was no way of knowing whether she had got it out for the summer, or had swapped it for the raincoat earlier in the evening. Whatever the case, it was not a happy sight. The jacket was there for another summer which its owner would never see. I took my shoes off in the hall and carried on into the house in my socks.

I discovered a more childish side of the late Agnes Halvorsen upstairs. On one of the bedroom doors, it said *Agnes' Queendom* in big red, green and blue letters, presumably a sign she had hung up when she was a girl, and which had just been left.

Behind the door, however, was the room of a now grown-up and serious young woman. There was a Norwegian Bible on the desk, and two German theology books, with long titles that I would struggle to pronounce correctly. The bookshelf was full of secondary-school books, as well as textbooks for theology and the university entrance exam. There were no children's books, with the exception of a children's Bible, and nor were there any books about ants or other insects.

The bed was neatly made with clean sheets, and there was not so much as a speck of dust to be seen on the bedside table. If Agnes Halvorsen had any idols, none of them had been given space on her walls. Nor had any possible loves. But there was a photograph from her confirmation, showing a younger Agnes together with her rather round parents and dark-haired older brother. And a class photograph from secondary school, where the only person I recognized, apart from Agnes Halvorsen herself, was her friend, Nora Jensen. I thought it was rather fitting that Agnes was the tallest and Nora the smallest in the row of girls, and that Agnes also towered above most of the boys.

The desk drawers contained chronologically filed notes from lectures and seminars, and a certificate for her final school grades, which were remarkable. But nothing else of any interest.

I didn't know exactly what else I had hoped to find when I opened the drawers, only that I hadn't found it. There were no secret love letters and no mysterious pictures of unknown people. In short, there was no trace of any potential murderer or any possible motive.

The late Agnes Halvorsen had indisputably been killed, but had so far proved to be a very unlikely victim.

On the back of the door was a timetable of her lectures at the School of Theology. I dutifully noted that she had no lectures the following day, but that she had been to one between two and four that afternoon. The lecture notes were lying on top of the pile in the top desk-drawer. The fact that Agnes Halvorsen had been to the lecture might throw light on her final hours.

The door to Agnes' Queendom had been unlocked when I

opened it. But on the way out, it occurred to me that I should check whether the other key on her key ring was for this door. And this proved to be the case.

As I stood there, the silence was suddenly broken when a large cuckoo clock in the dining room announced that it was one o'clock. It had a point. There was not much I could do to advance the case alone here in the dark. So I locked the parsonage door at Hovseter, as carefully and quietly as I had unlocked it, returned to my car, and drove home.

And even after I had fallen asleep, I was haunted by the blue tongue and staring eyes of the minister's daughter.

DAY TWO

A Missing Motive, Two Key Questions and Two Alarming Details

I

On Tuesday, 25 April 1972, I was woken by the alarm clock at seven, and was out of bed before the second hand had even completed a round.

Last night's murder had been discovered too late to be included in the morning papers. *Arbeiderbladet* once again expressed concern that Willy Brandt, the social democrat and friend of Norway, might have to step down as a result of the political crisis in West Germany and that this would in turn exacerbate the difference between east and west in Europe. *Aftenposten* focused on the EEC debate and whether it might pave the way for a new blue coalition government.

In the shower, I mused that it was almost a law of nature that my need to sleep disappeared as soon as I was working on a murder investigation. In quieter periods, I often found it difficult to get out of bed when the alarm rang. I had even been late to work a couple of times. But as soon as I had a murder investigation, I leapt out of bed in the morning and was wide awake straight away. My hunting instinct took hold and my adrenaline levels soared – and remained high until the investigation was over.

It was only four weeks since my last case closed, but I had had the time I needed to recuperate and was now ready for a new investigation. I reflected on the events of the night before as I ate breakfast and drove down to the main police station. I reached no further conclusion about Agnes Halvorsen's death, but this did not dampen my spirits. A new hunt had started and I was determined to finish it.

I was outside the door to my boss's office by five to eight, and he arrived, as usual, at eight o'clock on the dot. My boss was a serious older gentleman, who was rather formal. It was said that his children called him by their surname. But we were starting to get to know each other quite well by now. He nodded briefly at me and left the door open when he went into his office.

'I presume that you would like to lead the case involving the minister's daughter from Hovseter,' he said, as we sat down on either side of his desk.

This was said more as a confirmation and without a hint of humour. I replied in an equally matter-of-fact tone that I most definitely would, but my heart was hammering all the harder: to be taken off the case now would be a defeat.

My boss gave an almost imperceptible nod, before asking me to give him a summary of the case so far.

It took me no longer than ten minutes to fill him in on the previous night's events. I concluded that the case was, for the moment, pretty straightforward and would not require a large investigation. I added, however, that it was by no means a clear-cut case and so it might perhaps be best if I led it myself.

My boss nodded again – more obviously this time.

'And I would like you to do that too. But I would like another detective to be with you on the case from the start. What about Danielsen or Helgesen?'

I took a deep breath – and instantly knew the answer. Vegard Danielsen and I were still the two youngest detective inspectors in the force and had previously not seen eye to eye. But then we suddenly seemed to reach a mutual understanding during my last murder case. I could well have died, had it not been for the help I got from Danielsen, and he could have been dishonoured and unemployed, had it not been for the help he got from me. But following an unexpectedly emotional conversation at the end of the case, we had done little more than exchange routine information.

I was fairly sure that Danielsen would prefer not to work so closely with me again so soon. I would certainly be happier to keep a degree of distance. Vilhelm Helgesen was a very different kettle of fish: ten years older than me, a hard worker with a lower rank and no ambitions. He would no doubt be a good and unproblematic subordinate – and that was what I needed right now.

I said that I thought that Helgesen was perhaps best suited to this investigation. Then I added that it was of course my boss's decision – and that it might perhaps be best if he made any announcements himself.

'Certainly,' my boss said. Then he picked up the phone, dialled a number and said succinctly: 'Can you come in?'

Vilhelm Helgesen knocked on the door barely a minute and a half later. One of Helgesen's good qualities was that he was so unlike a policeman in many ways, and he did not dominate when he came into the room or when he sat down by the desk. He was of average height and slightly overweight, a middle-aged family man, who might equally well have been a taxi driver or a factory worker. But I did recognize a sense of excitement and the hunting instinct in him too. He straightened up in his chair when my boss explained the case to him in a few sentences. When asked whether he would he assist me with the investigation, he promptly replied: 'Of course.'

There was much that I appreciated about Helgesen, but right now, more than anything, it was the fact that he was not DI Danielsen. And what was more, he was efficiency itself and did not like to waste his own time or that of others. The same was true of our boss, who without further ado asked what my plans were.

I replied that we should get to work straight away. I would follow up the family and the friend who had found her. Helgesen could start at the School of Theology and as far as possible try to reconstruct what Agnes Halvorsen had done earlier in the day and whom she had met. If he had time, he could also check with local bus drivers to see if they could remember any passengers travelling to or from the stops near Hovseter between half past ten and half past eleven the night before. We could meet back at the station as soon as possible after lunch, and hopefully the pathologist would have his preliminary report ready by then.

'Good,' my boss said.

Helgesen asked if I would like him to bring anyone of interest from the School of Theology or Oslo Transport back here, and simply replied 'Fine,' when I said that I would leave that to his discretion.

We were just about to stand up when my boss unexpectedly spoke again.

'Check whether she has a man in her life, or several for that matter. When young women are killed, the answer often lies in their closest circle. But there is something here I don't like; a small detail makes me wonder if this case is in fact not that simple.'

'Are you thinking about the ant?' I asked.

My boss gave a curt nod, but said nothing more. Helgesen did the same.

I thought to myself that at the start of this investigation, we, the police, were all singing from the same song sheet, but were all equally perplexed. I hoped that we would find something at Hovseter or the School of Theology that might change this. At the same time, I thanked my lucky stars that I was already going to dinner in Frogner that evening. I was strangely certain that I would once again have need for my unofficial adviser, Patricia.

II

At twenty minutes to nine, I rang the parsonage at Hovseter. The voice that answered belonged to a young man, but was extremely serious. It was, as I guessed, Helmer Halvorsen, Agnes' older brother. He had been woken by the bishop himself ringing on the doorbell to tell of his sister's death, and had managed to contact his parents by telephone. They were on their way back from a visit to Telemark, but were not likely to be in town before half past ten. He would stay in his childhood home until they came, and would of course be available should the police want to ask any questions.

Helmer Halvorsen sounded calm and collected, and it would be a clear advantage if I could talk to him alone before his parents arrived. I therefore promptly agreed. Five minutes later I was in the car on my way to Hovseter again.

I recognized the man who opened the door from the family photograph I had seen in his sister's room the evening before. He still had dark hair and was slightly shorter than his sister had been. His face was serious, but showed no sign of tears, and his handshake was firm, if brief.

I politely declined the offer of tea or coffee. There was a large glass of water on his side of the table, but as far as I could see it remained untouched.

Someone had once described an older teacher from my secondary school as having drunk too much cold water. It struck me that this description might also be fitting for the twenty-seven-year-old Helmer Halvorsen. He spoke clearly and logically, but without any form of real engagement or emotion. Given the circumstances, I was impressed. I would certainly not have been so controlled if my little sister had just been killed.

Even as he answered my first question, I got the feeling there was not much help to be had here, despite the fact that he was clear and concise and appeared to have an excellent memory.

He started by saying that his sister's death had come as 'a bolt from the blue' and that he found it impossible to understand why anyone would want to kill her. According to her brother, Agnes Halvorsen had a 'very good and straightforward' relationship with both him and their parents, as well as the rest of the family. She did not have a boyfriend, as far as he knew, nor had she ever had one.

Helmer Halvorsen hesitated a moment when I asked if she would have told him if she had a boyfriend. His reply was that he might perhaps not be the first to know, which was plausible enough, but that he and his parents would no doubt have noticed pretty quickly. Agnes lived at home and did not go out much, other than to university.

When she was a teenager, Agnes Halvorsen had sung in a choir and played tennis, but she had then settled down to focus on her end-of-school exams and Christian activities. She participated in several of the parish youth groups, and every now and then met up with friends from school. Nora Jensen was the only name he could remember off the top of his head; she was a fellow student and the only friend who came to visit regularly.

Helmer Halvorsen had never considered his sister to be particularly interested in animals and even less so in insects. If anyone in the family was interested in science, it was him, though his sister had achieved good grades. Midges and wasps were the only living creatures he had seen his sister kill, he added with a cautious smile. The word 'ant' said nothing to him, and he was polite enough not to query why I had asked.

He told me that he himself had studied biology at university and now had a permanent job as a science teacher at Persbråten secondary school. He lived alone in Makrellbekken, but was engaged to a primary-school teacher and they planned to get married in the summer. His sister had been very happy about the engagement and had got on well with her future sister-in-law on the few occasions that they had met. As far as her brother knew, Agnes did not have any enemies.

Helmer Halvorsen hesitated a moment again when I asked if his sister's choice of study had caused any friction in the family. He then replied that there had initially been some pressure on him to study theology, and that his sister had in turn been encouraged to study something else. Both children had, however, managed to get their way, and their parents had respected their wishes. 'Our parents are somewhat conservative in terms of their religion, but they are very fond of me and adored Agnes,' was how he put it. I caught a whiff of a clue when he said that, but could not put my finger on it.

Helmer Halvorsen was equally calm and collected when he answered the more difficult question that followed. Now that his sister was dead, he was sole heir to his parents' wealth. The house came with his father's job and the family had 'always prioritized spiritual values over material values'. His parents had been open about the fact that they had around 30,000 kroner in the bank, and Helmer guessed that the total inheritance would be in the region of 50,000 kroner. But he was not likely to inherit this for a good many years, as his parents were still in their fifties and in good health. There was nothing to indicate that Helmer Halvorsen would need his sister's share of the inheritance, either now or later.

Helmer Halvorsen almost had an alibi for the time that his sister was killed, but it was only almost. His fiancée would be able to confirm that they had had supper together the evening before, and then spent the rest of the evening at his place, until she went to catch the bus at ten to eleven. This would make the timing tight, but not impossible. Makrellbekken was only a few minutes' drive from Hovseter.

It was an uncomfortable situation. However, Helmer Halvorsen understood very well that I had to ask questions about his parents' financial situation and his alibi for the previous evening, and he was helpful and precise in his responses. He repeated several times that he hoped I would be able to shed light on who had killed his sister, but he could tell me nothing that might help to identify who had done it. Even though I did not look forward to meeting the parents, it was almost a relief when I heard a car stop in front of the house.

III

Helmer Halvorsen jumped up and hurried out to meet his parents in the hall. Soon afterwards, they came into the living room to speak to me. Their son, however, only popped his head round the door to ask if I had any more questions for him, and then withdrew when I said I had none for the moment.

Reverend Valdemar Halvorsen was a tall, sturdy man, with dark hair and a serious, furrowed face. The resemblance to his son became apparent when I shook his hand; his grasp was equally firm, dry and brief. In contrast, his wife was trembling and she held my hand for some time. Henriette Halvorsen was slightly plump with greying hair. I could see a likeness to her daughter in her face, but not her build.

They accepted my condolences with the briefest thanks. Understandably enough, they both looked very sombre, but neither of them was crying. In this way, their son took after them, and I wondered if the daughter had been the same.

It was the deceased's father who unexpectedly broke the silence, before I had time to ask a question.

'The ways of Our Lord are often inscrutable even to those of faith. I have never found them more inscrutable than in the early hours of this morning. Our daughter, who was our little angel throughout her childhood, remained firm in her faith. We could not understand at first why God had taken her from us in this way. But now we understand that it was essentially we who betrayed both God and our daughter.'

His voice was muted and intense. The differences between the minister and his son were becoming more apparent.

I sensed a possible generational conflict in the family and therefore asked what he meant.

'We tried to let our children live their own lives. I am in no doubt that it was the right thing to do, but we perhaps let it go too far in terms of their studies. God told us clearly that He wanted Agnes to follow another path, not to become a priest. If we had been firmer with her, she might still have been alive today.'

I looked cautiously over at his wife, but she gave a resolute nod and agreed with her husband.

I was taken aback and initially did not know what to say. I tried to offer some words of comfort, to say that they must not blame themselves for their daughter's death. The killer alone was responsible, and the police would prioritize catching him.

I expected a positive response, but did not get one. They exchanged fleeting glances. Somewhat surprisingly, it was the minister's wife who broke the increasingly oppressive silence.

'Are you a believer, my young man?'

Once again, I felt I had to weigh my words like gold. My initial response was that my life philosophy was a private matter and of no relevance to the investigation. Then, when they still said nothing, I added that I was not a member of the state church or any other denomination.

'In that case, there is no point in discussing this aspect of the case any further. Ask whatever secular questions you wish, and we will answer as truthfully as we can. As far as we understand, it was a stranger who killed our daughter. We would of course like to know who he is and why he did it. But this stranger could never have killed our daughter if God was still watching over her. We will always feel that we are in some way to blame for that.'

The minister was sounding more and more like a prophet from the Old Testament. Again, I looked to his wife for her reaction, and again she nodded in agreement. They had obviously discussed it on the way here.

To me, as a younger non-believer, it seemed absurd. If I had been in their situation, I might possibly have lost faith in God, and would certainly not under any circumstances have assumed the blame. At the same time, I accepted that it was a personal matter that I could not change, and it was none of my business. I was obliged to respect the family's faith and perception of reality, no matter how misguided they might seem to me. Furthermore, it was not unusual for parents to blame themselves in some way for a child's death.

I therefore said that my job was to catch the killer, not to discuss questions of faith, and as such I wanted to ask some specific questions about their daughter and her life.

They nodded more or less in tandem.

The rest of the conversation was less confrontational and more constructive. The deceased's parents confirmed that their investments and property were worth roughly 50,000 kroner. They had always considered their relationship with their daughter to be good. With the exception of a few tentative suggestions about secretarial college and home economics, they had not wanted to cause any conflict about her choice of study. She had never asked her father for help with her studies, and he had not wanted to impose. They could not remember their daughter ever being particularly bothered about animals of any kind.

They gave the names of four classmates, but Nora Jensen was the only one they had seen since Agnes left school. Their daughter had never introduced them to any men, and they were pretty certain that she had never had a boyfriend. They were not aware of her being at loggerheads with anyone, be they man or woman.

As far as practical circumstances were concerned, the parents' statement tallied with that of the brother – and did not further the investigation by even a single step. Otherwise, the parents had been at a dinner party in Skien until around ten o'clock the evening before and therefore had an indisputable alibi.

They both stood up as soon as I did, and followed me out. The father shook my hand and wished me luck with the investigation, as did the mother, but with a slightly shaky voice.

We all hesitated by the door. It felt as though they wanted to say more, but in the end, the mother simply repeated that they were certain there had never been a man in her daughter's life, although if I discovered otherwise in the course of the investigation, they would appreciate being told the truth. They were of course keen for the case to be solved and would be ready to answer any questions I might have, whenever that might be.

I politely withdrew, just as the clock struck half past eleven. I hoped that the victim's best friend would be able to tell me more today, but I doubted it.

I almost bumped my head on the unusually low door frame on my way out, which seemed symbolic of my situation with regards to the investigation.

IV

Nora Jensen lived in a two-storey terraced house. From the outside, it was far less ostentatious than the parsonage I had just left. It looked as if all the lights were out. The outside door was locked and there was no response when I rang the bell first once, then twice. However, as I turned to go, I did notice a curtain moving upstairs, and the door was opened before I had a chance to ring the bell for a third time.

'Sorry I didn't open straight away. I couldn't sleep last night and don't really feel myself yet,' Nora Jensen said.

Her eyes were puffy and her voice and hands were trembling. She seemed to be even smaller and more fragile in daylight than when I had seen her the night before. Nora Jensen was, in other words, not a pretty sight as she stood there alone in the doorway, but I immediately felt great sympathy for her. She was perhaps weaker than Agnes Halvorsen's parents and brother, but appeared to be far more emotional.

I assured her that it was perfectly understandable that she was not feeling herself, given that she had found her best friend dead the night before, but I hoped that we could talk a little more about what had happened, all the same.

She said yes, and opened the door for me. Her parents had gone to work before she got up and would be back in the afternoon, she told me in a quiet voice. I realized that she felt more secure knowing that she wouldn't be on her own in the evening, but that she dreaded talking to her parents about what had happened. It was not hard to sympathize with these feelings.

There was a pot of coffee and a half-full cup on the

otherwise empty table in the living room. Nora Jensen disappeared out into the kitchen and came back with a cup for me, before sinking down into an armchair by her own cup.

'This can't be easy for you,' I said, by way of opening the conversation.

She let out a heavy sigh, but then leaned forward and answered in a stronger voice.

'Finding your best friend dead is a shock and a loss I wouldn't wish on anyone. And when you find her only a hundred yards from your house, you can't help but fear for your own life. They say that talking to someone about your sorrows and fears can help, and obviously, if I can, I really want to help you find the monster who killed Agnes.'

The word 'monster' was unexpected. I realized that Nora was possibly stronger than I thought. So I swiftly asked if she had anything to add to her statement from the night before.

This did not produce any results. Nora sighed and drank the rest of her coffee before she replied that unfortunately she did not. She couldn't think of anyone who might have had something against Agnes. And she couldn't imagine that anyone in their circle of friends would have a motive for killing her. Agnes Halvorsen's life had been so routine that it was hard to believe she had any secrets.

'If I was to say not what I know, but what I believe . . .' she said, tentatively.

I told her I would listen carefully to anything she had to say – I would listen to whatever people wanted to tell me, be it what they thought or knew.

She attempted a smile, but managed no more than to show a couple of rather large front teeth.

'Thank you. In that case, I believe more and more strongly

that Agnes must have been in the wrong place at the wrong time, and is a random victim. It doesn't make it any less tragic, but it does make the question as to why anyone would want to kill Agnes less incomprehensible.'

I had played with the same thought myself, but was not supposed to share my theories with her. And in any case, it was not a very uplifting thought. If the murderer was a man with no links to Agnes Halvorsen's life, we had no clues as to who he might be.

I dutifully jotted down what she had said. Then I asked if she knew whether there had been any conflict with Agnes' family and friends about her choice of study.

Nora Jensen tilted her head to one side, and then held up a hand. 'I refuse to believe that that's where you'll find a motive for murder. Agnes spoke about it a little when we first applied to the School of Theology. At the time she was upset because she could tell that her parents were strongly opposed to it, and she was very grateful to them that they didn't make a fuss. Her brother supported her choice, so there was no problem there. If they ever discussed it later as a family, she certainly never told me.'

My next question was about reactions and possible conflicts within the school.

'Agnes and I were the only female students in our year. We know that some of the male students were very glad to have us there, whereas others didn't want us there at all. The same is true of the lecturers. And while no one has changed their mind over the years, there has never been any outright conflict. I have to say I find the idea that a Christian man in Oslo in 1972 could strangle a Christian woman in order to prevent her becoming a minister absurd.'

She said this with surprising strength and conviction. The idea did seem utterly ridiculous to me as well. But I still found myself clutching at straws for want of a better explanation.

I switched tack and asked if Agnes had had a personal tutor. Nora Jensen replied faster this time.

'Yes, Oscar Fredrik Bergendahl. He's also my tutor. He's in his early forties and young to be a professor, but he's very clever and very nice. In fact, he's one of the most liberal theologians in the school. He's heavily involved with solidarity work in South America and an open advocate of women priests.'

I wrote down the supervisor's name as someone else we needed to talk to. Then finally, I asked if I was correct in thinking that the next lecture was tomorrow, and whether she was thinking of going.

Nora Jensen sighed heavily. Then she said in an even more subdued voice than before that there was a lecture at a quarter past twelve tomorrow, and that there would probably be some kind of memorial for Agnes. She felt that she had to go, but didn't know if she could face leaving the house. Just taking the bus without Agnes would feel like an ordeal right now.

I said that it would be good if she could go to the lecture, and that I had thought of going myself so I could pick her up on the way, if that made it any easier.

If I had hoped she would show any sign of pleasure at this, I was disappointed. Nora Jensen simply said 'yes please', in the same staccato voice, with the same expressionless face.

She must have heard that her own voice was not particularly enthusiastic. She certainly then thanked me more warmly for my 'very generous' offer and added that she looked forward to seeing me again tomorrow. It was just that fear and grief still hung over her and her home like heavy clouds.

Nora Jensen wished me luck with the investigation, and said she would be happy to answer any questions whenever needed, and that she would be extremely grateful for any further news about her friend's death. She hoped it might be easier to move on if she knew what had happened, she added hesitantly.

I left the house without looking back, but then turned around on impulse as I closed the gate. I couldn't see Nora Jensen from the road, but the movement of the curtains told me that she was standing by the window. If nothing else, I had to find Agnes Halvorsen's killer so that Nora Jensen could have her answer and move on with her life.

V

The police station was a little more frantic than usual when I got there at a quarter past one, after a quick lunch. Helgesen was still not back and had not phoned. On the other hand, more and more journalists from various papers were now calling about yesterday's death. I promised the switchboard that I would get a press release to them within the next thirty minutes, and then hurried to my office to write it.

There was a small, modest man in a suit waiting outside my office, who I immediately recognized as one of the best pathologists from forensics. His full name was Haldor Jørgensen, but here at the station he was simply known as Pathologist Jørgensen. No doubt as a result of his profession, he was terribly serious, and always correct and reliable.

As soon as he saw me, Pathologist Jørgensen said that the autopsy of the Hovseter victim was not yet complete, but that a couple of results were already clear. And he had come immediately to tell me in person.

I very much appreciated this and asked him to come into my office.

Without further ado, Pathologist Jørgensen started to give me a short report of the main points in his ever-steady voice.

'We will have to wait a day or so before the full autopsy report is ready, but the main conclusions are clear, given the physical injuries. The woman shows all the signs of death by strangulation. Given the marks on her throat, it would appear that this was done with bare hands. There is nothing to indicate that rope or anything else was used.'

'Can we conclude from this that the murderer is a strong man?'

The pathologist pulled a face, and shook his head hesitantly.

'That would simply be guessing. It is unlikely that the murderer is old or handicapped, and more likely that it is a man than a woman. But a young and determined woman, who was in good shape, would also be capable of this, particularly if the victim was taken by surprise. It is not unusual for shock to result in paralysis, and the victim's ability to fight back is quickly reduced if the attacker manages to get a firm hold and squeeze. It's most likely that it is a man between eighteen and fifty, but we can't rule anything out. And other than the marks on the victim's neck, there doesn't appear to be any clue on the body that might help the investigation.'

I looked at him in surprise and followed this up with another question when he didn't take the hint.

'That is to say, you haven't found any signs of sexual assault on the body?'

The pathologist did not say anything for a moment, but then carried on in the same steady voice.

'Quite the contrary, I would say. Her blouse had been buttoned up wrongly, and may well have been opened and closed by the killer. But her dress and underwear were intact. In fact, this is one of the few cases where one could say with absolute certainty that the perpetrator, if it was a man, has had no sexual contact with the victim. That is to say, no man has ever had sexual contact with her.'

I looked at him quizzically, but again had to ask a question to get him to say more.

'What you're saying, in other words, is that at the time of her death Agnes Halvorsen was still a virgin?'

'There is absolutely no doubt about it. She was fully intact.'

I suddenly did not feel like talking to the pathologist any more, and it seemed that he had no more to tell me either. So I thanked him for the information.

He said, 'You're welcome,' then stood up and left, without looking back.

I sat there on my own, deep in thought. It felt as though the little information I had been given only made the murder more inexplicable. At the same time it made the case even more tragic, as Agnes Halvorsen had been killed before she could experience real love.

I wrote a short, routine press release confirming that a young woman had been found dead by the roadside in Hovseter the night before, that the dead woman had been identified as twenty-one-year-old Agnes Halvorsen, and that the death was being treated as suspicious. I added a request that any witnesses who had been in the area between half past ten and half past eleven in the evening should contact Oslo police immediately.

I knew that I had only been half concentrating as I wrote the press release – and realized when I checked the spelling that I had not even been that. I fed a new piece of paper into the typewriter, forced myself to concentrate for three minutes, and wrote the press release again without spelling mistakes. I took it to my boss first, and then to the switchboard.

My boss had no comments on the press release, and no advice to give me with regards to the investigation. Helgesen had still not come back from the School of Theology. And I had no idea how to proceed with this unusually puzzling murder case.

So at ten to two I dialled one of the seven numbers, apart from my own, that I knew by heart. I knew the phone numbers of my parents, my younger sister and my boss, as well as the switchboard at the main station. Then there were two that I had not managed to forget but could no longer use: those of my former fiancée, Miriam Filtvedt Bentsen, at the halls of residence at Sogn, and of her parents in Lillehammer. The last and best number that I could remember was the one I now used: that of my friend and secret adviser, Patricia Louise I. E. Borchmann in Frogner.

VI

I felt more confident about ringing Patricia now than I had the first time I called her in connection with my previous murder investigation, just over a month before. Much had changed in the meantime. I was no longer engaged. And the conclusion of that case had brought Patricia and me closer, on a personal level, than we had ever been before.

This time we had continued to meet after the investigation had closed. I had asked Patricia out twice and been invited to supper at her house twice in the past three weeks. On Friday, she had come to my place for the first time. We had eaten together in the living room while her maid, Benedikte, had waited alone in the kitchen for several hours. Before she left, Patricia had remarked that it had been very pleasant, and invited me for supper again after work on Tuesday. We had agreed that I would be there at half past four, but that might now need to be put back. So in that sense, there was nothing odd about me calling her at all.

I had, truth be told, not been looking forward to it and had even considered postponing the meal. In contrast to our efficient and interesting discussions during my earlier murder cases, our meetings now felt unproductive and drawn out. We talked about everything and nothing, but without purpose. Patricia was less acerbic and much nicer these days, but also less interesting. Neither of us had shown any desire to talk about more difficult things, such as the loss of her parents and the traffic accident that had left her dependent on a wheelchair. And we were certainly not keen to discuss our previous relationships. On the whole, her life was not very eventful, and nor was mine, with the exception of my work as a police detective.

Our meetings were more exciting when we talked about my work and about earlier murder investigations. Patricia was particularly interested in our shared experiences and in what had happened to other people who were involved. But the big question as to whether we were a couple or just good friends remained unclear – as did the question of a possible future together. We hugged each other when we met and parted, but nothing more had happened. I was not sure if Patricia wanted anything more. She never refused an embrace, but always felt slightly tense when we hugged.

And even more unsettling was the fact that I was still not sure that I wanted any more physical contact myself. I was, more than ever, very aware that Patricia was now an attractive young woman. Especially when she gave me one of her teasing, slightly provocative smiles. Every time we met, my feelings swung this way and that. I felt more at a loss than I had done with any other woman before. In a way, we had known each other too well and for too long before our recent dates. We knew all the answers to the usual questions about parents, siblings, life and interests.

On one date, in the middle of the main course, Patricia asked what I thought about relationships where there was a considerable age gap. This was only lightly camouflaged by a reference to a recent article in the newspaper about the ageing actor Charlie Chaplin and his much younger wife, Oona O'Neill. I quickly replied that even their thirty-six-year difference was obviously not a problem, and that in our day and age when people were more enlightened and liberal, anything less than eighteen years should be acceptable to everyone, given that it was fine for the two people in question. Patricia gave one of her mischievous smiles and said that she agreed. A moment later, she added that here in Norway, fifteen years seemed to work well enough for the prime minister. Neither of us pursued the subject, but the subtext was clear. I was born on 15 March 1935 and Patricia on 12 January 1950. The age difference had never bothered me. I had had relationships with several younger women, most recently in the spring.

What bothered me more was the difference in our mobility. I had never been in a relationship with a woman who was physically handicapped, nor had I ever considered that I might. And now that I had to consider it, I found the principle easy enough, but the possibility challenging. Furthermore, both of us had been in a relationship with someone else only a matter of weeks ago. In a way, the fact that Patricia was on the pill and not a virgin made things a little easier. But I was still very uncertain as how I would deal with the situation if I was lying naked in bed with a woman who couldn't move her legs without my help. Especially when I also knew that she had lain there with another man only a few weeks before. The thought was less testing than it had been three weeks ago, and the night before last I had dreamed about it, but it had not only been pleasant.

The woman I was dating was possibly one of the richest young women in Oslo, but I did not give much thought to that side of the matter. I had a good and secure salary, and stood to inherit a tidy sum. Moreover, I was very happy with my current job and had no burning desire to do anything in life that I could not afford myself. On the other hand, I had once before, when I was in high school, known a girl first as a friend and study partner for a couple of years, before embarking on a romantic relationship with her. Our physical encounter, when it finally came, had been a disappointment, and, as a result, did not develop into the great love we had anticipated, but rather the loss of a friend forever.

I felt that I could not risk the same happening with Patricia. No one could ever know just how much she knew about my previous cases, and what was more, she might be invaluable to any future investigations. But I also realized that if she wanted physical contact and I did not respond, that might also lead to a break-up. And so I was doing what I had done all too often in my personal life: carefully treading water, leaving the dilemma hanging in the air.

Patricia answered the phone as soon as it rang – with an unusually bright 'Hello.' It sounded as though she had not only expected me to call, but was also very pleased that I had. An image of her sitting there in her wheelchair by the phone, waiting patiently in anticipation, the bookcases of her enormous private library behind her, flashed through my mind. And suddenly I realized that I had begun to fall in love with her. But of course I did not say that. Instead, I got straight to the point: 'Hello! Have you heard anything of particular interest in the news today?'

Patricia was, as I expected, immediately on the ball.

'You are of course thinking about the young woman who was found dead by the roadside at Hovseter late last night? They said on the radio that the death was being treated as suspicious. And given that you have called so soon, it is obviously murder and the police have no idea who did it. Unfortunately I can't tell you much more than that on the basis of the little information I have.' This was then quickly followed up: 'But I can of course set aside some time later this evening to talk about it, if you have more information and would like to hear my humble opinion.'

I replied that I would be more than happy to hear her opinion on the case later that evening. Then I said that I was now busy with the investigation and that it might perhaps be best if I used my time to gather as much information as possible first.

She answered that we could in that case meet a little later than originally planned. Her idle staff were not likely to have started preparing the food yet, so it would not make any difference.

This certainly confirmed that Patricia was her good old self, for better or worse, and I sent a sympathetic thought to her devoted and at times tyrannized staff. Out loud, I said that I hoped to be there by six, if that was all right for both her and the staff.

Just then, our telephone conversation was interrupted by a knock on my office door. Patricia said, 'That's fine.' I said, 'There's someone here. Speak later.' Then we both hung up at the same time.

VII

Detective Sergeant Vilhelm Helgesen was standing outside my door, together with a man and a woman who were unknown to me. They were both polite and tense.

Helgesen explained that he had two witnesses with him, but should perhaps have a word with me first. I waved him into my office.

'It all took a little time. None of the bus drivers at Oslo Transport had anything to report from Hovseter yesterday evening, unfortunately. But I've managed more or less to piece together the victim's last day at university. And I have with me two of the three witnesses who might be of interest. You can meet the third one later this afternoon.'

I asked him to give me a brief outline of Agnes Halvorsen's

last day at university and a quick introduction to the witnesses before we asked them in.

Helgesen took a notebook out of his pocket. The first few pages had more writing on them than mine usually would after only a few hours' work.

'Agnes Halvorsen usually took the bus to and from the School of Theology, and did so yesterday as well. She got there a little before half past ten, and then sat in the library until ten to two, when she went to a lecture. This finished at four, and she caught a bus home at a quarter past four, which got to Hovseter just after half past four. The bus driver on that route, Hilmar Lauritzen, was on the day shift from ten until five, so happened to drive the victim both ways. He's waiting outside with the library assistant, Astrid Marie Nordheim, who was on duty for the time that Agnes was there. Unfortunately, I don't think either of them have much of interest to tell us, but you can be the judge of that. The lecturer was Oscar Fredrik Bergendahl, who was also her personal tutor. He had to go to an important meeting with the school board, but is available later on this afternoon if you want to talk to him.'

I told him that Bergendahl was on my list of people to talk to as soon as possible, and thanked Helgesen for his good and efficient work thus far. This pleased him inordinately, and he said that it was a delight to work with such a young and positive inspector. I asked him to sit beside me at the desk when we spoke to the witnesses. He nodded attentively when I told him about my meetings with Agnes' brother, parents and friend, and about the pathologist's preliminary conclusions. If nothing else, the mood of the investigation team was still buoyant.

Hilmar Lauritzen was a relatively solid man of average height, who gave me an assured handshake. He told us that he was thirty-nine and had worked at Oslo Transport since he finished his military service. He drove on various routes, but generally worked the day shift and drove between Majorstuen and Hovseter two or three days a week. A small number of students from the School of Theology often took this bus, so he knew them by sight.

Agnes Halvorsen had been a frequent passenger on that route for about a year and a half now, and so was one of perhaps twenty or thirty 'regulars' that Hilmar Lauritzen 'nodded to, without knowing their names'. She had had her bus pass ready on the way into town, but on the way back to Hovseter, she had rummaged in her bag for it, so the bus driver just waved her on, as he knew she had a pass.

She seemed like a nice young lady and had made a friendly impression in their limited routine exchanges. Even though he hadn't known her personally, it was still a shock to hear that she had been killed only a few hours after her last bus trip.

The driver reckoned there had been around twenty passengers on the bus that afternoon, which made a full overview difficult. However, he hadn't noticed anyone following Agnes Halvorsen either on or off the bus, 'except, of course, the friend who was with her'.

But then it also seemed unlikely that anyone would follow her onto the bus at a quarter past four in the afternoon, and kill her more than six hours later.

The most interesting piece of information from Hilmar Lauritzen was about the friend Agnes had with her on the bus.

'I don't know her friend's name, but I've seen them together many times. Her friend is nearly a head shorter and has dark hair. She normally got on the bus behind Agnes and seemed to be more serious. They took different buses into town, but caught the bus back together. And actually, yesterday, there was something that surprised me a little . . .'

The bus driver paused for a moment, but then carried on as soon as I prompted him.

'Well, they obviously knew each other well and usually sat together near the front of the bus. But yesterday, they were clearly discussing something at the bus stop. The friend was unusually animated and swiped at Agnes just as the bus pulled in. She got onto the bus first. Agnes seemed a little agitated and was still looking for her bus pass when she got on. She then walked past her friend and sat down several rows behind her. It was probably just a normal tiff between friends. But I thought I should perhaps mention it to you as it was unusual, and then she was killed later that evening.'

Helgesen nodded and looked at me. I assured the bus driver that he had done the right thing in telling us, and that of course we would not jump to any hasty conclusions based on the information. When I asked if he could think of anything else that might be of interest, his reply was, 'No, I'm afraid not.' He did not have a business card, but wrote his address and telephone number down on a piece of paper, and said that we could contact him anytime if there were any further questions.

Helgesen and I exchanged a fleeting glance as the door shut loudly behind the helpful bus driver.

'You've already managed to get more out of him than I'd even thought of,' Helgesen said, without a hint of bitterness.

I magnanimously pointed out that, first of all, it was he who had brought the witness here, and second, it was not by any means a given that what he had told us would be of any importance. And in any case, we still had work to do. This was good news in what was turning out to be a difficult investigation.

The library assistant, Astrid Marie Nordheim, was forty-one and of medium height. She was, however, quite striking thanks to the combination of an unusually high, blonde hairdo and unusually thick glasses. She was a qualified librarian, and had worked at the School of Theology since finally leaving 'the ranks of housewives' two years ago.

Mrs Nordheim came across as a dynamic and observant lady, who knew the students by name and appearance. She even noted when people came and went, and so could tell us the precise times of Agnes Halvorsen's last visit to the library. It was hard not to notice Agnes as she was one of the few female students in the school. She was otherwise a hard-working and diligent student, and never a problem in the library. As far as the library assistant could tell, she had read two course books yesterday and taken notes.

Nora Jensen came to the library less often and for shorter periods, but had spent an hour there yesterday before the lecture. She had been sitting behind her friend. The library assistant had not seen any contact or communication between them. She had, on the other hand, noticed a short and whispered conversation between Agnes Halvorsen and a male student from the same year, Jan Ove Eliassen. He had gone over and started the conversation, which lasted no more than a minute or two.

The two did not usually talk in the library, but then again, it was not unusual for students to exchange messages. The observant library assistant felt it was only right to mention it to us, even though it was not likely to be of any importance – and she certainly did not want to direct suspicion towards anyone without grounds. She wrote down her address and telephone number as soon as I asked, and said that we could contact her whenever she could be of any use.

Our session finished with this mildly comical similarity between the two otherwise very different witnesses. I chuckled and Helgesen gave a careful smile. 'Well, you found a thin thread there that we might be able to follow up,' he said, tentatively. I told him what I thought: that it was an even thinner thread than the previous one, but that it was better to have vague clues than no clues at all.

I noted down a new and more critical question for Nora Jensen, and then added the student Jan Ove Eliassen to my list.

The only person left to talk to now was Agnes' tutor, Oscar Fredrik Bergendahl. I asked Helgesen whether he felt it was necessary to talk to the tutor that afternoon – and what he made of the case so far.

Helgesen scratched his head and thought for a while before answering. 'We now have a couple of key questions regarding the case, but still don't have anything that resembles a motive or a suspect. In that sense, the pathologist's conclusions are a bit of a blow. Young women are most often killed by a husband, boyfriend or lover who has already been jilted or is about to be. That seems less likely now that we know there was no man in her life. The first and most important question, then, is whether the murderer knew the victim or not. If he did, we still don't yet know who he is and why he did it, but it does mean there is a limited number of people to investigate. The girl lived a quiet and ordered life. There can't be many who have a possible motive for killing her, nor can there be many who knew where she was often to be found on a Monday night. If, on the other hand, it was a stranger and she was a random victim . . .'

Helgesen had said a surprising amount, but then stopped abruptly. It was about as far as I had thought myself, and I was pleased to be able to finish the sentence for him.

'. . . we are literally back to square one, with no physical clues at the scene of the crime. For the moment we can only hope that a witness will come forward who saw something in the area yesterday evening, or that the murderer gives themself away somehow or other. The picture of the ant remains a mystery.'

Helgesen agreed with me.

'As far as the tutor is concerned, I doubt that there's anything of real interest to be got there, but you have already managed to get more than I anticipated out of our two witnesses today. Oscar Fredrik Bergendahl is a likeable man, but he didn't have much to say about Agnes – except that she seemed to be a nice person, and was a diligent and talented student. He said that he would be back in the office by half past three and would stay there until five, if you wanted to speak to him. You will have to decide for yourself whether it's a good time to go and see him now. Based on what we've heard, it might be good to talk to her friend again. I finish my shift at four and have arranged to do something at half past, but will of course work overtime if you'd like me to.'

I took the liberty of asking Helgesen what he was going to do at half past four. He hesitated, then told me that it was his youngest son's tenth birthday – but repeated that he would work overtime if needed.

I thought about it for a second or two, then said what I had first intended: that I would go and talk to the tutor before talking to the friend again, and that there was no reason for him to come with me and run into overtime.

Helgesen held out his hand and thanked me for my understanding. We left the police station together just before four, but were going in opposite directions. Helgesen said that his son would be very happy to see him, as he had already called home to say that he might have to work late this evening.

I stood there on my own for a moment in the damp, rather cold spring air. I had no birthdays other than my own to celebrate – and no children who were looking forward to me coming home. That afternoon, a few weeks after my thirty-seventh birthday, was perhaps the first time that I felt a twinge of envy of my colleagues who did.

Fortunately it did not last long. Less than a minute later I was in the car and driving through the afternoon traffic towards the School of Theology.

VIII

By the time I got there it was twenty past four and most of the offices had been abandoned for the day. But Oscar Fredrik Bergendahl was there, as he said he would be, and even had his door ajar.

I recognized him without any trouble from the descriptions that Nora Jensen and Vilhelm Helgesen had given. Bergendahl was a trim man with a headful of dark hair and I would have guessed that he was in his thirties rather than his forties. My first impression was that he seemed to be somewhere between nice and overly friendly, and consequently I found it easier to imagine him as a car salesman than a theologian. Before the door had even closed behind me, he had managed to shake my hand, apologize that he had not been available earlier and thank me for coming to see him – as well as assure me that he would do everything he could to help solve this 'terrible and pointless crime'.

Oscar Fredrik Bergendahl struck me as being slightly false. But once all the small talk was out of the way and we had sat down, his shock and desire to help felt more genuine. He said twice, in a tremulous voice, that Agnes Halvorsen had been an extremely talented student and an exceptionally nice person. Her death was a great loss for the school and a tragedy for everyone who knew her.

When I asked about her academic performance, he was quick to say that her work had been outstanding.

'In theology, it takes considerable knowledge or understanding to be a good student, and Agnes Halvorsen was one of the rare people who had both. Bearing in mind that theological circles and higher education establishments in Norway are often divided by strong opinions, I think it would be safe to say that she was seen to be one of two exceptional students in her year. Even the more conservative staff who were actually opposed to her being here agreed that, in academic terms, she was an extraordinary talent. In fact, her academic performance had persuaded several lecturers to soften their stance on women priests.'

Oscar Fredrik Bergendahl hesitated slightly when I asked about Nora Jensen, and what he thought of her friendship with Agnes Halvorsen.

'Well, I would certainly be more cautious about making any bold statements about her academic work, and naturally I know very little about their personal relationship. However, they were the only two women in their year and had known each other since they were children. Their fathers had been friends before they were born and both called their daughters after Ibsen characters. I am possibly more positive about Nora Jensen than many others here. The truth is that she seems to be less motivated and hard-working than Agnes, and less intellectually gifted. Her performance is by no means bad, just weaker than her friend's, with whom everyone automatically compared her. I have often thought that having Agnes as a friend was both a blessing and a curse for Nora.'

I asked whether he had recently or previously noticed any tension between the two, be it about male fellow students or anything else.

He smiled broadly.

'No, absolutely not, I would say . . . First of all, I've neither seen nor heard anything to indicate that either of them had a boyfriend. And no, I have never noticed any disagreement between them. It seems very unlikely that there would be any kind of conflict, partly because they've known each other for so long and partly because Nora has always shown Agnes such great respect.'

'You said that Agnes was seen to be one of two exceptional students in her year. Who is the other?'

'Jan Ove Eliassen. They are at once so alike and yet very different. Jan Ove's family are members of the Pentecostal Church and he is in many ways far more conservative, but he and Agnes have both become better people through their discussions about divisive issues. To begin with, there was some rivalry between them, but that is no longer the case and my impression is that they get along well now.'

Oscar Fredrik Bergendahl spoke slowly and said this in a kind voice as he leaned back comfortably in his chair. Then it was as if something struck him; he leaned forwards over the desk and his speech was now fast and intense.

'But really – if you're looking for a possible murderer here among the students, I can assure you, you're on the wrong track. Of course there are tensions and rivalries; there are in any student environment. But the atmosphere here is devout to the point of pacifist, and I can't imagine that any of our students would take another person's life under any circumstances. It's an almost shocking idea.'

He said this with unexpected force. As he spoke, I caught a glimpse of a different Oscar Fredrik Bergendahl, a more passionate, serious and physical man, whom one might not want to get on the wrong side of. It was fleeting. He quickly calmed down and settled back in his chair again. Just then, I noticed something on the wall behind him.

Between two large bookcases, Oscar Fredrik Bergendahl had hung up a single photograph. It was a christening picture, showing two smiling parents and a howling child. I reckoned the photograph was no more than two years old – the father still looked very much the same.

For the second time in an hour, I felt a stab of envy when confronted with a man who had children. In what was more or less a fit of guilt, I expressed my hope that all was well with his family.

Oscar Fredrik Bergendahl drew a couple of deep breaths before he answered, but did not straighten up.

'Well, I'm afraid to say it definitely is not. You're looking at the last happy memory of my small family. My son died very suddenly in his cot the day after that photograph was taken, and my wife is currently in hospital with a serious lung condition. She has been so strong and brave, but then yesterday the doctors said that I should ready myself for letting her pass into our Lord's hands.'

I saw a tear twinkle in the corner of Bergendahl's eye, and hurried to apologize for my insensitive question. He kept his composure and held up a hand.

'On the contrary, your question was well meant and I appreciate you asking. I hope and pray for a miracle that can save my wife and give us another child, but more and more frequently have to console myself with the thought that the three of us will be reunited in Heaven one day.'

When he said 'Heaven', I remembered that I still had something to ask him – which was where he had been the previous evening between half past ten and half past eleven. It felt very wrong to ask about that now, even though it was simply a routine question. So instead, I gently queried whether he had been to see his wife in hospital yesterday.

If Oscar Fredrik Bergendahl realized what I was actually asking, he disguised it well.

'Thank you for your kindness. I drove straight to the hospital after the lecture yesterday and stayed far longer than was good for her. She dozed off around nine o'clock. I sat there watching her sleep, gazing at her peaceful face for another half hour or so, and drove home around a quarter to ten, when I realized that she wasn't going to wake up again before morning. She wasn't strong enough to talk much yesterday evening, but I hope she might be better today.'

I made a mental note that Oscar Fredrik Bergendahl did not in fact have an alibi for the timeframe when his student was murdered. But I both hoped and believed that he had nothing to do with the murder. Out loud, I thanked him for taking the time to talk to me, and wished him all the best.

The lecturer spontaneously gripped my hand and wished me luck with the investigation and my life. I hoped that he would not follow up by asking about my family life. And thankfully, he didn't. He struck me as a man who combined intellectual and social intelligence.

So we parted on a friendly note just before five o'clock.

IX

I was shown into the generously proportioned library at 104–108 Erling Skjalgsson's Street at two minutes past six. The table was set for two and the cauliflower soup had already been served.

Patricia sat as regally as a queen on her throne in her wheelchair; she was wearing a red dress that I didn't recall having seen before. For all I knew, the dress might have cost half a month's salary, but it was the tightest-fitting dress I had ever seen Patricia in. The combination of the dress and the candle on the table again made me acutely aware of my private dilemma.

The start of our conversation was, however, far from romantic. Patricia seemed to be in a slightly impatient mood and exclaimed, 'Finally! What more have you got to tell about the case? They just keep repeating the same old boring story on the radio about a young woman who was found dead at Hovseter late yesterday evening and that the death was being treated as suspicious. Any retard who can afford a radio will have long ago realized that she was murdered. But who was she, how was she killed and what do we know about her family, circle, friends and movements?'

What followed was one of those strange interludes when Patricia said nothing for what felt like a small eternity, but still felt so close that I could almost feel her breath on my cheek – even though there was a good three feet of mahogany table between us. It occurred to me that Patricia, despite her sharp tongue, was a remarkably good and patient listener. She was silent and focused while I spoke for almost an hour about the day's investigation, as we ate our cauliflower soup and tenderloin. Patricia had two notepads and five pens at the ready, but did not use any of them. Her thin arms only moved when she took a mouthful of food or a sip of wine, and the movement was mechanical.

I finished my account just as the maid slipped in discreetly to clear the half-finished plates after the main course.

'Hmm,' Patricia snorted with a hint of exaggeration, and took another sip of wine. We sat in comfortable silence until the door closed quietly behind the maid.

'Both a tragic and a mysterious case,' I said, expectantly.

Patricia nodded in careful agreement.

'More puzzling than tragic, I would say, as the case stands. And even though you have gathered a considerable amount of useful information today, there is still nothing to prove what happened or a motive. So far, the material only gives the basis for some fairly loose hypotheses.'

I said that in the current situation I would be more than happy to hear those hypotheses. I realized that this was a mistake even before I had closed my mouth. I should have remembered that Patricia disliked intensely saying anything that might later prove to be wrong.

She frowned and replied in irritation that her loose hypotheses were too loose to be discussed with anyone – even me.

'A key question must surely be whether the murderer is to be found in poor Agnes Halvorsen's closest circle or whether she was a random victim?' I asked in an attempt to make up for my mistake.

'Yes and no. To be precise, the key question is whether the murderer was waiting for Agnes Halvorsen, or whether he just happened to pass a suitable victim.'

'I personally am inclined to think it was the latter at present, but only on the shaky grounds that the murderer was not a jilted lover and there is no one that really fits the bill in her circle of family and friends.'

Patricia smiled, rather cynically.

'And I am inclined to believe it was the former, for the simple reason that it was a rainy and rather chilly evening, so not a particularly nice night to be wandering around at that time unless you had reason to believe that a suitable murder victim would appear. It clearly wasn't a humiliated lover, as Agnes Halvorsen had never let anyone close in that way. However, that does not rule out jealousy or unrequited love as possible motives. Any unmarried woman who carries two lipsticks in her handbag clearly wants to be attractive and may have ignited feelings she knew nothing about. There are two kinds of unrequited love: love for someone who has rejected you, and love for someone who doesn't know. And while the disappointment of rejection is usually worse, there are plenty of cases where the latter has resulted in murder or other crimes of frustration.'

I had never heard the expression 'crimes of frustration' either at police college or in my later work. But I was too curious about what it might mean for the case to quibble about semantics and terminology.

'So you think that jealousy could be the motive and Agnes Halvorsen was murdered by a man who knew her well but had understood that he would never have her?'

'Again, yes and no. It's possible that the motive was jealousy, yes, but of course not certain. And even if it was, that does not necessarily mean that the murderer knew Agnes Halvorsen well. He might be an acquaintance or even just a passer-by. Men have fallen in love in more incredible ways than that. If the murderer did not know Agnes, then all that remains is to answer the question we have already highlighted . . .'

The maid came in with the evening's dessert. Patricia stopped mid-sentence and gave me one of her teasing smiles as she tasted the pudding.

For a second I thought that Patricia was very attractive when she smiled like that, but then I snapped back to the questions we had mentioned, and attempted to finish her sentence.

'. . . in other words, how the murderer could know, without knowing Agnes, that she would pass by there around eleven o'clock in the evening.'

Patricia nodded in restrained agreement.

'Exactly. Though only if the murderer wasn't simply a raving lunatic on the lookout for a random victim. Which brings us back to the two crucial questions so far: did the murderer know that Agnes was coming? And if so, how did he or she know? Let us hope there is a witness who has seen the murderer. Whatever the case, it would still be interesting to know who knew that Agnes was going to visit her friend and then walk home alone at that time.'

I promised to follow this up the next day. I had to contact

her friend, Nora Jensen, regardless, to ask why she had not sat next to Agnes on the bus, as she normally did.

Rather unusually, Patricia seemed to agree with me today. She commented that it might perhaps be a sensible move to ask her that first. Then she swiftly added, 'For that matter, I have a question you could ask this Nora. I'm guessing that lectures in the School of Theology all start at a quarter past the hour, and I would like to know at what time exactly Agnes Halvorsen arrived. If she came just after two, then there's nothing more to think about. Whereas if she got there at ten past two, there is a window of time when we don't know what she did. There may be several natural explanations for this, for example, a cup of coffee or a bowl of soup. But it is certainly worth checking anyhow, when we have so little to go on.'

I agreed and obediently made a note of it. I had never gone to university or to the School of Theology and so had not thought or registered that the lecture would have started at a quarter past two.

'The explanation may simply be that it was her friend who did it. She knows the area well and is quick on her feet. Technically, there was nothing to stop her following Agnes, running past her under cover of dark, then waiting for her where she was found. The fact that Nora is shorter in build does not mean that she is physically weaker, particularly not if she caught her by surprise,' I said, tentatively.

I realized myself that the argument was more logical than convincing, but once again Patricia nodded in restrained agreement. Either I was making better suggestions than usual, or she was being more conciliatory for other reasons. I had the feeling that the latter was true – and was not entirely sure whether I liked it or not.

'Technically, it is definitely a possibility. To be fair, we only have Nora Jensen's word that she did not go with Agnes. And I think we should be careful about assuming that it was a man. Never underestimate what a determined woman can do, even if she appears to be physically inferior.'

This was said with a slightly self-deprecating smile, but it faded quickly and she became very serious.

'We must keep all options open. But you don't really believe that is the case, do you?' I said.

Patricia shook her head. There was no hint of irony now.

'No, I don't believe that was the case. There are two worrying details that we have not yet discussed that make me think we are looking for another type of murderer, far more dangerous than a jealous friend. Of course, both details could prove to be distractions and explained in several other ways. But for the moment, I do not like the picture of the ant one bit, and the buttoning on her blouse even less.'

I suddenly became aware of a slight tremor in Patricia's voice when she said this – and a tremble in her hand when she reached for her wine glass. Once again, it struck me that her normally so controlled exterior was in fact hiding a neurotic.

I said that both things had taken me aback, but as I had not been able to see any direct relevance to the murder, I had dismissed them as coincidences or red herrings.

As I spoke, Patricia drank the rest of her wine, then thumped the glass down on the table a little too hard. She suddenly leaned over towards me, as far as the wheelchair and the table permitted. When I then leaned over too, her face was no more than an inch or two from mine. I caught the scent of wine and perfume – and saw both anger and fear in her eyes.

'That may, as I said, also be the case. But after strangling a young woman by the side of the road on the outskirts of Oslo, most people would be in a hurry to get away from the scene of the crime. You have to be either pretty cold-blooded or in it for the thrill to take the time to put a picture of an ant in the victim's handbag. And even more cold-blooded and addicted to thrills if you then undo her blouse, only to button it up again. And even though I have never met Nora Jensen, I can imagine that a jealous, frustrated young woman might possibly strangle her friend, but I struggle to believe that she would do that afterwards. You've met her: can you picture her doing that?'

It was my turn to reflect. I was annoyed that in the course of a long day, I had not once thought about this aspect of the case, now highlighted by Patricia.

After a short pause for thought, I had to concede. Whereas I could possibly envisage Nora Jensen committing the murder, I could not imagine anything other than that she would run away immediately after. At a pinch, I might accept that she had planted a picture of an ant, but not that she had stayed and fiddled with her dead friend's blouse. And if she had done it as a distraction and to give the impression that the murderer was a man, it would have been more natural to leave the blouse open than to button it up again.

Patricia was surprisingly sympathetic once more.

'How nice that we agree on so much today. In that case, it's possible that the ant says something about the murderer's self-image and the blouse something about his views on women. If the murderer is part of poor Agnes' close circle, we will find the motive and perpetrator soon enough. If, however, the murderer is not from her closest circle, then we are dealing with the public sphere and have no idea who it is or what his motive might be. In which case I am seriously worried that we are not only trying to solve a very puzzling murder, but also racing against time to save more lives!'

She said this with great force. There were no windows in the library, but Patricia pointed emphatically at the wall. Her finger was shaking.

This intense emotion lasted only a few seconds, and she did her utmost to control herself afterwards.

'Sorry if I am being overdramatic; I certainly don't want to put any more pressure on you. But it really is not very nice to think that you might be racing against death, especially when you can't walk.'

I did think that Patricia seemed to be a little overwrought this evening. But the logic of her reasoning was convincing all the same, and her conclusion therefore alarming.

It was half past nine when I looked at the clock again. Our glasses were empty and what was left of the ice cream had melted in the bowls on both sides of the table. Patricia's lips were redder than I could remember and she was only an arm's length from me, but our conversation had been serious, and it certainly seemed to me that it had left us both in a sombre mood. So I said that even though there were perhaps other things we should talk about today, it might be better, given the situation, to focus on the investigation.

To my relief Patricia readily agreed, and added that I should call her when I knew what tomorrow would look like. I promised to call her regardless and rounded the table to give her a hug before turning and heading for the door.

'I hope that your investigation tomorrow will uncover the motive and the murderer in Agnes Halvorsen's circle of friends and family,' Patricia said, as I turned to leave. However, it did not sound as if she believed it would happen. And I understood perfectly, as I no longer believed that would be the case either.

X

I wasn't sure how the first night and day of my new life as a murderer would be, whether I would get away with it.

So far, it's been excellent. I fell asleep a little later than usual last night, but then slept soundly, and woke as soon as the alarm went off. Carried on with my working day as planned. I'm in fine fettle; in fact, I would say almost ecstatic. The adrenaline from yesterday is still there in my body. It bubbled up when I heard on the radio the news that a young woman had been found dead near Hovseter, and that the police were treating the death as 'suspicious'. They're talking about me on the news today. And tomorrow I'll be in all the major newspapers. I make decisions over other people's life and death. Tens of thousands, maybe hundreds of thousands of people throughout the country will be wondering who I am.

The police have also been calling for witnesses from last night. That means they have nothing to go on. I would love to know how many people are involved in the investigation, and how much they've understood today. They said on the evening news that the press release was signed by Detective Inspector Kolbjørn Kristiansen and that it was 'assumed' he was leading the investigation.

That was no great surprise. I read about him again in Aftenposten last week. The newspaper called him 'the young rising star of Oslo Police' and said that he was a man who could scale great heights: hence his nickname, K2. In all his previous investigations, he has caught the murderer and closed the case within two weeks. Let's see if I can't make that longer. That would certainly be quite a triumph, even if I did get caught in the end. But I've also heard people speculate that perhaps the nickname K2 in fact refers to all the air up top.

When I think about the murder, I don't feel any regret, only satisfaction. I still have no sympathy for Agnes. She was one of those useless and egotistical young women there are too many of these days. She wanted to focus on a career rather than having children, and wouldn't be ruled by any man. I've heard her say that with my own ears. She didn't say it to me, and probably didn't even think that I heard. Again, she underestimated me, and again, I understood more than anyone realized.

The only thing I regret today is the blouse. That wasn't planned. Having made sure she was dead, I put the ant in her bag as I intended. But when I saw her lying there lifeless at my feet, on a whim I decided that she would now show me the breasts that she hadn't wanted to show to any man when she had the chance. I unbuttoned her blouse on impulse. I never thought about pulling up her skirt or pulling down her panties, even though it would only have taken seconds. It would somehow have been undignified, vulgar. But her breasts were pure and beautiful. For a moment, when I saw them, I regretted having killed her, but I knew perfectly well that I would never have seen them if she had been alive. I stood there gazing at them. Then I buttoned up her blouse again and walked off into the dark.

The episode with the blouse took no more than thirty seconds and gave me a new rush of adrenaline as I stood there by the edge of the road holding a woman I had killed. But it was foolish. The danger of being seen increased with every second, even though I couldn't see or hear anyone. It's important to learn from your mistakes; I am not going to make that mistake again.

Otherwise, everything went smoothly and as planned. I have to say that I'm very pleased with both the planning and the implementation of my first murder. Passers-by and locals might easily have noticed an unknown car if it was parked there. The driver and passengers would remember the following day if a man got on the bus late at night close to where a murder had happened. But not many are likely to notice a man ambling along by the side of the road in the dark, and fewer still would be able to describe him the next day, especially if he was wearing a raincoat and scarf. I carried on at a leisurely pace in the direction that Agnes had been walking. I felt safe, as it was ten minutes before I passed anyone, but I still continued to walk for another half hour. By then I was a couple of miles from the scene of the crime, and could take the tram home.

Of course, I can't guarantee that nothing has gone wrong, despite my good planning. One of the drivers who went past might have seen me well enough to give a full description, or have recognized me from somewhere. I might also have left some kind of evidence that I didn't notice myself.

All evening I've been waiting for the police to come. My blood pressure shot through the roof when there was an unexpected knock on the door earlier this evening. It was just some idiot insurance salesman who stuttered and tried to sell me new house insurance. I slammed the door in his face, and then promptly took my pulse. It was over 150. Even now, sitting in the living room, relaxing with a cup of coffee and a piece of cake, it's nearly 100. So far, there's a fresh excitement and no side effects to my new life as a murderer.

I chose the ant as my symbol on purpose, but today I feel more like a bear: strong, wild and powerful – respected and feared by smaller animals. I remember that Grandpa once told me when I was very young that most bears stay away from humans, but once a bear has tasted human blood, it loses all respect for people and can easily attack again. They call them killer bears. I've lost any respect for other people's lives and have got a taste for the excitement of killing them. It's like a thirst, or an instinct, and I'll have to murder someone again soon.

In brief, I had a peaceful day off in my new life as a murderer. Tomorrow is another working day and will no doubt be very different. I have ant number two taped between pages 166 and 167 of the encyclopaedia, so that the police won't find it, should they turn up later on this evening or tomorrow. And if they do, I'm obviously a suspect and will just have to lie low for a few days more. If they don't come, ant number two will be used tomorrow night. I know what she looks like and I know where she's thinking of going.

XI

The time was now ten past eleven. I had watched the evening news on the television and then switched it off. The national broadcaster, NRK, had done little more than read out my press release at the end of the programme.

I was fully prepared for the case to be given more coverage in the morning papers, and that interest would increase when we released a statement to say it was murder. What Patricia had said about the danger of another murder was still rattling around in my head and worried me far more than any newspaper report. I stayed sitting on the sofa and ran through the day's events and those of the night before over and over again, without discovering any new details that might lead me to the murderer.

The key questions in the case were increasingly pressing, and the answers remained frustratingly unclear. There was no way to determine whether the murderer had waited for Agnes Halvorsen because he knew that she was coming, or had simply bumped into her and killed her at random, though the former seemed more likely. But how the murderer had known his victim's movements remained a mystery.

As I so often did when I was deadlocked, be it in a murder investigation or my private life, I stood staring out of the window in the final few minutes before going to bed.

My last investigation, which had resulted in dramatic changes in my personal life, had started here one Saturday only a few weeks earlier, when I saw a young lad on a rickety old red bike pedalling furiously up the hill towards the building. The boy on the red bicycle was now dead. And here I was again, looking out at an ordinary late Tuesday evening in Hegdehaugen. Most of the lights in my block and the neighbouring buildings had been switched off for the night.

Suddenly, my jaw dropped and I stood there staring. A young woman carrying a large book under her arm had appeared at the bottom of the road and was walking with determined steps towards the building where I lived. I stood there transfixed.

The shock didn't last long. Only seconds later I could see that it was of course not my former fiancée, Miriam. This woman was taller and obviously did not read books as she walked. I realized who she was when she stopped and rang the bell. There wasn't a sound in my flat, but I could hear a faint ringing in the flat to my left. I remembered that I had met the woman in the corridor a couple of days ago, when my neighbour took the opportunity to introduce his new girlfriend. I couldn't remember her name, but the names of my neighbour's girlfriends tended to change rather rapidly. This girlfriend was in fact closer to thirty than twenty, and worked in a bookshop, rather than being a student. I didn't think she was particularly attractive and did not envy my neighbour as a result. However, without knowing it herself, she was now an uncomfortable reminder of the woman who used to visit me here.

I had given the few things that Miriam had kept here to her neighbour in the halls of residence ten days ago. She told me that Miriam would be coming home from hospital the following day and hoped she would be able to sit the spring exams. The injuries she had sustained during my last murder case had apparently now healed. I had not heard anything about possible psychological damage. It felt wrong to contact her, after our break-up in the hospital. I hadn't heard anything from her and took that to mean that she did not want to talk to me. Seeing the neighbour's new girlfriend was enough to bring the memories flooding back.

It was as though a dam had burst, and the images came in uncontrolled torrents. I remembered my first meeting with Miriam – when I had stopped her crossing a road in Oslo with her nose buried in a book. I remembered our final meeting, when she was lying in a bed in the University Hospital and told me that she would have to live with the memory of what had happened during my previous investigation, and I would have to live without her. And countless other images from all our time together between these two encounters: meeting the parents, meals at restaurants, but most of all from my flat, here. It was only a month since she last stayed here. I could remember every detail of that evening and night, even though I didn't want to.

When I looked at the clock, it was already ten to twelve. I almost ran into the bedroom.

My body was tired, but my head was still too busy to sleep. I turned in towards the wall, imagined Miriam lying beside me as she used to do. The unexpected emotional storm stilled again slowly as I stared at the wall and tried to turn my thoughts back to the investigation and Patricia. When I finally fell asleep just before one, Miriam's face was the last thing I saw and the first to greet me in my dreams.

DAY THREE

An Extremely Dramatic Development

I

The morning papers on Wednesday 26 April gave little cause for worry. Both *Arbeiderbladet* and *Aftenposten* had written short reports in anticipation of further information, and included the appeal for possible witnesses to contact the police. *Aftenposten* gave the name of the victim, and added a sentence to say that, 'The well-known Detective Inspector Kolbjørn Kristiansen has been appointed to lead the investigation, which gives grounds for optimism that the tragic case will be closed quickly.'

I was not convinced that the tabloids would be as polite, but hoped and believed that time was still on our side with regard to the press. But only as long as there were no more deaths – and perhaps only until we confirmed that a crime had been committed. Officially, we could wait with that until the autopsy report was ready. I reckoned that we would have to confirm criminal circumstances at some point in the course of the day – and that media interest would then rocket.

My own curiosity about the case was growing and I saw no reason to prolong breakfast when I was on my own, so I was at the office by ten to nine. Helgesen arrived at the same time.

Sadly, there were no messages for us. Just as we were about to sit down to discuss the day's tasks, the telephone rang. The switchboard transferred a call from a man whom I guessed was a conservative businessman in his fifties, judging by his voice and language. This quickly proved to be the case.

'This may simply be a waste of your time and mine, as I only caught a glimpse of the person as I drove past, and there is no way of knowing if he had anything to do with your investigation. Apologies, my name is Arnold Eriksen and I'm a senior adviser to the Norwegian Employers' Confederation. I just read in today's *Aftenposten* that the police were hoping to contact anyone who was in the Hovseter area the day before yesterday between half past ten and half past eleven in the evening. Well, I drove by there at ten to eleven and did wonder a little about a man I saw by the roadside. So I felt it was my civic duty to contact you.'

I immediately assured him that it could be of great interest and asked him to think carefully and tell us whatever he could about the man by the side of the road.

He gave a small sigh.

'I'll certainly try, but unfortunately I don't have much to tell you. I was driving towards the centre at ten to eleven, after a private visit. I was slightly surprised to see the man by the roadside, as it was several hundred yards to the nearest bus stop or local train station. I wondered if he might have been involved in an accident of some sort, but could not see a car or a bicycle, and he made no attempt to stop me. In fact, he had his face turned away from the road.'

Helgesen had stood up and made a questioning movement with his hands. I pointed to the chair beside me and he quickly came over and leaned in towards the receiver. I noticed a vein throbbing on his temple. I could feel the blood pulsing through my own veins too.

'This could be very important. You have nothing more to say about his appearance?'

Eriksen's sigh was heavier this time.

'It's rather unfortunate, but I don't, I'm afraid. As I said, I only saw the man for a few seconds. He was standing, as I also said, with his face turned away. I was behind the wheel, so naturally had to keep my eyes on the road. I only saw that he was wearing a coat and scarf, but could not tell you the colour. And certainly not the colour of his hair or any facial features.'

I felt my irritation rising, but held my tongue. This could be our first glimpse of the murderer.

'You could perhaps at least guess his height? And are you sure that it was a man?'

'The person by the roadside was not particularly tall or short – possibly somewhere between five foot five and six foot. From what I could see and the coat, I assumed it was a man. But now that you ask, it could as well have been a tall woman in a man's overcoat. It's slightly worrying that I can no longer immediately say if it was a man or a woman.'

The latter was said as a joke, but he quickly realized that I was not in the mood for that kind of thing. His voice was more serious again when he continued: 'Well, I've done what I can to help. And I did say from the start that I had not seen the person clearly, but that I had passed someone by the roadside at Hovseter at ten to eleven the day before yesterday. Sadly I can't give you a detailed description. Do you have any more questions for me? Because if not, I'm actually calling you from work, and I should press on with it.'

I could understand his frustration – my own was growing

by the minute. The man was doing what he could to help, and could hardly be blamed for not being able to give a description. And what was more, there was nothing to gain by upsetting the only witness we had from the scene of the crime, so far.

I therefore reassured him that we very much appreciated his help and asked him to hold the line for a few moments.

I looked up at Helgesen, who said nothing. I recalled yesterday's conversation with Patricia. Suddenly I thought of a question that I was certain she would ask, if she had heard the phone call.

'Just one thing, and again, this could be important: did it seem to you that the person was just standing by the side of the road, not walking in either direction?'

The man who had called sniffed quietly on the other end, but checked his irritation before he spoke.

'That is precisely what I have been trying to tell you. I reacted to the fact that the person had stopped and was standing there, despite the fact that it was raining and late. I thought that he must just be waiting for someone. And now I really have to get on with my work.'

I disliked Arnold Eriksen inordinately, given that I had never met him. But he had phoned in, told us what he remembered and even given us some important information. I thanked him and wished him a good working day.

He put down the receiver without saying another word.

'You heard most of that, didn't you?' I asked Helgesen.

'Yes. How tall was the friend, did you say?' was his response.

'Just over five foot – certainly no more than five foot four. It could still have been her, but I don't think so,' I said.

Helgesen arched an eyebrow and sent me a questioning

look. I quickly regurgitated Patricia's reasoning about the blouse – without mentioning her name, of course.

'I hadn't thought of that. I'm impressed. It's unlikely that Nora is the murderer, but she may well know more of interest all the same. Perhaps there's more chance of getting something out of her if you go alone?' Helgesen suggested.

I agreed, but added that I would like him to come to the lecture. We agreed to meet outside the lecture theatre at ten to twelve.

I liked Helgesen more and more, but did not feel that I was very impressive myself. I felt slightly guilty about Patricia – and then wondered if that meant that I was now in love with her.

II

It was a quarter past ten when I got to Hovseter. I had initially thought that I would ask Nora my critical questions after the lecture, but I had obviously been infected by Patricia's anxiety regarding the time aspect. So at half past nine I had called to see if I could come a little earlier as I had some questions I wanted to ask before we went to the lecture.

She replied in a staccato voice that that would be fine. She didn't seem surprised and did not ask what kind of questions they might be. There was something oddly resigned about our short conversation.

There was no twitching of the curtains in the little house in Hovseter this time. I wondered for a moment if the bird had flown the nest. As it turned out, the explanation was more or less the opposite. Nora Jensen was ready and waiting by the front door, and opened it no more than a second after I had rung the bell. It was too quick, and she looked too apathetic, so I asked straight away if everything was all right.

She answered in a monotone voice that she had taken some sleeping tablets the night before, but still had not been able to sleep until early in the morning.

I said, as tactfully as I could, that perhaps the reason she had not been able to sleep was that she had not told me everything.

She made no attempt either to confirm or deny this. We moved into the living room and sat down in the same places as before. There was a pot of coffee and two cups on the table, but neither of us touched it. We just sat and looked at each other across the table for about a minute, which felt like both an instant and an age.

I held back slightly, and started by asking who else might know that Agnes used to walk home from here just before eleven on a Monday evening.

Nora Jensen seemed taken aback, and thought about it for a while. Her reply was to the point: that they usually met around that time on Monday evenings and that both families knew. But it was not something they talked about otherwise, though their fellow students, neighbours and others might, of course, have seen or heard about it.

I jotted this down and took a deep breath. And then I cut straight to the chase.

'You and Agnes had an argument the day before yesterday, didn't you?'

She hesitated for a second, then gave a stiff nod.

'It breaks my heart that we had to end like that. Agnes was five days older than me, and we grew up only a couple hundred yards from each other. We were best friends before we even started school, we sang in a choir together when we were teen-agers, started to study theology together when we were twenty, and had never really fought in all those years. But then we argued on the last day she was alive. In my confusion and despair, I only made things worse by lying to you about what had happened. God will never forgive me.'

Nora Jensen's slight frame suddenly started to shake as she spoke, and a tear ran down her right cheek. It is not pleasant to witness despair, but it was a relief all the same. Perhaps the case was not so puzzling after all. Something we hadn't known about was now coming to the surface.

'That can perhaps be rectified, but you must put all your cards on the table and tell me the truth. What did you and Agnes argue about the day before yesterday?'

Nora Jensen had stopped crying, but was staring at some invisible mark on the wall. Her voice was distant when she started to speak.

'Agnes and I used to joke that we were training to be women priests, who are more priest than woman, and so didn't have the same problems as other women. But in the end, it turns out that women priests are not so different, and in fact are more woman than priest. We fell out over exactly the same thing that young women so often do. A man. That's the long and short of it.'

She sat there in silence and looked at me with pleading eyes. But I was no longer in the mood to humour the deceased's best friend. I made sure I could get a look at her hands as I said in a more severe voice that I had to know both who the man was and why they had argued about him.

'It's very personal and I'm sure it has nothing to do with the murder,' she tried. But fortunately she continued without me having to push her.

'And now I'm sitting here talking behind my dead friend's back, which doesn't feel any better. But you've asked me to tell you the truth. And that is that Agnes had many attractive qualities that often disguised a very unattractive one. She would frequently boast to me about how many men were in love with her, and she was nearly always right. She often bragged that so-and-so was hooked now, and she would let him flounder for a while before setting him free. She would then justify this by saying that men had too much power and dominated so many women that they deserved to be put in their place now and then. I'm sure she left behind a trail of broken hearts in high school. But that was a few years ago now and I can't imagine anyone from back then would want to harm her for it – certainly not now.'

She bit her lip and was almost suspiciously calm where she sat in her armchair. For a moment I regretted not taking Helgesen, and continued to keep my eyes on Nora's hands. They lay motionless on her lap.

'So, what about the man you argued over?' I asked.

'He could never kill anyone, no matter what the situation,' she replied.

A gentle smile slipped over her lips as she spoke. I had seen it once before, and understood immediately who she was thinking of.

'So we're talking about Agnes' tutor, Oscar Fredrik Bergendahl?'

Nora Jensen nodded, and at the same time gave a contrary wave with two fingers on her right hand.

'Yes, but he wasn't just her tutor. He was my tutor too, and for practically all the other female students in the school. His circumstances were really tragic. Everyone felt so sorry for him last year when his son died. We all knew that he had been terribly unlucky and that his marriage was not a happy one even before that happened. And now his wife is dying too, so . . .'

She broke off and bit her lip – harder this time. I immediately tried to press her on it.

'So what you're trying to tell me is that all the women in the school deeply sympathized with him, at the same time that they all hoped that they would take his dying wife's place?'

She nodded – heavy with resignation this time.

'It sounds worse when you put it like that, but yes, more or less. There were five of us, all unmarried, who had Oscar Fredrik as our tutor. Six, if you include one who is engaged. I think all of us, including the one who is engaged, were or had recently been in love with him. Everyone except the one he perhaps was interested in himself. And that was of course Agnes.'

She said this with a grimace and a bitter undertone. A very different picture of the relationship between Nora Jensen and Agnes Halvorsen was starting to emerge. They might well have been born in the same month, grown up together and been best friends before they even started school, but Nora was still five days younger and had for all these years been the less confident, less beautiful and less clever friend. Agnes had always come first, even when Nora finally dared to fall in love with a man. It was a familiar story. Women had killed each other for less.

'I can't be sure about the others. But Agnes was convinced that he was in love with her, and she was normally right. I had the same impression.'

I was on the offensive now and asked her why she had got that impression, but before she had a chance to answer, I added another question: had she ever spoken about it directly with her tutor?

Nora Jensen was suddenly oddly on her guard and distant at the same time. She looked at me with eyes that were more alive than before, but her voice was still slow and flat.

'My feelings got the better of me towards the end of a one-to-one session, when he had been very helpful and seemed to be so interested in me and my studies. I plucked up my courage and rashly asked if we could go and have a coffee. It was stupid and inappropriate. He handled it well and was very considerate, and said that it was not really the right thing for a man with a very sick wife to do. I offered to wait until some time later in the spring. He then gently explained that he would respect his wife as long as she lived, and that any future plans were focused elsewhere.'

This was interesting news. If the tutor had made his feelings known to a student who did not return them, we had both a motive for murder and a possible scandal on our hands. I didn't waste any time.

'Do you know that it was Agnes he was thinking of with regard to his future plans? And did you get the impression they had talked about it together?'

Nora Jensen looked like a tired woman in a tight corner. She sat with her head in her hands for a few moments, as if it helped her to remember. Then she swallowed a couple of times, but her voice and words were just as monotone and steady when she finally spoke.

'I don't know for certain, no. I just put two and two together when Agnes later confided in me that he was in love with her.

As usual, she found it amusing that a man had shown an interest in her, and, as usual, the feeling was not mutual. That was when we started to argue. It wasn't her fault that men fell in love with her, and obviously she was under no obligation to return their feelings. But I thought it was mean of her to keep him on tenterhooks like that, when his wife was dying. And, of course, I still hoped that he might turn to me when he realized there was no future with her.'

She spoke faster than before, and for longer. And then suddenly she was exhausted. She leaned her head back against a cushion and stared at the ceiling.

'And that's what you had argued about earlier in the day. In which case, I would be very grateful to know what actually happened when you met again in the evening.'

She kept staring at the ceiling. A spasm in her neck showed that she was awake and had heard what I said, but it was about half a minute before she abruptly lifted her head and looked at me.

I could not be sure that I was looking at a murderer, but I was in no doubt that she was now feeling the pressure. As she talked, I see-sawed from sympathy to suspicion, moment by moment.

'I wasn't sure if Agnes would come as agreed after we'd argued, but she did. To begin with we both avoided the topic and talked about other things. Then just after ten o'clock, I took the bull by the horns and asked if she had thought any more about what we had discussed earlier in the day. She had, but still didn't feel she was under any obligation to resolve the situation. She thought it would be strange if she said anything to him about something they had never discussed. I got angry and said things that I should perhaps not have said, but luckily we sort of made up in the end. She was a bit more understanding and said that she would sleep on it. I followed her out and asked her to call me as soon as she got home, and she said she would. Then she walked off into the night alone, and was killed.'

Her voice broke when she said this. Nora Jensen was clearly vacillating between ambivalent feelings for her dead friend, and it felt as though she was still holding something back. So I chose to take the open approach and asked if she was hiding anything from me. It worked.

'There was another thing that we didn't speak about, that remained unresolved. I wondered more and more if Agnes, who had kept so many men dangling, had also fallen hook, line and sinker. And I thought to myself it wouldn't be a bad thing if she got a taste of her own medicine.'

Again, there was a spiteful undertone.

I said it was understandable that she should feel like that, and asked who she thought Agnes had been in love with, if it was not her tutor.

To my great satisfaction, I had guessed the name before she said it – though, to be fair, I didn't have many others to choose from.

'Jan Ove Eliassen. To begin with I was a little taken aback at how gentle she was when she spoke about him, even though he was opposed to women priests and pretty much everything she stood for. But as he moderated some of his more conservative views, they seemed to disagree less and less. And then recently she started to say things that surprised me and suddenly they seemed to agree. I tried to talk to her about it, to gauge how much she actually liked him, but she just looked away, which was very unlike her. He's good-looking, you've got to give him that. Apparently he's been going steady with a woman from his church for over a year, so if Agnes really had fallen for him, she may well have finally felt the pain of unrequited love herself. But if anything ever happened between them, she certainly never told me about it, so you'll have to ask him.'

I made a mental note to do precisely that. It was clear that I not only had to talk to Oscar Fredrik Bergendahl again soon, but also had to meet Jan Ove Eliassen for the first time.

In the meantime, I asked Nora if she wanted to change her statement about what had happened after Agnes left the house the night before last. She was quick to answer this time.

'No, I swear to God, every word is true. She was in a relatively relaxed mood and not at all bothered about walking home alone at night. Then I sat there waiting for the phone call that never came. I ran out into the dark and found her dead. I didn't see anyone else, but was so frightened that I ran back here to call the police. I don't want to change or add anything to my statement, now or ever.'

She said this in such a clear voice and with such conviction that I could not help but believe her.

It was now half past eleven. I said that we should perhaps drive over to the School of Theology. She nodded and stood up. We left the untouched pot of coffee on the table and went out to the car without a word.

We didn't speak in the car either. She had clearly said all she had to say. And I had more than enough to think about.

We really only had Nora Jensen's word that she was telling the truth about what had happened. She had lied to me two days in a row and there was a possible jealousy motive.

Oscar Fredrik Bergendahl could also have a motive, if he

had been rejected by Agnes Halvorsen in the days leading up to her death.

And the as yet unknown to me Jan Ove Eliassen could also have a motive, depending on what he and Agnes had talked about in the library, and on whether anything had happened between them.

I thought the case was now just as perplexing as before, but in a different way, because there were several possible murderers in the victim's close circle. And the mysterious strangler could in fact be sitting next to me in the car right now.

I did not really believe that to be the case, but I could not be sure. My passenger had once again closed down and sat in conspicuous silence, deep in thought all the way. She was slightly taller than I had at first thought, closer to five foot five than five two in flat shoes.

As I was about to park the car, I remembered the one specific question that I had not asked Nora Jensen.

'Can you remember when Agnes arrived at the lecture theatre for Monday's lecture? Was she there by two o'clock, or did she come at a quarter past?'

Again, Nora Jensen's eyes quickened as I spoke. Her mouth tightened before she answered.

'Now that you ask – I realized last night that I should have mentioned it to you, even though I doubt it's of any significance. Agnes was normally there in good time, but on Monday, she was actually late for the lecture. That had never happened before, so I started to wonder if she'd gone home without saying anything. But then she slipped in a few minutes late and sat at the back close to the door.'

Nora Jensen should certainly have told me that before. It was an interesting detail, which if proved to be true could indicate that Agnes had experienced something dramatic in the meantime.

III

Helgesen had come on the tram and was waiting for me outside the lecture theatre, as agreed. Nora Jensen greeted him briefly and then went in.

Helgesen and I stood by the door and watched a couple of dozen male students walk in and find places. Despite some variation in height, weight, hair colour and clothes, they were a remarkably homogeneous group. All of them were correctly dressed men in their twenties, with short hair. Only two women had ventured to join them at the last lecture on Monday. It was now Wednesday and one of the two was dead and other already seated. The atmosphere was subdued and sombre.

Things livened up when a group of students from Oslo University arrived, adding a splash of colour with their long hair, hippie vests and badges against Norwegian membership of the EEC and the war in Vietnam. The group of five also included two women. The young man sitting nearest to where I was standing was of medium height, slightly overweight and wore reading glasses with heavy frames. He spoke in a southern Norwegian accent and was energetically discussing the latest developments in the Socialist People's Party and the prospects for next year's general election. I thought to myself that even the School of Theology was changing and I kept my ears open to hear if he mentioned either the murder victim Agnes, or my former fiancée, Miriam.

Today, Oscar Fredrik Bergendahl was to lecture on Old Testament texts. He came in at twelve minutes past twelve, with a Bible and a bundle of handwritten notes under his arm. If the lecturer was either alarmed or surprised to see us there, he hid it well. His smile was perhaps a little stiff, but his handshake was firm when he welcomed me back. He then shook Helgesen's hand, but continued to look at me. In a quiet voice, he asked if I wanted to say something to the students before the lecture, or should he? The students had no doubt understood that we were from the police, and the chances of getting information were perhaps better if the request came directly from us. So I said that it might be best if he first called for a minute's silence for the deceased, and then handed over to me.

He was clearly happy to cooperate and said: 'Good plan. I'd thought of suggesting that as well.'

He then nodded twice, first to the person behind me and then to me.

I quickly turned my head. A dark young man in a suit, with short, dark hair and horn-rimmed glasses, had raised his hand in greeting as he came in. I noticed an engagement ring gleam as he lowered his right hand, and saw that he had a document holder under his left arm.

In terms of appearance, this student did not really stand out from the other correctly dressed men in the auditorium. He was possibly a little taller and more imposing than most, but was no more than five foot nine and not particularly broad across the shoulders. What was striking, however, was his confidence and determination. I would have guessed it was Jan Ove Eliassen, even without the lecturer's reaction.

The clock on the wall showed fourteen minutes past

twelve. The lecturer and I noticed at the same time, and we both went to find our places.

A quick headcount told me that there were twenty-seven male students and three female students in the auditorium when the lecture started. Nora Jensen sat on her own in the back row, with her back against the wall and her jacket still on. It was easy to understand why she might want to have an over-view and keep warm. I found myself wondering if Agnes Halvorsen had also tended to sit at the back.

Jan Ove Eliassen was also sitting on his own, but in the middle, with several empty places to his left and right. As far as I could tell, he was watching the lecturer and me with interest. I had no way of knowing whether he had been sit-ting in the same place at the last lecture or not, but just as we took our seats, he leaned back with an ease that demonstrated either immense self-confidence, or that this was his usual place.

And if that was the case, Agnes Halvorsen had then sat as far away as she could from him and her friend at the last lecture.

'Welcome to today's lecture, which sadly is a rather special one. As many of you perhaps already know, one of our flock was suddenly called to the Lord, all too soon, on Monday night. Our thoughts are with her parents and brother. Agnes' death is also a great loss for the school and all those who knew her. She was a remarkably gifted student and a remarkably good person. So let us begin today's lecture with a minute's silence in honour of Agnes Halvorsen.'

It was a short speech, but the lecturer's voice was sonorous and commanded respect. There was a charged silence in the lecture hall for the next minute. I could see tears in the eyes of several students, but no reaction in the two faces I was watching most closely. I thought that perhaps this was because they had already had time to think about the case. Or perhaps it was because they had seen some of the victim's less attractive traits.

Then the minute's silence was over. First there was a rustling of paper and the sound of pens on tables, and then Oscar Fredrik Bergendahl started to speak.

'Agnes' death is being treated as suspicious, and a representative from Oslo Police would now like to say a few words.'

He stepped back and left the lectern to me.

I gave my name, which provoked a couple of gasps from the audience. I did not expect any reaction from the back row, so I kept my eyes trained on Jan Ove Eliassen. His face was just as concentrated and showed no emotion.

I then told them that the death was being investigated as a possible murder, and asked anyone in the room who might have information that could be relevant to contact Oslo Police as soon as possible. We were particularly interested in what Agnes had done and said on Monday, but also in anything that might have happened in the weeks and months leading up to her death.

The room was silent as I returned to my seat.

I did not expect any of them to talk to me there and then, and even though Oscar Fredrik Bergendahl was undoubtedly an excellent lecturer, I had no desire to sit there for the next two hours listening to him talk about Old Testament texts, and nor was there any point. So I slipped out of the lecture hall as soon as it was possible. Helgesen had fortunately had the sense to sit by the door, and followed me.

'We can't really do any more now until the lecture finishes at two. Unless we were to take people out of the lecture, and we're not going to do that, are we?' Helgesen said in a quiet voice as we stood on our own outside the lecture hall. I suggested that we went back to the station in the meantime.

In the car, I updated Helgesen on my earlier conversation with Nora Jensen.

'It's not obviously untrustworthy,' he said, when I'd finished.

'Obviously untrustworthy' was one of Helgesen's favourite expressions. And in this instance, I had to say, it was appropriate. But Helgesen agreed that Nora Jensen's explanation would have been less obviously untrustworthy yesterday than it was today.

Neither of us said what we were both thinking: that we could not rule out the possibility that the friend was the murderer, but equally we could not imagine she was. The natural conclusion was therefore that we should go back to the School of Theology for the end of the lecture and have a chat first with the star student, Jan Ove Eliassen, and then with the star tutor, Oscar Fredrik Bergendahl.

IV

I learned, with mixed feelings, that there were no messages waiting for us at the station.

After a quick lunch, consisting of coffee and a Danish pastry, I flicked through the day's editions of *Dagbladet* and *Verdens Gang* to see what they had written about the case. *Dagbladet* was more cautious in its reporting, as *Arbeiderbladet* and *Aftenposten* had been. The paper was more interested in the liberal Hubert Humphrey's chances of winning the Democratic presidential nomination in the USA the second time round.

Verdens Gang showed more interest in the case and went further. Under the headline 'Minister's Daughter Murdered by Roadside', one of the paper's best crime journalists claimed that the police were dealing with a brutal murder.

This was within the limits of what was to be expected. The cause of death would get out sooner or later. What was more worrying, however, was the mention of 'a small picture or symbol found on the body' that had proved to be a bit of a headache for the police. It did not say that it was an ant, and the report made no mention of the blouse.

As a rule, I never rang journalists, but now I felt compelled to make an exception.

I had met the *Verdens Gang* reporter Knud Haasund a couple of times and knew him to be an ambitious scandalmonger, but also a straightforward and fair young man – which was precisely how he came across on the telephone. He of course wanted to have the best possible relationship with 'the police in general and you, in particular', he said, but he also had a duty to society and his editor to keep the readers as informed as possible.

Obviously he did not want to disclose his source – which was not unexpected, in the same way that he did not expect me to confirm or deny the information. And I assured him I did not want to create any problems for 'the newspaper in general and you, in particular', but warned that any further mention of details from the scene of the crime could be damaging to the investigation and so they could expect a reaction. Knud Haasund assured me that he and the newspaper were fully aware of their responsibilities and 'would not go further than necessary with regard to reporting details from the scene of the crime'.

We ended the phone call on a relatively friendly note, given the circumstances, but I was not at all sure that our mutual understanding would last until tomorrow's edition.

The lecture was not due to finish for another three-quarters of an hour and I had no idea how best to use the time. So I dialled Patricia's number.

She answered the phone as soon as it rang and listened to my summary of what Nora Jensen had said.

'It seems that we might be a little closer to finding an explanation in Agnes Halvorsen's circle of friends and family,' I concluded.

'Closer, yes, but there's still a long way to go,' was Patricia's prompt reply – followed by an unexpectedly heavy sigh.

She had no better suggestion than I did for what I should do now. And that seemed to bother her.

'We clearly need to get together later on today to discuss this further. But why don't we meet at your place rather than mine? Less because a change is as good as a rest, and it's good for me to get out, and more because you should be available if there are any new developments in the case,' she said with sudden determination.

It came a bit out of the blue. I said that it was a nice idea, but that I didn't have anything suitable to offer such a distinguished guest, and sadly would not have time to make supper.

Patricia had obviously thought of this. She replied swiftly that she and the maid could bring some food with them and prepare it in my kitchen, so there would be no extra work or cost for me.

It felt as though the matter was decided, but I wasn't particularly happy about it. I still did not like the idea that my neighbours might see a young woman in a wheelchair coming to visit me, especially in the middle of a murder investigation that was about to hit the headlines. But I couldn't tell her that and had no good arguments to deflect her. I had been invited to Patricia's for supper so many times that I could hardly say no if she now wanted to come to my flat with food.

So I asked instead if we could perhaps meet at seven o'clock, which she immediately agreed to. It was quite possible that Patricia understood that I was not finding things easy today, because she said in her least sarcastic voice that she was looking forward to it and that with our 'joint efforts' we would no doubt have a breakthrough in this investigation too.

It certainly helped a little to be reminded of our previous successes and to hear an encouraging voice. So I thanked her and said that I was looking forward to seeing her in the evening.

Patricia ended by joking that I had every reason to look forward to it.

And as Helgesen and I drove back up to the university, I speculated about what she had meant – and, to my irritation, couldn't even be certain of that.

V

We were outside the lecture hall again by ten to two, just in case the lecture finished early. But Oscar Fredrik Bergendahl obviously belonged to a small minority of lecturers who were both conscientious and precise. At exactly two o'clock, a subdued applause could be heard from inside.

The lecturer came out first. I went over to meet him and said that we would like to talk to him again later on in the afternoon. He said that he had a supervision session now, but that we could just knock on the door whenever we wanted to talk to him. He walked at a brisk pace as he spoke, and I realized that he did not want to be seen in conversation with the police.

The students followed. Some came out alone, others in groups of two or three. Nora Jensen came out on her own and surprisingly quickly. She was walking fast and seemed almost to swim through the crowd. She must have kept her jacket on and left as soon as the lecture was over. No one spoke to her, as far as I could see.

I asked if the lecture had been good and if she was happy to get the bus home. She answered yes to both questions, before floating away on the stream of students.

Both Helgesen and I started to wonder if Jan Ove Eliassen had managed to sneak past us in some mysterious way, but he was in fact the last person to come out, once all the others had disappeared. He had his document holder in one hand and a Bible in the other.

When he saw us, he stopped. There was still no reaction in his face. I got the distinct impression that he was an intelligent and grounded person, but also that he was hiding something.

'Are you Jan Ove Eliassen?' I asked.

He said yes, and we shook hands. His hand was supple and slender, and his grip was firm. I found myself thinking that this hand was possibly strong enough to strangle someone.

I asked if there was anywhere we could talk without being disturbed. He said that one of the seminar rooms up by the library should be free at this time of day and then led the way.

It took no more than three minutes, and not a word was said during the walk.

We found an empty room with a table and five chairs. Jan Ove Eliassen sat looking at us with an empty chair on either side, his back to the wall.

I started by telling him that, as a matter of routine, we were gathering information about Agnes Halvorsen from those who had known her, and asked what his impression of her was.

He was quiet for a few moments, then spoke for longer than I had anticipated, in a steady, controlled voice.

'I have to admit that I was sceptical when we first met last year. At the time, I was against women training to become priests, and very much influenced by my grandfather, my father and my uncles. But now I am open to it, largely thanks to Agnes. I don't think it will offend any of my male peers when I say that, certainly from a theoretical point of view, she was better than any of them. My impression of her as a person also improved over time. Our values and views became more aligned as I became less conservative and she became less radical. In fact, I would even venture to say that in recent weeks we got on quite well, and had developed a respect for each other, though we never met socially and were not close friends. I was first shocked, and then deeply upset when I heard from a fellow student yesterday that Agnes had been killed. And I have no idea of who might have done it.'

He looked me straight in the eye when he said this. I grabbed the opportunity and held his gaze when I asked my next question.

'You went over to talk to her in the library the day before yesterday, shortly before the lecture. Can I ask what you talked about?'

This didn't seem to surprise Jan Ove Eliassen either. He gave it about five seconds' thought, and showed no sign of emotion.

'When I sat down at my place in the library, I found a folded note from Agnes that said, *Can we talk before the lecture?* I considered for a while whether I should answer it or not and I came to the conclusion that it would be rude not to. I thought sending notes was childish, so eventually I went over and asked what she wanted to talk to me about. She said that she didn't want to discuss it there, but we could perhaps meet down the hallway by the stairs at ten to two. I agreed, but didn't particularly want to leave the library at the same time as her, so I went to the canteen, where I had a cup of coffee and a couple of doughnuts, then went to meet her as agreed.'

He stopped abruptly. Helgesen and I leaned forwards over the table at the same time.

'Did she come?' I asked.

Jan Ove Eliassen nodded – and suddenly looked up at a point on the wall above our heads, then continued.

'She came at the time we'd agreed, but our meeting was of a strictly personal nature. If you knew the truth you would understand why, if you were to ask what happened next, it would put me in a very uncomfortable ethical situation.'

It appeared that we were very close to something now. I replied, perhaps a little meanly, that we would have to hear the full story before we knew if we needed to know the whole truth. I added rather solemnly that the situation was critical and that he risked being added to the list of suspects if he refused to cooperate with the police. He of course had the right to talk to a lawyer first, if he so wished.

'When you have a clear conscience, there's no need for a lawyer. But I'm now faced with a difficult dilemma and would be grateful if you could give me a few minutes to discuss it with God before I make my final decision. I can assure you again that what was said between us has nothing to do with Agnes' death and solely concerned us, and that I have no idea who might have killed her.'

It was clear that Helgesen, behind his jovial appearance, could smell blood too: his chair was suddenly a good foot and a half closer to the table. He opened his mouth to say something, but then stopped when I held up my hand.

I said to Jan Ove Eliassen that he could have a few minutes to himself, but that he should not leave the room. He thanked me and said that we were welcome to stay there with him if we wanted.

Helgesen and I withdrew to the other side of the room and watched the rather unexpected scene from there. Jan Ove Eliassen sat quietly by the table, and shed all the confidence and control he had shown until now. Several times, his previously calm face twisted to the point where it was unrecognizable. Then suddenly he started to talk to himself, without the words making any sense. At first it seemed that he was answering questions, but then it was more as though he was responding to orders. 'Yes, of course,' he said, his face still contorting. 'No, I won't say that,' he said almost immediately after. There were a couple more spasms in his face, and then finally he said, 'Yes, that's how it must be. Forgive me my doubt.'

It was as though he was in a trance when he talked. But following the final and longest exclamation, he sat in silence again. His face gradually calmed. Then suddenly he turned and waved us over.

'God has told me that given the situation I can and should tell you the truth about what happened on Monday. But first I must tell you why I wasn't sure how to respond to Agnes' note. I had noticed over the past few weeks that she was keener to talk to me than before. Some of the other students noticed too. I said that I didn't think there was any romantic interest on her part, and there certainly wasn't on mine, though I have to admit that I found her more attractive than I had done when we first met. But I have had a steady girlfriend for over a year now, so I wasn't sure if it would be right to meet Agnes alone. And I have regretted over and over again that I agreed to it.'

Helgesen and I were both gripped by the story now. The young man's odd behaviour had certainly made me question his sanity.

'Are you absolutely sure that you need more details?'

Helgesen and I answered impatiently in unison that we did. He nodded in resignation.

'In that case, you should perhaps follow me to where it happened.'

He got up and left the room without waiting for an answer. We followed him obediently until he stopped a short way along the corridor by the stairs that led down to the lecture theatre. There was a door in the wall.

'This is where we met. I got here at ten to two and she came shortly after. I asked what she wanted to talk to me about. Without saying anything, she opened the door to the cleaning cupboard here and pulled me in.'

He held the door for us. We slowly shuffled in. The cupboard was just over six foot to the ceiling and about five feet wide. There was barely space for three people in there between the buckets and mops.

We both looked at Jan Ove Eliassen in anticipation. He

carried on talking without a prompt, but lowered his voice when he spoke.

'She pulled me in here, closed the door and turned the key. Then she threw her arms round me and whispered that she loved me more than anything on earth. I scarcely knew what was happening before I felt her tongue in my mouth. I registered – to my horror – that I was kissing her back. She was very beautiful and I was filled with an ungodly desire.'

Jan Ove Eliassen was only a couple of feet away and looked straight at me as he told his version of what had happened here two days earlier. The situation felt awkward – and his explanation was shocking.

'So what you're saying is that on Monday you had sexual intercourse with Agnes Halvorsen here in the cleaning cupboard, but that it was on her initiative?'

I exchanged a furtive glance with Helgesen, who was smiling discreetly over Jan Ove Eliassen's shoulder. We knew something that the student didn't – that Agnes Halvorsen had never had sexual intercourse with a man. If Eliassen said otherwise now, he was obviously lying.

All of a sudden, I had a clear picture of what had happened: it was him and not her who had hoped for a sexual encounter here in the cleaning cupboard. She had managed to get free and left. She had perhaps then, or later in the day, threatened to report him, which would cause a scandal. So he had followed her later that evening and strangled her – either out of jealousy or to save his skin.

My theory looked impressive for a few seconds, then collapsed like a house of cards when Jan Ove Eliassen carried on in an even more hushed voice.

'No. That's not what happened at all. It's what might have

happened – if I had wanted it to. I was completely unprepared for the situation and suddenly found her tongue in my mouth and realized that I was kissing her back. Her body was hot and wild in a way I had never imagined she could be. She grabbed my right hand and pushed it up under her top. I stood there with my hand on her stomach – and then noticed her skirt falling down her legs. She was standing there in only her panties and I felt her pulling my hand down towards them. I had never experienced such temptation. But then thankfully, with God's help, I managed to regain control. I pulled myself free, fumbled for the door and staggered out into the corridor. I tumbled rather than walked down the stairs. I have to admit, I felt an animal impulse to turn, go back into the cupboard and rip off all her clothes. But I didn't. I remembered the story of Sodom and Gomorrah and I did not look back. I was in the auditorium just after two. Sitting among my fellow students the whole thing felt unreal, and I had to ask myself several times whether it had really happened or was just a bad dream. Agnes did not appear until just after the lecture had started. When she came in, she sat down by the door and did not look at me. She didn't turn her head in my direction once during the lecture. Then I knew it was real. It's not a story I'm proud of, and I certainly did not want to talk about it after her death. You'll never hear her version, but you have my oath that it's the truth.'

Jan Ove Eliassen's explanation had come in a long but controlled stream of words that now suddenly stopped. He stood there looking at me, as did Helgesen.

At first, I thought the student's story sounded a little far-fetched. And yet he had told it in a very matter-of-fact way, and had kept eye contact all the time.

I found myself searching for questions that might expose the cracks in his explanation. I couldn't think of any. So in the end, I said that if what he had said was true, he would be able to tell us what colour panties Agnes Halvorsen had been wearing on Monday.

I thought for a moment that I'd hit the bullseye when a shadow passed over his face. But then he answered swiftly and clearly: 'I took great pains to see as little as possible of her panties, but I believe they were pale yellow.'

Which was right. It only proved that he had seen them, however, and barely even that. But his explanation was remarkably coherent.

Eventually I said that we only had his word for the fact that it was she who had taken the initiative. A witness had seen him going over to talk to her in the library, but no one had seen the note.

Without flinching, he put his hand into his trouser pocket and pulled out a wallet which he held towards me.

In the wallet, I found one fifty-kroner and two ten-kroner notes, three one-krone coins – and a piece of paper with exactly the words he had quoted. I immediately recognized the writing from Agnes Halvorsen's lecture notes.

Helgesen coughed and said that it was both foolhardy and brazen of Agnes Halvorsen to push things so far with a fellow student who she knew was already engaged.

The young man between us acknowledged the underlying question with a nod, and again looked straight at me when he answered.

'In her defence, and in the name of truth, she was acting in good faith at that point. I wasn't engaged on Monday afternoon. But I went home after the lecture on Monday and had a long conversation with God about what had happened and life in general. And I concluded that my girlfriend was the only one right for me, so I took a taxi to her house and proposed.'

This part of the story sounded even more preposterous to me. I could not imagine proposing after an experience like that, let alone asking God if I should. But then, from a deeply religious theology student's point of view, it was perhaps logical.

I now had only one question left to ask Jan Ove Eliassen, and his answer could free him from suspicion.

'As a matter of routine, I have to ask what you did for the rest of Monday evening.'

Jan Ove Eliassen clearly understood the purpose of my question. He gave a slight nod and let out a heavy sigh.

'I went to my fiancée's at around seven and was there until half past ten. We live very close to each other in Montebello, so it only took me about five minutes to get back, and then I was at home alone.'

There was silence in the cleaning cupboard for a brief moment.

'My parents came home from a fiftieth birthday party close to midnight, and my brother was out with friends as usual,' Jan Ove Eliassen added, with a hint of frustration.

I felt my anger flare against this unflappable young man. I fully believed that he had been at home. But the list of people who had been within striking distance in the west of Oslo and did not have an alibi was becoming frustratingly long.

I told him he was currently not a suspect and could go home, but that he should stay in town for the next few days in case we needed to ask any more questions.

Jan Ove Eliassen did not protest. I dare say he realized that he was still in a very precarious situation. He shook hands with me and then Helgesen, said once again that he was deeply shocked by Agnes Halvorsen's death, and apologized for what he had had to tell us. Then he opened the door and left.

He left as he claimed he had done on Monday. Quickly and without looking back. Again he had the Bible in one hand and his document holder in the other, as though it helped him to keep his balance. I could see that both his hands were shaking, and understood only too well that he might feel uncertain and confused in his current situation.

As he disappeared out of sight, I thought that if his story was true, Jan Ove Eliassen had, through no fault of his own, ended up in a situation where he might need strong faith to cope.

Helgesen and I stood in the corridor outside the cleaning cupboard. There was no one to be seen in either direction.

'We should probably get someone from forensics to examine the cleaning cupboard. This is a murder case after all, though it's not likely they'll find anything of use there,' I said.

'Yes,' Helgesen agreed.

We fell into our own thoughts again.

'Do you think I did the right thing?' I asked in a quiet voice.

'I think what you did was right, boss. His explanation was not obviously untrustworthy. And no matter what one might think, it was not enough to arrest him on suspicion of murder. A good lawyer would have had him released within a couple of hours,' he replied.

I agreed and suggested that we should go and talk to the next man on our list.

VI

A student was just coming out of Oscar Fredrik Bergendahl's office as we arrived. The student was a short young man with fair hair, who clearly lacked confidence. His eyes widened behind his thick glasses when he recognized us. For a moment he stopped and nervously wrung his hands, but then gave us a wide berth without shaking hands or saying anything.

It was almost as if the lecturer had been standing behind the door waiting for us. He opened it only seconds after I'd knocked and promptly showed us in.

'Welcome back. How can I help you with this tragic case?' he asked, as soon as we were all seated.

In an attempt to be friendly, I asked how his wife was. He thanked me and answered that her condition had not changed since yesterday evening, but that he hoped and prayed for an improvement today.

Then there was silence. We looked at each other in anticipation. I assured him that he was still not suspected of anything criminal, but that I had some more questions I would like to ask about the dead student and her friend.

I felt sorry for the man who now shuttled daily from his home to the office to the hospital. So I started gently by remarking that it seemed he was personal tutor to most of the female students in the school, and it was said that several of them felt a good deal of sympathy for him in his current situation.

He nodded to this, and leaned back in his chair before answering.

'I understand where this is going and I thank you for your

tact. I am in fact personal tutor to all our female students and am aware that people joke about it. But the fact is that I am the only tutor available who was born after the First World War and the only one who unequivocally supports women priests. I am an advocate of a broader and more accessible state church. And here in the school, I have championed a more open academic programme.'

It sounded more like a defence speech than an answer. He seemed to realize this and changed tack after drawing breath.

'But to answer your questions, a few weeks ago I had a supervision meeting with Nora Jensen which took a rather uncomfortable turn. She made it clear that she would like to meet me in more private circumstances. And I made it clear that I could not fulfil her wish, either now or in the future. She accepted this. And while I would rather not have been asked the question, I didn't feel the situation was awkward in any way after I had told her.'

So far, this tallied well with Nora Jensen's story. But it was not her I was asking about, and I was sure that he knew that. I therefore made my point more explicitly.

'That's all well and good as regards Nora Jensen, but Agnes Halvorsen is our main concern here. Was there at any point a similar conversation between Agnes and yourself, and if so, what happened?'

Oscar Fredrik Bergendahl held his breath for a moment, then shook his head vigorously.

'No, there wasn't. Anyone who says otherwise is a liar. As I said last time, I had a very favourable impression of Agnes and we always got on well. But she never mentioned anything of the sort you're alluding to – and nor did I.'

He looked less friendly and was breathing more heavily

than before, but still held my gaze. I was not convinced – so I leaned forwards and applied more pressure with an even more direct question.

'I apologize, but as the case stands, I am obliged to remind you of the ninth commandment and ask whether or not you had romantic feelings for Agnes Halvorsen and imagined that you might have a relationship with her in the future?'

As soon as I said this I realized I had gone too far. But the emotional outburst that I had in part hoped for, and in part feared, did not materialize. His voice had an edge to it when he answered, but he continued to lean back calmly in his chair.

'In that case, I apologize, and can only say that I am willing to answer you with regard to my words and my actions, but my thoughts will remain between me and God. The late Agnes Halvorsen and I never discussed the possibility of anything along the lines you're suggesting.'

There seemed to be little point in continuing. We had seen a glimpse of a more forceful and less friendly Oscar Fredrik Bergendahl, but that was all. His explanation was clear and, as far as we could tell, tallied well with Nora Jensen's.

I knew that I had pushed the limits and said in a more con-ciliatory tone that we unfortunately had to ask a lot of people very difficult questions in the course of an investigation.

Oscar Fredrik Bergendahl was still breathing heavily, but replied in a similar tone that he understood and hoped that we would find the killer. He said nothing more as we stood up and left.

VII

There was a young man waiting in the corridor when Helgesen and I came out of Bergendahl's office. The student we had passed on the way in was still hovering, flapping his hands, one of which he now held out first to me and then to Helgesen.

'The name's Trygve Andersen. This may perhaps be a waste of your time. I didn't really know poor Agnes. But at the lecture, you asked anyone who had seen something unusual involving her on Monday to come forward. I did see something on Monday, which was possibly quite harmless, but it was definitely unusual. So I thought perhaps . . .'

He flapped his hand again. To give him some encouragement, I said that he had done the right thing to speak to us. He pointed to a door further down the corridor, which proved to be an empty seminar room.

'I'm really not sure how important it is, but it was definitely very odd. I was sitting in the library reading a story from the Acts of the Apostles and had completely lost track of time, but fortunately realized it was almost ten past two. I rushed down the corridor and stairs to get to the lecture on time. And as I was coming down the stairs, I saw Agnes coming out of the cleaning cupboard,' he said, as soon as we had sat down.

Then he stopped and looked at me.

I told him that this was definitely of interest and ask him to continue.

'I'm afraid there isn't much more to tell. She looked very pensive – maybe even depressed. I thought that perhaps she wasn't feeling well. I stopped and asked if everything was all right. She waved me away without saying anything. I didn't want to push her, and nor did I want to be late for the lecture, so I hurried on and managed to find myself a place with only a couple of minutes to spare. She came in a few minutes later. It's the only time I can ever remember her being late for a lecture, and certainly the only time I've seen her coming out of a cleaning cupboard. But I'm afraid I can't tell you any more.'

I told him again that he had done the right thing to come forward. He thanked us and then left with hurried steps.

'So now we know. She was in the cleaning cupboard and was the last one to leave,' Helgesen said.

To which I could only agree. It was still possible that Jan Ove Eliassen had somehow lured Agnes into the cupboard, made his advances and then fled when they weren't reciprocated, but the evidence so far seemed to indicate that his version was the truth. In which case, having fallen suddenly in love, her desperate attempt at physical intimacy was a sad final chapter in Agnes Halvorsen's life. And it was very likely that it had absolutely nothing to do with the fact that she was murdered later that evening. According to his statement, Jan Ove Eliassen had kissed her only a few hours before she was killed and he was the closest we had come to a suspect. But we were still far from any formal arrest and the way forward in the investigation was still not clear.

'Well, what do you think? Was he really talking to God?' I asked my assistant in a slightly sarcastic voice.

Helgesen's reply was succinct and pragmatic, as always. 'It's of little consequence to the investigation whether I think he was talking to God or not. What's more important for us is whether he himself thought he was talking to God. And I do absolutely believe that to be the case. I've seen several of my deeply religious aunts and uncles behave in the same way.'

I had no idea that Helgesen had deeply religious relatives, but had no particular desire to know any more about them now.

'What do you make of his explanation otherwise?' I asked.

Helgesen gave an unexpected smile when he answered. 'It's strange: even detectives often still have things to learn from life. If you had asked me the same question six months ago, I would probably have doubted the credibility of his story. But today, I'd say he was telling the truth. And what we heard just now corroborates his version.'

I couldn't help asking Helgesen what had happened in his life in the past six months that made him believe Eliassen's story. He took his time, but then smiled wanly and replied.

'My quiet, kind eldest daughter came back from folk high school just before Christmas. She had been expelled because she'd been caught with a boy the same age in a clothes cupboard, but without any clothes on. My wife still doesn't see the funny side of it, but I do. And the boy is a very nice young man, so now we hope that they might get engaged. They both agree that it was she who pulled him into the wardrobe, but that they're both responsible, as he did nothing to stop her. To begin with, I thought it was just a sign of the times, that young people no longer had any respect for school or the Church. But then I remembered what I was like at school, and we got up to plenty of mischief too, both boys and girls.'

I thought about my own school days, and had to agree. I added, without giving any reason, that one should never underestimate what a wilful young lady might manage, even if she was physically inferior.

Helgesen nodded. It was only later that I realized I had quoted Patricia almost word for word without thinking.

VIII

There were no messages for us at the switchboard when we got back to the police station just before half past three. There were, however, two men in suits waiting outside my office. They stood up at the same time, and both indicated that the other could talk to me first.

I left the pair of them standing in the corridor while I went to get Helgesen. Then I called in Jørgensen the pathologist, having first said to Helmer Halvorsen that I needed to hear what the pathologist had to say before speaking to him.

As we went into my office, the pathologist said he wouldn't take more than a few minutes, and he didn't disappoint. He had a tightly written three-page report with him, but it contained nothing new of any interest. The cause of death was suffocation due to external pressure on the throat, applied, it would seem, by bare hands. There were no traces of the perpetrator on the victim, nor were there any signs of violence from the neck down. The victim had otherwise been in very good health and there was no trace of alcohol in her blood. The last two details were new, but no great surprise.

Helmer Halvorsen was a more interesting visitor. He started by thanking me for taking the time to speak to him in the middle of an investigation, and conveyed his parents' greetings.

I asked him how they were, and to send them my best wishes.

He paused, then said that they were increasingly weighed down by grief. They maintained that God would never have allowed this to happen if they had listened to him and been firmer with their daughter. It all seemed more and more futile and baffling to them. As a result, they had shown a great interest in what had happened and who had killed their daughter.

'We discovered something at home that was quite a shock for my parents. I said that we should tell you immediately. We found this in Agnes' room, under her pillow.'

He made a dramatic pause. Then he pulled from his coat pocket a transparent plastic bag that contained a small bundle of toilet paper.

And in turn, the bundle of toilet paper contained a half-full blister pack of the contraceptive pill.

I looked from the pills to Helmer Halvorsen a couple of times. The second time, he raised his hands in defence.

'Don't get me wrong: this doesn't bother me in the slightest. My parents also accept that young women use contraceptives these days. But none of us were aware that my sister had gone on the pill and there didn't seem to be any reason for her to do so. So we wondered if she perhaps had a boyfriend who she hadn't told us about.'

I kept looking from the pills to the very serious young man in front of me. Then I exchanged a quick look with Helgesen. He appeared to be waiting for me to say something. I thought that this further confirmed the story about the cleaning cupboard that we had heard earlier, and I absolutely did not want to tell the victim's parents and brother about that and thereby just add to their burden.

So instead I said that we had found nothing to indicate that his sister was in a relationship with a man before she was killed, which was actually true enough. I added that on the basis of the autopsy, we could in fact rule out that she had ever had a sexual relationship with a man.

Helmer Halvorsen was visibly relieved when he heard this. He spontaneously took my hand and said that this would be of considerable comfort to his parents in their grief.

I felt some sympathy for this quiet and supportive brother, and was not a little curious about his relationship with his parents. So I promptly asked him about his own values.

Helmer Halvorsen was open and friendly when he replied that he had kept his childhood Christian faith, but that it had perhaps become a little dustier over the years than his parents might have wished. And for that very reason, he added quickly, it was important for him, as their remaining child, to support them as much as he could in their tragic circumstances.

I thought to myself that Helmer Halvorsen was truly the incarnation of one of society's small cogs: a quiet young man who did what was expected of him in relation to his family and his employer, without demanding any recognition – which I thought he deserved. And I noticed that there was a redness to his eyes which showed that behind his mask, his sister's death had affected him deeply. So I said that he had dealt with the situation very well and again thanked him for his help. He acknowledged this with a small smile, then left.

It was now five to four. The working day was nearly over. And it seemed that we were no further forward in the investigation than at the start of the day.

'What do you think?' I asked Helgesen.

'The tutor – or no one, I'd say. Either him, because he was attracted to her and then rejected, or a complete stranger we haven't met and who she didn't know,' was his reply.

I found it hard to see Oscar Fredrik Bergendahl as a murderer – certainly not when his wife was dying in hospital. But I had no better suggestions.

'So, either it was Bergendahl – and we are a long way from being able to prove that – or it was someone we don't know and therefore don't know where to look.'

Helgesen was silent and studied the wall for a few moments before he answered. For the first time, he also seemed to be slightly disheartened.

'That's about the sum of it, boss. You made every effort today, no one could have done better. And yet we're stuck. Perhaps this is one of those cases where the murderer has been both calculating and lucky, and we won't make headway unless we get more help than we've had so far.'

It was not an appealing prospect, but a good and sobering summary of the case all the same. I was anxious about what *Verdens Gang* might write about it tomorrow. My hope was that, before then, Patricia would manage to squeeze some blood from the stone that was this apparently unsolvable murder.

I said to Helgesen that he had also done everything that could be done today, and could now enjoy his time off until tomorrow morning with a clear conscience.

I sat down reluctantly to write another short press release. This confirmed that Agnes Halvorsen had been murdered and that the investigation had made some progress, but as yet no arrests had been made.

Once I had done this, I asked two forensics officers to look for possible fingerprints or other technical evidence in the cleaning cupboard at the School of Theology. And then I could think of nothing more to do.

IX

I was home by half past four, but did not finish cleaning the flat until a quarter to seven. Everything was slow today. The investigation had become an obsession. My thoughts continued to circle around it and the people involved, even when I was at home. The progress I had mentioned in the press release was in reality still lacking.

Fortunately, the same was not true of the cleaning, but I did come across an unexpected problem in the bedroom which highlighted my personal dilemma.

As I washed the floor, I thought about stories and events from when I was younger. And the more I recalled, the more I realized that Jan Ove Eliassen's cleaning cupboard story was not so implausible after all.

I suddenly remembered the well-intentioned advice given to me by a male friend after a couple of beers sometime in the 1950s: always put clean bed linen on the bed if you're expecting a visit from a lady. This was given in connection with a story about how he had finally managed to charm a very attractive young woman home with him, having 'invested a great deal of time and money', only for her to turn around at the bedroom door with the remark that the sheets weren't clean. He never got another chance, and the trauma still haunted him several girlfriends later.

I stood there looking at the bedclothes that had been used for a few nights now. They did not look particularly clean and fresh. I had brought a clean set with me when I came into the room, but after a few minutes' reflection, I decided to put it back in the cupboard.

Initially I told myself that it was a practical matter, as I had a limited supply of electricity and water, and usually changed the bed only once a week. But then I was more honest, if only with myself, and admitted that it was in fact my ambivalent feelings towards Patricia that were at the root of it.

I had had a lovely evening with her yesterday and was looking forward to hearing her voice again. When I pictured Patricia in clothes, I thought she was incredibly beautiful. But I was still not ready to see her without clothes – and certainly not in this bed this evening. When I looked at the bed and thought of a woman, it was still my ex-fiancée, Miriam, that I saw.

I turned away, punched the door frame – and went to sort out the kitchen.

Patricia arrived at seven o'clock on the dot. It would not be fair to complain about her lack of discretion. The car she used was a Volvo, one of the largest models. And she had to be lifted out of it. I carried her up to the flat myself, and the maid, Benedikte, followed us up the stairs with the wheelchair.

Patricia said nothing on the way up, but smiled broadly and did not seem to find the situation awkward at all. I did. Fortunately we did not bump into anyone on the stairs, but I was not naive enough to think that my neighbours would not have noticed the large car and my little visitor.

I knew that I should not be thinking like that, but I wasn't entirely happy with the idea that news of my evening visit from a disabled woman might spread. Particularly as the fact that I discussed my investigations with her had to be kept top secret.

So the evening started with a bad conscience on my part, but then improved considerably behind drawn curtains. The maid quickly disappeared into the kitchen and soon the smells that wafted through carried the promise of the best meal in the building that year. Patricia was in good spirits as she waited by the dining table. She listened intently to my account of the afternoon's events, and gave one of her sarcastic, unsympathetic teenage laughs when I told her the story about the cleaning cupboard at the School of Theology. I humoured her by adding the story about Helgesen's daughter and the wardrobe at the Christian folk high school.

'One should never underestimate what a young woman in love might do,' Patricia said with a chuckle, when she heard the second story.

I happily agreed with this, without knowing exactly what I was agreeing with.

The day's meat course and rice cream dessert were exquisite. The only problem was that by the time we had eaten her food and digested my story, we seemed to have spent all our good cheer and fell into graver thoughts. To my relief, Patricia did not smoke. But for a while she looked more and more gloomy.

I realized that not even Patricia could see an answer – and that bothered her. Again she said that she hoped she could help me solve this case as well, but that she didn't have the necessary information to do so at the moment.

'There are not enough facts for anyone to say anything certain about the case,' she repeated twice. She said nothing when I asked if she had any suggestions as to how I could gather more information.

I tried to cheer her up, and prompted her into action by asking what she thought of Jan Ove Eliassen's statement. But that only resulted in a saccharine smile and an unexpected counter question.

'Let's do a little thought experiment. Let's imagine that Jan Ove Eliassen was Agnes Halvorsen or one of the other female students, and told a story about a fellow male student who had lured her into a cleaning cupboard and treated her in the way described. Would you have believed her story – given that it fitted with everything else you knew or found out?'

I was not used to thinking in this way. And when I tried, I quickly came to the conclusion that the answer was yes. 'I would probably believe her – or him, or whoever . . .'

Patricia smiled a little wider and a little longer.

'Excellent. Let's agree, then, that in this age of increasing equality, we can believe Jan Ove Eliassen, even if he is a man. Agnes Halvorsen was obviously in the cleaning cupboard with him, and from what we know, his explanation of how they got there and what happened appears to be true. But we still can't know for certain; nor does it rule him out as a possible killer, regardless of what happened there.'

I said that it seemed unlikely that Eliassen would kill a young woman only hours after he had become engaged to another.

'Well, that's debatable. No matter what happened in the cleaning cupboard, it's perfectly feasible that young Jan Ove Eliassen tracked her down and killed her later that evening. In which case getting engaged to someone else only hours before was a good move, in terms of both an alibi and a motive. But no, I don't think that is what happened either. His perception of reality may seem rather odd to those of us who don't suffer from deep faith in God, but there's nothing to indicate that he didn't say truthfully what he perceived to have happened.'

I quickly asked Patricia if she agreed then that the

alternatives were the lecturer and tutor, Oscar Fredrik Bergen-dahl, or someone completely unknown to us.

Patricia sighed – and then nodded reluctantly.

'There are other possible candidates among those you've met who don't have alibis. But I would tend to agree that the tutor with a dying wife and the young female admirers does seem to be the least unlikely. It's quite clear that he was attracted to Agnes. But it's quite a jump from that to telling her, and would be in very poor taste, given the timing and the fact that he will soon be a widower. And it would take an even greater leap from telling her to killing her in order to hide something that couldn't be proved – and which is not illegal, even if it could be proved. And what is more, Bergendahl, if he did have a life on his conscience, could deflect any suspicion by in fact admitting that he had strong feelings for her. The answer he gave could indicate that he's an honest man who does not want to be a liar. And Agnes said to her friend exactly what the tutor said to you: that they had never discussed the matter. So even though one should not overestimate an academic's rationality, I think we have to look for the answer elsewhere.'

Patricia suddenly stopped talking – and then started again just as quickly without letting me get a word in. She wrung her hands as she spoke.

'But was it simply a very unfortunate encounter . . . or had this unknown someone managed to find out that Agnes often walked past around that time on a Monday night? And how on earth, then, did they find out? If we are to believe Nora Jensen, everyone and no one might have known. Is it possible that . . .'

Patricia broke off in deep concentration for a minute or so, then shook her head.

'Oh, I give up. We know too little for me to guess how the

killer knew what time to be there. And even less who he or she might be. However ...' Again she stopped abruptly, but then quickly continued. 'However, we could look at what kind of motive this unknown person might have. I still think the combination of the ant picture and the misbuttoned blouse is alarming. Do you know the story of Leopold and Loeb?'

The names were unknown to me, and sounded like a British or American comedy duo. So, slightly irritated, I asked who they were and why they were relevant to the case. Patricia smiled triumphantly for a moment, and then carried on.

'Leopold and Loeb were two extremely intelligent and talented young students from very wealthy families in Chicago. In 1924, they committed a crime that shocked the whole of America, when they kidnapped and killed a boy from their neighbourhood in cold blood. Loeb was later killed in prison by a fellow inmate. Leopold was eventually released but, if one's to believe what was said in the papers, died a broken man in Latin America last year. Leopold and Loeb obviously have nothing to do with this case directly, but they and their almost fifty-year-old murder may be worryingly relevant to the murder of Agnes Halvorsen all the same. And do you want to know why?'

She might have said it as a question, but the tone was teasing and patronizing. And although this annoyed me, I was now too curious and fascinated to let it bother me. I found myself thinking that I really liked being tête-à-tête with Patricia like this. I leaned forwards over the table towards her and said that I would be very interested to hear more about how it might be relevant to our case – if she could and wanted to tell me. She of course did not let the challenge lie.

'Leopold and Loeb's motive was even more frightening that

the crime itself. There was clearly a good dose of old-fashioned madness there. They had been studying the German philosopher Friedrich Nietzsche and believed themselves to be two examples of his Übermensch – with the right to decide over the life and death of inferior people. But fundamentally, there were other psychological factors at play. They had committed increasingly serious crimes leading up to the murder, without getting caught. They finally took the life of a child, partly to get attention and prove that they could get away with murder, and partly because of the excitement of doing it. The victim in our case is a woman, not a child. Of course, there is nothing to say that our murderer is a highly intelligent person or that he or she has read Nietzsche. But I do suspect that he or she is driven by the same thing: a kind of madness that desires attention and recognition, combined with a repressed need for excitement.'

The story of Leopold and Loeb was new to me and I was interested. I asked how the police had caught them.

'Leopold and Loeb made several mistakes and were also unlucky, as their planned alibi was uncovered, and so they were arrested and sentenced after their first murder. If they hadn't been, I am quite certain that they would have carried on and killed again at some point. And I fear that that's what our unknown killer out there in the dark will do, if he gets away with the first murder. In that sense, he or she is a ticking human bomb; it's a frightening thought. It's impossible to know how impatient the murderer is or when he might see the next opportunity. I think we're racing against time, and I will continue to worry about the next murder until we have solved the Agnes Halvorsen case.'

This was said with unusual intensity. Patricia was leaning towards me now. And my table was far smaller than hers. I thought to myself that she really was beautiful when she dropped her cold mask and showed her true, passionate self.

I didn't say anything, though. I resisted the temptation to stand up, walk round the table and give her a reassuring hug. Instead, I said that I shared her fears and thought that her care for her fellow human beings was endearing.

We sat looking at each other. I glanced behind me to make sure that the door to the kitchen, where the maid was patiently waiting, was still shut. Patricia and I were otherwise alone in the flat and would not be disturbed. Her red lips were temptingly close. I could just stand up and kiss her, or I could put my hand on her arm. But I wasn't sure how she would react – and I was even more unsure about how I would want her to react.

The moment passed. Patricia pulled back to her side of the table.

I said it seemed we would not get any further with the investigation that evening. Then I added that it was almost ten o'clock and she was perhaps starting to get tired. But she promptly replied that she found my company invigorating and did not have to go to work in the morning, so it was up to me how long I wanted to have her company.

I could hardly say that her company was not wanted. So instead I asked how young she was when they discovered that she was exceptionally intelligent and at what age she had developed her interest in crime cases.

I couldn't decide whether I hoped Patricia would withdraw instead of talking about herself and her dead parents or not. Whatever the case, she most certainly did not. Instead, she livened up and said that she hadn't known I was interested. And then she chattered away happily. 'Leopold was said to have uttered his first words at four months. I needed another two, but then quickly accelerated,' she said, with a smile that was both self-deprecating and self-satisfied. She obviously did not find it difficult to talk about her early years and the time before the accident, when both her parents were alive and she could move around like any other child.

As the clock ticked on to half past ten, we had got to primary school and I remarked that it was perhaps unfair to keep the maid shut in the kitchen for much longer. But Patricia quickly replied that the maid was being paid overtime for every half hour she was here, at a generous rate, and also had this week's editions of two magazines with her in the kitchen. And given her reading speed, it would take a couple of days to get through them. The maid was not likely to complain, even if she had to sit there until early morning, Patricia joked.

I increasingly got the feeling that Patricia would not complain either, if I suggested she stay until the early morning, but once again I was uncertain whether I wanted her to or not. I let the opportunity go and we carried on talking about everything and nothing.

At a quarter to eleven, there was another moment of affection. After drinking some more red wine, Patricia turned back to the case. She said that it really was tragic, but she did not have a particularly good impression of Agnes. 'It sounds as if she was one of those women who likes to play with men, to lead them on and break them. And then one day in a cleaning cupboard she got a taste of her own medicine – and if she hadn't been killed a few hours later, I would have said she deserved it.'

Patricia gave one of her sarcastic teenage smiles when she said this.

I thought that her description was rather apt and found myself wondering if it might do the chronically smart and sarcastic Patricia a bit of good to have a taste of her own medicine too.

As I sat there wondering, Patricia leaned forwards and asked with dramatic intimacy: 'Do you remember what I said about a similar young woman involved in your first murder investigation? If you want to play in the kitchen, you have to put up with the heat.'

I saw Patricia's sardonic smile right in front of me. I felt myself getting annoyed again. Patricia knew perfectly well that I'd had a brief relationship with the young woman in question once the investigation was over. This time she had gone too far. Someone should wipe that smile off her face and let *her* feel the heat.

I got up from the table with the intention of lifting her out of the wheelchair, carrying her into the bedroom, laying her down on the not-too-clean sheets and taking off her clothes. I would of course stop immediately if she gave any sign that she didn't want it, but felt pretty sure that that wouldn't happen.

I noticed a sparkle in Patricia's eyes. I knew that she knew why I had stood up. And judging by the expression on her face, this provoked both tension and delight.

But I didn't get any further than standing up as, just then, the phone rang. I froze at the sound – and saw the colour blanch from Patricia's face. We were both thrown back into the seriousness and gloom of the case.

'I think you should answer that,' she said in a quiet, grave voice.

And as I picked up the receiver, the clock started to strike eleven, so I said, 'Kolbjørn Kristiansen, can you hold on a minute, please?' and waited until the last stroke.

X

So here I am again, waiting for another young woman. This time on a quiet road near Berg station. It's only a quarter past ten, but it seems that most people have turned in for the night already.

There's a slight breeze, but no rain. I would have preferred rain today as well, even though it wouldn't have been as pleasant to stand and wait. I can't imagine what kind of trace I could leave: at worst a footprint. But that could have been left by thousands of people in this city other than me. I'll burn the shoes I'm wearing tonight, to be on the safe side.

I can see two houses from here. But the people who live there won't be able to see me, standing behind a tree by the road. If anyone happened to be standing at the window looking at the road, they would need bionic vision or binoculars to see anything more than an outline of me. And I'm quite ordinary to look at. I have never been one to turn heads on the street, unless it's someone I already know. Just as no one would turn to look at an ordinary ant if it passed.

I've thought a lot about that image in recent days. I've lived my life like an ant – a quiet, monotonous and boring life with too much work and not enough excitement. I haven't distinguished myself in any way. No one has entrusted me with important decisions, let alone paid any attention to all my efforts. And now I'm going to use it to my advantage. I'm going to carry out my dangerous mission and then disappear amongst all the other people in this city, like an ant in a teeming anthill.

If an ant were to kill another ant on some small branch of a tree and manage to get away, who could then point out the killer on an anthill swarming in the summer sun? The answer is, naturally, no one. It's a question of being efficient when I strike and then getting away from the scene of the crime as soon as possible. Everything went well last time. And it will be fine this time too. And if I manage to get away from here, then this Kolbjørn Kristiansen chap and Oslo Police will have a hard time finding any links between the two women that would lead them to me.

The train I've been waiting for is coming now. I heard the first sounds about a minute ago, and could feel the tension rising in my body. The woman I'm expecting should be on that train. She normally takes the first train home after the club closes at ten.

There are two elements of uncertainty. The woman in question is semi-alcoholic and a promiscuous tart. She may have stayed in town, either because someone asked her to go on the razz or because she's been picked up by some man. She wouldn't say no to either – I've heard her say so herself. Alternatively, she might have brought a man home with her, even though she's admitted that usually doesn't work. If I see that she's got someone with her, I'll just walk by and take the bus home. And then I'll have to try for another woman on Friday – or wait here again next Monday or Wednesday.

There she is, at last. She's had no luck tonight. I can only hear and make out one person in the dark. She's not been invited back to anyone's house or managed to pull a man. And she's clearly made every attempt to drown her sorrows for the fact that the world doesn't realize that she's actually a musical genius. I've heard her say that she wants as many good-looking men and as few children as possible in life. She's a jazz singer, and a good candidate for the most immoral woman in town. So the moral fibre of Oslo would improve without this little sponging sinner of a woman.

She's weaving her way towards me slowly, irritatingly slowly. But step by step she gets closer. There's still no one else around. And now she's only about ten steps away.

I do the same with Lisa as I did with Agnes: hold out my hand to stop her when she's only a couple of steps away.

It's only now that she registers I even exist. She's more drunk than I expected. She staggers and her eyes swim up to meet mine, but she does stop. And eventually she recognizes me.

'Yooouu?' she says in an annoyingly slow and slurred voice.

She doesn't get any further. I am completely sober and much stronger than her. I reach out my hands, put them around her neck and squeeze. She tries to say something, but doesn't have enough air. It comes out as a low groan. But Lisa still manages to stay standing longer than Agnes. I keep squeezing and squeezing. I just need to keep focused and increase the pressure. It's like I'm obsessed. My hands are shaking with adrenaline. She doesn't try to fight me, just stands there looking at me, her eyes getting more and more blurred. Then suddenly a great spasm runs through her body. And finally she falls.

XI

I listened to the person on the other end until they were finished. Then I said, 'Very good. I'll come immediately.'

'Who and where?' Patricia asked, as soon as I put down the receiver.

'A young woman, as yet unidentified. Just by Berg station. Strangled, with a picture of an ant in her pocket,' I told her.

'That's a dramatic development indeed. Of course you must go immediately. But perhaps you should see me out first?' Patricia said.

I said yes, almost without thinking. It struck me later that Patricia would probably have been willing to wait if I had asked her to, and perhaps that is what she was hoping for. But by then she was already in my arms halfway down the stairs. She didn't say a word. I found her body sadly cold and she was shaking more than when I had carried her up the stairs a few hours earlier.

When the cool air hit us, she instinctively pressed her cheek against my arm. We had never been closer physically than this evening. A minute later she was in the back seat of her car and Benedikte had started the engine.

'I'll wait up at home. You can call me, no matter how late it is,' Patricia said, in a strangely formal tone.

I stood alone in the sharpness of the spring night for a few moments, then got into my own car and headed for Berg – and a new murder mystery.

XII

Two police cars and three policemen were at the scene before me this time. I was very glad to see that Helgesen was one of them. The case was becoming our mutual obsession – and our shared nightmare.

A dark-haired woman in a leather jacket lay dead by a tree on the quiet road. I guessed that she was around twenty-five and possibly just over five foot. She looked so peaceful where she lay, as if she was sleeping. But her neck was at an odd angle and there were several visible bruises.

A middle-aged couple from a nearby house stood in silence, with bowed heads, a few yards away. The woman had seen a person lying on the ground when she went out to the front step to turn off the outside light at twenty to eleven. She had also seen someone disappearing down the road, but had not managed to get a good look at them.

To begin with, I found it enormously frustrating that we were once again standing here with a witness who had seen the elusive strangler, but couldn't give a description. But then I realized it was difficult to know whether it had in fact been the murderer, or a passer-by.

They had both gone out to look at exactly a quarter to eleven, and called the police as soon as they found her. She had definitely not been there at nine o'clock when the husband had taken the dog out for a walk, so presumably had been murdered at some point in between.

The dead woman had three things on her. In her left trouser pocket was a purse which contained no more than a train ticket from the centre of town and some small change. In her right jacket pocket was an old iron key. And poking out of the jacket pocket on the left-hand side was a small picture of an ant from a children's book.

We found no identification, but the neighbours quickly cleared this up. The deceased called herself 'Lisa Elea' when she sang with various jazz bands, but her name was actually Lise Eilertsen, and she lived on the ground floor of a house just round the corner. No one lived on the first floor. Lise Eilertsen lived alone 'at the moment', but often had visitors, the neighbours told us with an arched eyebrow. She often went to Club 7 and other bars and clubs at the weekend, and came home late.

Lise Eilertsen usually took the train, but also used the bus now and then. It was reasonable to assume she had come back on the train, given the ticket in her pocket and the fact that she was found midway between the station and her house, which was four hundred yards or so from the station. She was lying in the least visible spot, by a large tree about fifty yards from the nearest houses.

Once again the murderer had struck on the west side of town, just outside the centre, but still well within the city limits – and again, under cover of dark. Beneath the leather jacket, the buttoning on Lise Eilertsen's blouse was fine, but the similarities to the murder two nights before were so marked that neither I nor Helgesen would have seen them as a coincidence, even without the picture of an ant.

As I stood there looking at the dead woman by the foot of the tree, I felt strangely certain that Patricia had been right. Agnes Halvorsen and Lise Eilertsen had been strangled by the same person – and neither of them had been random victims. The murderer had known roughly when they would come and had chosen where to wait with great care.

The forensics team arrived just before half past eleven. It was not raining, but there was a wind and the ground was hard. I doubted very much if they would find anything more than the single clue I could see with my bare eyes. And that was a footprint in the grass next to the tree. As far as I could tell, the footprint was medium-sized, around a size nine or ten. We didn't know yet that it was the murderer who had left it, but could only hope and assume.

The couple from the house nearby told us what little they knew. We also spoke to their neighbours, who had been watching their newly purchased television all evening, and so had neither seen nor heard anything. There was not much more to be gleaned here. When the ambulance arrived, I let them take away the body and left the forensics team to work in peace. Meanwhile, I took the key and Helgesen with me and went to the dead woman's flat.

If the similarities between the two murders were striking, the two victims' homes could not have been more different. Lise Eilertsen lived alone in a two-bedroomed flat on the ground floor of a small old house from the turn of the century. From what we had heard and could see, the first floor was unoccupied and empty. Downstairs, the paint was peeling from the walls and it was obvious the person who lived here was a bit of a bohemian. In the kitchen we found two days' worth of washing-up by the sink and a crate of beer in a corner – half the bottles were full, the other half empty. The living room seemed to be divided by an invisible line. On one side was a piano, two guitars, a drum kit and a record player. This part of the room was tidy and clean. On the other side, there was chaos, with clothes and shoes all over the floor between an old velvet sofa and three different brightly coloured chairs.

There was a very positive concert review pinned to the wall, along with a couple of black-and-white photographs of the late Lise Eilertsen singing with three or four men on two different stages. They all had long hair and looked rather dishevelled. Only one man appeared in both pictures. He was playing the bass guitar and was the tallest, broadest and darkest of them all. In both pictures he was standing closest to Lise Eilertsen and staring down at the photographer.

I said to Helgesen that we would have to speak to some of the men in the photographs and search the place properly in the morning, but it did not seem likely there would be much here. If Lise Eilertsen had been the first victim and had not had a picture of an ant in her pocket, we would have started to look for the killer in her immediate circle without delay. But as she was now the second victim, this solution seemed less plausible, unless we could find a connection between the two apparently very different victims, which seemed unlikely. There was certainly no murderer to be found in the flat and there was nothing to indicate that he had been there this evening.

So, at half past midnight, I said that we should perhaps call it a day, but asked Helgesen if he could be at the station by eight o'clock in the morning.

We locked the door to the flat where Lise Eilertsen had no doubt woken up that morning and eaten her last breakfast.

By the time we got back to the scene of the crime, her body was no longer there. The forensics team were frank and said that they had not found much, but promised to carry on their investigation for a few more hours. I thanked them and asked for a report as soon as possible in the morning.

Then I got into my car and drove home. I did not feel the slightest bit tired, but realized that there was not much more to be done here and now, and that I had to get a few hours' sleep if I was going to be of any use tomorrow. And I also wanted to hear Patricia's voice.

I need not have feared that she had already gone to bed. She picked up the phone as soon as it started to ring at a quarter past one. Patricia sounded just as wide awake as I was. Her first words were, 'Tell me,' and then she listened for the next ten minutes while I told her what we had found at Berg, in as much detail as possible.

I then hoped and waited for a miracle which I quickly understood was not going to happen. Patricia apologized that she still could not give me 'the name or address of the murderer'.

I told her it was perfectly understandable, but that everything would indicate that her theory about the murderer's motive had been right.

'Hmm, yes,' she said, with a heavy sigh.

As far as I could remember, it was the first time Patricia had ever been disappointed about being right. But the situation gave every reason to be pessimistic.

'It seems I only have one thing to add, and it's far from certain. But for what it's worth, I don't think the ant has anything to do with the victims, but rather says something about how the murderer sees himself,' she said, pensively, as I was about to finish the conversation.

'Well, in that case, we're possibly looking for a man who feels that he has worked for long enough without recognition, as just another anonymous person in the crowd,' I said.

Patricia was being very nice to me, whether because she was worried about the case or because she hoped that it might bring us closer.

'That's more or less what I thought at first. But there is another way of looking at it. Whatever the case, we can certainly call these the Anthill Murders, as a working theory. The murderer is an ant and it is impossible to differentiate him from the masses on first glance, so after committing two murders, he could be anywhere in the chaotic anthill that Oslo has become. He knows that it will be hard to find him here – and is almost using the little ant pictures to thumb his nose at the police.'

'What a nasty piece of work. And so far he's got away from the scene of the crime without being seen and disappeared into the anthill, where it's nigh on impossible to find him,' I said, both agitated and disheartened at the same time.

I could hear that my own voice sounded dejected. Patricia immediately said, 'We have to accept that this won't be easy. But somewhere out there, there must be tracks that lead back to that ant. And sooner or later, we'll find them and solve the Anthill Murders together.'

It was an almost touching end to a long and dramatic day. I thanked Patricia for all her help and good company. In return, she said she could wait to eat supper tomorrow until it suited me, and would stay by the phone in the meantime. She then wished me good night in an unusually soft and kind voice. I replied, 'Sweet dreams.'

By the time I regretted not using the opportunity to say how much I cared for her, she had already hung up. I sat there on my own with the silent receiver. For a moment I wondered if I should call her again, but then suddenly I felt not only lonely, but also very tired.

To my great relief, when I did finally get into bed, I fell asleep quickly. I barely had time to think about Patricia and the fact that Miriam now took up so little of my thoughts. The last picture in my mind was of the jazz singer Lise Eilertsen lying dead by the side of a road at the foot of a tree near Berg station. I wondered who she had been when she was alive. And even more, I wondered if she had seen and recognized the person who killed her.

DAY FOUR

A Possible Link

I

On Thursday, 27 April 1972, my alarm clock was set for seven, but I woke up ten minutes before it went off. Within seconds I was thinking about the investigation; it was taking over my life. But then I must have dozed off again, as the alarm rang. I was annoyed that I had not got up straight away, and hurried to the door to get the morning papers.

I caught a glimpse of my neighbour's new girlfriend as she was sneaking out, but thankfully she didn't see me. In those brief few seconds, she reminded me of Miriam. Only a month ago, I had stood here at the door and watched her leave for her morning lectures.

I quickly blocked out the memory by closing the door and reading the headlines. Neither *Arbeiderbladet* or *Aftenposten* mentioned the investigation on the front page. As expected, neither of them had included last night's murder. I wondered whether *Verdens Gang* might have managed to get it into the day's edition. Then I wondered how much all the newspapers would escalate their coverage of the case tomorrow, if they realized there was a connection between the murders of the two women.

I ate my breakfast in peace, but I found myself thinking it was the calm before the storm. It felt as though the floor was burning under my feet when I walked to the door at twenty past seven. I almost ran out of the building and drove to the main police station as fast as the speed limit would permit.

I had asked Helgesen to be there by eight. He knocked on my door at a quarter to. I appreciated his diligence and zeal. The situation was not at all good, and it felt marginally better not to be sitting there alone.

The forensics team had finished their work early in the morning, without finding any evidence that could help us trace the murderer. The autopsy report would not be ready until the next day at the earliest, but from what we had seen there was no reason to expect anything new.

It took me barely a minute to read the information held on Lise Eilertsen in the National Registry. I noticed to my surprise and slight irritation that Helgesen had finished reading before me.

Lise Eilertsen was born on 4 January 1950 and had moved from Røa to her current address in Berg in October 1968. Her father, a businessman, had been born in 1890 and died in June 1968. In the treason trials after the war, he had accepted a fine in lieu of a sentence for his membership of Nasjonal Samling, the Norwegian Nazi party. He got away with a 500-kroner fine as he was deemed to be no more than a passive sympathizer, and he had nothing else on his criminal record. Her mother was born in 1908 and still lived at the address in Røa. Lise had a brother called Lars, who was eight years older and lived in Rykkinn, and a sister called Lina, who was four years older and lived in Asker.

I said, partly to myself and partly to Helgesen, that we now had a new list of names to follow up. It was worth noting that the victims, despite their very different lives and the fact that they lived a fair distance from each other now, were born in the same year, less than a mile apart. And this increased the chances of a common connection to someone in their past.

There was a knock at the door. Our boss had found us before we went to find him, which only enhanced the seriousness of the case. Our boss was a patient man who normally had confidence in his subordinates and gave them time, but it was whispered in the corridors that if the boss came to see you without warning – particularly if it was before lunch – the situation was critical.

The boss listened to my account of the most recent developments without asking any questions. 'Hmm, what was already a difficult case has taken a very dramatic turn,' he remarked, when I had finished.

It was hard not to agree. I said that it was a complicated situation, but there were a number of possibilities to be followed up. We first had to speak to the victim's immediate family and friends from the jazz scene and Club 7. It might be as well for Helgesen and me to do that together today, rather than expanding the investigation to everything at once.

Helgesen chimed in with a brief 'agreed', but the boss said nothing. The atmosphere in the office was not particularly buoyant. Our boss eventually gave a small, somewhat reserved nod.

'Given the pictures of the ant, it seems more likely that we're hunting for a murderer with a penchant for young women than someone in their circle of family and friends. However, we still have to start there. It is possible that the murderer knew both Agnes Halvorsen and Lise Eilertsen in some way. The murders appear to be well planned, and the killer obviously knew when they would pass a secluded spot late at night,' I said.

This time my boss answered with a short 'agreed'. Helgesen said nothing to begin with, but then said: 'I'm not entirely sure about that.'

That was unexpected. The boss and I both turned to look at him.

'I absolutely agree that it's most likely that we're dealing with someone who is killing for the hell of it, but we should talk to Lise Eilertsen's family and friends first. There is another possibility we should be open to, at the same time. I recently read a novel by Agatha Christie, where the whole point was that the murderer knew one of his victims and killed the others so that the police would think that the murderer didn't know any of the victims. It's not very likely, but the murderer could either have read the novel or come up with the idea himself. In which case, the murderer could also be someone who would benefit from the death of one of them, and killed the other as a kind of red herring.'

I had no idea that Helgesen read novels, and felt slightly peeved that he had not mentioned this theory to me before-hand when we were alone. But I played along and said that it was definitely a possibility we should keep open in the on-going investigation.

'Good,' said our boss, as he stood up to leave.

'As far as the press is concerned, we must absolutely keep the ant drawings secret for as long as possible, and for the moment not say anything about the possible link between the two murders. I suggest that we put out a short press release about the murder at Berg last night, and call for any witnesses to come forward. And we should wait to identify the victim until we have spoken to the family,' I added.

My boss stopped for a moment by the desk, said, 'Good' again, and then left.

His movements were slower than I could remember. For the first time it struck me that my boss was getting older. He was due to retire in autumn 1973. People had started to speculate about who would take over from him. I had been asked if I had any ambitions to be head of the force before I turned forty, but had so far only given the rather ambiguous answer that I was perfectly happy in my current position as a detective inspector.

I was quickly pulled back to the present and the ongoing investigation when Helgesen asked, 'Should we speak to the family or to Club 7 first?'

I thought about it for a moment, then said that Club 7 was closest and that we should perhaps let the Eilertsen family grieve privately for a few hours more. Helgesen agreed with this, and we decided to go as soon as I had written the press release.

II

I had visited Club 7 at a couple of its previous addresses in connection with work. Its most recent home, in a basement opposite the as-yet-unfinished concert hall in Vika, was unknown to me, though. It was undeniably both bigger and more fashionable than the other venues I had seen. But it was still a place where the police should not really be seen, other than in the line of duty.

The idea behind the name Club 7 was that it should be about more than just *sex*, a play on the Norwegian word for six – 'seks'. And indeed it was. The legendary nightclub in Oslo might sound exciting to some and frightening to others, depending on who was talking. It had become one of the most popular meeting places for young people who were interested in music and culture. It was particularly popular with those on the left, and anyone who was against Norwegian membership of the EEC.

The place was less popular with the police. It was said that, compared with other bars and clubs in Oslo, alcohol consumption at Club 7 was average, violent incidents were average, prostitution was above average, drug dealing was above average, and the club was a clear winner when it came to long-haired men and short-haired women. Strictly speaking, the last two had never been illegal. It was also said, and was no doubt true, that the patrons of Club 7 were far more law-abiding now that antiquated laws prohibiting extramarital sex and sexual contact between people of the same gender had been lifted. However, Club 7's reputation within police circles was still not the best, and the fact that the club received money from the public purse was a constant source of debate and controversy in newspapers and the city chambers.

I personally was one of the people who believed that the activities at Club 7 had contributed to a reduction in criminality in the capital, rather than an increase – but it was not a view that I felt I needed to share with my boss and other more conservative colleagues.

On the other hand, I had shared it with my former fiancée, Miriam, who had apparently been to the club on occasion. I had of course also made it clear that it was not desirable for the fiancée of a well-known police officer to frequent such a place, and she had accepted this without protest. So when we arrived at Club 7 just after nine, the association made me think of my ex-fiancée, and for the second time that day I had to force her image from my mind by reading something.

This time I read a poster that was hanging by the door. It told me that there had been a jazz evening on the big stage yesterday and that the main attraction had been a black American guitarist called Paul Weeden. According to the poster, he was a man with 'five ex-wives, eighteen children and no enemies'.

Along the bottom of the poster were photographs of the three support acts. The middle photograph was of Lisa Elea, aka the now dead Lise Eilertsen. She was looking straight at the camera with a sharp, almost sarcastic smile on her lips. The photograph to the right was of a younger woman who was unknown to me, and who had the rather peculiar name Radka Toneff. And to the left was a photograph of a solid man in a leather jacket whom I recognized, even though I didn't know him either. He was playing the guitar and looking down in this picture too. According to the text, he was the 'mega-guitarist Steven Hanlon'. I was genuinely unsure as to whether this was his real name or not, but still jotted it down on the list of people we needed to talk to today.

It was very definitely the morning after inside Club 7. A drum kit stood alone on the stage and countless empty beer bottles lay abandoned around the room.

I tried to imagine what it must have looked like the night before, when the place was full of people shouting and laughing – when a woman called Lisa Elea was singing live on stage.

I could not conjure up any images. The stage was too quiet and empty.

The silence was then suddenly broken by a woman in her thirties with a bucket in one hand and a mop in the other, who asked who we were and who we were looking for.

I held out my police ID and said that we were investigating the murder of one of the artists who had performed there the night before.

The woman was stunned. She took a few steps back and, in a stammer, asked who had been killed. The bucket shook in her hand.

I paused for a beat and then said that it was Lisa Elea.

I immediately regretted this when I saw the cleaner sink to the floor, dropping the bucket. But it was too late. The water spilled everywhere. And the woman just sat in the middle, speaking in a staccato voice.

'Lisa. That's so terribly sad. I knew her – not very well. But she was – young. And she seemed – nice. Who on earth – would want to kill Lisa?'

I hesitated for a moment. Then I held out my hand to her. She took hold and almost involuntarily stood up when I pulled. I said that that was what we intended to find out.

'You'll have to talk to Atilo.'

She said this twice. The second time she pointed with a trembling finger out to the left. I walked through the river of soapy water, then felt rather disrespectful when I heard Helgesen jump over it.

The administration offices were also very quiet this Thursday morning. We found only one man there. He was sitting in an office with no sign on the door, which was half open. I recognized him straight away as the general manager, as I had seen several photographs of him in the papers, when he had talked about and in favour of Club 7.

Atilo Hovarth had apparently fled from Hungary when he was very young, when the Soviet Union invaded in 1956. Sixteen years later in Oslo, he was still only in his thirties, but was now nearly six foot five and quite probably weighed somewhere around twenty-two stone. He made me think more of a Russian bear than a Hungarian rebel. Without knowing who we were, he immediately stood up and held out his hand with a broad smile. My hand more or less disappeared in his great paw.

Hovarth's tone changed instantly from friendly to irritable when I said we were from the police; he gave an exasperated sigh and said that he had answered the latest letter from the tax office only yesterday.

I quickly assured him that our visit had nothing to do with the tax authorities, but was rather in connection with a murder investigation, as a Club 7 member had been killed on the way home last night. His mood changed again.

'Who?' he asked in a barely audible whisper, as he collapsed back into his chair. He sat there staring at us. 'Well, tell me, won't you?' he exclaimed, while I still dithered.

'The victim is called Lise Eilertsen, but was perhaps better known here as Lisa Elea,' I said.

An expression of pain ran across Atilo's face when I said her name. He held his head in his huge hands for a few seconds. What I then saw was a mixture of surprise and anger, and he had tears in his eyes.

'That's terrible. How sad. Lisa was here several times a week and sang only yesterday. She was a very talented jazz singer. I didn't know her well, but have never heard anyone say a bad word against her. She never argued about money. I find it hard to believe that anyone would want to kill Lisa.'

Atilo shed a few more tears. Then he added: 'It can't possibly be any of our members who killed her. So I'm afraid I can't really help you there.'

As I listened to Atilo talking about Lisa Elea, it struck me how different she was from Agnes Halvorsen, and yet they had one thing in common, which was proving to be a challenge for us. They were both very unlikely murder victims who had been strangled and left by the side of the road.

I asked Atilo how many people had been at the concert yesterday and if he could tell us when Lisa had left the venue. I suddenly realized I had obviously been influenced by the place and had started to call her Lisa.

Atilo told us that the jazz evenings were very popular, and he estimated that there had been around a hundred people in the audience when Lisa was on stage. The concert had finished around nine. Atilo thought he saw her 'hanging out' by the bar a few minutes later, but was sure that she hadn't been there when the bar closed at ten.

Helgesen commented that the number of tickets sold must surely be recorded somewhere. Atilo promptly replied that the number of tickets sold was of course recorded and could be checked if we were interested. But that was not necessarily the number of people present, as the board and staff and other artists all got guest tickets.

I would have asked the question myself, but was actually more interested in who Lisa might have left with than how many people were in the building. So I asked if he knew, or if she had 'hung out' with anyone in particular recently.

Atilo immediately knew what I meant. He said, first of all,

that he had not seen her with anyone in particular the night before, but then smiled carefully when he added that she was 'highly sociable in that sense'.

I felt that we understood one another. So I asked him straight out if Steven Hanlon was one of the people who Lisa used to socialize with.

Hovarth became serious again and nodded slowly.

'I was going to mention him. They played in the same band for a while last year and were together a lot. But then the band split up and I haven't seen them together much recently.'

I realized this was a possible lead and pressed on.

'So, what you are saying is that Steven and Lisa had a relationship last year, but that is no longer the case?'

Atilo's mood shifted again when he heard my question. Suddenly he was a reflective philosopher, and he shook his head slowly from side to side before carrying on.

'That depends on what you mean by "a relationship"... Steven and Lisa came together and left together a lot last year, but I haven't seen that at all this year. For a while, everyone took it for granted they were sleeping together, but as far as I know, they never lived together. If by "relationship" you mean that neither could be with anyone else, well, then they were not in a relationship. But if you were to ask who of our members knows Lisa best, I would say Steven straight away. As I said, I didn't know Lisa very well myself. I got the impression that most people said hello to her, but very few spent much time talking to her. She wasn't really the sort to have lots of girl-friends; she was more one of the boys.'

I recognized that Atilo, behind his slightly shambolic appearance, was a keen observer of people. I thanked him for the information and said that we would definitely have a chat with Steven Hanlon.

Atilo was on the ball. He said that it was probably very sensible, and added that he hoped we would find the culprit. He added hastily that behind his 'tough image', Steven 'was a good person and certainly not stupid'. Then he repeated that the murderer could not possibly be a regular at Club 7.

When I asked where we might find Steven Hanlon today, Atilo said that he was usually at home at 53 Osterhaus Street until about four. And it was possible that his real name, Stein Hansen, was on the door.

As I made to leave, Helgesen asked if we could check the ticket sales on the way out. Atilo said of course, and stood up again.

The secretary had not yet come in, but the door to her office was open, and a pile of ticket stubs marked 'Jazz concert 26 April' lay next to a small red cash box on the desk, which was tidier than Atilo's.

According to the stubs, twenty-three tickets had been sold. As far as I could see, that tallied with the amount of money in the cash box, if, as the poster said, tickets cost ten kroner. There were two fifty-kroner notes, a bundle of ten-kroner notes, and a handful of coins.

Atilo took a deep breath and said that he had perhaps over-estimated the number of people there. Then he said again that there were a number who got in free.

We thanked him politely for his help and time. We left him standing by the desk, puzzled, looking down at the cash box. I thought there was something quite comical, but also sad, about the large man and the small tin.

I remarked to Helgesen that no matter how talented the

jazz singer Lisa Elea was, Lise Eilertsen surely deserved to have more than twenty-three paying punters at her last-ever concert. To my relief, he agreed with me.

III

We didn't find the name Steven Hanlon on the mailboxes in 53 Osterhaus Street, but we did eventually find a Stein Hansen at number 55. But we still did not know which flat he lived in, and four of the nine flats had no name on the door. We had just asked an elderly gentleman in a coat, when we heard a heavy bass coming from the first floor. Helgesen saw the humour in it and smiled. The man in the coat did not.

'You just have to follow the noise. It's scandalous the way young people today just do what they like, day and night, without the slightest consideration for others. My wife and I have complained about the music several times, but the landlord is Hansen's uncle,' the old man sniffed on his way out.

The bass was coming from the middle flat on the first floor, and there was no doubt that the noise might be annoying to the neighbours above, below and beside. It only stopped after I had knocked hard on the door three times. It took another minute or so before the door was unlocked and opened, with the security chain still on.

'Hello, who are you and what do you want today?' Stein Hansen asked when he finally appeared in the opening. His hair was even curlier and longer than in the photographs we had seen, and his eyes were duller, but he was better shaved.

I held up my police ID. In a quiet voice I said that we would like to talk to him for a few minutes in connection with a murder investigation.

Stein Hansen was at once very focused and hastily undid the safety chain.

We followed him into the living room in silence. Half of the floor was taken up with a piano, a bass guitar and amplifier and a small collection of acoustic guitars, as well as a stereo player, and it looked as if there were more LPs than books in the bookshelves. Other than that, I thought, the flat was very unlike the now dead Lise Eilertsen's flat. This one was tidy and, as far as I could see, it was also clean. There were two leather jackets hanging in the hallway, but the man who lived here was dressed in relatively normal clothes – and as a result, possibly, looked smaller than he did in the photographs. At five foot nine, Stein Hansen was slightly shorter than me, but was considerably broader. He carried some extra weight round his middle, but his shoulders and upper arms were pure muscle. I looked at his hands and thought to myself that neither Agnes Halvorsen or Lise Eilertsen would have had a chance if Stein Hansen had put his hands around their throats and squeezed.

Stein Hansen gestured for us to sit down around the coffee table. 'Well, I have to say I'm a little curious now, but more scared, truth be told. Who has been killed and why do the police want to talk to me about it?' he said, with a slight tremor in his voice.

'Lise Eilertsen. She was killed by Berg station late last night,' I said.

His reaction was unexpectedly marked. Stein Hansen flinched and he fixed me with hard eyes. I noticed Helgesen tense in his chair, and was suddenly very glad to have him with me. But there was no danger. To begin with, Stein Hansen just sat there staring at us; then suddenly he burst into tears. He put his big elbows on the table and hid his face in his hands.

'I'm sorry, but that comes as quite a shock and makes me so sad. Can you tell me how Lisa died?' he asked, after a few minutes.

Helgesen turned to look at me. I thought about it for a moment, and then answered as tactfully as possible that we could not disclose the cause of death yet, but could say that she was killed close to her flat in Berg between half past nine and a quarter to eleven last night.

'Then I saw her less than an hour before she died, on the way out of Club 7. This feels totally surreal,' Stein Hansen said, sitting up straight again and shaking his head.

I quickly asked if he could tell us then when Lise Eilertsen left Club 7, and whether she left alone.

'I can't say exactly when she left, but it must have been between half past nine and a quarter to ten. Our set was finished by nine o'clock. I only saw her on stage, and in passing as she left. She was alone and I didn't see her speak to anyone else on the way out.'

I sighed mentally. The few leads we had were being snatched from us in quick succession. There was nothing to indicate that Lise Eilertsen had left with anyone, or that anyone had followed her when she left Club 7.

'Anyone else, you say . . . So she spoke to you?' Helgesen piped up. He was clearly not bad at picking up semantic subtleties.

Stein Hansen's emotions again got the better of him. He buried his face in his hands and stayed there longer this time. His long curls trembled.

'Yes, we exchanged a few words . . . It's so awful and it'll only be worse to have to live with it . . . As you're here, I guess you know that Lisa and I played, drank and slept together for a while last year?'

I said that we did, and asked him to be as open as he could about anything that might be of importance.

'Of course, I'll do my best, though I don't see how our relationship has anything to do with the fact that she's now dead. Lisa drank a little too much and slept with a few too many people, but the idea that she might die didn't even enter my head when we split up. Everything was fine to begin with. She was young, active and a seriously talented singer. We hit it off right away. Came back here the first night and were playing in a band together the week after. It all started well. Then later things got more difficult until one day we just hit a wall. And that was the end of the relationship and the band.'

Stein Hansen stopped talking for a moment and shook his head. His eyes were on Helgesen and myself, but he was looking far beyond us. I saw that Helgesen was about to ask him another question, and chose to pre-empt him by asking how long the relationship had lasted.

'Almost exactly five months – from mid-June to one day last November. I said later it was at least three months too long. It was heading in the wrong direction once the first rush wore off, but the physical attraction was still there. That was the main problem, really; that it was too strong. Do you mind if I smoke?' he asked, out of the blue.

It came as quite a surprise, as the flat did not smell of smoke. I said that he could. He thanked me, went out into the hall and came back with a pouch of tobacco. He took his time rolling a cigarette, and then barely smoked it once it was lit.

I suspected that he needed the time to think more than he needed the nicotine, as once he had lit the cigarette, he continued.

'To begin with, I was really happy that she was so hot, but then it never let up. She was insatiable. I realized over the course of the autumn that it wasn't good for her. And I didn't have the time or energy for my music. I'm a musician first and foremost, you see. Club 7 and other places are all about the music for me. The fact that there're women and drink there is a bonus. I realized soon enough that the opposite was true for Lisa. She had a great voice, but she didn't work hard enough and wasn't really interested enough. Lisa was unstoppable in bed, and lazy out of it. It was like music was a means for her to meet men. I knew that she'd had a lot before we met, and never thought for a moment I was the only one when we were together. I could live with that. At one point, in fact, I was glad of some respite: someone else could wear her out. But then one day . . .'

He stopped, sighed – and fell silent.

'One day at the end of November, something happened that affected you, the band and the relationship,' I prompted him.

He responded, leaning forwards across the table as he spoke.

'Exactly. To cut a long story short, I'd had some gigs on the west coast and Lisa had a spare key to the flat. I came home five hours earlier than planned because the last gig had been cancelled. So all of a sudden I was standing there looking at her bucking under another man in my bed. And to make things even better, it was the drummer from our band. That was the straw that broke the camel's back. It wasn't the fact that she was unfaithful in itself, but the combination of her being unfaithful with an old friend in my bed was too much. The next day it was over – the relationship and the band.'

I said that it must have been a very difficult situation for everyone involved. He nodded and took a drag on his cigarette.

'The drummer had let himself be seduced because he was drunk, and he apologized the next day. We settled our differences and I've played with him several times since. Lisa and I didn't say much more than hello whenever we met. I thought later that it wasn't really her fault either. One of her ex-boyfriends told me recently that he'd never met such a small lady with such a big sex drive, and I had to agree. Lisa got restless if she hadn't had a man for two days, and was almost uncontrollable after three. In the end she admitted it herself, but thought it was psychological, because she'd had so little love when she was a kid. But I think it was physical, though her moods did go up and down like a yo-yo. So I said to my friend the drummer, and others who asked later, that it was just as well that things turned out the way they did. It's fun to ride the rollercoaster for a while, but not to live on one.'

I thought the rollercoaster was a good analogy, something I could recognize in my own relationships and those of my friends when we were younger. But Stein Hansen had also given me an interesting angle to approach. I promptly asked if he had met her family, and what his impression was of her relationship with them.

'I actually never met any of them – other than her sister, who we bumped into once on the street. Lisa was the kind of girl who talked about her family a lot, but did not talk to them very often. She got on fine with her sister, even though they were very different both physically and mentally. The brother was much older, and their relationship was very cold.

Apparently her dad had been very fond of her and gave her a fair amount of money, but he was old and died a few years before she met me. The real problem was her mother. According to Lisa, she was incredibly conservative and intolerant. And there was a conflict about money. If Lisa ever mentioned her mother, it was generally to say she was scared she would cut her off.'

'Thank you, that's very interesting. I'm afraid we're going to have to ask you exactly what was said between you and Lisa yesterday,' I ventured.

'I understand that you have to ask me,' Stein Hansen said. His otherwise red face now paled and he stubbed his cigarette out straight onto the table. Then hid his face in his hands again. When he looked up, there were tears in his eyes.

'It's just so awful, and now I'm going to have to live with it for the rest of my life. I can see her and hear her. I thought she was really good on stage last night, and that it was perhaps time to bury the hatchet. So I gave her the thumbs-up and smiled as I passed her on my way onto the stage. She smiled back and pointed at me, teasingly. Then I spotted her sitting in the front row clapping when I was done. Later, about half past nine, I saw her in the bar. And then all of a sudden she was there beside me – with two fingers on my cheek. 'I'm going home now. Will you come and look after me?' she said, and smiled. It was typical Lisa: physical, honest and direct. I like that, and all my feelings started to well up. But she had too much make-up on and had drunk too much. And I could still feel the shock from the day it was over. She didn't tempt me. So I said that I couldn't right now and that maybe we could speak some other time. I was worried she might blow up, like she sometimes did when she was brushed off, but she just said it would be nice to see me again and that she hoped we could meet another day. Then she turned and tottered out. I thought to myself that she wasn't in a good state, and that maybe I should have taken her home or offered her a bed for the night. But in both cases she would be impossible, and we'd end up in bed together – and I couldn't face another rollercoaster ride. So I stood there and watched her stagger out into the night. And now I have to live with the fact that I let her.'

He hid his face again for a moment, but then held his hand out in thanks when I said that no one could have foreseen this and that he mustn't blame himself.

I mused that Atilo at Club 7 had certainly been right in his evaluation: behind his rough image, Stein Hansen seemed like a kind man, and he wasn't stupid. I asked what other interests he had apart from music.

He smiled sheepishly and said that he had originally started to study psychology, but he wasn't happy. Instruments suited him better than books, and he had realized that all he wanted to do was play music. And he could, because his parents were wealthy and he was an only child – and his uncle owned several properties in town.

Stein Hansen had regained his composure. And now it was me who needed a pause for thought. So it was Helgesen who broke the silence, when he touched me on the shoulder and asked if he could have a quick word with me in private. Stein Hansen immediately stood up and left the room without saying a word.

'I don't think it's him. But we only have his word for what happened yesterday, and if nothing else, there's a possible jealousy motive. So we should perhaps put a little more pressure on him, and talk to his drummer friend,' Helgesen whispered, as soon as we were alone in the room.

Given the way the conversation had gone, I no longer saw Stein Hansen as the murderer – and certainly not a double murderer, which was what we were looking for. I did, however, recognize the possible jealousy motive and could see that he had the physical strength to kill his ex-girlfriend if he so wished.

Stein Hansen had dutifully closed the door when he left the room, but was standing in the hall, and came back as soon I opened it again and waved him in. The pouch of tobacco was still lying on the table, but he leaned back on the sofa, with his hands in his lap.

As a warm-up, I asked if Lisa had ever used drugs. He shook his head vigorously.

'We knew people who smoked hash, of course, but agreed that it didn't seem to be good for the head. Lisa used to joke that her upbringing was far too conservative for that sort of thing, and that the hash girls should stick to solid doses of wine and men, like everyone else. She never took any drugs when we were together and I don't think she would have later either.'

There was a short silence again. Then I turned to look at him, and said that it was my duty to ask him where he had been after ten o'clock in the evening on Monday and Wednesday of this week.

'I can see why you have to ask me about yesterday, but Monday, I'm not sure . . . Whatever, I've got nothing to hide. After Lisa left the club, I went back to the bar and had another beer, but left without protesting when Atilo closed up with his usual 'Time to drink up and go home!' I was tired, so I went home and straight to bed. On Monday evening I had a gig in

Drammen, and caught the train back at half past nine. It got into Vestbanen station just after half past ten and I walked home from there. I don't have a car and have realized that I have to work to keep in shape now, so I've started to walk anywhere that's less than two miles.'

I said that it was without a doubt a good idea to keep in shape, but I made a mental note that Stein Hansen did not have an alibi either. He could have hopped in a taxi and made it up to Berg before Lisa, even though he left Club 7 after her. And on Monday, he could have got to Hovseter well before Agnes Halvorsen, especially if he got off the train before it got to Vestbanen.

The only thing that remained then was to ask Stein Hansen for the name and address of the drummer he'd discovered in his bed – with his then-girlfriend – one day last November.

He hesitated a moment, but then gave a clear answer.

'He's not a potential murderer, if that's what you think. A good drummer and a nice guy, who's got a new girlfriend, by the way. He's a good working-class boy from the east end and lives in a basement flat in Grünerløkka. Was still doing the morning shift at the Co-op on the corner last time I spoke to him, so there's a good chance you'll find him there if you go now. His name's Haug, Bjarne Haug.'

IV

We found Bjarne Haug at the Co-op at a quarter past eleven. He was on his way out of the storeroom with a pallet of fruit when we arrived.

Bjarne Haug looked a bit younger than Stein Hansen, but he

had shorter hair and was better groomed. He stood out from the rest of the staff as the others were older, but also because he had flaming-red hair that complemented the Co-op uniform. He seemed to be a level-headed young man. When I showed him my police ID, he arched his eyebrows for a moment and pointed towards a door at the back. This led into a small office with a table and four chairs.

I asked Bjarne Haug if he knew why we were there, to which he replied no. He was quiet for a moment when I told him it was in connection with a murder inquiry, then he asked who it was.

When I replied, 'Lise Eilertsen, also known as Lisa Elea,' he started. He frowned thoughtfully for a moment, then said, 'That's very sad – and quite a shock. She's one of the people I would least expect that to happen to.'

Then he was quiet again. Bjarne Haug seemed to be more reserved than Stein Hansen. I prompted him by asking what he thought of the deceased.

'I didn't know her very well, unfortunately. She was an amazing jazz singer and could have been an international star if she wanted to. Otherwise, she seemed like a genuinely nice girl who wouldn't harm a fly, even if she did live a little too hard and was a little too thirsty. As far as I know, she had no enemies at Club 7 or otherwise in the jazz scene. You'll have to look for the murderer elsewhere.'

This just tripped off his tongue – a little too lightly. I said in a slightly sharper tone that only last autumn he had apparently been very friendly with her.

This teased out the first sign of a sense of humour, but only enough to tug at the corners of his mouth.

'I know what you're talking about, obviously. But just

because you find yourself in bed with a woman at some point one year, it doesn't necessarily mean you know her well the next. Certainly not in Club 7 or any other jazz venue. I only remember three things from the evening in question. First, that I was sitting in the bar at Club 7 having a drink, and Lisa sat down beside me. Then that I was in bed with the wild little lady moaning underneath me – and a furious, shouting man beside me, who turned out to be Stein Hansen. He lunged at me and as a result I fell off the woman and out of the bed. The last thing I remember is walking home alone through a snow storm, promising myself I would never again drink so much that I didn't know whose bed I was in. And I've managed to stick to that ever since. So, not a great night, but it did teach me a good lesson.'

He stopped abruptly. But he had started to open up now. Out of the corner of my eye, I saw Helgesen nod encouragingly when I asked, 'And then what happened?'

Bjarne Haug shrugged lightly.

'If you're asking about Stein, Lisa and me, not a lot. Stein has more of a temper on a stormy day than one might imagine on a sunny day. When I realized where I was, I could understand his reaction. The band never played together again, but Stein and I made up over a beer a few days later. He said that the relationship was on its last legs anyway, but asked me to use another bed next time I wanted to pull one of his girlfriends. I assured him that it was me who had been pulled, and that I had been very drunk, and it would never happen again. Lisa didn't get in touch, and I didn't feel the need to apologize to her for anything. So I don't think the incident left any of us with hard feelings. I certainly didn't have any. And since then I've found myself a new band and a new woman.'

Bjarne Haug had said more than I'd expected. And then he sat in silence. He didn't ask any questions about what had happened to Lise, and seemed almost disconcertingly uninterested.

I thought that either he had put the whole thing behind him or he was unusually self-controlled. The feeling was only strengthened when he then asked if he could get back to work.

I said he could go shortly, but first I had to ask where he was between ten and midnight yesterday and on Monday.

Bjarne Haug didn't query why I was asking him about Monday evening. Instead he simply replied that he had been at Club 7 the night before and left just before ten, then took a bus home to Grünerløkka. And on Monday evening, he had been playing in Drammen and taken the train back at half past nine, then caught the bus from Vestbanen station.

When I asked if he had taken the same train as Stein Hansen, he said yes. He added that it had been a last-minute job and that they hadn't been sitting in the same carriage. Then he stood up and went back to work.

Helgesen and I left the Co-op in silence. Helgesen nodded in agreement when I pointed towards a bakery on the corner of the street, rather than the car. We each bought a Danish pastry and found a corner table where we could talk without being disturbed, but even then kept our voices down.

'So, what do you think?' I whispered.

'That the victims came from two very different worlds, even though they grew up in the same part of town. But I'm afraid I don't have an answer as to who might have killed them,' Helgesen whispered back.

I said that that was more or less my conclusion too, and added that it was perhaps time to meet the jazz singer's family and find out more about the apparent conflicts there.

V

Caroline Maria Eilertsen's house in Røa was surrounded by a large garden that was vibrant and in full bloom. The atmosphere inside the house, however, was more in keeping with the overcast skies. 'Widow Eilertsen' presented herself in a very formal tone.

Caroline Eilertsen had agreed to meet us when I rang, and was waiting at the door when we arrived at a quarter past twelve. She had silver hair, and despite her sixty four years, was still straight-backed, with a clear voice. Her handshake was firm, without so much as a tremor. For me, she was the epitome of a dignified and controlled well-to-do lady. I was surprised, all the same, to note how little emotion she showed for a woman who had lost one of her daughters.

Her husband, Anton Eilertsen, had died four years earlier, but was still very present in the form of a large portrait in the drawing room and lots of photographs. According to a plaque on the wall, he had been a bank manager for twenty-five years and had retired from working life in 1960. The house bore his mark, and that of good old-fashioned wealth, with its plush sofas and armchairs. In this house, all that was old was a thing of great value. And it was almost clinically clean and tidy; I could not see a crumb on the tables or a speck of dust on the floors. There was something unreal and perfect about it, and it reminded me of a doll's house.

Widow Eilertsen fitted in perfectly here, and only a few minutes after arriving I found it hard to imagine the house without her. But equally, I found it hard, if not impossible, to imagine the young and vivacious Lise Eilertsen here. And that, no doubt, was why she had moved away from home so early and barely been back since. There were only a couple of photographs on the walls of her as a child.

The table in the drawing room was set for four with coffee and cake. We sat down, leaving the place closest to the door empty.

'My son was in an important meeting at the bank when I called, but will be here by one o'clock. If you wish, I can of course answer some questions now,' Mrs Eilertsen said.

I thanked her and tactfully remarked on how well she seemed to be coping with the painful loss of her daughter.

'It is only painful because I actually don't feel any great loss. It was a shock, of course, when the minister came to the door this morning. But as soon as I saw him, I knew what he was going to say. Over the past few years I have accepted, with growing certainty, that things would not end well for poor Lise. It was more a question of when and how, than if.'

I flashed a glance at Helgesen – and felt fairly certain we were thinking the same thing. In other words, that the now dead Lise Eilertsen had lived in a completely different world from the late Agnes Halvorsen, but their childhood homes were remarkably similar. Agnes had accepted it, whereas Lise had rebelled.

'So many people warned me against marrying a man eighteen years my senior. But I did not once regret it. We were very happy together for thirty-one years, until the day death really did us part. The only thing we ever disagreed on was little Lise. I was forty-one and he was fifty-nine; he was of the view that the two wonderful children we had already were enough: he had a son and a daughter. But I desperately wanted to have a third child before it was too late, and he was a good husband, so he gave in. Then we got this changeling, who from the start was not like any of us. Paradoxically, as things turned out, my husband understood her better than I did. I did not feel too old to have a baby at forty-two, but at fifty-eight I did feel too old to be bringing up an uncontrollable sixteen-year-old. It must have been in her blood, though heaven knows where that came from. Even at Sunday school she was unruly and loud – and she started chasing boys in primary school.'

Mrs Eilertsen had a clear, controlled voice. I could not decide if I was impressed or appalled, but guessed it was the latter.

I said that she mustn't blame herself, and asked how much contact she had had with her daughter after she moved out.

'It was almost a relief when she moved. She was hardly ever at home anyway, and when she was here the entire house shook with her ungodly music. Any respect she might have had died with my husband, but his death meant that she inherited some money and no longer needed to live at home. I didn't protest when she moved out, but said that perhaps having to deal with the realities of life might make her a better person. I still hoped that she might grow up one day, even if it was a few years later than others, but it never happened, and eventually I lost hope of it ever happening. When she first moved out I would call her every week or so, and then that extended to a month and eventually every four months. She never rang me back and showed no interest or respect when I called her. She just wanted to talk about things she knew I did not want to hear. If you were to ask me about my youngest daughter's life over the past twelve months, I'm afraid I wouldn't be able to tell you much. Now and then I read that she had sung in a concert, and I heard from others that she spent a lot of time in that club that has now been given a home close to the long-planned concert hall. And I am under no illusion that she was in any way less sinful than any of the others who frequent that den of iniquity. I'm ashamed to say, the dream of a miracle lived with me until the minister came knocking, but in reality I had given up on my youngest daughter. Her short life started as a mistake and became a tragedy long before she was killed yesterday.'

Her voice was still steady, but I detected a trace of emotion when she took a couple of deep breaths before continuing.

'I would be grateful to be spared the details of my daughter's life in the past few years. I hope that she didn't suffer too much when she died. And if the police manage to solve the case, I would of course like to know what happened and who was responsible for her death, but I'm afraid I really don't have much to contribute. I didn't really know my daughter any more; she lived in a world that was very different from the one she grew up in. And quite clearly, you should look for the murderer there and not in our peaceful family.'

I felt slightly resigned myself, but promptly told Mrs Eilertsen that her youngest daughter had been attacked and strangled close to her home in Berg and that she died quickly. We had, however, not arrested any suspects.

'I'm afraid I'm going to have to ask you a couple of questions that may seem rather odd, but your answers could be important to the investigation. Did your daughter or any of her friends have a particular interest in ants?'

The widow raised her eyebrows and gave me a pitying look.

'Now that is an odd question indeed, but as it is the police who are asking, I will of course take it seriously. We have never had any anthills in the garden or at the summer house, and Lise was not particularly interested in animals. In fact, even when she was only twelve, if anyone asked what her favourite animal was, she said "boys". No, if ants have anything to do with her death, I'm afraid I'm at a loss.'

'Can you remember your daughter ever talking about a girl of the same age called Agnes Halvorsen?'

Mrs Eilertsen thought for moment, but then shook her head.

'There's something familiar about the name . . . Agnes Halvorsen, is that not the name of the young woman who was killed at Hovscter, the minister's daughter? I read about it in *Aftenposten* yesterday. In which case, I can understand why you might ask. Hovseter is nearby, but we don't know anyone who lives there. And I can't remember my daughter ever having any contact with this Agnes Halvorsen – but then again, I have no idea of who my daughter might have met in the past three years.'

Just then, the doorbell rang. A smile spread over Caroline Eilertsen's face, and there was a sudden energy in her movements as she got up.

'That must be my son. He always comes a few minutes earlier than agreed. Just one moment, then you can speak to him.'

She was unexpectedly nimble on her feet as she hurried out into the hall.

VI

Lars Eilertsen turned out to be a man of around my age. He was about an inch shorter than me, and also quite a lot darker. In fact, he was in many ways a remarkably black-and-white man. His hair was short and black, in contrast to his pale, white skin, and his suit and tie were black, in contrast to the white shirt and socks. When I glanced at the picture on the wall I saw that his face was the same shape as his father's, but when I offered my condolences, his handshake was the same as his mother's: firm, fearless, and utterly without warmth.

He sat down on the fourth chair at the table. His mother took her seat again, and I didn't have the heart to ask her to leave.

'The news of my sister's unexpected death is both tragic and terrible. I cancelled as much as I could at the bank today, and naturally will do whatever I can to help the police. But unfortunately I am not sure that I can be of much help, as I've had only very limited contact with my sister in recent years.'

His mother nodded eagerly, which convinced me straight away that we would get nothing more out of the conversation.

But I still dutifully asked the same questions of him, and got more or less the same answers. That his sister's lifestyle was 'totally alien' to him and that his few attempts to make contact had never produced much response. They had had very little contact over the past two years, but there was 'no conflict whatsoever'. He was 'not surprised' that his sister had had boyfriends, but unfortunately did not know what any of them were called.

He had never had any interest in ants, nor had he noticed that either of his younger sisters did. He only knew the name Agnes Halvorsen in connection with the murder earlier in the week.

Sometimes an interview could feel like you were simply banging your head on a foam mattress. This was one of those interviews.

The time was now a quarter past one, and I had a dilemma.

In the end, I didn't ask the brother or the mother if they had an alibi. It felt disrespectful in a situation where neither of them appeared to have any motive. Instead, I concluded by saying that even though we clearly need not look for an answer in the immediate family, we would still need to speak to the victim's sister.

The mother and brother both nodded to this. The mother said that her daughter unfortunately had had to stay at home with her sick child, but would be more than happy to talk to us if we were willing to go out to Asker. She handed me a piece of paper on which she had already written down the address and telephone number, and said I could use the telephone here if I wished.

I took the piece of paper and suddenly felt an acute need to get away from the house. I didn't have much hope that we would learn anything new from the sister, so I said that as things stood, it was not urgent. I then thanked them for the coffee and cake, and stood up just as the clock struck half past one.

The atmosphere from the family home trailed after us out to the car, where Helgesen and I sat in silence for the first couple of minutes.

'I'm sure it's not easy to have a child you feel you have nothing in common with, especially when you are getting on a bit. But I would still have more photographs on the walls and shed a few tears if the child died.' Helgesen broke the silence.

I agreed with him, but also pointed out that breaking all contact with a family member was a long shot from killing them.

On the way back to the station, we had concluded that there was no reason to believe that this was a family murder.

The rather uncomfortable reality of this, as both of us knew but did not verbalize, was that our trip to Røa had not contributed a jot to solving the case. Nothing more was said until we reached the station.

VII

The morning papers had come by the time I got to my office at ten to two. The report in *Dagbladet* was no more than two columns and did not say much more than *Arbeiderbladet* and *Aftenposten*. The victim remained anonymous, but the paper did go as far as to say that she was 'a woman in her early twenties who was known on the Oslo jazz scene'.

As I feared, *Verdens Gang* was better informed, or less respectful. The fact that the newspaper had named the victim and included a photograph from an earlier concert review was bad enough. What was worse was that the report included a fairly detailed description of the scene of the crime, including the information that 'a small picture or symbol' had been found on the body, 'that had also been found at the scene of Agnes Halvorsen's murder, close to her home on Monday night'.

The newspaper hinted, without giving any details, that there were similarities between the two deaths, and concluded that 'there may be reason to fear that a murderer with a penchant for young women is at large on the streets of Oslo. And if that is the case, we can only hope that the police find the murderer before he finds his next victim.'

I felt a chill spread through my body as I read the article. At first I was indignant and wondered how the newspaper had got hold of all this information, but then it could have been gleaned from a few conversations with the witnesses and the family.

Instead of calling *Verdens Gang*, I went to find Helgesen and got him to read the report while I went to the switchboard to see what was happening there. The general public did not seem to be panicking yet, but there was growing unease. All the other national papers and a few of the local papers had called the station, as well as a handful of nervous mothers who wondered if it was safe to let their daughters go out on their own at night.

I went back to the office and wrote a standard press release, confirming the identity of the new victim and the fact that the death was being treated as suspicious. I added a sentence to say that the police were widening the investigation and looking at the possibility that the two deaths were linked.

Helgesen read over my draft and said that it was 'well formulated'. I went to deliver the press release and when I got back, he was still sitting looking at the report in *Verdens Gang*. It was perhaps just my imagination, but I thought he was sitting a little heavier on the chair and that his cheeks were slightly flushed. His face was definitely graver. There was not a trace of a smile on his lips today.

'What do you make of the situation?' I asked.

'That this is just a taster of what it might be like if there's another death. We may find the ground burning under our feet, so I suggest we don't sit here any longer than necessary,' he replied.

His voice was quiet and controlled, as always, lending his words all the more weight. Without answering, I took out the piece of paper with Lise Eilertsen's sister's address and phone number on it. She was not a lead that I thought would go anywhere, but she was the only lead we had. Fortunately she answered the phone as soon as it rang, just as her mother had promised.

VIII

Lina Eilertsen, whose surname was now in fact Vallestad, lived in green and pleasant surroundings just outside Asker. The house and garden were smaller than her childhood home, but still generous. There was no car outside when we arrived at three o'clock, but the tyre marks on the verge of the road indicated that a car was usually parked there. And a pram stood ready at the front door.

In contrast to her mother's house, however, Lina's home felt very much alive. She opened the door with a big smile, and a one-year-old on her arm. It was the first real smile that I'd seen all day, I realized, as I followed the mother and child into the living room.

We sat down on a sofa and chairs arranged around a triangular table. On it lay the day's papers and a couple of red photograph albums.

I now understood what Stein Hansen had meant when he said that the Eilertsen sisters were very different both physically and mentally. Lina was about five foot six, with blonde hair and a rather long face that reminded me of her mother – but any similarity stopped there. Lina was lively and friendly, and smiled when she shook my hand.

'I do apologize that I couldn't meet you at my mother's. My husband is away on business and has the car, and my daughter was coughing so much last night that I didn't want to take her out. So it's very kind of you to come here, and I will of course do all that I can to help the investigation.'

I started tactfully by saying that we understood that family relations were perhaps not the best, but that we had also been led to believe that she was the one who was closest to her sister. She responded immediately.

'That's probably true, yes, especially now that Dad is dead. I was like the zebra crossing in the family, with Lise going one way and Mum and Lars going the other way on the opposite side of the road. Lars was a boy and a lot older, and Mum had been brought up strictly in another age, and did nothing really to try and understand Lise or where she was coming from. She was pretty out of control, truth be told, from about the age of ten. I was closest to her in terms of age, and could understand the choices she made, even though I didn't make the same choices . . .'

She was interrupted by her little daughter who started first to cough and then to cry, but after a little attention she was smiling again and her mother continued where she had left off.

'. . . even though I didn't make the same choices. But I'm really not sure how much I can help you. I know a lot about my wild little sister's upbringing and childhood, but almost nothing about her life in the past few years. I've been busy getting married, having a baby and looking after my little girl for the last couple of years, and Lise was doing quite the opposite. We drifted apart, I guess. I was a little disappointed that she didn't show more interest in her niece, but whenever we met we always got on fine, if not brilliantly. I know nothing about her friends and boyfriends or anything like that. I bumped into her once with a good-looking guy, who I think was her boyfriend. He was called Stein. But I didn't ask and neither of them said anything.'

This tallied with what Stein Hansen had said. I explained to her that he had been Lise's boyfriend at the time, but was not any more.

'That sounds reasonable enough,' Lina said, without any further explanation, only a gentle smile.

I was obliged to ask her about the ant and the name Agnes Halvorsen. Neither rang any particular bells for her. So instead I asked Lina what she knew about her sister's financial situation.

She told us that her little sister had always been better at spending than saving, but that she should have been all right financially. Their mother had inherited their father's estate, but each of the children had received 150,000 kroner when their father died.

'Evidently her rent was low and she earned some money from her singing. I don't think she struggled financially, though again, I can only say what I think, not what I know. But there was also . . .'

She bit her lip, and stared down at her daughter for a few moments, but carried on as soon as I asked her to tell us everything that might be of interest.

'The issue of money is a bit fraught in our family . . . I'm pretty sure that Mum didn't tell you that she's seriously ill.'

I replied that her mother had not mentioned anything about ill health, and had in fact looked remarkably well for her age.

'Mother is Mother and will keep up appearances to the bitter end. She has cancer and no one knows if she will beat it or not. She told Lars and me a couple of weeks ago. It was so typical of Mum, for better or worse. No tears, no complaints and absolutely no sentimentality. Just the fact that she had cancer, that it was uncertain what the outcome would be, and that we should perhaps talk about our inheritance. If she died, everything left by Father would be divided equally between the three children, but Mum thought it would be both irresponsible and morally wrong to give Lise so much money. She proposed leaving the house to Lars and the summer house to me, and dividing the bulk of the inheritance between the two of us. Lars was all for it, but I wasn't sure. Lise is – was – still young. I thought it was a bit harsh to deny her her inheritance for good, and wasn't sure that it would make her situation any better. So we agreed to compromise and to see what happened with Mum and the cancer, and to think things through. I felt then that it was wrong to divide up the inheritance in advance, and feel the same now, only more so. But it's no longer of any practical importance.'

I realized that the inheritance question could give the brother a motive, and asked roughly how much the inheritance was worth.

'Mum inherited a fair amount of money, and Dad a lot, which he then invested well. So we're talking somewhere in the region of two million, including the house and the summer house. But . . .' she suddenly rolled her eyes, then looked at Helgesen and me with something akin to accusation, 'but you can just forget the idea that anyone in the family might want Lise dead for that reason. Mum was free to give away what she liked, and Lars would get both the house and half the money if he wanted. And he's an honest auditor and happily married father of two, and has never broken the law in his life, as far as I know. He's so straight and law-abiding that it's almost annoying; the sort of person who tells you if you're even a mile over the speed limit.'

I raised my palms in defence and said that no one in her family was suspected of anything, but we had to look at all possibilities in an investigation.

The little girl started to cry again, but it was hard to tell whether it was because her mother had raised her voice or not. Lina sounded in no way unfriendly when she almost shouted at us over the howling child, 'Don't get me wrong, I of course want to know what happened to my poor little sister, and will do whatever I can to help. But I'm going to have to feed my daughter soon. I dug out two photo albums from Lise's childhood, in case they were of interest.'

She pointed to the albums on the table.

Helgesen looked at them, and then at me.

I thought, well, when needs must, and said that we would very much appreciate having a quick look, if it was not an inconvenience.

She shouted that it wasn't at all, and just to say if we would like coffee, then made a hasty exit to the kitchen with her wailing daughter.

For a few moments, with the toddler's cries ringing in my ears, I tried to see it as positive that my engagement had been broken off before it resulted in screaming children. Then I carefully opened the cover of the photograph album lying on top.

We went through the first one rather quickly. Even Lise Eilertsen had once been a sweet little girl, surrounded by proud parents and a smiling older brother and sister. But as she got older, it was possible to see the friction around her, even in black-and-white photographs. The girl was looking in every direction other than the camera, her parents looked increasingly serious, and her siblings' smiles were more and more forced. She stood out in class photographs as the only one pulling faces at the photographer.

Apart from her family, I recognized no one in the first album.

I leafed through the second album, which started on her tenth birthday, more slowly. There wasn't much of interest to begin with. Lots of pictures from garden parties, but not an anthill to be seen. She no longer pulled faces in class photographs, but instead looked straight into the camera with defiant eyes.

In her confirmation photographs, her father was more or less bald and her mother's hair was turning grey. Her older brother Lars was dark and lean, and easily recognizable, but appeared less and less frequently. Lina was a head taller than Lise, and her kind smile was not to be mistaken. She was also to be seen less often. There were simply fewer photographs, and the captions underneath, written in an old-fashioned hand, presumably her mother's, became shorter. Following the five pictures from the confirmation, there were suddenly only one page and two photographs left from Lise Eilertsen's childhood.

Underneath the second-to-last photograph in the album, it simply said, *Lise's fifteenth birthday*. Her father now had a walking stick, but was the only one smiling, even though there was an enormous cake on the table between the mother and her daughters.

I glanced down at the last picture in the album with some resignation – and then jumped up from the chair in surprise. Helgesen remained seated, but gasped when he saw the photograph.

The last picture was labelled as *Practice with parish choir*, and was of five girls aged around fifteen.

A man in his twenties was sitting at a piano in the background. Lise Eilertsen was easily recognizable: she was standing in the middle and was about half a head shorter than the others. The two girls to the left were completely unknown. The tallest of the five girls was standing to the far right, a fair-haired girl with a cross pendant and quite unmistakably the face of Agnes Halvorsen. And I was in no doubt that the shorter, darker and slightly blurred girl standing between Agnes Halvorsen and Lise Eilertsen was Agnes' enigmatic friend, Nora Jensen.

'Well, well, perhaps we've found our link,' I said.

Helgesen gave an excited nod. We raced over and knocked on the kitchen door.

'You said the name Agnes Halvorsen meant nothing to you – but we are more or less certain that there is a photograph of her in this album,' I said, as soon as Lina Eilertsen opened the door, and held the picture up for her to see.

'The choir only lasted for a few months, and I never got to know all their names. But now that you mention it, yes, I think there was an Agnes. Mum was very active in the church, and when one of the youth leaders suggested starting a choir, she thought it might be Lise's salvation. There weren't enough girls to form a choir in either Røa or Hovseter, so two friends from Hovseter came here. I should have remembered,' she said, and bit her lip.

We assured her in stereo that it was a perfectly understandable slip. Then I asked if she could remember the names of any of the others.

She sighed.

'No, I'm afraid that's all way back in my memory. Remembering is not one of my strong points. Even though Mum has suppressed it, it was actually me and not Lise who was not particularly bright at school. Having said that, I seem to remember that Agnes and Nora were always mentioned together, but I've no idea what Nora's surname was. The other two from Røa . . .'

She sighed again and put her finger on the two girls to the left. They were standing side by side, arms touching, and looked like best friends too. They were each wearing a cross around their neck, but any physical resemblance stopped there. One was blonde, tall and athletic, with a serious, almost sullen expression on her face. She made me think of a grumpy greyhound. The other girl had auburn hair and looked as though she still hadn't grown into her woman's body, but her freckled face was all smiles. She had her hair in plaits, so it was hard not make the obvious association with Pippi Longstocking.

'I don't think these two were in Lise's class, and I can't remember them ever coming to the house. One of them might have been called Kari, but I'm afraid I can't remember any of their surnames. But I do remember the pianist, I think, because he was only a year or two older than me and played at my confirmation. He was very passionate about music and singing, but was otherwise a man of few words. His name was Tore Pettersen, I'm pretty of sure of that. But I have no idea where he lived. Don't think I ever saw him apart from in church, and I wasn't there very much after I got confirmed. I really am sorry not to be of more use.'

I told her that the albums had proved to be very useful indeed and that I was certain we could identify the other girls in the photograph if we could take it with us.

'Of course,' was her response.

The mood was friendly when we left at half past three. The little girl waved happily to us from her mother's arms, as Lina stood on the steps. I could well understand why the now dead Lise had preferred her sister to her mother and brother. But it struck me, all the same, that even Lina, despite all the care she had given her daughter and us, had not shown any real grief at the loss of her sister. As far as I could tell, we were investigating the death of a young woman who had been known to many, but would really only be missed in Club 7.

'Shall we go to the parish office in Røa?' Helgesen asked when we got into the car.

'Let's try Hovseter first,' I said. I felt we had been given a boost.

IX

I went in alone this time. Helgesen himself suggested that he should wait in the car and I didn't protest. It seemed that the chances of Nora Jensen telling the truth were greater when we talked one-to-one.

We both feared that she might not be at home, but the curtains upstairs twitched as I walked up the path and the door was opened as soon as I rang the bell.

I asked how she was and she forced a tight smile and thanked me for asking. Things were a bit better, but not great, she said.

I asked whether there was anyone at home with her.

She told me that her parents were at home in the morning and evening, but both worked during the day.

'I suppose you've come to ask me something,' she said.

'Yes,' I replied.

We went in and sat down in the living room, in the same places as before.

'Have you heard about the murder at Berg last night?' I asked.

'Yes, I heard about it on the radio, but they didn't give any names,' she responded. Her blue eyes were strangely devoid of expression, like a still sea with no waves.

'The woman who was killed called herself Lisa Elea, but her real name was Lise Eilertsen,' I said.

'Oh,' was Nora Jensen's only reaction. She showed no sign of being upset. But something did move somewhere deep down below the surface.

I pulled out the photograph of the choir and showed it to her.

'Both you and Agnes knew Lise Eilertsen,' I said.

'It was such a long time ago. Like another happier world. Lise . . . she came from another neighbourhood and was very different from Agnes and me,' Nora Jensen said.

She didn't even look at the photograph, just at me. I held the picture up between us, but she still didn't look at it.

'We didn't really know her back then either, and we only sang in the choir with her for a few months. It was in spring 1965, from February to April, I think. We had choir practice every Tuesday evening from the mid-term break until Easter. Then one day after Easter, we got a letter from the parish council to say that the choir had been wound up.'

'That's a bit odd, isn't it? And you were not told why?' I wondered.

She shook her head, almost imperceptibly.

'It didn't say in the letter. When my mother called the office, she was told that the choir leader had left. Which seemed to be true, because we never saw him there again. No one said why he had left so suddenly. Agnes and I speculated about it for a while . . .'

I felt my pulse increase. The possibility of a drama in the small group of five young girls and a young male choir leader had already crossed my mind, though I still couldn't see a connection between that and two of the girls from the choir being killed seven years later. But all of a sudden, it felt as if we had tripped over the answer. So I pressed on and asked what they speculated about.

'Agnes thought that the choir leader was in love with her. She had relished the thought on several occasions. Only his eyes had given him away, she said. I hadn't noticed any special interest on his part. He was a quiet man, and not particularly attractive. But he was over twenty, and we were fourteen, fifteen. Nothing had happened either with Agnes or me. We wondered whether something might have happened with one of the other girls, but didn't know them well enough to ask. So I can't tell you any more than that. Do you think that he killed Agnes?' she asked, rather abruptly.

The direct question was unexpected. I looked down at the seven-year-old photograph of the choir leader. In the picture, he was a clean-shaven young man in his early twenties, with short fair hair. He was sitting in the background, half hidden by the piano. The image of him was slightly blurred. I said that for the moment I didn't think so, but that I would of course have to speak to him and the other girls in the choir.

She took the hint and blinked several times. There was definitely some turbulence beneath the waters now. Something was coming to the surface. Again, I found myself thinking that she was sharper than one might at first guess.

'The girl without the plaits is Kari Evensen and the one with the plaits is Heidi Olsen. They were both from Røa, so we never saw them otherwise. I have no idea where they lived then and even less where they might be now. But my parents happened to bump into Kari's parents last autumn. They told them that Kari had converted to Catholicism and was now a Dominican nun. So she might be somewhere abroad or with the Dominican Sisters of Notre Dame de Grâce at Katarina Convent in Majorstuen. But that's all I know, I'm afraid. The choir leader was called Tore Pettersen, but I haven't a clue about him.'

I was honest and told her that that was fine, and that I could no doubt find out where the others lived now, if they were still alive, based on what she had told me. The latter was simply an official formulation but in the current situation took on a rather sinister tone.

I asked her to take care until we had fully investigated this lead with the choir.

Nora Jensen swallowed, and then said that she would stay at home and not let in anyone she didn't know, and that her parents would be home again in the evening.

I asked whether she would like a policeman to guard the house. She declined, saying that she would rely on Our Lord's protection for the moment, but promised to let me know if she changed her mind.

Her voice shook slightly when she said this, and I realized that her friend's death had come as an extra shock to Nora, precisely because she had always trusted that Our Lord's protection was enough. It was not only her sense of security, but also her world picture that had been shaken.

I did not trust in Our Lord's protection as much, but I did not want to challenge her faith and was now also keen to get on. So I thanked her for her help and got up to leave. She again gave one of her minuscule nods, but did not get up so I let myself out.

I hesitated outside the house for a few seconds. I did not like the idea of leaving the door unlocked. But Nora Jensen was clearly more alert than she gave the impression of being, and I heard the lock click only moments later.

X

The Dominican Sisters had a young 'Sister Kari' at Katarina Convent in Majorstuen. She was the youngest of the novices, but very devout and hard-working, the Mother Superior told me.

Sister Kari was at prayer when we arrived at twenty past four, but came into the visiting room no more than ten minutes later. Her hair was covered, but the fine and graceful features under her coif still belonged to a beautiful young woman. Her face was as serious as it had been in the choir photograph. She still reminded me of a greyhound, but seemed to be less anxious now.

Her handshake was very slight and she pulled her chair back a touch when she sat down. We were sitting by a bare wooden table under a large photograph of the author Sigrid Undset.

I started by asking Sister Kari if she had heard about the two murders in Hovseter and Røa this week.

Her voice was surprisingly deep and somehow did not suit her slight frame. But her reply was believable enough: that prayers and work had taken up all her time and she had not read the papers or listened to the news this week.

I explained that we wanted to speak to her because the two victims were Agnes Halvorsen and Lise Eilertsen.

She rolled her eyes lightly, and folded her hands. This was followed by a short and intense prayer in a language I can only assume was Latin.

'May the Almighty have mercy on their souls. Lise had no faith in Our Lord when I knew her and I can only pray that she found the way later. Agnes, on the other hand, had strong faith in God, albeit in the wrong church,' she said, in an even deeper voice.

I said that was undoubtedly the case, but that we were duty-bound to find the killer, regardless of their faith. As I said this, I took out the photograph of the choir and placed it on the table in front of her.

She nodded twice, first at what I said, then at the photograph.

'We fear that the murders may be connected to something that happened when you all sang in the choir together,' I said.

I am not quite sure what sort of response I had expected, but it was certainly not the one I got.

Sister Kari was not at all surprised, but stayed completely still on her chair. When she finally replied, she simply said, 'I have no right to share with anyone other than God secrets told to me in confidence.'

'In other words, you know about something serious that happened when you were in the choir, but you won't tell us what it was? Withholding evidence from the police is a serious crime,' I reminded her, with mild irritation.

Sister Kari was not to be swayed. She sat perfectly still when she answered.

'Better to have a strained relationship with the secular state than to have an impossible relationship with oneself and God.'

Helgesen looked at me. And I focused on the wall for a moment or two. Sister Kari's reasoning was starting to annoy me. The implication of what she was saying was clear enough. Someone had confided a secret in her, and it seemed reasonable to assume that that someone was her friend, to whom we had not yet spoken.

'It is of course a dilemma whether you should share something told to you in confidence or not. It's another matter when you have seen or experienced something yourself. And if I have understood correctly, you neither saw anything with your own eyes or experienced anything personally that might be of relevance, is that correct?'

Sister Kari's eyes were steady. She did not blink in the two seconds she took to think before she answered. 'I am more than happy to share my own secrets with you. It's those given to me in confidence by others that I cannot share without betraying a friend, myself and God.'

I replied that the context was clear and that we would have to respect her faith and morals as far as was possible.

She thanked me for this.

I added that two of the four others in the choir had now been killed, so that if she was intending to go out alone at night in the next few days, she should be vigilant. We could also provide police protection if she so wished.

She thanked me for the warning and said that she seldom left the convent, and that she always trusted in the Lord's protection if she did.

I asked in conclusion if she could remember where Heidi Olsen had lived. A hint of a smile twitched at the corners of her mouth.

'Back then, Heidi Olsen lived at 52A Røa Gardens, two houses away from where I grew up. And I'm sure that I heard more recently that she now lives in the black houses up by Grini Station. I believe the street number mentioned was 17C.'

Thus she offered me the opportunity to finish our visit with heartfelt thanks and a smile. We had finally established a sort of mutual understanding despite the obstacles that her faith and moral standpoint represented.

Helgesen ruined this somewhat by asking if the secret she had been told had in any way influenced her later decision to become a nun.

Her pale cheeks flushed a faint red, as she replied in a serious, slightly sharp voice that her reasons for becoming a nun were a matter between her and God.

It was now well past the end of our shift. On the way out, I asked Helgesen if he wanted to call it a day now. 'You must be joking,' he said, with unexpected and boyish cheer.

XI

Grini was still best known for the concentration camp that had been there during the war. Grini Way was not within view of the former concentration camp, but was close to the old brickworks. It took us a while to find the right number amongst all the identical black-stained wooden houses.

The next problem was to find the right flat. We discovered that there were nameplates for five of the six flats, but did not see the name Olsen on any of them. This could of course be explained if Heidi Olsen had got married and therefore changed her name. After a brief discussion, we eventually decided to knock on the door with no nameplate first.

And we struck lucky first time. The woman who answered the door no longer had plaits, but still definitely had freckles. Without them, we might not have recognized her: she was taller and had a much wider girth, thanks to being around eight months pregnant, I guessed. There was no longer a cross around her neck, but she did have a wedding ring on her finger.

'And how can I help you?' she asked from the doorway. Her words were friendly, but her voice was tense.

Behind her, I could see a standard two-room Selvaag flat, with the furniture pushed up against the walls. The main room was sizeable, with a living-room area in one corner and an open-plan kitchen. There was a cot standing in the room, but no evidence of any children other than the unborn baby, and the husband did not appear to be at home.

I asked if she could confirm that she was Heidi Olsen, and held out my police ID card.

No more was needed. The colour drained from her face and she had to lean against the door frame for support. Then she waved us quickly in and closed the door, before sinking down onto an old sofa by the coffee table. When she spoke, her voice was muted and trembling.

'I'm not called Olsen any more . . . But yes, that was my maiden name. I of course know why you're here.'

I still did not know why she thought we were here, but my desire to know the secret behind this long-since disbanded choir was now growing. Once again, I pulled out the photograph and said, 'If you think we're here in connection with the choir you were in some years ago now, where something happened that should never have happened, then you're right.'

She let out a heavy sigh, and looked up at the ceiling briefly before answering.

'It was a long time ago. Why suddenly come and rake over that old story now?'

'Because two of the other girls have suddenly been killed in the past three days,' I replied.

Heidi's freckled face seemed to fall apart when she heard this. Her right hand was clamped over her mouth, while her eyes darted back and forth between myself and Helgesen, and her whole body, including her big belly, started to tremble alarmingly.

'What are you saying . . . Who has been killed?' she asked in a barely audible voice.

'Agnes Halvorsen was murdered on Monday night, close to her childhood home in Hovseter. And Lise Eilertsen was killed in Berg, where she now lived, yesterday evening. It seems likely that there is some kind of connection with the choir, which is why we are here now,' I explained.

She sighed again, but kept her eyes trained on me.

'That's awful, and so sad. I didn't know either of them particularly well and haven't spoken to them for years. But they were both the same age as me, and they seemed to be nice, each in their own way. Peace be with them. But I really don't see how it could be connected to the choir. It all feels so long ago and what happened had nothing to do with either Agnes or Lise.'

'No, that was between you and the church youth leader, wasn't it? He liked underage girls a little too much, perhaps,' I ventured.

She nodded, but also flinched slightly. Her voice was louder and sharper when she carried on. 'Yes, but – it was my fault, not his. He fell in love with me, but was too decent to show it or make any kind of advance. I was young, looking for adventure, and intoxicated by being in love for the first time. It was me who asked one day after practice if he could give me some extra singing lessons at home, when I knew my parents and little sister weren't going to be there. I used the excuse of my fifteenth birthday and said that there was a present I would love to have. It was me who put my hand on his thigh when he sat next to me at home. I asked for it, and have never accused him of anything.'

'But he was an adult and you were a minor – and you were discovered?' I prompted her.

She sighed heavily again, and gave a bitter smile.

'Yes, and it was my fault. I forgot the time, and then my mum and little sister came home earlier than expected. We were still in bed when my annoying little sister suddenly ran in. She burst out laughing and thought the whole thing was hilarious. But my religious mother most definitely did not, and all hell broke loose in Røa. My parents wanted to take him to court for sexual assault, to begin with, but then they couldn't bear the idea of the scandal or any criticism about the way they had brought me up, because I insisted that I had invited him into the house and into my bed. He took full

responsibility, in terms of both my parents and the congregation. He lost his job, his flat, and had to move away, within the
space of two days. My bed was thrown out and I had to sleep
on the floor for a month. It was nearly a year before my mother
spoke to me again, but the whole thing was kept absolutely
secret, so any scandal was averted and there was no trial. And
to this day, I have only ever discussed it with my little sister and
with Kari, who was my best friend and confidante at the time.
She was deeply shocked, but crossed her heart and swore that
she would never tell a living soul. But none of it had anything
to do with the other three girls in the group, and as far as
I know, they never found out.'

I had no reason either to believe that the other girls in the
choir had known, but I did see a possible connection and
answer here, all the same. This Tore Pettersen chap was apparently interested in several young girls at the time, and had done
something illegal with one of them. One possible explanation
was that he, as a result of mental issues or further disappoint-
ments in life, had now started to wreak his revenge on those
who had once rejected him. Perhaps both Agnes and Lise had
done just that. And maybe Nora, Kari or Heidi herself would
be his next victim.

Just then, there was a noise at the outer door. The flat was
small and not very well sound-insulated. Helgesen and I turned
towards the door, while Heidi stayed sitting where she was,
without moving.

'No need to worry. It's just my husband. He normally
comes home from work around this time. We can carry on
talking,' she said.

'Do you have any idea of what happened to this Tore
Pettersen later and where we might find him now?' I asked in

a hushed voice. It struck me that the pregnant woman's husband might not know about the story we had just heard, and I did not want to cause a family crisis or put her in an awkward situation.

Heidi still looked very serious, but smiled when she replied. I got the distinct impression that in a more relaxed situation she could be both cheerful and charming.

'Yes, in fact, I do. The very same Tore Pettersen is standing right behind you.'

Helgesen and I turned our heads again, in time to see her husband come into the room.

He was taller and more solid than he had seemed in the photograph, with darker hair and a bit more stubble, but it was clearly the same man. His initial reaction was surprise, and then slight indignation.

'What's going on? And who are you?' he asked, with some tension in his voice.

'They're from the police, and are here to talk about the choir. Agnes and Lise have both been murdered!' she explained, before I had managed to get a word out.

It was as though her husband had been shot. He clapped his hand on his heart and staggered a few steps over the floor. Both Helgesen and I jumped up to support him, but instead he leaned back again the wall, and held up his hand to stop us. He stood there only a few feet away, gasping for air for a few seconds.

'I read about Agnes in the papers at lunch today. I didn't know about Lise. That's terrible,' he then managed to stammer.

I asked him to come and sit down, and then went back to my chair. He did as he was told, moving more or less mechanically. He sat down beside his wife on the sofa. She put her hand on his thigh and he put his arm round her shoulder.

'We have always feared that one day the police would knock on our door to ask about what happened back then. So I'll say now what I have always thought I would say, which is that it was all my fault. I was a grown man who fell so totally in love with a young girl that I lost all control, and if I have to go to prison for that, I will. But the fact that Agnes and Lise have been murdered . . . We don't know anything about that, and I don't see how on earth it can be connected to the choir.'

He said this with unexpected and forceful passion. His wife nodded vigorously in agreement.

'So first of all you engage in illegal activities with an under-age choirgirl and then you contact her again later to start a relationship?' I remarked.

They both shook their heads. It was she who answered in a strident, almost indignant, voice.

'No, no, it really wasn't like that. You mustn't think badly of the best man in the world. I engaged willingly in those illegal activities. He later sent me a letter with no return address, asking me to forgive him for all the problems he had caused me, and promising that I would never see him again. But I didn't forget him. I continued to worry about him. I wasn't able to fall in love with anyone else. So the day I turned eighteen, I mustered my courage and phoned every Tore Pettersen I could find in the Oslo telephone directory. Eventually I found the right man, in a tiny basement flat in Sagene. At first he was frightened and upset, but then all the happier for seeing me again. I was so glad when he told me that he had finally managed to get a job after having been unemployed for some time, and I was even happier to discover that he was living on his own and had not found another woman. And, well, here we are.'

He nodded a couple of times as she spoke, and gave her a quick hug when she had finished.

It was certainly an unusual love story, and I had to admit that I found it rather touching. And they seemed to be genuinely in love, sitting there together with a baby on the way.

I was frank and told them that we were here solely to investigate the murders and that they need not worry about their first date being a little too early. If the girl was over fourteen, cases like that rarely went to court unless it was formally reported.

'Thank goodness, and thank you for telling us. We made a mistake and are painfully aware of it now. And we've tried to make amends for it subsequently. I don't earn a fortune as a janitor's assistant, but we have what we need. We just want to be left in peace and to see our children growing up. And let me tell you, the children from around here grow into fine young men and women too,' he said quietly, placing his hand gently on his wife's belly.

Tore Pettersen did not look like a murderer. In fact he looked so unlike a murderer that I almost dismissed the idea completely.

But then suddenly Helgesen was there beside me, holding a slim book in shaking hands.

'I found this in the bookshelf,' he said.

I had never seen the book before, but immediately understood its significance. It was a children's book, with a picture of two ants, a beetle and a wasp on the front cover. The picture of the ants was very similar to those we had found at the two murder scenes.

We started to leaf through it right away. Helgesen held the book and I turned the pages.

'What's happening now? Surely it's not illegal to have children's books even though you don't have children?' Tore Pettersen exclaimed from the sofa.

Helgesen and I both ignored him. We were too engrossed in the book. There were pictures of ants on nearly every page.

We whipped through the book, impatiently searching for two missing ants. Any missing pages or cut-out ants would provide strong grounds for arresting a possible suspect.

We scanned every single page, without finding anything suspicious. When we had gone through the whole book, Helgesen snapped it shut with audible frustration.

All the pages and all the ants were there.

The Pettersens sat hand in hand in silence, watching us with bewilderment. By their own admission, they had for several years feared that the police would show up unannounced because of what they had done when they were younger. Unless one or both of them knew more about the murders than they had admitted, it was easy to understand why they might look on in disbelief at two policemen frantically leafing through a children's book.

'I'm very sorry, but we have no idea what's going on now. I read that book when I was a girl, and I can promise you it's in no way dangerous. We want to start reading to our child as soon as possible, so we've gathered together some of our children's books from when we were small. But does that mean we're suspected of doing something criminal?' Heidi ventured.

I tried to answer with as much tact as possible and said that neither of them was suspected of anything at the moment, but that the book might be of considerable importance to the investigation, so we would have to take it away with us. And

I was also obliged to ask Tore Pettersen where he had been between ten and midnight on Monday and Wednesday.

He swallowed a couple of times, but his answer was measured: 'I am trying to earn as much as I can now before the baby is born, so I was doing some overtime on Monday evening, as we had an evening event, and got home around half past eleven. And I was here all evening yesterday.'

The woman at his side nodded emphatically.

'My husband was at home with me all of yesterday evening. And anyway, it's unthinkable that he would kill anyone in any case. Why on earth would he want to kill them now?' she cried.

I did not have the answer to her question. Tore Pettersen could have killed Agnes on Monday night and we only had his wife's word that he was at home with her on the night that Lise was killed. If it had been shortly after he had lost his job in the church, while he was unemployed and living in Sagene, I would absolutely have suspected him. But why he would want to kill them now, when he had a wife and a baby on the way, was beyond me. It seemed completely irrational that he would now suddenly decide to kill these women when, as far as we knew, he had not had a relationship with either of them, or any conflicts. And even though Tore Pettersen was perhaps not someone to make a lasting impression, he was certainly not unsympathetic or irrational.

In other words, it felt as though we had now followed the choir lead as far as it would go, without finding an answer to who had killed the two former choirgirls.

I smoothed things over as best I could. I thanked them for their help, and once again assured them that they could sleep safe in the knowledge that their past sins would have no repercussions, then added that we had absolutely no reason to suspect either of them of being involved in the murders. However, it was my duty to say that a situation where two out of five former choirgirls had been killed was very alarming indeed. So in conclusion I asked if they would like police protection.

They gave each other a quick hug. Tore Pettersen said that they had nothing to hide and they would certainly feel safer if there was a policeman nearby, at least when he was out at work.

I promised them that a policeman would be there on duty later on that evening and asked them to telephone me if they remembered anything else that might be of importance. They chorused their agreement, then thanked me for freeing them of 'the heavy, invisible burden' of fear that their earlier misdemeanour had become.

As I looked around, it struck me that there was no sign of anyone else here, except for the unborn baby's cradle. There were some black-and-white photos on the wall, but only one of him, one of her and one of the two of them together. That was it.

The lyrics of the Seekers' hit from a few years back, 'A World of Our Own', popped into my head.

I stood there with the words running through my mind. It fitted. These two people just wanted to build a world of their own in here.

We finished on a friendly note. They stayed sitting on the sofa, while Helgesen and I found our own way out. One advantage of the Selvaag flats was that everyone could always find their way out. All we took with us was the children's book with the drawing of two ants, a beetle and a wasp on the front – and I unfortunately did not have much hope that it would bring us any closer to solving the murders of Agnes Halvorsen and Lise Eilertsen.

XII

'So no witnesses have come forward with interesting sightings near Berg yesterday?' Patricia asked, before taking her first sip of wine during dinner.

It was now five past eight. A glass of red wine had been waiting for me too when I arrived a good hour earlier. And Patricia had said, 'Yes, of course,' without any great upset when I said that I could not drink alcohol because of the investigation, and also because I had the car. She had only drunk water herself until now.

She had listened with great concentration to my account of events earlier in the day, and had not asked any questions. Now that I had finished, she only had one question to ask – and my reply, unfortunately, was negative. Then there was silence.

The atmosphere at the table was not bad, but was very definitely tense. I hadn't even noticed what kind of soup we had had, and had only paused for a moment to compliment the beef and Béarnaise that we were served for our main course. Patricia, for her part, had said rather vaguely that it was fine.

'Did you establish whether the ant pictures from the crime scenes were taken from the same book as the one that the Pettersens had on their bookshelf?' she suddenly asked, when the silence was starting to feel oppressive.

'Yes, it certainly seems so – unless there are other books that use the same illustrations. Several of the drawings are identical to the two we found with the bodies, but there were no ant pictures missing from the Pettersens' copy. And it's the same paper quality, so it looks as though the ants may have been cut out directly from a book.'

Patricia sighed.

'Which tells us nothing, really. He may of course have had two books and disposed of what was left of the other copy. But if you got rid of one, it seems rather odd to keep the other on the shelf.'

'You don't think it was him either, do you?' I remarked.

Patricia shook her head firmly, then took another sip of wine.

'Of course I don't think so. Why would he suddenly kill the two girls now, when fate was finally smiling on him? And why would his wife then support him with an alibi? The Pettersens might well have wanted to kill one of the others, if she knew something and was blackmailing him or threatening to expose him. But there's nothing to indicate that any of them were doing that, and that they both should do it at the same time would be pretty far-fetched.'

I had to agree, and asked, 'What do you think, then?'

Patricia released an even heavier sigh, and drank some more wine.

'I think that so far we know nothing about the murderer's identity. It's extremely frustrating that you're gathering in more and more information, but there's nothing more that I or anyone else can squeeze out of it. This murderer appears to have planned everything exceedingly well and has also had his fair share of luck. I am not ruling out any connection with the choir story, but I don't think that is where we will find the link we are looking for. If one were to believe that the murderer is either the choir leader or one of the other girls, the problem of the motive remains. Another question is how the murderer could know, so many years later, when Agnes and Lise would pass the spots where they were killed. That is the greatest riddle, really, no matter who the murderer is. He or she may of course have spied on them, but you normally need to know someone's movements pretty well to know for sure where they will be at a given point in time. And that is particularly true of Lise, who lived a far less regulated life than Agnes. But it is possible that . . .'

Patricia broke off mid-sentence and sat with her chin on her hand, staring at the wall.

I knew her well enough to know she had a theory, but that she did not want to say anything about it as it was still too uncertain. And I knew her more than well enough to know that she would only get irritated if I pushed her about it. I therefore let her contemplate in peace while the maid cleared away the main course and served the dessert. Once the maid had left the room, I started to eat my cake, taking care not to disturb Patricia's trance-like concentration.

'Remarkable coincidence, really. The chances that two women who are killed two days apart just happened to have sung in the same choir when they were fifteen must be pretty slim,' I tried.

My voice was clearly what was needed to rouse Patricia again. Within seconds she was back in the conversation.

'Yes, the chances of them meeting in a choir when they were fifteen are against the odds. But then, what are the chances that two women who were born in the same year and grew up less than a mile apart from each other had met at some point when they were growing up?'

Considerably greater, and very likely, I had to admit. Patricia sent me a fleeting smile.

'Good to know we agree on that. And the chances that someone may mess around with someone they ought not to mess around with are always relatively high when young and slightly older people get together, whether it is a Christian congregation or otherwise. So let's be open to the possibility that there is a link between the murders and the choir, but let's not assume that there has to be one.'

I was just about to say that there had been more than a little messing around in the choir, but stopped myself just in time. The point Patricia was making was valid regardless. But I did wonder if there was anything behind her formulation 'young and slightly older people'. In the end, I somewhat hesitantly said that I thought the Pettersens' story was charming and touching in the midst of everything else.

Patricia responded immediately.

'Absolutely. One might vote red for less,' she quipped.

As far as I could remember, it was the first time I had heard Patricia say anything that might turn the conversation to Norwegian politics. I had simply assumed, given the size of the house, her family background and wealth, that she would vote Conservative and that I would therefore struggle with her arguments if we were to have a political debate. I realized I actually had no idea where she stood politically. Her views on relationships between men and women seemed to be very liberal, but if what she had said was an invitation to be more personal, I did not feel the desire to take it up there and then. It was not that I was thinking of Miriam, but rather that my attention was focused on Agnes Halvorsen and Lise Eilertsen and their still faceless killer out there in the dark.

Patricia also seemed to be affected by the case. Following a short pause for thought, she carried on in a more serious tone, 'I have to say that I am more and more puzzled by this case. Never before have we had so few clues and been so far from solving the case three days after the first murder. If the murderer, as I think, has no close links to either of the victims, we really are looking at the curse of public space. The murderer could be pretty much anyone in Oslo and the surrounding areas. As long as he or she managed to leave the scene of the crime unseen, we will find it very difficult to identify the perpetrator, and even harder to prove that it is them. So at the moment, the water is black as far as the eye can see.'

Patricia stopped for a moment and bit her lip, but then carried on with the same grave face and underlying indignation in her voice.

'The very idea that anyone should strangle young women who are out alone at night is disgusting. I fear that more lives may be lost, and that is partly because I think this killer has much in common with Leopold and Loeb. The murderer is possibly killing for thrills and attention rather than any rational reason, which makes the relatively short space of time between the two deaths even more alarming.'

'You're worried that two days between the first two murders means that there is a danger there might be a third by the end of the week?' I asked in a muted voice. The thought was horrifying.

Patricia nodded brusquely, and then gulped down the rest of her wine.

'In the worse case, I fear we may even have a third and a fourth death this week. There have not been many serial murderers in Norway since the war, so there is not much to build on, but the experience in the United States, Great Britain and other countries is that they often wait longer than that.'

My knowledge of serial murderers was limited. But I could not think of a single example from Norway and could only agree with what she said about serial killers in other countries. In most of the cases I had read about, there was one, or a maximum of two victims a year.

'So this murderer is possibly out of the ordinary. Not just a ticking bomb, but a fast-ticking bomb. Did you ever watch *The $64,000 Question?*'

The question was so out of the blue and seemed totally irrelevant in the middle of a serious conversation, but based on previous experience, I reckoned that Patricia had a reason for asking. So I said that I had preferred the young Bjørnsen to old Haarberg as a presenter, but had watched most of the programmes.

'It was my favourite programme when I was a child, and I still hope that it might come back soon – with or without Bjørnsen. But my point is that this killer may share some of the psychological traits of the participants. The murderer is completely focused on himself or herself, and his or her interests, and has been planning this for a long time. He or she enjoys the attention and excitement, which increases with every success. A lot of the participants understand that they should stop in time, but very few of them manage to do it. The board and the booth get the better of them once they are in. In this case, the murderer succeeded on the first attempt and so doubled the stakes, and succeeded again. I think he or she will double them again, and I fear that it won't take long.'

I heard a slight tremor in Patricia's voice as she spoke. There was a mildly comical moment when, with her eyes fixed on me, she put the wine glass to her mouth, without seeing or noticing that it was empty. I immediately pushed my glass gently over the table. She gave a quick nod in thanks and took a big mouthful.

Then we just sat there looking at each other, saying nothing.

I thought to myself that the telephone call about the second murder seemed to have put a new wall between Patricia and me. The physical attraction that I had felt for her when we were sitting in my flat the day before was gone, now that we were sitting here in her house today. She was quite literally more distant, as her table was double the size of mine. But above all, it was the gravity of the situation and our fears about what might happen next that dominated my mind. It made it impossible for me to think of my life outside the investigation. And it also made it impossible for me to think of Patricia as a woman.

The clock on the wall behind me struck nine as we sat there and pondered.

'Thank you again for your help. I'll ring as soon as there is anything new, and I hope that we can meet again tomorrow. Because we're not going to get much further tonight, are we?'

Patricia's nod was barely perceptible.

'No, we are not going to get any further. I hope that tomorrow will be a better day, but fear that it may be even worse. Call me if there is any news, and let me know what time you would like to have supper.'

I said that I was very grateful to her, for this evening and for the food. I stood up and then hovered for a moment. I was unsure as to whether I should go round the table and give Patricia a hug or not, or indeed, if I wanted to. It felt like the most natural thing in the world now, the way things had developed – and yet, at the same time, one of the hardest. I genuinely did not know if Patricia would be cold and tense, or warm and alluring. I guessed that she would be the former, but I was very uncertain as to how I would react if she was the latter. So in the end, I simply said goodnight and left.

There was a chilly wind blowing through Oslo that spring night. I felt cold and unsettled inside as well and found myself glancing furtively at passers-by as I walked to my car in Frogner, and when I got home to Hegdehaugen. None of them looked like the murderer I was pursuing. But then there was one major and increasingly frustrating problem: I still had no idea what the murderer I was pursuing looked like.

Once indoors, I went straight to the telephone and called the main station. The pathologist had left a message to say that the autopsy report would be ready by nine the next morning, but there was no other news.

'Black water as far as the eye can see,' I muttered to myself as I put the receiver down. Then I stood there and ruminated on how quickly Patricia influenced my way of thinking and speaking, even when she was not there. It was an expression I had never used before.

It felt like time had almost stopped. I tried to read the first chapter of a new novel, but even though I could see that it was well written, my thoughts quickly returned to the murder case.

At half past eleven I was done with the day. I fell asleep with an image of Patricia's sombre face staring at me, and a mixture of unease and tension about what tomorrow might bring.

XIII

I'm already impressively good at planning a murder.

Everything went more or less as planned yesterday too. The depraved little singer was more resilient than I thought and stayed on her feet longer than the arrogant minister's daughter. But I kept a cool head and just pressed harder and harder around her throat. It felt like a physical triumph when she finally slumped to the ground and gasped her last. And once she was down, she was completely dead: no breath, no pulse.

But one little detail still annoys me. My hands were steady when I was strangling her, but afterwards they were shaking so much that I dropped the picture of the ant on the ground. I picked it up again, but I'm not sure if I managed to get it properly into her pocket. And if I didn't, it might have blown away. In a moment of madness, I even thought about phoning the police today from a telephone box and asking in a distorted voice if they had found it. I didn't see how anything could go wrong, but decided not to all the same.

There was no reason to worry yesterday. I was more in control than I was aware of myself. There was no one to be seen when I killed little Lisa, or when I left the place afterwards. I jogged for the first couple of hundred yards, and then carried on walking when I was well out of view of the scene of the crime. I forced myself to walk calmly past Ullevål Stadium and Vestgrensa and then got on one of the last trains to Blindern, in the end carriage. The driver didn't see me and there were only two other passengers at the far end of the carriage when I got on.

If the police can and want to check who got on the buses, trains and trams in the vicinity, they are not likely to include a station so far from the crime. And if anyone did see me walking along the road or on the train, they won't be able to give a description. I'm not unusually tall, or unusually small or unusually fat.

Last night I lay awake wondering if ants actually have a face, something that makes one stand out from another. I've been a person without a face all my life. And for the first time, I now see that it has its advantages.

Yesterday's murder was mentioned on the news this evening, but there were very few details. They certainly didn't mention specifically whether the police had linked the two killings. But I'm sure they have, whether they found the ant picture or not. The choice of place and method is the same, and it is interesting that they are choosing not to say anything yet. I had a little debate with myself over a cup of coffee whether this was a good or a bad thing. I think it's a good sign. There is certainly no reason for the moment to think that they suspect me.

None of the morning papers carried any reports about yesterday's death, and the later editions had only short two-line notices. I had expected that, but it was a bit of a disappointment all the same. I read the papers with more interest now than before I became a murderer.

I obviously have to kill someone earlier in the evening if I want to read about it in the papers the following day. Which fits perfectly with my plans for tomorrow.

People like her should not be allowed to live here. The town is better off without her. But most of all, it's a captivating thought that I, a person without a face, who has never turned a head on the street, now have the power to decide over other people's life and death. It's an exciting, almost compulsive feeling. I didn't get to sleep until two in the morning, and am still wide awake now, and it's close to midnight.

When I lie here alone in bed and think about yesterday's murder, I feel the adrenaline surge. It's in my blood now. Twice this evening I was overcome by the desire to have that thrill again tonight. And both times I managed to stop myself, thanks to my impressive self-control. I got no further than the hall.

There are no doubt plenty of young women out there alone in the *dark, but I don't know who they are or where they are walking. It would be far more risky simply to roam the streets looking for a random victim. This evening, I have no plans and no victim. Tomorrow I have both. It will be the most exciting day yet. So I'm about to go to sleep now, just before midnight, with high hopes and great expectations of what Friday, 28 April will bring me in terms of experience. Life as a murderer is far more exciting and invigorating than I ever imagined.*

DAY FIVE

An Expected Murder and an Unexpected Telephone Call

I

Faced with the slow progress of our investigation, I had suddenly felt very weary before going to bed on Thursday, 27 April, and had therefore set my alarm clock for twenty past seven. Before I fell asleep, I guessed that Friday, 28 April would be one of those days when I was woken by the telephone, but that was not the case. I was woken by the alarm clock and ate breakfast alone in a quiet flat.

Both the bread and the cheese were a bit dry and my mood was heavy. I missed having someone to talk to, and dreaded looking through the morning papers. When I finally forced myself to do it, I saw that both *Arbeiderbladet* and *Aftenposten* had written about the investigation on the front page. Fortunately, both only had a one-column report, below the headline news about Norway's relationship with the EEC. The reports in both papers were far from bad news, but definitely not good news either. They were clearly based on the feature in *Verdens Gang*, and now included both the name and a photograph of the dead jazz singer. *Arbeiderbladet* described her as 'radical and very talented', whereas *Aftenposten* said she was 'very gifted, if rather unconventional'. Both hinted that there might be a link to the murder of Agnes Halvorsen, but did not offer anything conclusive.

I was at the office by half past eight, and was told, to my disappointment, that nothing of any interest had come in. The only phone call about the case that morning came from an old woman who claimed she was psychic and declared that she knew that both the women had been killed with a shotgun by 'two dark and dreadful Sami boys'. I resisted the temptation to state out loud that she clearly did not have psychic abilities, and instead finished the conversation as quickly as I could at ten to nine.

At two minutes to nine, Helgesen knocked on the door, and Jørgensen the pathologist came in five minutes later. His report was matter-of-fact and informative. Lise Eilertsen had been killed in the same way as Agnes Halvorsen, by strangulation. It would appear that the murderer had used his or her bare hands, and had very strong fingers. Lise Eilertsen's lungs were damaged by smoking and her liver by alcohol, but otherwise she was in good form. She had a high blood-alcohol content at the time of her death, but there were no traces of any drugs. She had not been a virgin, but there was nothing to indicate any sexual activity in the last forty-eight hours of her life.

I nodded as the pathologist told us this and once he had left I said to Helgesen that it was more or less as we had expected, and there was nothing to help us move forwards.

He agreed and then we sat there in silence. By ten past nine, I suddenly could not bear to see Helgesen or my office any longer. So I asked him to hold the fort and said that for want of any better leads, I would go and talk once again to the person who was the closest thing we had to a suspect.

II

There was not much activity at the School of Theology, but Oscar Fredrik Bergendahl was one of the few people around and was in his office. He was talking to one of his young female tutees. She was a long-haired, short-skirted woman of around twenty-five, who offered to wait out in the corridor as soon as I knocked. She had a cross on a chain round her neck, but as far as I could see no ring on her finger.

Bergendahl did not look happy to see me. His smile vanished within seconds of recognizing me. I could understand why, and had to admit that he kept up appearances very well. His handshake was firm and his voice steady when he asked how he could help me today.

I explained that I wanted to find out if Agnes Halvorsen had ever mentioned the names of people who were now part of the investigation. Lise Eilertsen, for example.

'That's the singer who was murdered. There was a report in *Aftenposten* today and it said that there were similarities with Agnes' death. I've already given the name some thought, but no, if there was any connection, Agnes certainly never mentioned her to me. The name was unknown to me until this morning.'

When I said the names Tore Pettersen and Heidi Olsen, Bergendahl's answers were short and negative, but he hesitated slightly when I mentioned Kari Evensen.

'There is something familiar about that name,' he said. His

face showed intense concentration, and he looked up at the ceiling. He thought hard for a few moments, then suddenly looked back at me.

'Is that the young woman who converted to Catholicism and became a nun? Agnes did mention that she had met a childhood friend who had done just that and that it had been a rather uncomfortable experience. It was a few months ago now. The name is definitely familiar, but I'm not sure.'

I said breezily that it might well be – and made a note that there might be reason to visit Katarina Convent again. Then I got straight to the point and asked Oscar Fredrik Bergendahl where he had been between ten and midnight on Wednesday.

'Do you really think that I killed my student and friend Agnes on Monday? And that I may also have killed Lise Eilertsen, who is a complete stranger to me and of no interest whatsoever, on Wednesday? That's absurd,' he said.

I assured him that I suspected him of nothing for the time being, but that it was my job to look at every possibility. And I would be only too happy if he could rule himself out by giving me an alibi.

I almost jumped when Oscar Fredrik Bergendahl abruptly turned his head. This time he did not look at the ceiling, but out of the window. He sat like this for almost a minute, before slowly turning back.

'In that case I am glad to say that I do have what you might call a watertight alibi for Wednesday evening. I went to the hospital straight from work and was there until around midnight,' he said, eventually.

'That is definitely a sound alibi, if it can be confirmed by either your wife or a member of staff at the hospital,' I replied.

'Sadly, my wife has left me. She started her final journey at ten past ten on Wednesday night. But the doctors and nurses will be able to confirm that I was there for her till the end, and that I left the hospital a couple of hours later. I sat and talked to her for a while after she had died, and then there were all the papers to sign and things to tidy up.'

He said this with a faint tremor in his voice, but no tears in his eyes.

I assured him that this definitely ruled him out of the murder investigation. And I offered him my condolences on his loss.

'I thank you for both. It has been an extremely demanding week. Agnes' death was a great shock and very sad. She was so young and alive. My poor wife had been very weak of late, so it was not unexpected that God finally called her home,' he said.

I looked at him and thought that he seemed almost relieved. I ventured to say it must have been a very painful time for him and that he now hopefully could get on with his own life.

He gave a small smile and said that yesterday had been such a difficult day that it certainly felt a little like that today. Despite his grief, he was grateful that his wife no longer had to suffer.

We parted in a lighter mood. He gave me his hand as I made to leave and wished me luck with the investigation, and added that if there were any questions that he might be able to answer, I just had to ask.

The woman with long dark hair and a short skirt was waiting patiently outside the door, and slipped in past me as I came out. I thought that she might be the reason he was at work two days after his wife had died, and that it was perhaps best if I didn't mention her to the already hard-tested Nora Jensen.

Oscar Fredrik Bergendahl's relationship with his female students was no longer of interest to me.

III

It took several telephone calls to the council before I eventually located Tore Pettersen in a school corridor in Sagene just before half past ten.

It was about halfway through the second class of the day, so all was quiet in the corridor when I arrived. He was standing there with a large brush and a small pot of paint, painting over something that someone had written on the wall. I detected no pleasure, but equally no upset when he saw me. His face was devoid of expression and his movements were as steady before and after. He covered the last letters in the white paint. Then he pointed to a door on the other side of the corridor and walked towards it without waiting for an answer.

It opened into a small school library. We closed the door behind us and sat down at two desks designed for fourteen-year-olds.

'Heidi said yesterday that you were bound to come and talk to me again today. I lay awake half the night thinking about what I should say, but I don't really have anything more to add. I was a desperate and lonely young man when I made the mistake of taking the love that was offered. I have since been a law-abiding citizen. It was a shock to hear that Agnes Halvorsen and Lise Eilertsen had been murdered, but I'm afraid I know nothing that might help you find the murderer,' he said in a muted voice.

'You didn't tell me yesterday that you were working in a

secondary school. The principal would not be very happy to hear the story you told me yesterday,' I pointed out.

'He wouldn't like it at all, but he's heard it before. The principal is a man of honour. He could tell that something was bothering me when I started, so called me into his office and asked what was wrong. I couldn't lie, and I told him the whole story. I expected to be fired on the spot. He said that of course it should never have happened, but lots of things happened all the time, even to good people, and that after years without work, I deserved another chance. And I have worked hard for three years to prove that. My job would not be in danger, even if someone who knew my background were to call the principal.'

Tore Pettersen gave a lopsided smile when he said this. I thought to myself that either he was a good person, or very good at pretending to be. But I still followed up with the question I had not wanted to ask yesterday – about his relationship with his parents and parents-in-law.

'My parents have not been around for many years, and Heidi never had the opportunity to meet them. My father died in a work accident when I was fourteen, and my mother never got over it and drank herself to death when I was sixteen. The relationship with Heidi's parents is not great, but it's getting better all the time – that's what we tell ourselves. Her mother will never be able to forgive me, but at least now she is talking to me. They are both looking forward to having a grandchild. I hope and believe that with our child's help, things will get better.'

He said nothing for a few moments, but then carried on without prompting. 'My life is a bit like my relationship with my mother-in-law – still not easy, but improving steadily. Last year at this time I had only 120 kroner in the bank; now I have fifteen hundred and I'm going to be a father. But most of all, I have Heidi. As long as everything goes well with the birth, I have nothing to complain about. I had never dreamed, after what happened, that I would be as happy as I am now.'

Even though this was of no consequence to the investigation, my curiosity got the better of me and I asked how he and his wife now viewed the Christian faith.

'We have both kept our faith, albeit in a slightly different form. After everything that happened, I no longer believed in a God who saw everything and looked after everyone's best interests. We have both abandoned our childhood belief that we can trust in God to sort everything out. But over the past years, we have rediscovered our faith and the belief that there is a kind God and a greater justice up there somewhere.'

He pointed to the ceiling while looking me straight in the eye when he said this, and in that moment, I was convinced that he was a good person. I finished by asking if he had then not been in contact with any of the girls from the choir other than Heidi since that time. He thought for a moment or two before answering.

'No, or that is to say . . . I never saw Agnes or Lise again. I often thought about the choir in the years that followed, but more or less ran away; I moved out of the neighbourhood. I did bump into Nora in the centre of town a couple of years later. We recognized each other and said hello, but then quickly went our own ways. I don't think she had any idea about what happened with Heidi and me, and I was glad about that. We both met Kari last year, when we were down in Majorstuen. I didn't recognize her in her habit, but was astonished to see a nun turn on her heel and run down a side street.

Heidi recognized her and found the whole thing rather upsetting. They had been best friends; then Kari found out what had happened. According to Heidi, Kari had promised not to tell anyone. And Heidi is convinced that Kari will never break that promise, even though they later chose to go different ways. So I accepted that and tried to think as little as possible about her and the other girls from the choir. Heidi is the only woman in my life and we have decided to look forwards rather than back.'

Just as he finished saying this, a bell rang somewhere in the building. The janitor's assistant in him sprang to life. He stood up, grabbed the brush and said that he should get back to work, unless I had any more questions.

I didn't, and so just wished him good luck.

For some reason, I did not want to leave the school with all the children swarming around. So I stayed sitting at the slightly too small desk until the bell rang again a few minutes later.

As I walked out of the school alone, I reflected that the person who was now closest to being a suspect in a double murder case was a Catholic nun – which did not feel like a promising lead. So I drove back to the main police station rather than going to Katarina Convent.

IV

The actual murder in the morning went according to plan.

She walked confidently towards me as I'd expected, without seeing the danger until my hands were tightening around her soft little throat. But to be fair, I moved in quickly and forcefully. I had planned it well.

We looked each other in the eye for a few seconds as we stood there, and as far as I can remember, I felt no sympathy for her. I am clearly a hard-hearted person. But then, I didn't really know her. If she had a personality or any kind of individual worth, I certainly never noticed it. She didn't seem to have two brain cells to rub together and for me was simply a means to an end.

I felt only relief and no regret when she fell. And by then it was too late. I stood and looked down at her for a few moments. She looked so still and relaxed, as if she was just taking a little nap. But within seconds she had died and was gone forever.

I felt no great thrill when I strangled her. But now, in the face of my next and more critical challenge, I feel enormous excitement.

Her body is going to be left here, in the building I'm entering now, with hundreds of people milling around. I'm ready to drop her on the spot and run if anyone screams. But so far, I just hear a constant murmuring of voices and no screams. People are even less observant than I thought. I'm no more than a few feet from where I had planned to hide her. It's just a matter of getting there, putting her down and leaving without being noticed. If I manage that, then I can relax – and make the phone call I've been longing to make.

V

At twenty to twelve I was sitting on my own in my office with my packed lunch when the phone rang, between two sandwiches. I had asked the switchboard not to transfer any calls that were not of direct relevance to the case. So I put down the second sandwich and lifted the receiver.

'We have someone on the line who doesn't want to give their name, but claims to have important information regarding the investigation,' the switchboard operator said.

Her soft voice was then followed by the sound of the call being transferred. After the distinctive click, I heard pips that told me the call was from a telephone box. And following the pips came two sentences that had me on my feet immediately.

'I am the mysterious ant murderer. You might like to know that my third victim is now ready and waiting for you in Tveita Shopping Centre.'

The voice was slow and muffled. It sounded as though the man on the other end was talking through a handkerchief, and also speaking slowly in some strange accent to make it harder to identify him later. And with great success. There was nothing familiar about the voice or intonation – and I was not even sure that it was a man I was talking to.

I could think of nothing sensible to say in such an unexpected situation, so I said that if this was some kind of sick joke, he should confess immediately and apologize.

The person on the other end paused for a few moments, but then continued to speak in the same irritatingly slow and muffled voice.

'I am not a joke. And now I have to move on to my next victim. Good luck with the investigation. We may speak again.'

Then the receiver was put down, not slammed down, but put down with the same annoying deliberation.

My immediate thought was that whoever had made the call was either a morbid joker or a remarkably callous murderer. I hoped it was the former, but feared it was the latter. The words 'ant murderer' had a particular impact in a situation where, to my knowledge, the fact that pictures of ants had been found at the crime scenes had not been mentioned in the newspapers, or on the television or radio.

I rushed out to the switchboard and asked them to contact

the telephone company immediately to see if they could trace the call. Then I spoke to the operator who had transferred the call. She had also registered that the voice was distorted and found it disturbing. All the person had said was: 'I have an extremely important tip-off about the case involving the murdered women. Put me through to Detective Inspector Kolbjørn Kristiansen immediately.' She also thought that it had been a man, but could not swear that it wasn't a woman, and had not been able to identify the accent.

I still hoped that it was some morbid prankster who somehow or other had heard about the ant pictures found at the crime scenes, but I felt chilled to the bone as I ran down the corridor. The first thing I did was to ask any patrol cars in the vicinity to go immediately to Tveita Shopping Centre to look for a potential murder victim. Then I knocked on Helgesen's door and asked him to come with me.

VI

Tveita was one of the city's newest major retail projects: an experiment to gather a score of shops under one and the same roof, so that customers could go from one temptation to the next without getting wet. I had gone there myself a couple of times before Christmas and found it to be so practical that I was certain there would be more shopping centres in the future. My father, on the other hand, still believed in cooperatives and was convinced that Tveita Shopping Centre would go bust within a year.

Apart from the fact that there were four police cars in the car park, the shopping centre appeared to be running as normal, so I held on to the hope that the phone call had been no more than a distasteful prank. But there was a policeman standing guard at the entrance and the back door, and around fifty staff and customers were huddling just inside the entrance. No one said anything, but they were all looking in the same direction.

She was lying on the floor between two police constables, full length beside a grey mail sack. As soon as I saw her I thought that I had seen her somewhere in a photograph or newspaper, but I could not for the life of me remember where. And I did not yet know who she was. She was around five foot two, slim and well dressed, and had no doubt been an attractive woman when she was alive.

But now she was lying there with her eyes shut, looking for all the world as though she were asleep. The clear white skin of her face contrasted with her black hair and red lips. My initial thought was Snow White, but then I thought of Sleeping Beauty, who slept for a hundred years in my childhood fairy tales. But I was an adult now, and this was real, and this woman would never wake up again. There was not a drop of blood to be seen anywhere on her body, but she had marks on her throat which gave away how she had been killed. This was no real surprise when I took into consideration the picture of an ant that was lying beside her on the floor.

'The mail sack was discovered in the caretaker's cupboard just around the corner here, beside the fire extinguisher and some packets of soap. The picture of the ant was in the mail sack with her, as was her handbag,' one of the constables told me in a hushed voice. 'The sack fell out when the caretaker opened the door to show us the cupboard,' the other constable added.

I asked to speak to the caretaker, who turned out to be a greying, slightly overweight man in his fifties. He looked deeply unsettled by the situation, and took long, deep breaths every time he answered a question. But the answers in themselves were clear enough. The cupboard had not been locked, as apparently the fire extinguisher had to be easily accessible. There had been no mail sack in the cupboard when he went there to get some soap at ten o'clock. He was the only caretaker on duty that day and definitely had nothing to do with this. He had no idea who the woman in the cupboard might be. Any of the staff or customers who passed the cupboard after ten o'clock could in theory have dumped her there.

'I saw him!' a loud voice said beside me. I turned round and looked straight into the distressed face of a fur-clad lady in her fifties, who squinted at me from behind a pair of narrow glasses, under a large, flowery hat.

I almost dragged her around the corner with me, out of view of the others. Then I asked her to tell me exactly what she had seen.

'I saw the man who killed her, I just said. It must have been sometime after eleven, because that is when I got here. I was about to go into that clothes shop there to buy a dress for a friend's birthday, but hadn't made up my mind. I saw a man come in the entrance carrying a large, grey mail sack, which he put in the cupboard and then left. I wondered what it might be. He was wearing blue overalls and a cap, so I presumed he was one of the caretakers. I should have looked more closely. But of course, I didn't think there might be a dead body in the bag . . .'

Her voice slipped into a whine as she said this and she took off her glasses to wipe away a couple of tears. I said it was totally understandable, and asked if she could describe the man in any way.

'I'm so sorry, but I'm afraid I can't. I didn't have my glasses on and my eyesight isn't what it used to be. He was wearing the kind of blue overalls that caretakers often wear. And he was wearing a cap, which I think was black, so I couldn't see his hair, but his beard was dark. He was wearing the kind of dark glasses that young people wear these days in summer. I was surprised at the glasses, because there still isn't much sun, and certainly not in here. I should have guessed something was wrong, but I'm afraid I didn't. He put the bag in the cupboard and then walked calmly towards the entrance, and I didn't see him again.'

I could not be angry with a witness who was trying so hard to help, but still felt the frustration bubbling as she spoke. We had never been closer to getting a description of the murderer. And yet we were no nearer.

I asked a few more questions, but that only served to make both of us more frustrated. When I asked how tall he was, she said with a sigh that he was 'neither very tall nor very short'. Nor was he particularly fat or thin. And she certainly wouldn't like to guess his age. When I asked her if we could at least be certain that the person in the overalls was not a woman with a false beard, she replied that she couldn't rule that out. She thought it was a man, because he did not seem to have any problem carrying the mail sack, but she couldn't be sure. Young women could also have muscles these days, she said with a sigh.

I thanked the woman in the flowery hat for her help, and shepherded her back around the corner. She pointed out the assistants from the clothes shop, but they had been inside the shop and had not seen the man with the mail sack.

So we had a clear idea of how the body had ended up in the cupboard, but a frustratingly unclear picture of the person who had left it there – and a crowd of around fifty people waiting only yards away. They had started to move and talk again now. Several of them were already late for things they had planned.

I went over to them, told them my name and title, and said that we needed to take a note of their names and addresses and to ask a few quick questions before they could go home. We would divide them into two groups and get started in about five minutes. This went remarkably well. They quickly formed two queues, with only a bit of jostling between those at the front.

I said to Helgesen that we should each concentrate on one group, and ask what they had seen in the shopping centre and in the area just outside.

The dead woman on the floor had a diamond engagement ring on her right ring finger. In passing, I wondered who her fiancé was and how he would take this.

I guessed that the dead woman was somewhere in her early twenties, but there was something doll-like about her which meant that I would not have been surprised to learn she was eighteen or thirty-two. She was in fact twenty-two, according to her driving licence. We found this in her handbag, along with a purse, a lipstick and a small set of keys.

Her name was Amalie Meyer-Michelsen, which sounded very grand. And given that she had also been walking around with four hundred-kroner notes and one fifty-kroner note in her purse and was wearing a diamond ring, and a gold chain round her neck, there was every reason to assume that she came from a wealthy background. But I did not realize just how high in society she was until Helgesen remarked that she must be the daughter of Christoffer Meyer-Michelsen. 'Or what do you think?'

I did not answer straight away and instead looked through the side pockets of her purse. There were two photographs there. One was of her with a fair-haired young man who was grinning broadly, and they were both holding their gold rings up to the photographer. I did not recognize the young man. I did, however, know the older man standing next to her in the other photograph. It was indeed the hotel magnate and multi-millionaire Christoffer Meyer-Michelsen. I had never known that he could smile, but he was beaming in the picture. I suddenly remembered where I had seen a picture of the dead woman. It was in *Verdens Gang* a few weeks ago, under the headline 'Hotel Heiress to be Wed'. Her father confirmed that his daughter was now engaged and that he was delighted, as was she, but she preferred not to comment, as was her wont.

I had heard Amalie Meyer-Michelsen described as being 'timid as a deer' on a couple of occasions. When I looked down at her again now, I suddenly saw the Disney character Bambi instead of Sleeping Beauty.

I wondered if the Anthill Murderer was aware of whom he had chosen as his third victim. And I thought with dread of the hell that would be let loose when the press found out that the latest victim was the daughter of one of Oslo's richest men.

VII

It was half past three by the time Helgesen and I left Tveita Shopping Centre. In the last few minutes we were almost alone on the ground floor. Despite loud protests from the director, the centre had closed for the rest of the day. Amalie Meyer-Michelsen had been put on a stretcher and driven to the pathologist for an autopsy. The forensics team were combing over the walls and floors and would of course examine the mail sack she was found in. But in my melancholy state, I had little faith that it would get us any further. For the third time in a week, I was standing where the murderer had left a young victim no more than a few hours before – with no idea of who he was and where he had gone.

The problem at the two previous crime scenes was that no one other than the murderer and the victim had been there. And the problem here was the opposite: the murderer had been able to leave unnoticed because there were so many people around. It was entirely in the spirit of the murderer. He had been able to come and go without attracting attention in the crowd of shoppers, like an ant on an anthill.

In the last two hours, I had seen around fifty people, the faces of men and women from different social classes and different parts of town. The youngest had been fourteen and the oldest over eighty. All of them wanted to help us. The problem was that none of them were able to.

There had been a total of one hundred and two people in the shopping centre when the body was found in the caretaker's cupboard, and it would seem that the victim had been lying there for some time by then. Most of the shoppers had already arrived at the centre when she was left here, and the staff had all been busy in their shops. Two other people had seen someone in blue overalls come into the centre carrying a mail sack. One of them had registered the fact that he was wearing gloves indoors. But neither of them could remember the time or what he looked like. Nor could anyone remember seeing the victim alive earlier in the morning, though many said that they would not have noticed her even if they had.

Judging by what people had told us, Amalie Meyer-Michelsen had been left in the cupboard between eleven and half past eleven. Where and when she was murdered remained a mystery. Helgesen suggested that perhaps the murderer had driven the body there in the mail sack, but had no answer when I asked why he would take such a risk. My preliminary theory was that the murder must have taken place in or near the shopping centre, and that the murderer had dumped her here rather than taking the body with him.

This theory was given some weight by a discovery in the car park outside. At a quarter to four, there was only one car left. It was a red Toyota that looked like last year's model. A car that cost more and drove better than most others, without being ostentatious. I was not at all surprised when the car key found in Amalie Meyer-Michelsen's handbag fitted the lock. The registration documents confirmed that the car belonged to her.

I alerted the forensics team and asked them to examine the car for fingerprints and other possible clues. But unless the murderer knew her well and had driven here with her, I didn't hold out much hope. There was much to indicate that she had driven here alone and then been killed somewhere inside or just outside the shopping centre. In which case, we were dealing with a truly cold-blooded murderer. But then his decision to go into the centre with the body in a mail sack, and then to call me, reinforced Patricia's theory that this Anthill Murderer was doing it for thrills rather than for any rational reason.

There were a dozen or so journalists waiting when we left Tveita. I confirmed that there had been a death inside the shopping centre that was being treated as suspicious. After a moment's hesitation, I replied 'Yes,' when the *Aftenposten* reporter asked if I could confirm that the person who had died was a young woman. However, I refrained from making any comment when *Verdens Gang* asked if a picture of an ant had been found, thereby linking it to the two other murders of young women that week. The flashes went off as we made our way back over to the car park. I tried not to think about what would be written above the photographs on the front pages of the morning papers.

We drove back to the main police station, where the telephone lines were glowing. All the papers in the country were now on the case. And between the phone calls from a growing number of journalists came a steady flow of calls from increasingly desperate parents who were worried about daughters they could not reach. I gave the switchboard operators permission to rule out all names but the one correct one.

Then I asked for an external line and called Meyer-Michelsen's office. I was afraid that they might have closed for the day, but managed to get hold of a woman with a deep, pleasant secretarial voice. She told me that the director was still there, but that he would be unavailable for the rest of the day due to an important meeting.

I said that I did not want to go into details over the phone, but that I was calling from the police and that it was imperative we speak to the director as soon as possible.

There was a short silence on the other end. Then the secretary replied in an equally pleasant but slightly tenser voice that the director was in an important meeting with his business partner and the partner's son. He had given strict orders that they should not be disturbed, and she wondered if we could possibly come to the office and talk to him once the meeting was over. If we were able to do that, she would let the director know and ask him to wait for us, if he came out of the meeting at any point.

I did not feel I could say any more over the phone, so I agreed to her suggestion.

Helgesen waited patiently while I spoke. Then he followed me dutifully to the boss's office.

According to younger colleagues at the station, the boss had three facial expressions: one serious, one even more serious and one very grave indeed. He was wearing the latter when he said, 'I have been invited to appear on the seven o'clock news, and see it as my duty to go.'

About once a year, the boss was invited to talk on the news about an unsolved case, and I knew that he disliked it intensely every time.

I said that he must of course decide himself whether he wanted to or not, and if he did, what he was going to say. And if he did go, it would seem only natural to confirm a third suspicious death and to imply that all the cases were linked, but at the same time to emphasize that we were holding all options open. And of course to say that the case was now our highest priority.

'I agree. Who else would you like to work on the case?' my boss asked.

I exchanged a quick look with Helgesen, who was sitting there watching and waiting.

'At the moment no one, other than the forensics team who are working at the new crime scene. We should ask all patrol cars to report any men loitering around or displaying other behaviour that might be linked to the murders. Apart from that, we don't have much to go on. We have no more leads to follow up on the two earlier victims, and now we have to talk to Amalie's family. It would take us more time to get any re-inforcements up to speed on the case than would be of any value,' I said.

My boss nodded slowly and gave a heavy sigh.

'You are right, of course. But we can expect criticism from both the police force and elsewhere if it gets out that there are so few people working on the investigation. We can't really say that we don't need any more people – especially not if we have to say it is because we have no leads and don't know where to look for more. Let me know whenever you need more help, and be prepared, I may need to ask Danielsen or another detective inspector to join the investigation tomorrow.'

He sighed again and then continued. 'The name of the latest victim will increase interest in the case. When the daughter of one of Oslo's richest businessmen is killed in a shopping centre and the body has been seen by so many people, we haven't got a cat in hell's chance of keeping it secret. The rumours will be spreading as we speak. So we may as well release the name this evening.'

This was a statement, rather than a question. I immediately

took the hint and told him that we would contact the victim's father and fiancé immediately.

'Good. As soon as possible,' the boss said. Then he sat in silence looking at the wall, and Helgesen and I stood up and left the office.

Not a critical word was said against me or my handling of the case, but based on what was not said and my boss's body language, it felt as though, for the first time, he doubted that I was the right person to be leading the investigation. It was not a nice feeling. This was partly because I was unwilling to work with Detective Inspector Danielsen, but mostly because I myself was starting to doubt that I could find the murderer – with or without Danielsen's help.

I said to Helgesen that I hoped he realized that some overtime would be required this afternoon. He said that he was fine with that, and that he would not have enjoyed any free time today anyway.

We left the station in silence. The air felt a little less oppressive outside, but we had to give three journalists and four photographers a wide berth.

VIII

Meyer-Michelsen & Wendelmann A/S had their offices on the fifth and sixth floors of a large, grey building close to the town hall. Looking up, it was clear to see that the builders had not skimped on the concrete or windowpanes.

We did not get there until a quarter to five. There was no one else in the office other than the secretary I had spoken to on the phone. She was sitting, as promised, at her desk by the door. She was younger than I had imagined, given her deep voice, and was a shapely, red-haired woman in her early thirties. Her movements were quick and youthful. She shook my hand and introduced herself as Rikke Johansen, then told me in a hushed voice that the director was still sitting in the meeting. She understood that our visit was important, but had not wanted to disturb Mr Meyer-Michelsen without knowing what it was about, she said, in an even quieter voice. So he was still unaware that we wished to speak to him, but would hopefully be out soon, she almost whispered.

As she spoke, she pointed towards a large oak door at the end of the room. It was very solid and the lettering on the sign was large enough to read from where we were standing: *Meyer-Michelsen, Director*.

I certainly did not want to go through that door to tell Director Meyer-Michelsen that his daughter had been found dead. However, I doubted that delaying the matter would make it any easier, and reminded myself that he should be told as soon as possible, out of consideration both to him as a father and to the investigation. I was just about to say that we should let him know that we were here, when the door was wrenched open.

Out came two men, one of whom was around fifty, the other around twenty-five, both dressed in suits and carrying briefcases. I did not recognize either of them, but it was easy to see that they were related. The older man was greying and had a squarer face, but they were both around five foot eight and of a lean build, with the same brown eyes and slightly crooked nose. I quickly concluded that they must be Mr Wendelmann and his son.

I did not have time to reflect any more on the pair, as

Meyer-Michelsen himself came out straight after them. I recognized him immediately. He was even bigger in life than in the photographs I had seen in the newspapers. I understood straight away why it was often said that he made a powerful and almost intimidating first impression on people. The hotel king was nearly six foot five and towered a good head above the other two. Even though he was well over fifty, his hair was still raven-black and his biceps bulged beneath his white shirtsleeves. Meyer-Michelsen was the epitome of a dynamic businessman, and positively exuded power and determination. I reckoned that he must weigh at least fifteen stone. His right hand was like a club as he punched his fist in the air in front of Wendelmann senior's face in obvious anger.

Then he noticed our presence and spun round to look at us.

'What's this, Rikke? Who are these gentlemen and why are they here? Was I not clear when I said that no one was to be let in today?'

The secretary suddenly lost her composure in the face of her boss's irritation. She more or less wilted under his gaze. Pearls of sweat suddenly appeared on her cheeks and brow, and her eyes were glued to the floor when she spoke.

'I'm so sorry, but ... these two gentlemen are from the police and said they had to talk to you about an urgent police matter that could not wait.'

Meyer-Michelsen glared at us with perplexed and wary eyes. He took three steps towards us, while the other two hovered by the door to the office. When he was a few feet away from us, he looked down at me with piercing eyes.

'A police matter that cannot wait? What on earth is that urgent?'

Meyer-Michelsen stared at me without blinking. His eyes

felt close, hard and almost hypnotizing. There was a faint flush in his cheeks now and he made me think of a charging bull. While I felt great sympathy for his loss, I was also becoming increasingly angered by his behaviour.

I wondered for a moment how to tackle the situation. I tried to resolve it by saying that it was deeply personal and we should perhaps go into his office. But he just continued to glower at me – his face getting redder and redder.

'Spit it out, man. I have never broken the law and have nothing to hide from my business partner and my secretary. So what is that the police want with me?'

I hesitated for a few seconds, but no longer dared to do anything but tell him the truth.

I said, as gently as I could, that we were there because his daughter had been found dead earlier in the day.

Christoffer Meyer-Michelsen stared at me for a moment longer. He still did not blink. Then there was tiny spasm in the corner of his mouth and a cramp-like trembling in his legs.

And suddenly he collapsed.

Wendelmann junior rushed forwards and caught the sinking giant just before he fell. They stood swaying in the middle of the room until I managed to prop up Meyer-Michelsen from the other side. Wendelmann senior took a step forward, but then stayed where he was, a passive onlooker.

Christoffer Meyer-Michelsen's eyes were closed, and as far as I could gauge, he was only semiconscious. 'Ama,' he whispered in a broken, distressed voice, as we sat him down on the closest chair. He slid back and sat staring up at the ceiling.

His secretary was completely paralysed to begin with, but then rushed over with a wet handkerchief that she laid on his brow. Then she ran to get a glass of water for him.

I asked Helgesen to keep an eye on Meyer-Michelsen, and indicated that Wendelmann and his son should follow me to the other side of the room. Over by the reception desk, the father introduced himself as Henrik Harald Wendelmann and his son as Harald Henrik Wendelmann.

His son said in a shaken voice that they had of course met Meyer-Michelsen's daughter and that it was terrible news. Despite his stern appearance, her father had been deeply attached to his only child, he added.

Wendelmann senior agreed with his son that it was indeed 'terribly sad'. His voice sounded somewhat forced when he said this. He then promptly asked if there was any point in them staying here any longer.

I replied that they could leave shortly, but that I had to ask them a few quick questions first.

I began with how they perceived Meyer-Michelsen's relationship with his daughter, and whether she was in any way involved in the business.

Mr Wendelmann replied, 'They were, without a doubt, extremely close. Meyer-Michelsen has been a widower for many years, and his daughter was his only child. But she had no involvement whatsoever in the business and as far as I can remember I have never seen her in the office.'

What he said sounded reasonable enough, but his mechanical voice and expressionless face gave the impression that he was without feelings.

'I can only agree,' his son said swiftly, but he was clearly still upset. It struck me that though the father and son were very similar in appearance, they were very different in temperament and personality. I had the feeling that I had seen the son before, but I could not remember where.

I turned to him and asked if he had met the late Amalie Meyer-Michelsen in other social contexts. He shrugged theatrically before answering. The movement somehow reinforced my feeling that I had seen him before, but I still could not think where.

'I have known about Amalie for as long as I can remember, but have never really known her. I said hello whenever we met in town, but I never stopped to speak to her. We were practically neighbours growing up, as we both lived on Kristinelund Road in Skøyen, and we went to the same schools. But Amalie was a couple of years younger than me and was never one to draw attention to herself. I couldn't really say that I knew her well. I've seen her and her fiancé at the National Theatre a couple of times, but they were in the audience, and I was on the stage.'

As soon as he said this, I realized where I had seen him before. It was of course at the National Theatre. I had seen a new production of Ibsen's *The League of Youth* there with my ex-fiancée, who was very interested in the arts. It must have been in January sometime. It was certainly the last time we had gone to the theatre together, and also the last time I had been to the National Theatre. It had not occurred to me to go without Miriam. I remembered her commenting that the young Wendelmann was very good as the landowner Monsen's son, and that he was apparently a very talented young actor. I had felt a little stab of jealousy when she said this. Obviously without any reason – and for which I now felt slightly guilty.

I quickly asked the father and son if they knew Amalie's fiancé.

Mr Wendelmann shook his head silently. His son said that he had only seen the fiancé a couple of times at the theatre. He had not paid much attention to his name when he read the engagement notice in the newspaper, but seemed to remember he was the son of a pharmacist from Frogner.

This took me down an unwanted track of associations. The very mention of Frogner made me think of Patricia, and I wondered if she might know the fiancé. I found myself thinking that I hoped she didn't. I quickly parked the thought by asking the father and son how long their meeting with Meyer-Michelsen had been and what it was about.

'My son and I got here just after midday, and have been in the meeting until now. The meeting had been planned and was about company matters that I can guarantee have nothing to do with the deceased. And now I really do hope we can go, as we are already late for an important dinner appointment. I really don't think we can be of much help to the investigation, though you are of course welcome to contact us if needs be,' the father replied.

As he spoke, Henrik Harald Wendelmann took a business card out of his wallet and handed it to me. It had his home address, office address and telephone numbers written on it in gold lettering on a black background. I noticed the Wendelmanns had an office a few hundred yards down the road, even though Mr Wendelmann was a partner in the company that clearly had ample space here in this building. I thought that as it had been a very long meeting, any link to the day's murder seemed unlikely, so I let them go.

Mr Wendelmann left the room with quick steps, his patent shoes clicking on the floor; he did not look back once. His son left almost without a sound, showing his hands in apology as he followed his father out. The son had definitely made a better impression than the father, but there was still no reason to believe that the father had anything to do with the murder. For a moment, I regretted that I hadn't checked what they had done before the meeting, but I went back to the victim's father on the other side of the office, rather than chase after his business partner.

IX

Christoffer Meyer-Michelsen was still leaning back in the chair when I returned. Even though his eyes were open, I seriously doubted that he was fully present. I could not remember ever having seen such a rapid change in someone as I had witnessed in the man on the chair, and I thought of his glare only minutes before. The apparently invincible giant had crumpled, both physically and mentally, in front of my very eyes. And now it was suddenly me who was looking down at him.

In a way, I liked him better now. One could say a lot of things about the businessman Christoffer Meyer-Michelsen, and he had made a pretty brutal impression when we met. But he was the first family member in this investigation to show any great emotion at his loss.

'How did Ama die?' he asked, in a whisper that was barely audible.

I was sparing with the facts and told him that she had been found at Tveita Shopping Centre a few hours before and it would appear that she had been strangled. No one had been arrested yet.

I feared that this piece of information might provoke an outburst, but it seemed that Christoffer Meyer-Michelsen had no anger left, only grief and despair. When he abruptly raised his hands, it was only to hide his face. I could not see if he was crying, but his voice was choked when he continued.

'It's my birthday today. This morning at breakfast, Ama said that she was going to go to Tveita to find me the best gift.'

I exchanged a quick look with Helgesen, who took the hint and nodded back. My theory that she had driven to Tveita and then been killed either inside or just outside the shopping centre was reinforced by what her father had told us.

I said that he must not blame himself in any way, and apologetically explained that in order to find his daughter's murderer, we would have to ask him some questions. He just sat there with his face in his hands, and I was unsure if he had heard what I said.

His secretary came to the rescue. She asked if we might perhaps see first how many of the questions she could answer, to give him a few more minutes. She had worked there for seven years and knew both the business and the people involved fairly well, she said.

As I was not entirely sure that we would get any sense out of the director anyway, I thanked her for the offer and pointed to her boss's office.

At first glance, Christoffer Meyer-Michelsen's office was like an engine. It was immaculately tidy, with all his pens and papers in place on his desk and all the files neatly stored on the shelves. There was a large mahogany table in the middle of the room, with four chairs around it. We let the largest chair stand empty and sat down on the other three.

As I sat down, I saw the photograph. It was the only sign that a human being worked here. It was on the director's desk, and was of a younger Amalie; she looked to be around seventeen. She was standing outside, wearing a light summer jacket

227

and smiling at the camera from under her dark fringe. She had smiled at her father from the frame ever since the photograph had been taken – and as recently as that afternoon, when in the harsh reality of the world outside, she was in fact dead.

I sat and looked at the photograph for a few moments, but my attention was eventually drawn by the secretary.

'You'll have to forgive Mr Meyer-Michelsen. Despite all appearances, he is a man with a big heart, and his daughter meant the world to him, especially after his wife died.'

I tore my eyes away from the photograph and said that was easy to understand, and then asked how long Meyer-Michelsen had been a widower.

'I can tell you exactly: it was the day before Christmas Eve 1965, and I had started to work here in August. We all knew that his wife was ill and had a weak heart, but none of us were told that she had died on 23 December until we came back to work in the new year. And there was no notice in the newspaper until early January. When I asked Mr Meyer-Michelsen about it later, he said that he had not wanted to ruin Christmas for me or any of the staff. At the time, you would never have known. He was very fond of his wife, but the death was expected, and he has since confided in me that he then poured all his love into his daughter. She was all he had left, and your news was a bolt out of the blue. In fact, when he came in to work today he said that his daughter had been in a very good mood this morning and had asked him what he would like for his birthday.'

Her voice was controlled, but she was clearly upset. It seemed to me that Meyer-Michelsen talked very openly with his secretary and I wondered how close they were. But I did not want to ask her that right now. Instead, I asked what her impression was of the now dead Amalie.

She said nothing for a moment, and took a deep breath. I took the opportunity to encourage her to be honest.

'It's just that it's not always easy to know what one should and can say about a person who has been taken from us so young. But with my hand on my heart, I can say that I have never seen Amalie do anything to hurt another person. As a teenager, she found it hard to be the daughter of such a famous and controversial man. She resolved this in her own way, by living as quiet a life as possible and not seeking attention. She didn't like to take the bus or the tram, because sometimes people recognized her and would ask her about her father. More recently, she either drove to wherever she was going, or took a taxi. She never said much, but I have never heard her say an unfriendly word. If I were to say anything critical, it would be that she was perhaps a little lazy and liked an easy life. She started university when she finished school, but gave up after only a few weeks and never bothered to look for a job. But that was also partly due to her background and family. She was the sole heir to a business empire. In a way, her job was to find herself a suitable husband and to have children who could carry on the family line. She was the princess of her father's kingdom and her only responsibility was to ensure it carried on.'

She stopped abruptly, which gave me the chance to ask the well-informed secretary if she knew the late Amalie's fiancé.

'I've never seen him here, but I have met him at family dinners. His name is Rolf Johan Svendsen, and he is the only son of a pharmacist from Frogner. He is twenty-six years old and has just started work as a lawyer after achieving an excellent degree. He is quiet and very nice. I met him for the first time last autumn and immediately thought that they were perfect for each other. He lives in a flat close to his childhood home, at 32C Tostrup Street, if I'm not wrong. They were of course going to buy a house together after the wedding.'

The secretary was remarkably well informed about the fiancé as well, so I used the opportunity to ask about the relationship between Meyer-Michelsen and his future son-in-law.

'As far as I know, the director was a little put out that his daughter spent so much time with her fiancé last year, and dreaded the day when she moved out. But he seems to have come to terms with it now. Recently he has said more than once how happy he was about the engagement and that he hoped he would have a grandson within a year or so. The young couple seemed to be very happy together, not even a hint of tension. In fact, I can't for the life of me think who might want to kill Miss Amalie,' the secretary concluded.

I said there was much to indicate that the murderer did not know his victim, but that we were obliged to investigate every possibility. I therefore had to ask whether Amalie's fiancé would now become the heir.

'When they got engaged, they drew up a joint will to say that they would each inherit everything from the other. I have a copy of the will in the filing cabinet. But it won't make her fiancé rich. Amalie only has a couple of hundred thousand to her name: a small inheritance from her mother, confirmation money and the like. Everything else is held by the company or in her father's name. And I don't know that anyone has considered who might inherit from him, if Amalie were to die. It might perhaps be his late sister's two children. But that is of course up to Christoffer himself, and I am fairly sure that he's not thinking about the money right now.'

We looked at each other. There was something unsaid here. The secretary was too well informed about the Meyer-Michelsen family, and the fact that she had now called the director by his first name was the nudge I needed.

I asked, somewhat tentatively, if other members of staff were usually invited to family dinners.

The secretary immediately understood and smiled, despite the tragic circumstances, and then answered: 'On the contrary, I would say. Christoffer normally keeps a clear divide between his public and personal life, and calls most people here by their surname, even when they have worked here for years. I am the only one, other than himself of course, who you might see here and in the family home. In answer to your next question: I was never invited there while his wife was still alive, but at the time there was no reason to ask me either.'

So far, I liked this secretary. She had social skills and appeared to be honest. If the situation regarding the investigation had not been so serious, and had I not already got two women vying for my affections, I might perhaps even have found her attractive. But the relationship between her and her boss was clear and I had no reason to believe that it had any implications for his daughter's death.

I did ask, however, how Amalie had taken the secretary's presence in the family home after her mother's death.

'I wondered a bit about that myself. She was only fifteen when her mother died, and I did not start going to any family arrangements until at least two years later, out of consideration for Amalie. She was a bit like a tortoise in social settings: she sat quietly and said very little, and I often found myself wondering what she was thinking. At first I thought she didn't like me or the fact that I was there, but then I realized more and more that she was just like that. And in the past six months or so, she became more confident and lively. She even put her arm round me in the hall after lunch last Sunday and said how much she appreciated that I looked after her father so well, both at home and in the office. If Amalie was ever upset or annoyed with me, I never noticed. I can say with my hand on my heart that we had a very good relationship now.'

The picture of our third victim was becoming clearer. She was in many ways very different from the first two, but like them, had no known enemies. We were now investigating the third murder of a very unlikely victim. I was increasingly convinced that we would not find the answer here, and that we were looking for a serial murderer who was at large out there somewhere.

I did, however, ask quickly if Amalie had been an active churchgoer, if she had ever been involved in a choir or if she was interested in animals and insects in any way.

The secretary replied that Amalie had thought of getting married in church, but otherwise only went to the Christmas Day service with her father. She listened to music on the radio, and her interest in animals was limited to the few years when she had taken riding lessons and owned a horse.

The answers were as expected and feared. There was no obvious connection to the two previous victims. I thanked the secretary for her help and we left the director's office together.

The office in itself had made no real impression, but the photograph of Amalie stayed with me, even though I consciously looked in the other direction when I stood up.

Christoffer Meyer-Michelsen no longer had his face buried

in his hands and was now very much present, though he was still slumped in the chair when we came out. The secretary went over and put her arm round him, and for a moment he put his big right hand round her hip, but then it dropped back into his lap again. This moment of tenderness in the midst of tragedy only served to increase my sympathy.

I offered my condolences and said there was no need to bother him further at the moment. Thus far it would seem that the murderer had nothing to do with the family and we would have to look elsewhere. We did, however, still need to search the house to see if we could find any clues. It was possible his daughter might have received some threats or letters that were of significance.

'She definitely didn't receive any threats. She would have told me about that, but please, go ahead,' Meyer-Michelsen said, and held out a big bunch of keys.

I thanked him for his trust, and then said that the house key was no doubt one of those on the key ring we found in Amalie's handbag. So, if her father was happy for us to do so, we could go there straight away. I added that we would of course be careful with her things and not move or touch anything unless strictly necessary.

'Thank you,' was Christoffer Meyer-Michelsen's simple reply.

Then he turned away, and looked out of the large office window. I doubted that he was looking at the spring sunshine outside, but guessed he was looking back to happier days when his daughter was still alive. Whatever the case, I felt deeply sorry for him.

I left the office and the building as quickly as possible, with an unusually silent Helgesen in tow.

It was still a beautiful day outside – possibly one of the best so far that year. But the sun was lower in the sky and our mood was even darker when we left than when we came.

X

As we drove out to Skøyen, I remarked twice that it was perhaps unnecessary. The first time Helgesen replied that we didn't have any other clues, and the second time he said we should leave no stone unturned. And I had to agree with him on both occasions.

So at a quarter past five, we parked outside the house where Amalie Meyer-Michelsen had woken up that morning and eaten breakfast some eight or nine hours ago. The tyre marks from her car were evident on the ground, but the car was still parked outside Tveita Shopping Centre, and she would never come back here.

The house was even larger than I had expected, and surrounded by a big garden. The lawn was recently mown and the house had clearly been given a fresh coat of blue paint. My initial impression of Christoffer Meyer-Michelsen's house was that it was neutral to the point of sterile, in much the same way as his office. The sign on the mailbox simply read *38 Kristinelund Road*, and there was no nameplate on the heavy brown oak door.

Once inside, the ground floor was really rather dull: a tidy, spacious and almost irritatingly perfect rich man's house. There was nothing lying on the floor, no piece of furniture missing. And nothing looked any older than ten years.

Judging by the clothes on the hangers in the hallway, cupboards and wardrobes, Meyer-Michelsen lived on his own on the ground floor. His home reinforced the image of him as an inveterate businessman with no other interests. There was a large television set and the newest model of radio, but no stereo player or records. On closer inspection, the only book-case contained three files of accounts and various books on the economy and financial magazines. There were no plants or flowers on the windowsill and no paintings or other art of any kind.

Once again, what made the difference and transformed the house into a home were the pictures of his daughter. There were nine framed photographs on the walls. With the excep-tion of a wedding photograph dated 13/6/1948, Amalie was in all of them. Christoffer Meyer-Michelsen was not smiling in the picture from 1948; he looked the very essence of a serious and responsible businessman even on his own wedding day. But he was smiling broadly in the next black-and-white photo from his daughter's christening and in a large colour photo-graph from her confirmation.

The most recent and biggest picture showed the father and daughter smiling with a fair-haired young man, who I assumed was the fiancé. It was too much for me – I turned away and said that it seemed she had lived on the first floor. Helgesen pointed to a staircase in the centre of the house.

The flat on the first floor was clearly Amalie's, and less tidy. A pink teacup stood abandoned on the coffee table, beside a large pile of ladies' magazines. In addition to books from pri-mary and secondary school, the bookshelves contained solely novels, the bulk of which were paperback romances. She had a radio, a television and a record player, and her LPs included the Beatles and Kirsti Sparboe.

There were fewer pictures on the wall than downstairs. A rather painful photograph showed Amalie when she must have been around fifteen, together with her thin and visibly ill mother. But the most recent pictures were more cheerful. Her father was in some of them, but in the last two he had been replaced by her fiancé. The most recent photograph was dated 5 April 1972, and was of what appeared to be a kind of engagement dinner at the Theatre Cafe.

It was the flat of a privileged young woman with a kind father, who was only lacking a husband and her own home. I could just imagine the reserved young Amalie sitting here alone reading her romantic novels, with her pink teacup in hand and a Beatles LP on the record player.

For a moment I hesitated before stepping into her bedroom. But there was nothing much to be afraid of. Her wardrobe was full of clothes, but only clothes. She had a double bed, but only half the bed had been slept in. Her fiancé smiled at her from under his blond fringe in a framed picture on the bedside table, but there was no other trace of him in the room. Nothing to indicate that anything dramatic had happened.

The only thing of any possible interest we found in a small desk standing in one of the corners. There was nothing in the lower drawer, but the top drawer contained a pink diary, symbolically closed with a small, gold-coloured padlock. The key was nowhere to be seen. And while I did not believe that Amalie could see us, I felt a little uncomfortable when I finally lost patience and broke open the lock.

The diary was full of entries, both short and long. The most recent was from the evening before and finished: . . . *Decided this afternoon that I would go and buy a birthday present for Dad – and a new pair of shoes for me. Tveita Shopping Centre and the weekend, here I come!*

The story of an excited and optimistic young woman who would shortly enter into married life and adulthood ended abruptly there, without any explanation as to what had happened. I didn't feel like reading any more there and then, with Helgesen. Instead, I said that we should take the diary with us, though it was not likely that we would find much there.

Helgesen agreed and replied, 'The house doesn't explain anything or make it any easier. Perhaps we should go and hear what her fiancé has to say instead?'

I longed to get out as well and had no better suggestion, so we clattered down the stairs and out of the door without looking back.

As I swung the car out onto Kristinelund Road, Helgesen pointed to another house. 'That must be where the business partner lives,' he said. The name Wendelmann was written in big letters on the mailbox and it was unlikely there were any others with that name in the neighbourhood. The house was only a hundred yards away from the Meyer-Michelsens.

I made a note to check the history of their partnership and how they had come to live more or less as neighbours. It might indicate that they had once been closer than they were now. But I simply could not imagine either Wendelmann senior or junior as a murderer. There were no lights on in the house, so having first slowed down for a moment, we drove on towards Frogner and the home of a fair-haired young man who presumably by now had been told that his fiancée had been murdered.

XI

I feared another emotional meltdown when I rang the bell outside 32C Tostrup Street – and felt that I was ill-prepared for it. But the twenty-six-year-old Rolf Johan Svendsen had been told the news before we got there and had taken it with remarkable composure. He briskly shook our hands and showed us indoors. The red rims round his eyes indicated that he had cried, but had now dried his tears.

'They announced on the radio this afternoon that a young woman had been killed at Tveita, and I knew straight away it was Amalie. She told me yesterday that she was going there this morning, and I'm sure that she would have contacted me if she had been there when another young woman was killed. I called her home and got no answer, so I called her father's office, and was relieved when the secretary said she hadn't heard anything. But then she called me back a quarter of an hour ago and confirmed that it was Amalie who had been murdered. I just don't understand who would want to kill her. It feels unreal – like a nightmare and I can't wake up,' he said, as we went into the living room.

Without anything being said, we sat down around the coffee table. He sat on the sofa, leaving the armchairs to Helgesen and myself. There was a photograph of Amalie on the table, with a burning candle beside it. As we sat there, he carefully took off his engagement ring and placed it beside the picture. One of the pictures I had seen in her flat was hanging on the wall here too: that of the happy couple and her father at the engagement dinner.

The situation was depressing, even though her fiancé was

controlled and friendly. For a moment I tried to imagine her here beside him on the sofa, where she had no doubt sat a hundred times in the past. But now she was gone and I could not even imagine her there. Her fiancé sat there alone.

I was worried that he might get angry, so after I had offered my condolences, I cautiously asked where he had been when he heard it on the radio. It was often said at the station that young women were generally killed by their husbands or fiancés.

If Rolf Johan Svendsen had understood why I asked the question, he certainly gave no sign of it when he answered.

'At work. I'm an associate in a law firm based at Majorstuen. I start a little later on Fridays, so went in as usual for ten. I heard the news on the radio at two o'clock. I called Amalie's flat first, and then her father's office. But I couldn't concentrate any longer, so I was given permission to go home at three o'clock. And I've been sitting here since then waiting for a phone call or news about what has happened.'

I noted that if this was true, Svendsen had a strong alibi. I then asked if he had noticed if his fiancée had been emotional or anxious recently.

'Quite the opposite, in fact. Amalie had not had an easy life, and was quite nervous and lacking in confidence when we first started dating. But in the past six months I haven't noticed any anxiety or fears about anything. If she had been anxious, she would hardly have gone to Tveita Shopping Centre alone. Dear God, I should have asked yesterday if she wanted me to go with her. I thought about it. But then I had to go to work and I knew that she liked to go shopping in the morning when there were fewer people. Amalie sometimes found it hard to breathe when she had to go to places where there were lots of people.'

We sat in silence for a short while. Then I said what I had said to Stein Hansen the day before: that no one could have foreseen this, and that he had done nothing wrong and mustn't blame himself in any way.

He thanked me for this, hesitated a moment, and then asked how she had been killed.

It was my turn to hesitate, but I replied that it would appear that she had been strangled.

Rolf Johan Svendsen gasped and put his hand to his throat. I realized that he could almost feel his fiancée's pain.

I wondered myself how it had happened and what she had thought and felt in her final moments. Had the murderer been a stranger, or someone she recognized? If it was someone she knew, it was clearly not her fiancé. I wished we could just take our leave, but knew that we had to follow every lead. So I asked what he meant when he said that she had not always had it easy.

'Well, obviously, she didn't need to worry about money. But she had no siblings and lost her mother at a young age. She's always had a good relationship with her father and he worshipped her. She only ever called him Dad, but he had a pet name for her, Ama. I can't bear to think how he must be feeling now. But having a father who was so well known and controversial was not easy. She avoided all possible conflict. To begin with, she didn't answer if anyone on the bus asked her if she was his daughter, and then she stopped taking the bus. Amalie was kindness itself and a good person in every way. She wanted for nothing materially, but longed for her own life and her own family. When I asked what she wanted for Christmas or her birthday, she said that it didn't matter, as long as she didn't lose me.'

I asked if perhaps there were any former boyfriends or admirers she had rejected who might have killed her out of jealousy. He quickly shook his head.

'No, I can't imagine that, and she certainly never mentioned anyone. I went out less than my fellow students, but have still had a couple of girlfriends before Amalie. She said that she had been in love before, but had never had a boyfriend. She was very careful like that. I think she was telling the truth and that there had never been another man in her life. It certainly felt like that, both mentally and physically. We met just over eight months ago now, and I can't say much about what happened before that.'

I took the opportunity to ask how they had met. He took a deep breath and thought for a few moments, but then the words came tumbling out.

'It was a strange coincidence really, as our families don't know each other and she was rarely out in town. I had no idea who she was. She was sitting outside a cafe in the centre of town one August afternoon when I walked past. I was on my way home after a lecture in a series I had decided to attend, as it was relevant to my work. She was alone, and had the kind of dark-haired beauty that I like. I was feeling lonely as I had relatively recently split up with my former girlfriend. So I asked if I could sit down and we chatted about this and that. She was fairly reserved to begin with, but then loosened up a bit later. Asked where I came from and nodded when I said that I had studied law. She wasn't unfriendly, but did seem rather distant and unattainable. So after a short while, I said that I had to go. On the way home it struck me that there was something familiar about her. But then I forgot all about it and didn't think about her again.'

He swallowed – and stopped. I saw his jaw tremble when he closed his mouth.

'But you met again?' I prompted.

He carried on the story.

'Yes, the following Monday. I walked home the same way after another lecture in the same series. She was sitting at the same table and looked a little down in the mouth, but then lit up and waved when she saw me. This time I stayed longer. I still had no idea who she was. She just said "Amalie" when we met the first two times. I thought that she either didn't want to tell me her full name yet, or she had a name that she didn't want to be known by. She seemed to be quite upper-class and a little precious – like a doll or a princess. I thought it might alarm her if I asked her back to my place, but eventually I dared to ask if I could take her to dinner. She immediately said yes. There was an awkward moment during the meal when I asked what her full name was. I was relieved to discover it was only because she had a father who was a well-known businessman. She was visibly pleased when I said I had nothing against him and in any case was more interested in her than her family. And from then on, I think you could say that things just got better and better.'

He finished with a little smile, which somehow seemed inappropriate and quickly vanished, given the serious mood. But I had seen it – and warmed to it. It was a charming story of two lonely young people who bumped into each other by chance and yet had made a determined effort to find each other – and who had never doubted since that they had met the right one. Once again I thought of the Seekers and my favourite song, 'A World of Our Own'. For a moment I envied this young couple their fast and deep conviction. I felt desperately sorry for Rolf Johan Svendsen, sitting there alone on the sofa. He was still composed, but pale.

When I looked around the flat, I saw through the open bedroom door that he too had a double bed, but that only one side had been slept in.

'And soon you ended up back here,' I said, my eyes still fixed on the open bedroom door.

Again, I expected an angry reaction. But again, he remained calm and talked in a steady, controlled voice.

'Oh, yes. Though it wasn't until Saturday that week, after our second date. It was also my birthday. At first she seemed so doll-like that I scarcely dared touch her, but I soon discovered there were two Amalies in the same body. The one everyone could see was distant, careful and reserved. The other, who only I saw, was intimate, energetic and open. Her dreams were simple in many ways. She had never wanted to be a politician or a pop star, nor had she ever wanted to take over the family business. All she wanted was her own life and her own family. Two children would be perfect, she often said. Three would be a bit too much work and too many to worry about. She had grown up as an only child and had always missed having a brother or sister. I'm also an only child and so knew how hard it was, and we quickly agreed that two children would be perfect.'

He closed his mouth, and again there was a tremor in his jaw.

I saw no reason to ask for any further details. There was nothing so far to indicate that the dead young woman's love life was of any significance. Suddenly the silence was crippling, so I quickly asked when they had got engaged and if they had set a date for the wedding.

'We've only been engaged for a couple of weeks. Since the Saturday before Easter. We went skiing up at the family cabin in the Jotunheimen mountains. I proposed as we stood looking out over the peaks. She threw her arms around my neck with such force that we fell down into the snow. It was a very emotional moment, but not unexpected for either of us. On the way home we talked sensibly about the practical aspects and we agreed that we wanted to get married in the summer, but that we would wait to set the final date.'

It seemed slightly odd to me to get engaged after only knowing each other for seven months, and then to plan to get married within the space of three or four months, and yet not set a date. So I asked him about it.

'Neither of us had many friends and we both came from small families, so it would be relatively easy to plan. But there was also a very practical reason for not setting a date. It was a very personal one, and I can assure you that it had nothing to do with her death . . . I am happy to tell you now, but would rather that it was not recorded in any reports that might be read by anyone else.'

Without looking at Helgesen, I told him to go ahead. The young man on the sofa hesitated for a moment, but then leaned forwards and opened up.

'You have to understand, Amalie and I loved each other and had no doubts about wanting to get married. Neither of us was religious, but we were both practical. Having children to carry on the family on both sides was important to both of us, as we were only children. My parents and her parents had wanted more children, but were not able to conceive, and her mother's sister had no children. So we made a pact and said that we would set the date as the first possible Sunday after she got pregnant. I personally had never thought of using it as a reason to get out of the marriage. But ensuring the family lineage was particularly important on Amalie's side, so I did not want her to be bound to me before we knew we could have at least one child.'

His voice was still steady. I listened with growing astonishment. I veered between alarm and admiration for this serious young man. If his story was to be believed, he was both exceptionally considerate and exceptionally pragmatic. He might also, like his dead fiancé, be two people in one body. And it was always important to be alert to men with split personalities in criminal cases.

I said, somewhat casually, that the expectation and uncertainty must have been very demanding for him. Then, following on from that, I asked if he knew what her inheritance was worth.

For the first time he frowned, and looked almost indignant.

'Believe it or not, we never spoke about that. I never asked and I don't think she would have told me if I had. Her father and his business are inseparable and were always there like a mountain in the background. Some of my colleagues have joked about how rich I will be one day. They calculated the value of his hotel chain at around thirty to forty million, even double that if he was successful with his latest acquisitions and construction projects. Amalie's father is in his early fifties and looks set to lead his company single-handed until he's a hundred, so we thought it would not be for decades yet. I would carry on working as a lawyer, regardless, and am set to inherit a million or two from my own family, so the money was not important to us. But for the record: now that Amalie is dead, I guess I will only inherit a few small things and a paltry sum from her.'

The twenty-six-year-old lawyer, Rolf Johan Svendsen, was unwavering. His voice was almost irritatingly controlled, but what he said was absolutely credible and he did of course have a point. His fiancée's death would undoubtedly amount to a substantial financial loss for him. And what was more, he was at the office when she was killed. This was clearly a dead end, of which there were now a frustrating number in the investigation. It felt as though we were caught in quicksand, and slowly being pulled under.

I assured him that he was not suspected of anything and thanked him for his help. Then I informed him that, with her father's permission, we had already searched Amalie's flat, but so far had only taken a diary away.

The word 'diary' provoked the man's most obvious emotional outburst so far. He flinched, rolled his eyes and took some deep breaths before saying anything.

'I of course fully understand that the police should take her diary as part of the investigation, but I would greatly appreciate it if I could have it once the investigation is over. Firstly because I don't like the idea that more people might read it, but also because I would like to have it. That diary is a chapter in our story in itself.'

Rolf Johan Svendsen stopped abruptly, but then carried on speaking when I asked him to. There was nothing to indicate that he needed time to think of an explanation.

'As I've said, Amalie was an only child and had always longed for a sister. She was one of the few young women I know who did not have a best friend. In a way, her diary was the sister and best friend she never had. It even had a name.

The diary is called Anna. Apparently it was the name her parents wanted to use if they ever had another daughter. Amalie has confided her most private thoughts to Anna for the whole time we've been together, and she would not let me read them. She kept the diary closed with a padlock and hid the key in a secret place, so she would know immediately if I had opened it. There was a strange little episode the first time I stayed over . . .'

He fell silent, gave a sheepish smile, looked up, and then continued.

'There was a strange little episode the first time I stayed over there. I got up before her and saw the diary lying on her desk. I reached out teasingly to pick it up, as she was lying naked on the duvet. "Don't even touch her," she said. "You have free access to me, but no access to my best friend." And she meant it. I doubt that there is anything unfavourable about me in there; I certainly hope not, but I will always wonder if I'm not allowed to read it. Other than my own memories and a few photographs, it's the only thing that remains of our story.'

He looked me straight in the eyes when he said this.

And suddenly shed a tear.

A single tear that slid silently and slowly down his left cheek. And for that very reason, it made a far greater impression on me than the expected floods of tears and sobbing.

XII

It was a quarter to six when we left. I was only a few hundred yards from Patricia's house in Frogner, and wanted nothing more than to go straight there. I suddenly realized it had been such a hectic Friday that I had barely given Patricia a thought, and yet somehow I missed her. I longed to hear her voice.

However, not only did I have to keep my contact with her secret, I also had to go back to the main station to check if there was any news. The radio had been silent, but that did not necessarily mean that no important information had come in. So even though I would gladly have swapped Helgesen for Patricia right then, I went back to the station with him.

'It is increasingly clear to me that we have not yet met the murderer, but are chasing a faceless serial killer who is still walking free out there somewhere,' I said, glumly.

To my surprise, Helgesen protested.

'I'm actually not so sure about that. I don't know if I believe that the murderer is someone we have spoken to in the past few days, but I would not rule it out. This victim was heir to a considerable fortune, which is always a possible motive. Did you notice, by the way, that Svendsen didn't ask any questions about what had happened to his fiancée or how the investigation was going? He didn't ask to see her or anything. Apart from wanting to know what she had written about him in her diary, he seemed to be rather uninterested.'

I was not in the mood to be contradicted, certainly not by a subordinate, and felt a rising resentment. I was on the verge of saying that the death of Amalie Meyer-Michelsen was in fact the strongest indication yet that we were dealing with a serial murderer, but instead simply remarked that her fiancé actually had an alibi.

Helgesen was not going to give in that easily.

'If she was killed at Tveita Shopping Centre after ten o'clock, granted, he couldn't have done it. If it can be proved that he was at the office all the time, then clearly he didn't leave her in the cupboard either. But (*a*), we only have his word for it, and (*b*), he may have got someone else to commit the murder. Or he may have killed her himself in the morning, and then got an accomplice to dump her so he had an alibi. Even if he only inherits a few hundred thousand, money and revenge could both be motives if she was about to break off the engagement. He even admitted that they had waited to set a date for the wedding because one or both of them were not yet certain.'

I was about to pooh-pooh this, but realized in time that not only did Helgesen have some good points, but also that I was simply being grumpy. This extraordinary investigation with a growing number of deaths and no clues as to who the murderer might be was getting to me more than I could remember any previous case doing.

So I got a grip of myself and said that of course we had to keep all possibilities open.

I realized that I had spent far too much time together with Helgesen over the past four days. And fortunately, I had an idea as to how I could have a day without him the next day.

I said that he had a valid point and that we should perhaps check the alibis of everyone we had met that week. If one of them had committed all three murders, this would become apparent if he or she did not have alibis for the times when the three murders had taken place.

Either Helgesen genuinely believed this, or he was glad at the thought of a break from me too. Whatever the case, he answered compliantly that this was a very good idea and that he would be happy to spend a couple of hours this evening and the day tomorrow following it up.

I felt a pang of guilt and said that he could go home to his family now. But behind his calm exterior, Helgesen was obviously just as involved in the case as I was and more optimistic than expected. He replied that his family had been sent off to visit his mother-in-law in Østfold for the weekend and he would be more than happy to do a couple more hours' overtime.

So Helgesen got to work on the alibis straight away – having first established that there was no more news at the station. The newspapers were calling with greater frequency and urgency, as were ordinary citizens, both with and without daughters. But nothing of any interest had come up.

If it was the murderer who had phoned me around lunchtime, he had definitely not called back later. The telephone company apologized profusely and said that they could not trace the call as it had been made from a telephone box, and was over before they were contacted. It would probably not have been of much help to us anyway to know which of the many telephone boxes in the city he had called from. Practically anyone and everyone could have been there and the murderer was not likely to leave any fingerprints if he was calling the police. I was more and more convinced that it was he who had called. But even this direct conversation with the murderer had not given me any clues.

It was now a quarter past six and all was quiet in the station, except for the persistent ringing of telephones further down the corridor. I had no idea whether this was in connection with my case or not, but they were a reminder of the mounting pressure.

I dialled Patricia's number. She answered on the second ring and said, 'Of course,' when I asked if it would be convenient if I came for supper at half past seven.

No more was said, and yet it felt like the most uplifting conversation of the day.

XIII

When I was shown into the library at twenty-five past seven, she was sitting in her wheelchair waiting in her usual place, at the end of the table furthest from the door. The table was set with fish soup, wine glasses and a lit candle.

'Finally. They said on the radio that a third victim had been found at Tveita Shopping Centre and I realized immediately that it was connected to the other two. I presume that a picture of an ant was found with the body and that she had been strangled. But who was she, and what happened? Sit down and tell me!' Patricia said, as soon as the door closed behind the maid.

I sat down and started to tell her about the day. I did not get very far. As soon as I said: 'Her name was Amalie Meyer-Michelsen . . .' Patricia interrupted me.

'So it really was Amalie . . . as I suspected. The latest news bulletin on the radio indicated that the victim was a young woman from Skøyen and the daughter of a well-known businessman. This is starting to become very unpleasant indeed . . .' she said, in a tense voice.

Patricia shook her head from side to side in a peculiarly angular and fretful way as she spoke. Then she stared at me without blinking.

I asked if she had known the victim.

'We haven't seen each other for years now, and she has never been here. But we knew of each other and met several times when we were little, yes. Amalie did not live far from us and our parents were often invited to the same parties.

251

Sometimes we were taken along too, and often we were the only two children there, but we never became close friends. She didn't say much and I remember at one point wondering what she thought about, then concluding that it couldn't be much. But it's sad, all the same. I do know that she didn't have a mean bone in her body. And it's rather worrying that the Anthill Murderer has now started to attack rich young women from Frogner and the west end as well.'

This could have been taken as black humour, only there was no hint of laughter in her voice.

I told her that I had probably spoken to the murderer earlier in the day, but still had no idea who it might be.

'Tell me more,' Patricia said.

Then she sat and listened for nearly an hour without interrupting me at all. Neither of us touched what was without doubt a delicious fish soup. The maid looked at us disapprovingly when she came in to collect the soup plates, but Patricia just waved her away again.

I took the hint and carried on with my account of the day's events, as soon as Benedikte had shut the door. Patricia had rubbed her hands impatiently on the table as the main course was being served. She only ate a few mouthfuls of the superbly prepared veal and took a couple of sips of water while I spoke.

'So, after all that has happened today, can you tell me anything more about the murderer?' I asked when I had finished updating her.

Patricia let out a heavy sigh – and then took her first drink of wine.

'There are some differences between this murder and the first two, but there are also some interesting similarities. It seems increasingly likely that the murderer is a young to middle-aged man, and possibly someone who feels he has been slighted in some way and has a difficult relationship with women. But this is all still very uncertain. And what is more, that could be any number of the thousands living within the city boundaries. I can only say one thing for certain about the murderer, which is not likely to be of much use to us at the moment. And that is that he must have exceptional hearing.'

I looked at Patricia, fascinated, and asked how she could be so sure of that.

'Before this third murder, I had at least one other theory about how the murderer might know when these young women were going to be in suitable places at suitable times. But now, there really is only one plausible explanation. He hears with his own ears what they are going to do in the next few days. The first two may have been overheard in public, but poor Amalie steered clear of such places. So there can be no other explanation than that the murderer heard her talking to her fiancé, her father, herself or someone else on the street. The streets of Oslo are the only place where all three women may have been overheard. The murderer is quite possibly someone who simply walks the streets listening out for possible victims. Most of us would have to be so close to hear that it would attract attention if we were to follow the person. And from what I remember when we were younger, Amalie had such a quiet voice that even I, with perfectly normal hearing, could not hear what she said only a couple of feet away. So in order to get hold of the information without attracting attention, the murderer must have exceptional hearing.'

I was amazed. Patricia sent me a triumphant smile before she carried on.

'We have a tendency in murder investigations to think that

all criminals must have normal or reduced abilities. Which is quite natural, I might add. But more people than one might think have additional opportunities precisely because they have extraordinarily well-developed senses. My mother wrote a chapter about it in one of her monographs, so it was discussed frequently at the dinner table for a while. As a twelve-year-old I found it hard to accept that there were people on this earth who could, for example, read a car registration plate from no less than half a mile away. But there are. It is unfortunately very difficult to see whether people have such highly developed senses. So keep your ears open in case you meet anyone in the course of the investigation with exceptional hearing.'

Patricia slowed down and her voice shook faintly when she talked about her parents. When she was thirteen, she and her mother had been involved in a car accident that had left her mother, who was in the front passenger seat, dead, and Patricia herself, who was sitting in the back, paralysed. She had presumably seen her mother die. But she seldom spoke about her and never about the accident, and I had chosen not to ask any questions. And this time as well, we turned swiftly back to the present and the investigation.

'It must have been a terrible shock for Meyer-Michelsen. He has a reputation for being hard on everyone except his daughter, who he adored. It is frightening to have such a small family. You're so vulnerable when someone dies. And it's rumoured that Meyer-Michelsen's business is more exposed than ever before. He has always taken risks, but has now evidently excelled himself with a series of acquisitions and expansions. In two years he will either be the richest man in Norway or bankrupt, so they say.'

A new side of Patricia appeared as she spoke. I could see the makings of a businesswoman, but did not yet have any idea what that might mean. I only knew that she had inherited a fortune when her father died. It would appear that she had kept herself well informed about the market as well. But she stopped there and turned back to the murder investigation.

'That's definitely of interest. It seems that the relationship between him and his partner was not the best. But surely none of this is of much relevance, as we're looking for a murderer who kills for thrills,' I said.

Patricia gave a cautious nod.

'Possibly, yes. Though I'm not sure that you haven't met the murderer, and I am very interested in the alibis that Helgesen is working with at the moment. They could either rule out or weaken some of the possibilities I'm keeping open, and maybe . . .'

Patricia suddenly stopped mid-sentence. She looked straight at me for a few seconds – and yet did not see me at all. I was very curious as to who she was thinking about, but knew her well enough now to know that she would not tell me if I asked.

We sat like this for a minute or so, in comfortable silence. The maid sneaked in, cleared up the dinner plates and left two bowls of ice cream in their place. Patricia still said nothing for a few seconds after she had left the room.

'I'm sorry I just blundered in like that. I should have thought that you and Amalie might have played together as children,' I said, when the silence was starting to feel oppressive.

I immediately regretted saying it, as I knew from experience that it was not a good idea to interrupt Patricia's thought process, especially when my investigation was at a dead end. However, she did not react as I feared she might.

'Not at all. I only ever played with my parents until I started to read, and once I had started to read, I didn't play with anyone,' Patricia replied in a relaxed, almost ironic voice.

I fished a little in the muddy water and remarked that she surely did not agree with Helgesen's theory about the deceased's fiancé. The sharper Patricia was back in a flash.

'Only an officer would suspect someone who first of all has no motive, and second, has an alibi. Though to be fair, it says more about the investigation in this case, unfortunately. So no, I don't suspect Rolf Johan Svendsen. But this murder does have some striking differences from the first two. How the murderer found out where the victim was going to be and when is even more of a mystery, as the victim was so quiet and unassuming. We may perhaps find something of interest in her diary. If you don't have any better suggestions, we could perhaps spend the rest of the evening doing that – reading the diary?'

I obviously cared more for Patricia now than before, and on top of everything else, was worried that she ate too little. So, in a cheerful voice, I suggested a compromise: that we first eat our pudding and then read the diary.

She gave a measured nod and picked up her spoon.

The ice cream tasted good, but I found myself sitting there wondering if I'd made a mistake. Patricia had after all suggested herself that we read the diary – but was she actually asking something else? I tried to imagine what I might do in a similar situation if I had been sitting with a young woman with no disabilities who had asked me for supper, and she then asked if I had any suggestions as to how we could spend the rest of the evening. Again, it seemed to me that Patricia's physical handicap represented a mental divide between us.

If Patricia felt in any way slighted or disappointed with my answer, it passed quickly. Within a couple of minutes she had finished her ice cream and emptied her glass. Then she drummed on the table impatiently while she waited for me to finish.

The moment I put down my spoon, she said, 'It's not practical to read the diary at such a large table. Can you help me over to the sofa?'

It was a question, but sounded more like an order. I obeyed without protest – though I had my reservations. Patricia was no doubt right that it would be impractical to go through the diary with each of us sitting at opposite sides of the table. I might have said that it would be easier just to move my chair round than to move Patricia over to the sofa, but it felt a bit insulting, almost unacceptable, not to lift her onto the sofa when she had asked me to. Again, her physical handicap made our relationship more complicated.

I had seen both the sofa and Patricia many, many times before. But I had never sat with Patricia on the sofa, and was a little anxious as to whether she would be able to keep her balance or not. But she seemed to sit upright. It struck me that Patricia had remarkable control over her body, despite the fact that she could not walk. She sat beside me on the sofa in her high-heeled shoes and knee-length blue dress.

I tried not to look down at her legs, but that was hard, as she put the diary down on her knees. From what I could see, there were no scars of any kind on her legs. On the contrary, her legs were shapely, if thin. I realized that in the middle of this depressing murder case, I was most definitely deeply in love with her. I wondered for a moment how she would react if I put my hand on her thigh.

But then the diary on Patricia's knees was opened and we both entered a closed world that the late Amalie Meyer-Michelsen had wanted to keep entirely to herself. It felt strange and not entirely comfortable for me, whereas Patricia seemed to have no reservations about leafing through the book.

XIV

The first entry in Amalie Meyer-Michelsen's pink diary was dated Saturday, 10 October 1970, and it said:

> *Let's see if I manage to keep a diary for more than a couple of weeks this time. I need someone to confide in. So you, Anna, will be the little sister I never got and the best friend I have never had.*

Patricia rolled her eyes humorously and quickly turned the page.

The final months of 1970 were sad reading. If her diary was to be believed, Amalie Meyer-Michelsen had no interest in politics or sport of any kind, nor in finance or business. She went to the theatre or cinema once or twice a month, with her father or alone. When she wasn't reading magazines she read novels, preferably the kind of easy reading romantic novels that were never reviewed in the papers. And in between short entries about these and her daily activities was the occasional thought-provoking reflection about how she viewed her life.

> *Wednesday, 4 November 1970: I turned twenty-one today –*
> *and am the third richest heiress in Oslo under thirty, if today's*
> Aftenposten *is to be believed. But I still have no qualifications –*
> *and am still unkissed. What's going to happen to me?*

Sunday, 6 December 1970: The second Sunday in advent, but there is no Christmas feeling here this year either. Mum is dead, Dad is away on business, my school friends have all moved on with their lives, I have no brothers or sisters and I have never had a boyfriend . . . Feel like the world's loneliest person in the midst of all the Christmas decorations.

Thursday, 24 December 1970: Lovely dinner with Dad, but still think about Mum every Christmas. Cried as I decorated the tree yesterday. Remember Mum and I decorated the tree together so well.

Thursday, 31 December 1970: Hope the new year will be better, but do not dare to believe it. This year, like last year, I stood alone with Dad by the window and watched the fireworks at midnight.

There were two blank pages at the end of 1970 and the start of 1971. I noticed with no surprise, but a flicker of irritation, that Patricia read about twice as fast as me. She noticed herself, of course, and said, 'Just turn over when you're ready,' in a voice that was both helpful and sarcastic. As a result, my hand hovered around her knee. We were sitting close together on the sofa, but there was no physical contact. It felt good – and strange.

The diary continued to be depressing through the first half of 1971. Amalie Meyer-Michelsen was not a great stylist and was rather self-absorbed. But there was an honesty about what she wrote, and her human longing made it engaging reading all the same.

Wednesday, 10 February 1971: Let Dad persuade me to go with him to one of these high-society parties. Good food, but horribly long speeches. Talked to two young bachelors, but was disappointed to discover that they were both more interested in Dad and his business than in me. So tired of people like that who only think about numbers. Did not meet anyone else it might be interesting to know, and took a taxi home at half past ten.

Tuesday, 9 March 1971: Tried to take the bus into town today, but was immediately recognized and pestered by a man who hated my father because he had been sacked from one of his hotels. An elderly woman came to my rescue, but then two others joined in. I asked them to leave me in peace and when they carried on, I said I had to get off at the next stop. Dad is not a slave driver – and in any case, I am not my father. I won't be taking the bus again for a while. Hailed a taxi to take me into the centre, but in the end asked the driver to take me home.

Friday, 19 March 1971: Finally got angry with myself for being so self-pitying. Thought about the poor little bookworm, Patricia Borchmann, who I played with a few times when I was little. She's now even more isolated than I am, sitting alone in an even bigger house having lost both her parents – and she can't even walk. I am at least fit and healthy and my darling father is still alive.

I found it wisest not to ask about this entry, and instead just pointed at it tentatively. Patricia simply wiggled her head and turned over to the next page.

Saturday, 10 April 1971: Easter holidays in the mountains; even though the weather was super, it felt like I was being crucified. Painful memories of Mum still linger in the walls at the cabin. But Dad is a sweetie and gave me Easter eggs like he did when I was little. It still feels sad to be sitting there alone with him and his secretary day after day. Eventually said to them that they should have a child, if they wanted to. It would make me happy. She looked so sad and he said that it was not on the cards. Perhaps he is the one who cannot have children, even though it was Mum who was ill. Dad's happiness and continuing the family line is now down to me. And I am just as chronically lonely and single after the Easter holidays as I was before.

Monday, 12 April 1971: Locked myself in my room and read the personal ads in Dagbladet on the last day of the holiday. Not many temptations there. There are a couple I could try if my name were not so well known. The fear of rumours and parasites has stopped me from answering any personal ads or putting one in myself. The fact that Dad is so rich is limiting my freedom. I feel like a canary in a golden cage.

Sunday, 25 April 1971: Am considering applying to university again in the autumn, more to meet new people than to study a particular subject – but can't decide what I want to study and what I could manage. My first attempt with maths the year before last was a fiasco – luckily I got out before it became too embarrassing. My grades are not the best, and not only because I was sick of school. My teacher at secondary school said in front of the whole class that it was a good thing I didn't need a university degree. It still hurts. Next month it is two years since I finished school, and I have not achieved anything other than passing my driving test. Think Dad is disappointed, even though he is too kind to say.

Friday, 21 May 1971: Saw a new production of A Doll's House at the National Theatre. A few very good actors on stage, but no interesting young men in the audience tonight either. I went alone, sat alone, and came home alone. Sometimes I think I live in a doll's house too.

Saturday, 26 June 1971: Warm summer day. I wandered around in town in my light summer clothes for a few hours with nothing *particular to do, in the hope that something exciting might happen. Nothing happened, of course, and in the end I could not walk any more because my legs were so tired. Stopped down by the harbour and looked at the water. Was gripped by the sudden desire to end it all and jump, but quickly thought better of it. It would kill Dad if I was to disappear and I am too much of a coward to die young. Even though it was a bright day outside, I was dark inside.*

Following this ominous end to the first six months of the year, there were two more blank pages, and it was another six weeks before Amalie wrote anything else. Patricia looked disgruntled and I quickly turned the pages. The second half of 1971 soon proved to be far more interesting.

Wednesday, 18 August 1971: Got a cold and feel miserable. Will get over the first soon, but not sure about the latter . . . If nothing happens soon, the autumn chill is not likely to brighten my mood more than a sunny day.

Monday, 23 August 1971: Woke up feeling better. A sunny late-summer Monday. Lots of young people out and about in town this afternoon, on their way to and from university or work. Walked around aimlessly for a few hours. Eventually sat down outside a cafe and ordered a cup of coffee. Then got unexpected company. An attractive, well-dressed young man with blond hair and no wedding ring asked if he could sit down. I of course said yes. If this was my big chance, it was unexpected and, as always, I was reserved and boring. He politely thanked me for my company and left after only a few minutes.

I did not want to tell him my surname, so I just said Amalie. And naturally he then only told me his first name. So all I know is that he is called Rolf Johan and is studying law. I sat there berating myself for always being so reserved and banged my head against the wall when I got home. Did not make my mind any clearer. Tried looking through the telephone directory, but gave up after I found thirteen Rolf Johans in the first seventy pages.

Tuesday, 24 August 1971: Dreamed about Rolf Johan last night. A very nice dream, but woke up alone in my bed. Got up around eleven. Annoyed that I was so vague yesterday. But at least I now have a purpose in life. Want to find out who he is. Going to the law faculty tomorrow.

Wednesday, 25 August 1971: The faculty office apologized, and said they did not give out students' personal details. I was disappointed, but had guessed that might be the case. Wandered around for a couple of hours but did not find him. I, on the other hand, was found by three students who all asked if I was Amalie Meyer-Michelsen and if I had started to study there. I lied to the first one, and said I wasn't me. Gave the second one a wide berth when he asked, and escaped after the third one. Do not want to attract attention by being there or be recognized again, and have no idea when Rolf Johan goes to lectures.

Friday, 27 August 1971: Have tried telling myself to give up, but still dream about Rolf Johan every night. Had another idea today. Unless it is an introductory course of some sort, lectures are usually on the same day at the same time. So he might walk the same way again on Monday. I am going to take a chance and sit at the same cafe at the same time and see.

Monday, 30 August 1971: The most exciting day in my adult life so far! Was so wound up last night that I didn't get to sleep until four in the morning and then slept until midday today. Was still tired and did not feel great when I sat down at the table outside the *cafe at a quarter to four. I counted over a hundred people walk past, and was about to give up when he appeared, as I had hoped, at exactly the same time as last week. My heart was in my mouth when I waved to him. Was terrified that he would just scoff and walk on. But he waved back – and stopped. I was shaking so much I thought I might fall off my chair when he came towards me. But kept my balance and think I managed to be a bit more interesting today. Had thought a lot and planned what I could say to make a good impression.*

I was worried every time he opened his mouth that he would say something about a girlfriend. But he didn't, until finally he mentioned in passing that he had had a girlfriend in the spring, but they had broken up a few months ago. By then it was nearly half past four. He eventually said that he had to go as he had arranged to have supper with his parents, but that it had been very nice getting to know me a bit better.

I said brazenly that it had been lovely talking to him, and it was a shame that he had to go so soon. He suggested that we might meet another day instead. My heart was pounding so hard that I could hardly hear what I said. Something like, I would no doubt be able to find time for that in my diary – depending on what days suited him best. He suggested Wednesday. I pretended to think for about ten seconds and then said I should be able to make that. He looked a little surprised when I suggested Grand Café, but said it was fine before I could suggest anywhere else. The hours have dragged by today, but this is the most exciting week I have had this year.

Tuesday, 31 August 1971: A torturously slow day is finally coming to an end. Have used it to plan questions and answers for when I meet him tomorrow. Must not be boring, but don't want to be tiring either. Dad once said that it is important in business not to appear to be desperate – especially when you are. The same could apply to love. Have gone through my wardrobe twice – and in the end decided that I should go out and buy a new dress tomorrow morning.

Wednesday, 1 September 1971: Did not get to sleep until half past four in the morning, but woke up feeling bright at eleven, all the same. Incredible how refreshing being in love can be. Drove to Tveita and spent two hours looking around before buying the most expensive dress there.

He came on time and smiled when he saw me. I have eaten at Grand Café many times before, but have never gone in with a young man. It was a new experience – and very exciting.

We spent three hours at Grand and the evening was everything I had hoped for. There was a nerve-wracking moment when Rolf Johan asked what my full name was, so I had to tell him. There was no visible reaction even when I told him who my father was. He asked a little about my parents, but seemed to be more interested in my mother's story than my father's business. He said nothing about inheritance or anything like that.

He is an only child too, from a good family on both sides. My two greatest worries were laid to rest: he is not religious or a communist. I said over dessert that we had a lot in common. He smiled and we drank to that.

The only disappointment was that he did not ask me home with him. Not that I necessarily expected him to do that, but I hoped that he would. I had tidied and cleaned my whole flat, and changed the bed, just in case he asked where I lived. I thought it might be a bit off-putting if I were to ask him back. And as he didn't ask me, I can only presume that he is still unsure about what he wants to do.

So in the end, I asked if I could invite him out for a good dinner in return. It felt like a critical moment. I don't think I would have been able to hide my disappointment if he had said he didn't have time. But that is not what he said. Instead, he got out his diary and asked if Saturday would suit. I had planned to give myself five seconds to think if he suggested another date, but did not dare wait for more than two before saying yes.

We parted with a hug outside Grand Café around nine. His cheek was unexpectedly hot and burned against mine. See you again, I said. I certainly hope so, he replied. I almost flew to the taxi rank. Shed a few tears in the back of the taxi, but this time it was tears of joy.

Sunday, 5 September 1971. Did not manage to write in my diary yesterday, but for very good reasons, as I did not get home until late afternoon today!

Took a chance and wore the same dress again yesterday, as it did not seem to put him off the first time. The dinner with lovely piano music from the waltz king and excellent food at Ribo restaurant was beyond expectations. I felt free and happy and was more open than I can remember being with anyone else, ever. We laughed a lot, about things that were funny and others that were not really that funny.

I had planned to ask about seeing where he lived, but was very relieved that he asked me home with him first. Everything felt right. He lives in a well-looked-after flat in Frogner, and if any other women have been there, there was certainly no sign of them now. There was a bouquet of flowers on the table when we came in, which made me nervous, as I had not sent it. He tried to hide it away, but when I asked, he told me it was from his work as it was his birthday.

I was deeply touched and encouraged by the fact that he had chosen to spend it with me. I was intoxicated, even though I had only drunk one glass of wine for fear of saying something silly.

Things went very fast after that. I said that I had a present for

*him, but was not sure whether he wanted to unwrap it today. He
gave me a mock-stern look, then we leaned in towards each other
at exactly the same time and kissed passionately on the lips. He
whispered in my ear that exciting presents should of course be
opened on the day.*

*I don't remember much until later when I was lying on the bed,
thoroughly unwrapped, with his head on my chest.*

*Felt a stab of fear when I woke up alone in the bed this morning.
Worried at first that the whole thing had been a dream, and then
that he had run away. But five minutes later he sauntered in from
the bathroom in only his underpants and said, 'Good morning.
Well, I guess we're a real couple from today on. What do you say?'
I almost squealed with delight.*

The diary went from being a depressing account to an
uplifting story. I flicked through the pages so I could read what
happened next. Patricia was smiling broadly. I thought it must
also be an encouraging story for her, despite their obvious differences. It felt like Patricia's leg was pressing against mine – but
I was not sure if she was aware of it.

The entries for the next few days were much shorter, but
showed a marked change in spirit.

*Monday, 6 September 1971: His first day back at work felt endless,
but the evening was all the nicer for it. Still incredibly happy.*

*Thursday, 9 September 1971: First supper at home with his
parents. Was nervous, but they were very welcoming and friendly.
They knew my father, but did not seem to have anything against
him. There was not a cloud in the sky when I left and I thought
to myself that my life had changed from rainy and grey to pure
sunshine.*

Saturday, 11 September 1971: Another relief – Rolf Johan's first meeting with Dad went very well. Dad was more than happy with his potential son-in-law and thought it was nice that he stayed over. We had our first little confrontation when Rolf Johan showed an interest in you, dear diary. Obviously, I don't want him to see how desperately lonely I was before he came into my life. When I said that he could have free access to me but not to you, he accepted it without argument. He said that he would then rather concentrate on me, and I did not protest at that . . . So our first little tiff ended happily. And that must be a good sign.

Sunday, 19 September 1971: Stayed with my boyfriend all weekend. Very good mood and lots of activity. In one incredible month I have gone from having a cold and feeling desperate to being pampered and in love. Definitely a great improvement!

This entry seemed a little vulgar to me. Patricia seemed to be enjoying it more and more and let out a chortle when she read it.

Monday, 20 September 1971: Still so in love and dazed after the weekend that I forgot to vote. I have never been interested in politics anyway and it feels completely irrelevant now.

Over the next few weeks, there were fewer and shorter entries, but these did confirm that things were going well for the young couple.

4 November 1971: I turned twenty-two today – and for the first time since primary school, I was happy to celebrate my birthday. Got a new car from Dad, but was even happier to get the biggest bouquet in town from Rolf Johan when he came to surprise me first thing in the morning. Understood today how the ugly duckling

must have felt when it discovered it had become a swan.
Called myself the happiest woman in the world before going to
sleep.

 The first longer entry was the second to last one of the
year.

3 December 1971: A terrifying moment – followed by a joyful
shock. We were eating supper here at home and everything was
fine. So I jumped a little when he said that there was something
serious we should talk about before Christmas. Naturally, I was
terrified that he had found someone else or was bored with me. For
a few moments, it felt as if the ground had opened up beneath me.
But all he wanted was to know if we had a shared understanding of
any future family plans – as he put it, in his legal language. I was
worried he was going to say that he wasn't sure if I was the right one
to have his children, and that he did not want any for a few years yet,
anyway. But instead, he said the opposite: that he wanted to have
children with me, and that he hoped we would not have to wait long.
I burst into tears and cried on his shoulder. Then I went into the
bathroom and came back with my pills and asked if we should burn
them. We melted the last one over an advent candle. Very romantic.

31 December: The happiest new year ever. Standing here watching
the fireworks with my boyfriend. Pretending that it is all in our
honour. The end of a magical year. I have the man I have always
dreamed of – and hope to be standing here with a baby in my arms
next year.

There were a couple more blank pages after this happy end
to the year. For the first three weeks of January, there were no
entries of any kind – and then there was a less optimistic start
to the year.

23 January 1972: Five months since we first met – and today has been my worst day since then. Suddenly overwhelmed by my one remaining fear. A month since I stopped taking the pill, but still no sign of any changes in my body. I know that doesn't need to mean anything dramatic, but it worries me all the same. Mum only had me and my aunt has no children, so am scared it might be hereditary.

17 February 1972: Still no sign of pregnancy, and it's certainly not for want of trying. The first time Rolf Johan and I have talked about it. I needed to talk about it and could not wait any longer. Was terrified of how he would react. He took it well and was as calm as always. Said that he had been thinking about it too, but that it was not unusual for it to take a few months. We just have to hope for the best and do what we can, he said. I was relieved, but still uneasy.

2 March 1972: Optimistic yesterday when I felt unwell and nearly five weeks had passed since my last period. Physically and mentally dulled when it started today. I wasn't pregnant, I just had the flu.

13 March 1972: Despite all my other worries, I have always had a good relationship with my own body, but now we are at loggerheads. Nothing is happening and my frustration increases by the day. Have been to the doctor, who said it was quite normal that it took a bit of time, and we should just wait and see what happens. He also thought that we should get married before we had children. Which did nothing to lift my mood. I would happily say yes if Rolf Johan asked, but don't feel that it's the right time to bring it up. His mother is very excited about the prospect of grandchildren, and has already started knitting baby clothes. Dad has been busier than ever with work, but I think he also hopes to have a grandchild and heir within the year.

20 March 1972: Went to a new doctor. He was nicer, not so moralizing, but had no better advice. There was no reason to worry as long as we were both young and healthy, he said. But that is what they told my aunt, apparently, and she has been unhappily childless for nearly thirty years now.

Maundy Thursday, 30 March 1972: Easter holidays in the mountains, at Rolf Johan's family cabin in Jotunheimen for the first time. Am happy here, but also worry that it may be the first and only time I come. We haven't argued once, but I can feel that the situation is wearing him down too. Hard for either of us to think about anything else. This evening, Rolf Johan said with a tear in his eye that maybe it was his fault. His mother had also had only one child, and he was operated on for a hernia when he was a boy. This was not good news, but in a strange way it did take some of the pressure off me. In the end, we're the same, and in the end, we love each other. It makes things a little easier.

Easter Sunday, 2 April 1972: Beautiful weather – and Rolf suddenly proposed to me when we were out skiing! I threw my arms round his neck and said yes. But the gravity of the situation was there all the time. On the way back to the cabin, we agreed that we would announce our engagement, but would wait to set a date until we knew that I was pregnant. He said he hoped our engagement would have a positive effect, but I am not so sure he really believes that.

Sunday, 16 April 1972: Lots of congratulations on our engagement, but still no date for the wedding . . . Cannot imagine life without Rolf Johan – but the thought of a life without children is almost as bad. Dad seems a bit gloomy these days and I worry that all this is getting him down. Rolf Johan's mother is constantly pestering us. What on earth are we going to do if we can't have children?

Wednesday, 19 April 1972: Dad has looked even more depressed in the past couple of weeks, and today I couldn't stand it any longer. Asked him what was bothering him. He did not want to answer at first, but when I said it was important for me to know, he told me that they had to make some serious decisions in the company, and he and his partner disagreed vehemently about what they should do. He assured me that it was purely business matters that were getting him down and nothing to do with me. I have never liked Mr Wendelmann, but don't really know him or the business. Just have to hope that Dad has everything under control, as he always does. It was a relief, though, to know that it was not the lack of a grandchild that was bothering him.

Following this there was an odd little entry. The heading *Friday, 21 April 1972* was clear enough, but underneath there were only two words written in pen, which had been scored out. From what we could make out, they were *Unexpectedly met,* but any attempt to make sense of them was pointless. The next entry was legible and immediately drew our attention.

Monday, 24 April 1972: The closest I have come to an argument with Rolf Johan. He was unshaven, looked tired and was so glum at supper that I realized that something had happened. I demanded to know what was wrong, and he told me reluctantly that his mother suspected that I might not be able to have children. And if that was the case, she thought he should break off the engagement and find another woman. I howled like a stuck pig and then he got angry with himself for telling me. He reassured me that he had totally dismissed the very idea. But when I then suggested that we might

*as well set the date for the wedding, he was reluctant, and said we
should perhaps wait a little longer.*

 Suddenly we had come to Amalie Meyer-Michelsen's last
two days alive.

*Thursday, 27 April 1972: Lovely meal at home, just the two of us.
But I still really hope that there will be three of us this time next
year, and that in time we will have the two children we dream of.
Have stayed at home the past couple of days. Don't feel one hundred
per cent, but think it is just a touch of flu – don't dare to hope any
longer. Am staying at Rolf's on Saturday night, so we can keep
trying. Decided this afternoon that I would go and buy a birthday
present for Dad – and a new pair of shoes for me. Tveita Shopping
Centre and the weekend, here I come!*

Then finally, there was the heading *Friday, 28 April*, but
nothing more had been written.

Patricia turned back and read through the last entry from
the day before. Then she snapped the diary shut and put it
down on the table in front of us.

We sat in silence for a while. Patricia, who had been chuck-
ling halfway through the diary, was now serious to the point of
sombre. I wondered how much of that was due to the situation
regarding the investigation, or to the story itself. The fact that
Patricia had known the victim, if only vaguely, was one thing,
but another, more serious aspect was that Amalie's life had in
some ways resembled her own. She had been isolated in luxury
for years now – a bit like a canary in a golden cage. I knew that
Patricia had also longed for a boyfriend. And I was not sure if
she could have children as a result of the injuries sustained in

the accident. During my previous investigation, she had made a comment that seemed to infer that she did not know either.

'Well, I have to say that the diary is pretty much in line with what her fiancé told me,' I said, tentatively.

'Goodness, yes,' was Patricia's reply.

We said nothing more until Patricia suddenly released a great sigh.

'How the hell did this hideous murderer know that Amalie was intending to go to Tveita the next day, if she had stayed at home for the past few days and only decided yesterday to go?' she hissed. Her slim right hand hit the table with unexpected force.

I voiced one of my possible theories – that perhaps the murderer had in some way been tapping the victims' phones.

'You mean that someone from the surveillance services or some kind of technical genius is on the loose? It is of course perfectly possible that there are potential murderers in both categories, but there is nothing to indicate that Amalie spoke to anyone on the phone about it. She told her fiancé when he was there yesterday, and her father at breakfast today. What on earth is the link here?'

'Is it possible that Amalie might simply have been a random victim, even though the murderer was waiting for the other two? Or that he might somehow have heard this morning where she was going?'

Patricia shook her head and seemed to be almost angry.

'Oh, for goodness sake . . . Poor Amalie started her car right outside her front door and parked only a few yards from the main entrance at Tveita. I think we can safely rule out the idea that she may have picked up an unknown hitchhiker en route. And it is also highly unlikely that the murderer strangled her just outside the main entrance. There are clear sightlines in every direction, and people going in and out all the time. The murderer would have to be stark raving mad and incredibly optimistic if he thought he could find a suitable young victim in the shopping centre. And in any case, there are witnesses to say that he was carrying the mail sack when he came into the mall. And does that mean he took the body out first, only to come back in with it in a sack? It seems highly unlikely, and would be madness.'

I had not thought about it like that – and had to admit that my theory that she was killed either in or close to the Tveita Shopping Centre did seem less likely. I reluctantly repeated what Helgesen had said, that perhaps the murder had been committed earlier.

'It would certainly be very interesting to know if the pathologist can give us a specific time of death. The fact that her car was in the car park does not necessarily mean that she parked it there. The murderer may have driven the car to Tveita, with the body in it. But then there must be a reason for taking that risk, instead of just dumping the body by the roadside. He must have known that she planned to go there. It is all so odd that one might even wonder if Helgesen . . .'

I waited with bated breath for her to finish the sentence, but having first spoken very fast and with unusual passion, Patricia now quickly closed her mouth mid-sentence – only to carry on: 'No. I can see that this was well planned, but I don't see how the Anthill Murderer could have planned it, certainly not if he planned and carried out the murders of Agnes and Lise. I don't know what to think. And that is both unusual and unsettling for me.'

She said this with a hint of self-irony. All of a sudden,

Patricia looked tired, and her grim mood was almost aggressive. It was no more than half an hour since we had sat there smiling as we read Amalie and Rolf Johan's love story, yet the hope of any romantic development between Patricia and myself now felt very distant. And I still did not know what I wanted. I too was tired and bewildered. When I looked at my watch it was a quarter to ten.

I thanked her for supper and for her help and promised to contact her as soon as I had anything new.

'Will you help me back into my wheelchair before you go?' Patricia asked.

I of course said yes, but now dreaded even the most superficial physical contact. Her body was tense and she was shaking when I picked her up. I gave her a proper hug once I had set her back down, and she gave me a small smile back.

On my way to the door, I suddenly stopped to ask one last important question: 'Do you think we need fear another murder this weekend?'

'I don't know, but it does worry me. The murderer has struck every second day so far, so we can only hope that nothing happens on Saturday. Today he struck in the morning, and in a shopping centre, so who knows where he might be at the weekend. The murder today was more or less expected, only we didn't know where or when it would happen. I personally thought that the murderer would continue to operate after dark. Now he has raised his stakes and won in broad daylight, so I expect that the Anthill Murderer will strike again relatively soon, but I have no idea when or where. For all we know, he might be out there stalking another victim right now.'

Patricia said this with a heavy sigh. Then she turned away and looked at the candle that was still burning on the coffee table. She sat there watching the flame as I left the room, serious and still as a Red Indian chief by the fire.

It had been a demanding day, and my body still held the tension. When I got home at a quarter past ten, I immediately called the main police station, before even taking off my shoes. My boss had been on the seven o'clock news, which had devoted the first half of the programme to the case. The number of calls from the public and the newspapers had of course risen dramatically through the evening, after this. But otherwise, there was nothing new to report. Still black water as far as the eye can see, I thought to myself.

Suddenly I had to shut myself off from the case, so I went to bed at ten to eleven, without waiting for the last news of the day. Before I turned off the light, I moved the telephone to my bedside table, beside the alarm clock.

I lay there alone in the silence. It felt as though it had never been so quiet in my flat. As I drifted off to sleep, I heard myself saying Miriam's name, without knowing why. But the face I saw in those final minutes of the day was Patricia's, still staring intensely into the candle flame.

XV

Tonight was a cock-up.

Two hours later I'm now safely at home and under the duvet. But it still maddens me to think about what happened.

I was prepared for the possibility that something unexpected might occur, of course. But I had fuelled my expectations throughout the day. For the first time I was going to kill someone in the centre of town. And

I was going to kill a woman I hate and despise more than those I have killed before.

Whatever one might say about my previous victims, they at least belonged here. She was a stranger in our country – a cuckoo who ate all our food. And she was younger and more cautious than the others. That's to say, she was far more alluring prey and it would be harder to get my hands around her neck.

My pulse was well over 150 for the ten minutes that I stood waiting for her in a dark side street by Young's Square just after ten. I could look up to the party offices above the People's Theatre and the citadels of power in the People's House, though obviously none of the great men were to be seen. They all went home at four. A few people walked past, but not many and none close. And in any case, they wouldn't be able to see much of me behind the coat and scarf.

One of the passers-by was a dotty old man who was talking to himself. It annoyed me beyond reason. I had to listen to him babbling on about what vegetables to buy tomorrow for nearly a whole minute. What the doctor said to my mother the day before my sixth birthday was true: exceptional hearing is a blessing in some situations, but overall, it is more of a burden than a gift. I have often wondered what my life might have been like without the handicap of exceptional hearing. I think it might have been better. But you can never know for sure, and I have accepted the fact that I will never know.

My victim is called Fatima. Have you ever heard a more foreign-sounding and unsuitable name for a woman in Norway? And as far as I know, her parents are Muhammadans as well.

She eventually came round the corner of the People's House, ten minutes late and without a care. I heard her footsteps before I saw her. But I also heard some other footsteps.

One of the problems I had feared and anticipated happened tonight. For some reason, Fatima was walking home with a friend.

Her friend was a blonde young woman in her early twenties, wearing one of those fashionable shapeless hooded jackets and carrying a big book under her arm. Fatima called her Miriam.

As far as I can remember, I've never seen the friend before. I have, however, seen and heard Fatima close by several times in recent weeks. And I've wondered if she will recognize me when we're standing face to face – when I put my hands around her throat.

They talked and giggled like two annoying teenagers. As far as I could make out, they were laughing about a young man who no doubt meant well, but had not had much success when he tried to talk to Fatima at the socialist meeting they had just been to. Without knowing who he was or what had actually happened, I could sympathize with him. Fatima's friend had an unusually derisive laugh. For a second, I wanted to kill her instead. But I know nothing about her, other than her first name, and have no idea where I could find her alone. She is at least white.

They walked arm in arm down Møller Street. It was disgusting to see Fatima's dirty brown hand against her friend's beautiful white skin. It makes my stomach turn whenever I see dark people like that walking around in our streets. This time, my disgust was stronger and actually made me feel sick. I wanted nothing more than to get my hands around Fatima's neck and squeeze the living daylights out of her. But I realized in time that it would not happen this evening. Her intensely irritating friend had ruined everything.

I swallowed my disappointment and managed to control myself exceptionally well, though I say it myself. Within ten seconds of the pair turning the corner, I moved off in the other direction. If they saw me, they probably just thought that I was turning out from the side street. I was too far away for them to see my face. In the worst case, they will have seen that I was wearing a light-coloured coat, but then, so does half the town.

No one knows that I was standing there with a mind to murder – and a picture of an ant in my pocket. Fatima, her friend and all the others who passed have probably forgotten me already. Who would remember a stranger and passer-by from an evening when no one was killed?

Little brown Fatima was luckier than she deserved, and got away this evening. But that's not going to save her pathetic little life – only extend it by another day. She talks too much and too loudly. I know where she's going tomorrow evening now.

I can still hear her carefree, almost mocking laugh in my ears as I lie here trying to sleep. She shouldn't have shunned that man who tried to talk to her this evening. It might have been her last chance to experience a man's love. She should have been grateful that a Norwegian man wanted her. But she's arrogant like that and won't take just anyone. I hate her more than I can remember ever hating a woman before. And that is saying something.

But the unsuccessful murder has wound me up more than I thought. Fatima must not and will not get away tomorrow. The possibility of getting caught becomes more and more certain. In the past twenty-four hours, I have come to accept that it will happen, sooner or later. Just not before I have killed my third victim.

But I have a nagging worry: could it be that the newspaper reports about my other murders have frightened little Fatima so much that she doesn't dare venture outdoors alone? She said nothing about them yesterday. But you never know what these self-centred young women might think of next. Fatima is fast becoming an obsession.

It's going to be an exciting Saturday. Sleep still evades me, and my alarm clock shows that the new day has arrived. Another countdown has started, without my victim having the faintest idea. I now decide over other people's life and death. And I'm still very happy with that.

DAY SIX

Seven Missing Alibis and a Glimpse
of a Serial Killer

I

The start of Saturday, 29 April 1972 felt unusually grim. A lack of sleep through the week caught up with me and I overslept by ten minutes.

The main story in *Arbeiderbladet* and *Aftenposten*, albeit from different angles, was a recent opinion poll that showed that the majority of Labour voters were now anti-EEC membership. But an old photograph of Amalie Meyer-Michelsen still looked at me accusingly from the bottom corner of the front page of both papers, all the same. And they both wrote about the ant pictures that had been found at all three crime scenes, and therefore understandably presumed that there was a serial murderer on the loose in the capital, with a penchant for young women. *Aftenposten* was concerned that 'even women living in more law-abiding parts of town' were not safe from the killer. They had dubbed him the Ant Murderer. *Arbeiderbladet*, on the other hand, wrote that we were all in danger. Fortunately, neither of the newspapers mentioned the head of the investigation by name, though both did imply that the investigation had still made no progress. As far as *Aftenposten* was aware, 'a number of people have been questioned in connection with the three murders, but so far no arrests have been made'.

In other words, the morning papers did nothing to lift my already miserable mood. And outside, the clouds were dark and the air was heavy with rain. When I arrived at the police station ten minutes late, there were no new messages or information waiting for me. And when I got to my office, I found DI Danielsen outside.

It was not entirely unexpected. I could well understand my boss's decision to expand the investigation team, if for nothing else but to demonstrate to the newspapers and public that the case was top priority. But my mood did not improve when I saw my old rival outside my office.

Danielsen himself seemed at ease with the situation and did his best not to make my mood worse. He said that the boss had ordered him to join the investigation, but that he had every confidence in my leadership and hoped that I could give him something meaningful to do.

I thanked him and asked him to come into the office. My ability to keep face in uncomfortable situations had improved over the past couple of years.

The time I spent updating Danielsen on the case was so free of friction that I almost wondered if we had started to like each other. I said that I would give him as complete an overview as possible of the investigation. He thanked me, and noted down names, times and other details that I gave him.

I hoped primarily that I would see some new links or clues myself as a result of this, and secondly that Danielsen would. But neither happened. When I finished my account at a quarter to eleven, we both sat in silence. Danielsen looked over his notes; added a comma here and there. I also hoped that we might be helped along by a phone call with an important tip-off. But the phone remained silent.

'It really is not easy to know what to do next. If the murderer has no connection to any of the victims, it's hard to know where to look for him. But if the murderer does have some kind of connection to one of the victims, the list of alibis is of utmost importance. So perhaps it might be best if I help Helgesen with his list today?' Danielsen ventured, eventually.

I agreed and suggested that the three of us should meet again when the list of alibis was ready. I would in the meantime follow up the latest murder and question the victim's father and his business partner again. Danielsen said that that sounded like a good plan.

When he left, I sat alone in my office with an empty desk and a silent telephone. I picked up the receiver and dialled Christoffer Meyer-Michelsen's home number. There was no answer. When I rang the office, however, the phone was immediately picked up by his ever-helpful secretary. She told me that her boss was still 'clearly very affected' by his daughter's death, but that he was busy in his office all the same. We agreed that I would come to the office around one o'clock.

I had just put down the phone when there was a knock at the door. I thought I recognized the efficient two quick raps, and I was right. Pathologist Jørgensen was waiting outside, and offered to give a report on the late Amalie Meyer-Michelsen.

I was touched by the zeal that was hidden by the man's easy-going nature. It was not normal for top pathologists to come into the station at the weekend, and I knew that Jørgensen did not usually work on Saturdays. So I thanked him and said that I would very much like to hear his report.

Jørgensen sat down on the chair opposite me and put three sheets of paper down on the desk between us as he reeled off the main findings with his characteristic calm and dignity. The late Amalie Meyer-Michelsen had been strangled in the same way as the two previous victims, by a person putting his or her hands around her neck and squeezing until she died due to lack of air. The injuries to her throat indicated that the murderer had very strong hands and used them effectively. It was most likely that the murderer was a man who was 'over fifteen, but under fifty', though given all possible eventualities, he did not dare rule out that it could be an older man or a 'strong and determined woman'.

Amalie Meyer-Michelsen had been dead for between three and five hours when she was taken in for autopsy. This meant that she had been killed at some point between half past nine and half past eleven. There were no findings that determined whether she had been killed indoors or outdoors, so the question as to where and when remained unanswered.

'The victim was otherwise in good shape, without any visible injuries or illness above or below the neck. However, there is one medical condition that I thought you should know as soon as possible, though I'm not sure how relevant it is to the investigation. Amalie was pregnant.'

It was like a punch to the stomach. I felt a wave of nausea and asked Pathologist Jørgensen if he knew how far gone she was.

'No less than three weeks and no more than five, but too early to know whether it was a boy or a girl. And it is quite possible that Amalie herself did not know she was pregnant when she died. But she was, and so, in a sense, two people have been murdered.'

I said that as far as I was aware she did not know, and thanked him for the information. He in turn thanked me and then left the office. Once again I sat there alone staring at the door. The office suddenly felt icy cold, even though the radiator was on.

I imagined the diary entry that Amalie Meyer-Michelsen would never write, telling of her enormous relief and great joy at the pregnancy. I thought that the foetus that had died in her womb would have been a much longed-for child, irrespective of whether it was a boy or a girl. Amalie and Rolf longed to be parents, and it would be the first grandchild for all their own parents. For the first time, I felt a deep and personal hatred for the murderer.

My thoughts were interrupted by the telephone. The switchboard operator said that she had someone on the line who claimed to have important information about the murder at Tveita Shopping Centre, but refused to give it to anyone other than me.

The first thing I heard when the call was transferred was a series of pips, which told me that it was being made from a telephone box. The second thing was a strangely gruff and deep voice, which I immediately presumed belonged to a man over fifty who had been smoking for years.

'Is that K2?' he asked. I confirmed that it was straight away.

'The paper said the Tveita murderer was a man who walked into the shopping centre with a big mail sack over his shoulder. If it was, I saw him close up. Thought there was something dodgy about him. Can tell you more, if you come and meet me later, alone, somewhere outside,' the rough voice continued.

I said that I definitely would like to hear more, but it would be best if he could come down to the station.

'No way. Don't like police stations. Whenever I've been in one it's taken way too long to get out.'

He said this very openly, with a hint of irony. Suddenly I got the picture – there were two possible alternatives. Either the caller was a criminal himself, but still wanted to help solve the murders, or it was an attempt to lure me into a trap.

The pips returned to tell us that his time was soon up. He spoke even faster.

'No more coins. I'll be outside the caff in Rosenkrantz Street in half an hour. Will make myself known if you come. But come alone, or else I'll leave.'

The connection was broken before I had a chance to answer.

I was firmly convinced that this was not the same person who had called me at the same time the day before; it was not just the language, but also the intonation that was different. It struck me that if you were planning to attack a policeman, a cafe in Rosenkrantz Street, with witnesses everywhere, was not the best place. And I was more and more curious about who the caller could be and what he had seen at Tveita. So I decided to go and meet him.

11

There was only one cafe at the end of Rosenkrantz Street, and only one person loitering around outside when I got there. My first thought was that it couldn't be him. But it was. He came over to me immediately and spoke in his distinctive gruff voice. 'Buy me a coffee, then?' he asked, as the waiter approached.

The waiter sent me a questioning look, then bowed slightly when I asked for two coffees and two Danish pastries.

My witness sat with his elbows on the table, the right side of his face covered by his hand. I thought to myself it was unlikely that that hand could have strangled any of the victims. I mused that if the gruff voice belonged to a man in his forties or fifties, then the dark and evasive eyes under the cap certainly did too. But the boy was no more than fifteen and of slim build. His denim jacket was worn and his jeans had been patched in several places. This was not a witness who would be taken seriously in court. And yet I believed he would tell me the truth.

I said that I appreciated his openness, and that I perhaps should not ask why he was at Tveita Shopping Centre. He nodded. The shadow of a smile flickered on his lips, but vanished as soon as he started talking.

'I'm no mummy's boy, no. But I might have been if I'd actually had a mum, instead of growing up in a children's home.'

We were interrupted by the waiter, who came over with the coffee and Danish pastries. I gave him two ten-kroner notes and said that he could keep the change. He took the hint and retreated quickly.

My guest sipped his coffee with the left-hand side of his mouth, and did not take his hand away from the right side.

'What interests me is not who you are or what you were doing at Tveita yesterday, but what you saw,' I said.

My young witness leaned forwards over the table and lowered his voice when he replied.

'I saw a bloke in blue overalls. He walked across the car park and came into the centre, and he was carrying a big mail sack over his shoulder. I noticed him cos of the sack, and cos he didn't chase me off, like most of the janis do when they see me. There were three possibilities: he was new to the job, he was an undercover agent, or he was a criminal of some sort hisself. Didn't want to get caught up in nothing, so I left him well alone and went outside. Hung around outside for about five minutes, but didn't see him again. Ran off when I saw one of the other janis, the old fat one, come out and head in my direction. But when I heard on the radio last night that a body'd been found in a mail sack at Tveita Shopping Centre, I knew there was a connection. And when I read the paper today, there it was. So I called you.'

I said that was a good move, and asked if he could give me a description of the man with the mail sack. I then hastily asked whether he was sure that it was a man, to which he nodded vigorously.

'Dead certain it was a man. Hair on his arms and nothing exciting under his shirt. He was wearing a cap, dark glasses and beard, which was probably false, mind. Taller than me, which is not saying much. Smaller than you, and he seemed to be pretty fit. I'd guess in his twenties or thirties, but not easy to say, really. Kind of normal body. Dark-brown hair, but might have been dyed or a wig, right enough.'

I listened with fascination. If the boy was telling the truth, this was the clearest picture we had of the shadowy Anthill Murderer. In other words, we were talking about a man who was between five foot five and five foot nine, which certainly disqualified some, but fitted a number of the men I had met, and thousands more I had never met.

'I'm not a reliable witness. I know that much. I'd never appear in court and no one'd believe me if I did. But I rang you, so I've done what I can. There were loads of posh people there in nice clothes who must've seen him too, but I bet they haven't called.'

I thought quietly to myself that he had a point, but instead asked him if he had seen which car in the car park the man had got out of, and whether he had the mail sack with him then.

'Sorry, didn't see what car he got out of. But he had the sack over his shoulder when he came over from the far side of the car park and there were only four cars standing there. A big black 1969-model Mercedes, a red Toyota – think it was last year's model – a blue 1950s Amazon and a yellow 1965 Peugeot with a taxi light on the roof.'

I scribbled this down and remarked that he certainly knew his cars. A faint smile played on his lips again when he replied.

'Thanks. Have to be good at something, I suppose, and I've got a thing about cars. Dream about getting my own one day. But that won't be for years yet.'

As he spoke, he lowered his hand from his right cheek. I immediately understood why he had kept it there for so long. There was a wound with three straight sides, as if someone had carved a triangle there.

I could not help staring at the wound. He noticed and put his hand up again.

'No connection. Got this on Wednesday night – a work conflict, let's say. It hurt then and doesn't look too good now, but time heals all wounds, as they say. And I could do worse than a scar on my cheek.'

His coarse, old man's voice drawled when he said this. Then he drained his cup of coffee, put what was left of the Danish pastry in his pocket and stood up abruptly. He paused for a moment when I asked why he had phoned me.

'I rang cos I don't like men who strangle young women,

even though I don't have a great relationship with the police myself. And for once, I had the chance to talk to someone decent.'

I told him it had been very useful, and held out my hand. His handshake was firm and brief, and he gave another wan smile. Then suddenly he was up and away. I saw him slip into the crowd out on the street.

I stayed where I was and pensively ate my Danish pastry. It was rather chewy.

I considered getting up and running after my kind helper. Miriam had done that kind of thing on a couple of occasions when we were out together. But she wasn't here and I was not Miriam. I wouldn't know what to say if I did, and then before I had the chance, he was gone.

I sat there wondering how he had ended up in a children's home – it must have been sometime in the late 1950s – and who had carved the triangle on his cheek this week. In a way, both things were irrelevant. He was not a potential suspect; his was just another sad story about a young person who had not had a good start in life. And neither he nor I could answer the big question as to where his life would go from here.

III

It's been an unusually quiet Saturday today. I haven't left the house, and haven't heard a voice other than my own.

Yesterday evening's fiasco is still playing on my mind and under my skin. I've left the newspaper lying by the door, front page down, and have not switched on the radio. I know it will feel humiliating to hear news reports where I'm not mentioned. It shouldn't have been like this today. And it will be different tomorrow.

This morning I dreamed I was back at Young's Square. Her friend wasn't with her. I had my hands around Fatima's throat and was squeezing hard. Her body spasmed and she was about to collapse, but then some faceless people came running towards me. I stood there, debating whether to let go and run. I woke up before I had made a decision.

The possibility of being arrested came up again, and I lay there thinking about it. I have prepared myself for being caught, ever since the first murder. Every morning this week, I have woken and thought the police would be at my door before breakfast. But they weren't, and not today either. I'm not just surprised, but almost a little disappointed.

I had accepted the idea of an extensive trial and prison sentence long before I committed the first murder. I'm looking forward to the trial with all the photographs and attention, but I can't say that I'm looking forward to life in prison. I do think it might be better, though, than the lonely captivity I live in now. For years I've trudged the same boring path, without any acknowledgement for the work I do. I might even meet some like-minded people in prison. Apparently murderers get lots of letters, love letters and letters from people who want to know who they are. That would make a nice change, as all I've received in the post in the past few months is bills. I've already started to think about answers to some of the questions they might ask about who I am and how I became a murderer. Maybe it will be the start of a better life later. If I'm sentenced to ten or twelve years, I still won't be old when I get out. Life will still have plenty to offer. Whatever the case, anything would be better than the increasingly irritating and boring life I've been leading for the past few years.

The thought of being killed myself is less attractive than being arrested. I've considered that possibility too, of course. The police will be itchy on the trigger now, and you can never know for certain that the victim or some random passer-by is not armed. Today I thought that *maybe it would be the best thing. If I'm killed, my boredom dies along with me and I avoid all the discomfort and disadvantages of a prison sentence. My name would live on. The newspapers would call me a mystery. Books would be written about me, and perhaps a famous actor might even play me in a film. It would be a bit of a shame, though, not to stand up in court and not to be able to answer those letters. But apart from that, it would be fine. I would still have done this, even if I knew it would result in my own death. The value of a life can't be measured in the number of days lived. Better to have lived a short life full of excitement and to have been someone, than to live a long life without excitement or meaning. I have lived my life as an anonymous ant for long enough.*

Ahead of this evening and the next chapter in my life as a murderer, I feel the thrill of anticipation, but no fear. The hours drag by so slowly it's unbearable. I don't feel like going out. But it's almost midday now, so I can at least make myself some lunch. Wonder what that Kolbjørn Kristiansen and the police are doing today. They should have been on my tail by now, if they were going to save young Fatima. But there's nothing to indicate that they even suspect me. I've managed to hide away in this anthill of a city. Everyone is talking about the Ant Murderer, but only I know who he is – and who will be his next victim.

IV

At ten to one, I was back in the office of Meyer-Michelsen & Wendelmann A/S. There was a medium-sized bouquet from Wendelmann on the table closest to the entrance, with a card that read, *With my deepest condolences.* But Mr Wendelmann himself was nowhere to be seen. The place was empty, as the rest of the staff had finished for the day at noon. Christoffer

Meyer-Michelsen was in his office. I waited outside, with his flaming-haired secretary.

Rikke Johansen had smiled bravely when she saw me, and had said she would appreciate it if I could wait until one before disturbing the director. He seemed to be better today and very much in control, but it might be best to stick to the agreed time. I knew that people who were grieving could often get very upset by surprises, and trusted that she knew him well.

In the meantime, I looked through the morning papers. A report on the significance of the EEC debate for the Liberal Party was at the top of the front page of *Dagbladet*, but the greater part of the page was dedicated to the murder case, under the headline 'Multi-Millionairess Strangled by Serial Killer in Shopping Centre'. They had all the information included in the early morning editions and tried to outdo them with an even bigger photograph of Amalie Meyer-Michelsen and a drawing of an ant. However, there was no new information of any interest in the report and the only slightly uncomfortable reading was the final comment that 'The police do not yet seem to have a suspect in their hunt for the evil ladykiller.' I noted, to my relief, that Mikael Grundtvig Sparde had been given the case. He was an unusually popular reporter down at the main station, in part due to his competence and understanding, but largely due to his patience and tolerance for the police. Sparde could be uncompromising when it came to publishing new information as soon as he got it, but had, on the other hand, always shown respect for the police and the judicial system.

The article in *Verdens Gang* was less pleasant reading, but also a little more interesting. The paper had put the EEC to one side for a day. Young Knud Haasund had splashed the murder case over nearly the whole front page, under the headline 'Serial Murderer at Large'. The photograph of Amalie Meyer-Michelsen was even bigger and supplemented with a picture of her father. The third photograph on the front page was of the queue waiting to give statements at Tveita Shopping Centre. And the fourth was an old picture of me, with the text: 'Detective Inspector Kolbjørn Kristiansen has been remarkably unforthcoming, giving grounds to fear that the police still have no clear leads when it comes to the murderer.'

The interesting information was printed under the photograph of Christoffer Meyer-Michelsen. *Verdens Gang* stated that 'This personal tragedy comes at a very difficult time for the hotel magnate as his business empire is on the brink of collapse.'

I read this twice. And after reading it a second time, I waved the secretary over and asked her what her impression was of the relationship between Meyer-Michelsen and his business partner, and what they had talked about at yesterday's marathon meeting.

Her mouth tightened. She spoke quietly when she replied, and there was a sharpness to her voice.

'Apparently they were once close friends, but that must have been a long time ago. When I first started working here, the tone between them was very businesslike, but it has become more and more strained recently. Mr Wendelmann and his son have spent as little time here as possible over the past twelve months. The son arrived about a quarter of an hour before the meeting was due to start, but the father got here on the dot and didn't even say hello. The director is very frustrated about the situation. He's in the middle of new building projects here in Norway and there are some excellent opportunities to expand abroad, but his business partner is like a ball and chain. The problem is that Christoffer is just as aggressive and ambitious as he always has been, even though he's now over fifty, whereas Mr Wendelmann has become increasingly defensive and risk-averse.'

There was no doubt as to where her sympathies lay; there was a marked contrast in the way she talked about Mr Wendelmann and Christoffer. She was aware of this and remarked that she was perhaps a bit biased. She certainly tried to rectify this before I could even ask another question.

'In his defence, Mr Wendelmann is no doubt more worried about his son's future than his own. He is also a widower with only one son, and behind his stern facade is perhaps just as tied to his son as Christoffer was to Amalie. But whatever the case, he and Christoffer are drifting further and further apart.'

I realized that this conflict could be a possible motive. So I probed a bit more and asked what specifically yesterday's meeting had been about.

Rikke Johansen gave a deep sigh. For the first time, she seemed neither young nor dynamic herself.

'The same as all the countless phones calls and discussions they've had in the past few weeks. Wendelmann, with encouragement from his son, wants to split the company and to realize his equity. From a business point of view, it's madness to want to leave the table at a point like this. It's also impossible, legally. Christoffer made sure that he had all the necessary powers before embarking on his last offensive, and Wendelmann can't pull out until the end of 1973. Legally, Christoffer has nothing to worry about, but the constant nagging from his business partner is clearly very wearing. The other day he remarked that battling on two fronts is four times as tiring as battling on one.'

The secretary broke off when the door to Meyer-Michelsen's office opened. It was exactly one o'clock when he appeared in the doorway, correctly dressed in a black suit and white shirt. His back was straight, he looked fit and his handshake was firm. It was impossible not to be impressed.

All the papers had been tidied from his desk when I went into the office. The photograph of Amalie smiled at us as we sat down. I so desperately wanted to find her murderer, for her sake as well as her father's, and for all the others left behind. But unfortunately there was not much help to be had here either.

Christoffer Meyer-Michelsen looked at me intently and answered all my questions clearly and succinctly, but was not interested in elaborating. He didn't know of any earlier boyfriends or scorned admirers who might have a motive for killing his daughter. As far as he knew, she had never had another boyfriend nor refused any offers. She was very happy with her fiancé. Even though he knew that there was considerable anxiety about the ability to have children, he had seen nothing to indicate that there was any tension. He simply could not understand who on earth would want to harm her.

'I can understand that a lot of people might not like me, but my daughter had done nothing to hurt anyone. The only explanation I can find is that she was the random victim of a murderer who didn't know her,' he concluded authoritatively after a five-minute conversation.

I pointed out that it was still a mystery how the murderer could know that she was going to Tveita Shopping Centre.

Christoffer Meyer-Michelsen furrowed his brow and

thought for a moment, but couldn't come up with anything. He had only been told at the breakfast table that his daughter was going to Tveita, and had mentioned it to no one other than the secretary later. His daughter had not said whether she had told anyone else, but then she rarely discussed her day-to-day activities with anyone except him and her fiancé.

I remarked that it seemed slightly odd that a wealthy young woman from Skøyen should go shopping in Tveita. He gave a sharp nod, and a shadow of a smile twitched at his lips when he replied.

'That is, of course, correct, but Amalie was a little eccentric that way. Where other young women clamour for attention, all she wanted was to be left in peace. The reason for this was quite simply that she had been stopped a number of times by acquaintances and strangers in Steen & Strøm and other shops where wealthy young women from Skøyen usually shop. So she tried Tveita Shopping Centre last year, and was pleasantly surprised by the selection of shops and the fact that no one had recognized her. My poor daughter went to the east side of town to avoid attention. In a way it's typical of her endless search for a peace she never found.'

This was more than anything he had said so far, and his voice was thick by the end. But in contrast to his outpouring of emotion the day before, Meyer-Michelsen now seemed to be controlled, if resigned. He was serious and spoke in a quiet voice, so obviously still affected by his daughter's death. I got the impression, however, that he had not only accepted that she was gone forever, but that he had also come to terms with his own fate.

Only once in the course of our conversation did his emotions betray him, and that was when I told him that his daughter had been pregnant when she died. He covered his face with his hands briefly, and then asked if the baby was a boy or a girl. Without waiting for an answer, he added that it was strange that his daughter had mentioned nothing to him.

I told him that it was not possible to know the gender of the child as Amalie was only a few weeks pregnant, and she might not even have been aware of it herself.

He said that sounded reasonable.

A question that I did not particularly wish to ask still hung in the air, and I could not leave without an answer. So eventually I asked it in a roundabout way, by saying that his loss must be all the harder when, as I understood it, so many demands were being made of him in connection with his business.

To my relief, he didn't make a fuss. He simply answered curtly that any reports in the papers about his business were unfounded and that even major deals felt small at the moment. Furthermore, he believed that the disagreement between him and his business partner would be resolved very shortly.

He said this with such calm and certainty that I immediately believed him. I reckoned that he now planned to accept dividing up the business and letting his business partner go his own way. But from what he had told me, his business had nothing to do with his daughter's death and therefore was no longer of interest to me.

When we parted at a quarter past one, the mood was cordial. I wished him luck with his business and future. He thanked me and said that he had every confidence that with time I would manage to catch the murderer.

I was stopped by the secretary on my way out. She asked if I had got answers to all my questions, and whether the director was holding up.

I told her honestly that his composure was impressive, but that the loss of his daughter was obviously hard to bear and that it was good that he had her to support him in the period ahead.

She gave a careful smile and was about to say something, but then froze.

'NO!' she screamed, and pointed a shaking finger over my shoulder.

As I spun round, I couldn't see anyone. But the secretary continued to point at the large window facing the street. I immediately understood why – and stood there as though paralysed myself.

Christoffer Meyer-Michelsen was standing just outside the window, his body turned away from us. But there was no veranda or balcony out there for him to stand on.

For a moment I had the unreal feeling that he was standing on thin air. Then I realized he must be balanced on some kind of cornice or ledge.

The secretary regained her movement before I did. She ran over to the window and put her hands out towards him, but they were stopped by the glass. The sound made Meyer-Michelsen turn towards us.

For a brief moment he raised his hand in a final greeting. His face was without expression, as though carved in stone.

He jumped like a diver, head first.

Through an open side window, I heard the thud when he hit the ground and then the shouts from the street below.

The secretary stared petrified at the window, then threw her arms around me with unexpected force. I could feel her heart hammering furiously and heard her gasping for air. I thought she might faint and that she should definitely not look out of the window. So I carefully disengaged myself, led her over to a chair and asked her to stay there. She nodded almost imperceptibly, her eyes fixed on the window.

I went over alone and looked out. Meyer-Michelsen was lying on the pavement below; his neck was twisted and he was not moving. Four or five passers-by had stopped and were standing almost devoutly beside him. The traffic on the road had stopped completely.

Christoffer Meyer-Michelsen had been a man who made an impact on his environment and attracted attention to the very end. But now he was dead. I had only met him for the first time yesterday, and my first impression had been poor, but now I felt that his death was a great tragedy and that I had witnessed the fall of a giant.

There could be no doubt as to the reason for his deadly plunge. As far as I knew, the director, his loyal secretary and I were the only three people on that floor. He had been alone in his office when I spoke with him a few minutes earlier and no one could have gone in after me without passing the secretary and myself. But in the end, I could not stop myself going into his office, instead of towards the exit. There was obviously nothing I could do down on the street. But up here, I might find something that would throw light on this increasingly tragic murder investigation.

The draught from the open window hit me as soon as I opened the door to his office. There was no evidence of any struggle there. As far as I could see, the only change was that the photograph of Amalie had been moved from the desk to the mahogany table, where it stood on top of a folded sheet of paper.

Christoffer Meyer-Michelsen had been a consummate businessman to the last. The piece of paper under the photograph was a will, dated 29 April 1972, with the signatures of two witnesses, as required. The text was short and concise.

> Even though they are the children of my late sister, I do not want the two greedy parasites to benefit from my daughter's death. I therefore leave half my property and fortune to the only person other than myself who loved my daughter: her fiancé Rolf Johan Svendsen. The other half I leave to the only person who has loved me after the death of my wife, other than my daughter: my secretary, Rikke Johansen.

I read the lines about six or seven times. On the final couple of readings, I realized that I would now have to talk to the two who had been heirs to tens of millions only the day before, but now, without knowing it, had had everything taken from them.

I jumped when I turned around. She had slipped in silently through the open door and was standing stock-still only a couple of feet from me. She still didn't say a word, just stood there looking at me askance.

'This is a new will that leaves half of everything he owned to his daughter's fiancé – and half to you,' I said.

'Oh,' she replied in an apathetic voice, with no sign of interest on her face.

Then she fainted.

V

Rolf Johan Svendsen read it with a frown.

I imagined that that was how he read legal documents at

work too. I had to admit that his apparent equanimity was both impressive and annoying. He had looked a little surprised when he heard that his future father-in-law had committed suicide, but had not shown any signs of upset. And now he knew that the death had made him a multimillionaire he still looked a little surprised, but showed no signs of delight.

'I had no idea,' he said. He put down the copy of the will and looked over at the wall. I struggled to catch his eye, and even more to understand who he was and how he thought.

I asked if he had spoken to Mr Meyer-Michelsen after the news of his daughter's death yesterday.

'Yes, but only very briefly. I called him at home around seven in the evening, to convey my condolences. Rikke, his secretary, answered the phone, but let me speak to him when I said why I had called. Meyer-Michelsen himself was very sombre and weighed down by grief, but still composed. He thanked me for everything I had done for his daughter, and said that he was enormously grateful for the consideration I had shown him. Then he politely, but very definitely, made it clear that enough had been said.'

As far as I could tell, he was still telling the truth. When she had regained consciousness, the secretary had said that Rolf Johan Svendsen had called between seven and half past the evening before, and that the conversation with Meyer-Michelsen had lasted no longer than a few minutes. She had made a note of all other callers and taken messages. The director had remarked several times how pleased he was that Amalie's fiancé had called and said he was disappointed that neither of his sister's children had done the same.

'But none of us knew he had any plans to change his will

– and certainly not that he planned to take his own life,' the secretary had said, in a shaky voice.

I believed her. And I still saw no reason to suspect Rolf Johan Svendsen, other than that I found it hard to catch his eye. The fact that he did not ask or show any interest in the value of the will was both agreeable and inclined to inspire trust.

I had one card left to play. I consciously chose to use his fiancée's first name and kept my eyes glued on him to see if there was any reaction.

'The autopsy has shown that Amalie was in fact in the very early stages of pregnancy when she was killed,' I said.

The response was striking. And yet it was what I had expected. I felt that I was finally starting to understand him.

To begin with, there was no reaction, other than a slight lifting of the eyebrows. Then he said, 'I didn't know about that either.'

Rolf Johan Svendsen had suddenly and silently shed a single tear for his fiancée the first time I came to speak to him. Now he shed another, just as suddenly and just as silently. I sat there and watched the tear slide down his cheek and wondered if it was for her or the unborn child. Then the tear vanished, and I had run out of questions.

He came with me to the door, and just as he was about to open it, he started to speak.

'A Knud Haasund from *Verdens Gang* was at the door about an hour ago. And then *Dagbladet* came shortly after. Neither of them knew that Meyer-Michelsen was dead or about the will, but they both asked me about Amalie's death, if I would inherit her share and the implications for her father and his business. I confirmed that I was engaged to Amalie, but said that I was grieving and would make no further comment. They both respected this, but no doubt now they'll be back again soon. Do you have any advice on what I should and should not say to them?'

My first thought was that I was glad that there would be no newspaper editions until Tuesday, because of the first of May. The mass media's interest in the case could be expected to soar following the dramatic suicide of the hotel king.

So I said that he was free to say what he liked about himself and his possible inheritance, but that I would appreciate it if he said as little as possible about his contact with the police and anything that might be of significance to the case. He promised to be very selective about what he said to the press.

VI

The two people referred to only as parasites in Christoffer Meyer-Michelsen's will were in fact called Rakel and Robert Enger. They were twenty-six and twenty-eight respectively, and lived at two different addresses in Eidsvoll. But both were now sitting in my office at the main station. I understood what Meyer-Michelsen had meant, but could not decide whether it was true or not.

'You'll have to excuse the fact that we're not showing any sorrow at our uncle's death. His daughter's fate was truly tragic. But our uncle treated our mother very badly, and our sympathies of course lie with her,' Rakel Enger said. She was a tall, voluptuous, perhaps slightly overweight blonde who seemed to be honest. Her eyesight was obviously quite poor as she squinted at me over the desk.

'It's shameful the way he treated Mother and us. But now that wrong will be righted. We must be his closest family, as his daughter died before him and he had no other heirs,' Robert Enger chimed in, and looked at me enquiringly.

He was shorter, slimmer and darker than his sister, and he gave the impression of being better read, perhaps thanks to his horn-rimmed glasses. But I still liked him less. I found it distasteful that someone should ask so directly about the inheritance so soon after a close relative's death. My sympathy for Rakel Enger also dwindled when she nodded eagerly to what he said – and looked at me enquiringly.

I produced a copy of the will and placed it on the desk between us. Their eyes immediately dropped to look at it, and I watched them carefully as they read. He read it faster than her, but the only reaction was a furrowed brow and a small sigh.

Her reaction was stronger. She hit the table and then burst into tears. 'That man was loathsome to the bitter end,' she cried.

Her brother gave another sigh – deeper this time. Then he gently put an arm round his sister's shoulders. He said nothing. Just sat there with his arm round her. Her whole body shook with emotion, but he was just as calm and collected.

I thought that even though they were apparently very different, they were suspiciously in agreement when it came to their late uncle. There could quite possibly be a motive for one or more murders here, especially if they thought that their cousin's death sooner or later might give them an inheritance of several million kroner. I asked straight out why they had such ill feelings towards their uncle.

Once again, their reactions to the question differed, but

they appeared to be finely tuned. She tried to say something, but the words got stuck in her throat. So she sat there biting her lip, and he did the talking. There was a slight tremor in his voice, but the words were well chosen and the sentences well articulated.

'To be honest, it's a shameful family story that we, personally, have no reason to hide. Our maternal grandfather was a successful businessman, who agreed to transfer all his companies to his son before his death. Our mother was only given a small amount as compensation, but with the promise that the difference would be levelled at the next generation, so that her children would get a share of the companies equal his. When we were close to coming of age, our grandfather died, and our uncle denied any knowledge of the agreement. Our mother had grown up in the shadow of her dominating brother, and absolutely trusted his word when he said the agreement had been made. She should of course have insisted on having it in writing, and blamed herself for that until her dying day. Mother drank heavily and in the end lost her house in a forced sale, while her brother bought more and more hotels. His daughter got anything and everything she pointed at and wanted for nothing. My sister and I, on the other hand, had to look after ourselves and our drunken mother, and get a job like most normal people. We hope that you can understand why we don't feel any grief at the loss of our uncle – and that we are genuinely disappointed that even after his daughter's death, we won't inherit any part of the wealth that should rightly have been shared with us long ago.'

I really did not particularly like the formulation 'like most normal people', but it was clear that this brother and sister and their mother had been treated appallingly, and their reaction was therefore understandable. I probed a little more and asked where they worked. The question provoked some more sobs from her, and another long tirade from him.

'I am, with help from the public purse, a qualified teacher and work in a secondary school. My sister has not managed to motivate herself to get any training, so she has had various badly paid jobs. For a while she was actually a receptionist in one of our uncle's hotels, but was then suddenly fired without explanation. At the moment, she works as a cleaner at the school where I teach. Can you think of a more insulting and humiliating situation for a woman of her background?'

I could in fact think of many more humiliating situations than working as a cleaner. But my feelings vacillated between considerable irritation at this pair's open sense of superiority and a degree of sympathy for their situation as a result of losing their mother's inheritance. I also felt that this was the closest we had got to a motive for murder. I therefore asked if they had had any contact with their uncle and cousin recently.

They glanced quickly at each other. He nodded, but then it was suddenly she who spoke.

'We only met her a few times when we were little. How much she knew and what she thought about the matter, we have no idea. But it was inevitable that we disliked her when she had unfairly got our mother's money, whether it was intended on her part or not. As we never heard anything from her, it didn't seem natural to send her birthday presents, especially as we had so little money. We talked about sending flowers and our condolences now that she was dead, but weren't sure how her father would react. We put off making a decision until after the weekend. Perhaps not the right move.'

It certainly wasn't, I thought to myself. Only a couple of hours ago, the secretary had told me that the director had remarked: 'Not a word, not so much as a flower from them; they're no doubt rubbing their hands with glee at the thought of getting Ama's millions! Those parasites make me sick!'

I did not feel like mentioning this. Instead, I turned to look at her brother, and asked if they had had any direct contact with the director himself in recent years.

'Yes, but no, is perhaps the right answer. We invited him to Mother's funeral, and later sent a couple of letters asking for a modest amount to help us get on in life. I remember I sent him a letter asking for financial help when I wanted to start studying. It would be both financially irresponsible and humiliating for someone with my background to go through university on a student loan. But we never got an answer, not with regard to my mother's funeral, or my studies. And we had nothing but my mother's side of the story, which we knew would not hold up in court. So we gave up, and in the past few years we've just tried to forget our uncle and all the millions he swindled from us. It hasn't been easy, as there are constantly photographs of him in the newspapers and reports about how many hotels and how much money he has.'

'But then yesterday, the hope of getting an inheritance was revived,' I suggested. To my surprise, it was she who answered this time.

'Yes. It sounds awful, but we can at least be honest. We tried not to have any strong feelings against his daughter, but we certainly didn't care for her. Neither of us believes in divine justice or anything like that any more, but after the initial shock, yes, we did think that finally there might be some kind of recompense for us. An old dream of a new and better life was rekindled yesterday and then promptly extinguished when you showed us the new will.'

I told them that I appreciated their honesty, and then asked about their civil status.

'We have both had steady partners at various times, but are single at the moment, and think perhaps it's best that way. Our father soon disappeared when Mother started to drink too much, and has shown no interest in us since then. And that, along with the story of our mother and her brother, means that the idea of family is perhaps not as attractive to us as it is to many others. Or certainly not in my case,' he said.

'Or mine,' his sister added. Her voice was sullen and did not invite any further questions on the matter.

Instead, I asked where they had been on Monday evening between half past ten and half past eleven, Wednesday evening between ten and eleven, and the morning before between ten and twelve.

'Do you really suspect one of us of murder?' she cut in, her voice shrill with indignation.

'He in fact suspects one of us of being a triple murderer. But he is only doing his duty and we should not be offended. And in any case, neither of us has anything to hide. On Monday and Wednesday evenings I was at home, alone, unfortunately. And on Friday morning I should have been at work, but was instead at home in bed with a cold,' Robert Enger informed me.

His sister caught her breath a couple of times and then sat very still before speaking, with hard-won composure.

'I'm afraid I'm not much better. On Fridays I only work after classes are finished, so I was at home in the morning. On Wednesday, I cleaned until six and then was at home for the rest of the evening. And on Monday, I was invited out to dinner by a man after work, but went home alone around nine.'

This was said with a slight flush in her cheeks.

'I didn't know, I'm sorry to hear that,' her brother said.

It struck me that they genuinely cared about each other, but showed little interest in anyone else. That is perhaps what happens, I thought, when there are only two of you and you share a family history like that. Particularly if you do not have your own family.

'Is there not even a shadow of a doubt that this is valid and will be accepted by a court?' she asked suddenly, and pointed at the will.

I replied that I was not a lawyer, but that we currently had no reason to doubt the validity of the new will. The content was clear and the formalities were in order, given the signatures of both the deceased and the witnesses.

'Our heartless uncle, true to form, kept his papers in order if not his morals. I'm afraid I have to go and catch the bus so I'm not late for work – unless you have any more questions?' she said in a bitter voice.

I had no more questions and had no wish to add to their burden. So I thanked them for coming at such short notice and wished them well

He replied tersely: 'Thank you for that.' She said nothing.

I had seen a glow of hope in her face when she shook my hand on arrival, and a glimpse of anger when she punched the table. But now, as she left with her hands deep in the pockets of her jeans, she seemed to be utterly resigned.

Her brother once again put a supportive arm round her shoulders as they left. I thought that he was no doubt a good big brother. And I found it hard to imagine that the hand that now lay on his sister's shoulder had tightened round his cousin's neck the day before. But I could not rule it out. He was a man with a motive and no alibi. If he had been too ill to go to work yesterday, he had got better faster than most of the capital's inhabitants normally would when attacked by the lurgies of spring.

VII

'I was deeply shocked,' Henrik Harald Wendelmann said.

The effect was slightly comical, as he said this in a completely monotone voice and with a stony face. But the atmosphere in my office was very sombre indeed.

Mr Wendelmann was not talking about Christoffer Meyer-Michelsen's death, but about his business partner and the way the business had developed in recent years.

'I met him for the first time when we were about twenty-five and was immediately impressed by his self-confidence and aggressive business style. But that confidence became excessive over the years, and so his strength gradually became his weakness. In the early years, he listened to the advice and objections of others, including myself, behind closed doors, and often changed any decisions based on this. Then there was a period when he listened, but took less and less account of any such advice. And in recent years, he rarely listened to anyone other than himself. I said from the start that this most recent expansion was overambitious and came at the wrong time. The danger signs were ever clearer; he still didn't see them and simply refused to listen to those of us who did.'

'You didn't seem very surprised or upset when I told you that your partner had committed suicide,' I said.

This sounded slightly offensive, and that was the intention. But Mr Wendelmann was not a man to be provoked. He continued to talk in the same monotone voice and his face remained just as stony.

'I have to admit that I was neither particularly surprised, nor particularly saddened. I still remember the day in 1932 – I was no more than a youth at the time – when I woke up to the news that the Swedish industry magnate Ivar Kreuger had shot himself, in a situation where his apparently impressive financial empire was in fact on the brink of collapse. In the past few months, I have thought on several occasions that there were alarming similarities between Kreuger and my partner. Kreuger had no children to live for, and nor did Meyer-Michelsen, after his daughter's tragic death. Only this morning, I realized that this might now happen. And when I heard that it had, I thought it was a sad end for a great man, but realized that it would also save the company and us. And by us, I mean myself and my son.'

'From what I understand, you had for a long time been trying to find an alternative solution for you and your son – as you discussed yesterday,' I said.

'Yes, that's true. I tried to be as solicitous as I could, and said that either we worked together as partners again, and that he actually listened to what I had to say, or, as friends, it was time for us to dissolve the business partnership and go our separate ways. But he was not willing to consider either option. He accused me, as chairman of the board, of wanting to jump ship in the middle of a storm and said that things seldom turned out well for mutineers. In the end, I got angry and said that, as captain, he was about to run his ship aground. He said that behind the storm we would soon see a whole new continent, and that I would later thank him for not letting me abandon ship. And yet the figures made for more and more alarming reading with each week that passed. Reason was on my side, the formalities on his. I could not dissolve the company and save my assets for another eighteen months at least, and increasingly feared that there would be nothing left to save.'

He paused for a moment, then carried on.

'I have been a good sleeper all my life and never worried about my own circumstances. But recently I have lain awake at night worrying about my son's future. I invested all the money I inherited from my father in the company, and it was a galling thought that I now might have risked it all and would leave my son with nothing.'

Henrik Harald Wendelmann was on a roll, and did not need me to ask questions.

'He's all I have now, after my wife's death. I understood only too well how Christoffer must have felt when he lost his only child. At the same time, I hoped that it would be the saving of my son's future, something I had thought about every day for the past year. Everyone thinks about their own children first, especially those of us who only have one.'

He still spoke in his irritatingly monotone voice, but I did now have a more favourable impression of him. The fears about his only son's future were understandable enough, even for someone who did not yet have children. And I told him so, then asked if he had had a better relationship with his business partner in the past.

'Absolutely, yes. We met when we were both students at the

School of Economics just after the war and, back then, got on like a house on fire. He had lots of ambitious plans and some family money to back them, and was looking for a sensible business partner with more capital. I needed a business partner with more ambition and drive than I had. So it was a perfect combination that for many years gave good results. The company was successful and we got on very well. Our wives were best friends and we often joked that we hoped a romance might blossom between our children in the future. It felt quite natural to buy homes in the same street, and for many years we were constantly in and out of each other's houses. But that's a long time ago. After my wife died, ten years back now, family parties were less and less frequent, and even more so when his wife died too. And given our disagreement about business matters in recent years, what was left of our friendship has evaporated. It's sad, but true.'

I mused for a moment that when you spoke to Wendelmann one-to-one, and managed to get behind the mask, it was possible to understand and even sympathize with him. I said that Meyer-Michelsen had apparently had a conflict with his late sister, and asked if he knew anything about this.

'If he ever mentioned it to me, it must have been so long ago that I can't remember,' was his answer.

Wendelmann only paused a beat before he said this, but it was just long enough for me to understand the truth in what he said. We looked at each other afterwards and both of us knew exactly what had happened. Meyer-Michelsen had told him about the demands that his sister and her children were making. The reason that he no longer mentioned it was probably because those demands were more or less justified. Wendelmann's answer did not deny that that was the case, but was vague enough not to have negative consequences for him and his son. Should it later be discovered that Meyer-Michelsen had in fact spoken to him about it, we could still never prove he remembered it when I asked.

'Meyer-Michelsen was a man who kept his papers in order,' I said.

Wendelmann did not respond to my comment, in words or with a gesture. I took that to be a confirmation of the story regarding Meyer-Michelsen and his sister.

I then went on to ask where he and his son had been on Monday evening, Wednesday evening and Friday morning.

'Your assistant, Mr Helgesen, has already asked me about this in detail. And I will of course tell you what I told him. On Monday evening I went to the National Theatre to see my son performing in a play. On Wednesday, I was invited to dinner at eight with a business contact and his wife, and was there until around midnight. And on Friday, I was in my other office from nine until eleven, and then had an early lunch with my son before our meeting with Meyer-Michelsen.'

That all sounded plausible enough, and thus gave him an alibi for all three murders. I was not sure that I would trust Wendelmann in any situation, but I could not imagine him as a murderer, sneaking around with drawings of ants in his pocket. So I thanked him for his time and cooperation and then asked his son to come into my office.

Harald Henrik Wendelmann was not as stiff as his father, and still made a far better impression. He agreed with his father's statement on most points. With slightly theatrical pathos, he confirmed that his father's relationship with Meyer-Michelsen had been 'close, if not always warm', but more recently had been 'distant and icy'.

After yesterday's sensational news about the murder of Amalie Meyer-Michelsen, the news of her father's death was less of a shock. His father had said that he was not sure that Meyer-Michelsen would survive the trauma.

'Father also said it would be hard for him to find the will to live if anything similar should happen to me, which is a reflection of his feelings about life and being a father. So no, it wasn't such a surprise.'

Wendelmann junior also admitted, with refreshing honesty, that he had not felt any great sorrow.

'It felt strange, because Meyer-Michelsen was such a big and powerful man, and when I was a boy I thought he was immortal. As an adult, of course, I now know that everyone dies and is vulnerable, and that those who appear to be the greatest and strongest are often the most vulnerable. Please don't get me wrong, though; I in no way wanted Meyer-Michelsen to commit suicide, but when he did, I hoped that it would be the end of a nightmare that has plagued my father for at least a year now. Our meeting yesterday gave me no reason to feel any sympathy for him. You could say that when I heard of his death I was perhaps relieved, but certainly not glad.'

Wendelmann and his son reminded me in a way of the Enger siblings. Once again I was talking to two closely related people who were very different in personality and nature, and yet remarkably unified in their narrative. This was true of their alibis for the murders that week as well.

'On Monday I had a performance, so I was on stage between nine and eleven, and didn't leave the theatre until after midnight. I spotted Father in the auditorium several times during the show. On Wednesday evening, I was at a friend's birthday party, and left between half past ten and eleven o'clock. Then on Friday morning, I got up late as I'd had a performance the night before, and met my father for what he called lunch and I called breakfast, at eleven, ahead of the meeting at midday. And we were with Meyer-Michelsen until we met you.'

He talked with insight and energy. I thought to myself that he really was an actor by nature, and I would not trust him in all situations either. But I did not think he was a serial killer; he seemed a bit too rational for that, behind his theatrical bluster. And in any case, he and his father had the best alibis so far. So I let him go at three o'clock.

I sat on my own in the office for five minutes, feeling a bit hopeless, in terms of life in general, and the investigation in particular. So I called Patricia. She answered right away, and said in a strained voice, 'Has anything happened?'

Hearing her voice, even if it was tense, put me in a good mood for a few seconds. So I replied blithely that there had been no breakthrough in the investigation, but I would still appreciate being invited to dinner this evening. Her reply was prompt, and just what I had hoped.

'Well, in that case, I hope we can have dinner at yours today. My maid will of course bring everything with her: food, drink and the like. I think it might be prudent for you to be available to answer the phone this weekend. And it's good for me to get out. So as we were here yesterday and the day before . . . And it was so nice when I came to your flat last time . . .'

As usual, she was prepared. I could not argue with this without appearing to be petty and ungrateful. So I said that it would of course be fine to have dinner at mine, and suggested that we meet there at seven. She said, 'Perfect, see you then,' and hung up before I had the chance to say anything more.

VIII

At half past three there was a knock on my door. Detective Inspector Danielsen came in without waiting for an answer, with Helgesen at his heel. I realized that it was serious and that we were obviously in the same boat. The pressure was mounting on us all. Instead of commenting on the fact that they had just marched right in, I welcomed them and said how pleased I was that the list of alibis was ready. I had presumed this, as they were now standing in my office, and Helgesen was holding a sheaf of handwritten papers.

'I'm not sure that it will be of much help, unfortunately. But we have at least identified some parties we no longer need to worry about, and others we might like to follow up a bit more,' Danielsen said, and flapped a hand at Helgesen and his pile of paper.

'If we start with the first murder, we can definitely rule out the parents, Valdemar and Henriette Halvorsen. They were in Skien the evening their daughter was killed, and were with friends who had come to give their condolences on Friday morning. They only had each other as an alibi for Wednesday evening, it's true, but I think we can safely rule them out,' Helgesen began.

In my mind, I wondered if the ever-diligent Helgesen had perhaps made the list a little too comprehensive. Out loud, I said that his report was clearly very thorough, and asked him to continue.

'The brother, Helmer Halvorsen, is on shakier ground. In fact, he is one of five people on the list who doesn't have a watertight alibi for any of the murders. His fiancée has confirmed that she was with him on Monday evening, but she caught the bus home at ten to eleven, so left the flat a few minutes before that. He didn't go to the bus stop with her, so could have got to Hovseter by eleven to wait for his sister. On Wednesday he was at home alone all evening. And he took the Friday off work so he could go with his parents to the funeral director's, but got there a bit late at half past ten.'

Helgesen took a dramatic pause, and look up at me questioningly. I waved him on without comment.

'Agnes' friend, Nora, was at the School of Theology again on Friday, where she first had a lecture and then a short meeting with her personal tutor, Oscar Fredrik Bergendahl. Other people have confirmed that they were both there yesterday morning. We also established that Bergendahl was at the hospital visiting his wife on Wednesday evening. The library assistant, Astrid Marie Nordheim, can also be ruled out. She was home with her husband and several children on Monday, at a parents' evening in school on Wednesday and at work on Friday morning. The bus driver, Hilmar Lauritzen, also seems to be fairly sound. He was on the buses in the west end of town all day on Friday. But he was at home alone on both Monday and Wednesday evenings, though he says that he called his mother between half past ten and eleven. His mother is nearly eighty, and a bit forgetful. She assured us more than once that she had a good son who called her every evening, and that he had rung her just before she went to bed for the past few months. So it's not really worth spending much more time on him.'

I agreed and again commented that he really had been very thorough in his work. Helgesen thanked me, but was not put off his stride, nor did he accelerate.

'You asked me to check the alibis of everyone we had spoken to, and in this case, I would rather make three phone calls too many than one too few. The next person on the list is Arnold Eriksen, the senior adviser to the Employers' Confederation, who called and said that he had seen a man standing by the edge of the road at around the time that Agnes was murdered. He was not particularly cooperative, but then suddenly changed his tune when I threatened to call him in along with his wife. He promptly told us that he had had a very private meeting with a much younger woman in Østerås. The woman has confirmed this, and that he left at ten to eleven. But that is not to say that he didn't stop and kill Agnes Halvorsen himself. On Wednesday, however, he was celebrating his wife's birthday with guests, and he was at work all day on Friday. So he too can be struck from the list.'

I swung between admiration for the detail in Helgesen's work, and irritation at his long-windedness. So I made a gesture for him to speed up, which was only partially successful. He kept talking, but did not pick up pace.

'Then we have Agnes' fellow student, Jan Ove Eliassen, who attracted our interest. He was at home alone on Wednesday night, but on Friday morning, he was at the School of Theology as well. However, someone who was not there, and who does not have an alibi for Wednesday evening, is the other student, Trygve Andersen. He is the one who told us that he'd seen Agnes coming out of the cleaning cupboard. When I mentioned his name, the library assistant remembered an incident from the week before. Trygve Andersen had broken the silence in the library and made a snide remark to Agnes, because she was reading a book by the liberal theologist, Jacob Jervell. But this kind of minor disturbance was relatively usual and there were no other signs of conflict. Trygve Andersen claimed that he was at home alone in his bedsit on Wednesday evening and that he hadn't felt well enough to go to the lecture on Friday morning. And yet when I went to talk to him in his bedsit in Majorstuen, he seemed to be fine, there was an obvious anxiety in his voice and he didn't want to look at me. It might be worth asking him a few more questions, even though he doesn't strike me as the killing type.'

Again, I agreed. The rather weedy and careful Trygve Andersen did not look like a murderer to me. But he clearly could not be ruled out.

'So, Trygve Andersen is the second person who doesn't have alibis for any of the murders. If we now turn to Lise Eilertsen's friends and family, her mother seemed to be more upset at being asked about this than she was about her daughter's death. But when she did finally give an answer, her alibis were in order. She had been with her younger sister on Monday evening, and was visiting neighbours the evening her daughter was killed. On Friday morning, she was with her other daughter and her baby. We can also strike off Lise's sister: she was at home alone on Monday evening, but her husband was at home with her on Wednesday evening and her mother was with her on Friday morning. So they both have alibis, and in any case, it's doubtful that they physically could have been the murderer. The brother, however, is on thinner ice. His wife is in Bergen this week, visiting her sick father, so Lars Eilertsen was at home alone on both Monday and Wednesday evening, and on Friday he was at work in the bank, but did take a longer break than usual from half past ten to midday. He says that he went home, but there is no one who can confirm that. He is the third person without alibis for any of the murders.'

'So who are the last two?' I asked with some impatience.

'When we now look at the choir, the Pettersens are solid. He was at work and she was at the doctor's on Friday morning. So, even though neither of them has an alibi for Monday evening, and they only have each other for Wednesday evening, I think we can safely rule them out. The nun, Kari, is the fourth person who lacks alibis. She claims that she was at Katarina Convent at all three critical points. But as there were no prayers, services or other activities, God is her only witness. Earlier on Wednesday evening, she was seen by the sink washing up the most enormous pile of plates and pots and pans, which would surely have taken her all evening. But neither washing-up nor God qualify as good alibis here.'

I asked about Lise Eilertsen's male acquaintances.

'Atilo Hovarth was at the club on both Monday and Wednesday evening. He slept late on Friday morning, but met a couple of musicians down at the club around midday. So he has a watertight alibi for the first two murders, and a fairly good one for the third. Lise's one-night stand, Bjarne Haug, was at work in the Co-op from ten until five on Friday, so even though he is not on such solid ground for the first two murders, he can be ruled out of the third. Her former lover, Stein Hansen, however, is the fifth person who does not have an alibi for any of the murders. He stuck to his original statement regarding Monday evening, in other words that he had been on his way home from a gig, and claims that he went straight home from Club 7 on Wednesday evening. His only alibi for Friday morning is his bed. He says that he woke up alone at around eleven, but that no one saw him until he met a friend for a beer at one.'

I jotted down Stein Hansen as the fifth name on my list of

people who lacked alibis for all three murders, and asked if we were nearly finished with his report.

'Almost. Amalie's fiancé arrived at work as he said around ten o'clock and was sitting with some colleagues when they heard about the murder at Tveita on the radio around two o'clock. The Wendelmanns appear to be high and dry, bearing in mind that they gave each other an alibi for Friday morning. On Monday, they were both seen by lots of people at the theatre, and on Wednesday they were both out. The friend that Wendelmann junior was with happens to live in Tåsen, only a few minutes away from Berg, but several of the other guests have confirmed that Wendelmann left with them just before half past ten, some ten minutes after Lise was killed. Anyway, his performance at the theatre on Monday clearly rules him out. The secretary, Rikke Johansen, is not so lucky. She says she was at home with Christoffer Meyer-Michelsen on Monday and Wednesday evening, which is not entirely implausible, but hard to confirm now that he's dead. But several other employees have confirmed that she was in the office from nine o'clock on Friday. And you were going to talk to Meyer-Michelsen's niece and nephew. How did you get on?'

'Yes. They both say that they were home alone, so neither of them have alibis for any of the murders,' I told them.

Helgesen nodded emphatically and added their names to his list. 'In that case, we have a total of seven people without alibis. And I think the murderer's name is among them.'

He put the list down on the desk in front of me: seven names, with two question marks after each of them.

Helmer Halvorsen. Trygve Andersen. Lars Eilertsen. Kari Evensen. Stein Hansen. Rakel Enger. Robert Enger.

I read through the list of seven names three times, but it

was still no clearer to me who the murderer might be. 'Which of them do you think it is?'

Helgesen thought carefully before he answered

'I haven't met the niece and nephew. But they could have a very strong motive if they thought that the death of Miss Meyer-Michelsen would give them an inheritance worth millions. But otherwise, I would point the finger at Lise Eilertsen's brother. He also has a motive involving an inheritance worth millions. And there are those who have killed three people for less. If not him, her ex-lover, and the least likely is the nun. But I think the murderer knew at least one of the victims.'

Danielsen was leaning unusually far back in his chair, staring at the wall, deep in thought. But he turned his head sharply back as soon as I asked him who on the list he thought was the murderer.

'None of them. I think the murderer is an irrational, calculating person out there somewhere whom we haven't met yet. This list is an important piece of work, and Helgesen has done an excellent job of it, with a little help from me. But I don't think the murderer is rational, and I don't think he knew any of the victims personally.'

'And what do you think we should do, then, to find the murderer?' I asked.

'I see the cars that were in the car park at Tveita Shopping Centre as our best bet. The murderer has been clever and lucky, and the truth of the matter is we don't have any other clues. We can only hope we discover something – either because of a tip-off of some kind, or because the murderer is less clever and less lucky next time. And I think there's a good chance of that.'

'But the danger is that one or more young women will lose

their lives in the meantime. If your theory is correct, no one can predict when or where the Anthill Murderer will strike again,' I said.

Danielsen let out a deep sigh – and answered briefly that I was unfortunately right.

We sat there in gloomy silence. Eventually I said that they had done an excellent job with the alibis, and could call it a week now. I would follow up the few leads we had, including the cars parked at Tveita and the missing alibis.

Both of them thanked me as they left, but the mood was still unusually sombre. Fortunately, I met no one in the corridor when I sneaked out of the station at five to five.

IX

After breakfast, I sat here alone on the sofa. I questioned why I still didn't feel any sympathy whatsoever for my victims or the people who cared for them.

I realize myself that there must be something wrong with me, as I still don't feel anything. I have no empathy. I sat there all morning thinking about what I might have missed out on as a result. Even as a child, I found it difficult to create bonds with other people, both in the family and outside. Perhaps it's because of my overdeveloped hearing.

It started early. I still remember the day when my mother took me to the doctor because she was worried there was something wrong with me. I was five. She was worried because I seemed to be so sensitive to noise, and because I showed so little interest in playing with other children. This was certainly the case, but whether the two were related or not, it was hard to say.

The doctor was a rather dour old man, but I think he was a very good doctor. He was quick to give a diagnosis and to explain in such a way that even Mother could understand.

I have always been able to remember what other people have said about me. I can still remember word for word what the doctor said.

'Your son has what might be called a reverse handicap; in other words, he has exceptionally well-developed hearing. In some situations this might be an advantage, but it can also cause problems. Some of the few children who suffer from this withdraw from others in their childhood, almost instinctively, in order to avoid noise. It is also possible that they hear things it would be best not to hear, particularly when meeting with peers.'

My mother thought everything would be fine and was just happy that there was nothing seriously wrong with me. But the doctor was right in what he said. I remember as a child being constantly irritated by the noise of other people. Loud children's voices can hurt the ears. And younger children in particular could say so many stupid things. It was much more comfortable to sit at a distance and listen to what they said at a normal volume.

Keeping a distance worked well in those early years, but it became harder when I was forced to be with other people at school. You can't hide away in the changing room or a classroom, certainly not when you hear everything that is said. I knew that the other boys in the class thought I was an anti-social loner, and more. I also knew that the girls, in between all the giggling fits that come with puberty, had me at the bottom of their list of boys to fall in love with.

Maybe things would have been easier if I hadn't known. Maybe I would then have made friends with some of the boys. Maybe then I wouldn't have learned to hate the stupid, beautiful young girls. A hatred that has accompanied me through life. As an adult, I've had relationships with some who are less young and less beautiful, but my hatred for the young and beautiful has always simmered below the surface. And that must be why I've struggled to make the few relationships I've had work.

The beautiful young girls still pass by without paying much attention to me – as though I were an ant or some other insect they don't need to bother about. I still hear and remember what they say. The few that do say anything about me rarely say anything to make me happy.

I heard a lot of things I shouldn't have heard, both at school and at home. I heard my parents discussing their concerns and worries about how things would turn out for their only son. They had such high expectations of me. I heard Mother and Father having sex, and it didn't sound like fun. I heard Father hitting Mother as well. For some reason, my father never hit me, only my mother. But I heard him hitting her and the fear that he would one day hit me too never quite disappeared. I can still wake up to the sound of his belt hitting Mother, even though I know he can no longer touch me.

And so I became what I became: a quiet, lonely child who feared his father, despised his mother and didn't trust his sister. I was a child who always knew too much and kept all my frustrations in.

The doctor who diagnosed my far-too-good hearing was also able to say that I could in fact hear everything that was said. And it was there, when I still only a little lad, that my life as a man who knew too much started, a man who has been underestimated by everyone. I am quite sure that my life would have been very different without my reverse handicap. I think it would have been better.

When that Sergeant Helgesen phoned at around midday, I was busy making some food. My heart started racing as soon as I recognized his voice. It was so gratingly loud, even when I held out the receiver. But it seemed they were simply compiling a list of alibis for anyone who was in any way connected with the investigation or one of the victims, as a matter of routine. He just said, 'Very good,' when he noted down where I was at the time of the murders, even though my alibis weren't perfect.

But I was taken aback by one of the times he asked about. It might have been just to confuse me and other possible suspects. Can't see any evidence of surveillance around the house. The fact that the police obviously have me on a list of names only adds to the adrenaline.

The hours have crept by so unbearably slowly, but now, at last, it's a quarter past four. The countdown has begun. Only four hours left before I leave the house and go to my long-planned and longed-for meeting with young Fatima.

X

I went to stand by the window at seven minutes to seven. And just in time: the car pulled up a minute later. I immediately ran down to get them into the flat as swiftly as possible.

We passed almost, but only almost, unnoticed. Mrs Borgen on the first floor opened her door just as I was carrying Patricia in. I hurried on and pretended not to have seen her. But Patricia gave her a winning smile over my shoulder that rendered the old lady speechless. I had no illusions that she would not say anything later. Anything that Mrs Borgen knew tended to spread like wildfire from neighbour to neighbour. Mrs Borgen had been married to a drunken war sailor who apparently had been totally uncommunicative for a decade, so she had an urgent need to talk to people whenever she had the chance. Her husband was now in a mental hospital, so I found it hard to get annoyed. But today, for the first time, I cursed Mrs Borgen and her loose tongue. For reasons I still could not decide on, I wanted as few people as possible to know that I had been visited by a young handicapped woman on Saturday evening.

I had had enough time to do the washing-up and dust the tables in the living room, but I had not managed to wash the floor. And I had certainly done nothing with the bedroom. The bed-linen would just have to stay on, even though I had used it for eight days now. If I was to be perfectly frank, I had very strong feelings for Patricia, but they were still so confused that I didn't really know what I wanted. And the idea of any physical contact with her, over and above carrying her up the stairs, still felt alien. The murder investigation dominated my mind and mood, and no doubt it was the same for Patricia. She stopped smiling as soon as Mrs Borgen disappeared from view. Her slight, young girl's body was stiff and fizzed with tension in my arms.

But we were a little closer, all the same. This time, I put her down on the sofa and then sat down beside her. It felt perfectly natural that we, having sat beside each other on her sofa, should now do the same in my far smaller flat. But I did not feel the need to initiate any more physical contact than that. I deliberately sat several inches away from her.

Patricia smiled as I put her down, but was soon serious again. She listened silently and patiently as I told her what had happened over the course of the day. The maid had disappeared out into the kitchen and had clearly been instructed to interrupt us as little as possible. When she slipped in three-quarters of an hour later with two servings of tenderloin for us, Patricia was brusque and simply pointed to the coffee table. I had thought that we would eat at the dining table, but let her decide. So there we sat, with our delicious food in front of us and an unsolved murder case hanging in the air. We had never been so close and yet so far from each other.

'So, what can you tell me after all that?' I probed gently when I had finished.

'Pass,' was Patricia's reply, after a few seconds' pause.

We sat in tense silence for a while. Patricia's movements were unusually sharp and angular when she turned to look out of the window.

'It really upsets me that I haven't been of more use thus far in the investigation. But there's not a man or woman in the world who could have got more out of it. Your work is producing more and more information, and yet we still can't see any links. Somewhere out there, in the world beyond that window, is a serial killer with a predilection for young women. And we still have no idea who he is or when he will strike again.'

As she spoke, it struck me that our partnership had always been based on me gathering information that Patricia would otherwise never have access to, and on her seeing links that I would never have been able to see. In this case I had gathered more and more information, but she had not been able to see any links. The situation was taking its toll on the balance of our relationship, and on her mood.

I agreed with her that no one else would have been able to get anything more out of it, and added a little more tentatively that I still very much enjoyed her company. She still didn't look at me and sighed as she repeated what she had said before. I realized this was gnawing at her confidence. And I thought that for the first time, she seemed older than her twenty-two years.

I had taken a photostatic copy of the list of alibis for her, and now put it down on the table between us. But Patricia didn't look at it; she just continued to gaze out of the window.

'Shall we have a look at the list of people lacking alibis? First up we have Trygve Andersen, a fellow student of Agnes Halvorsen, who came forward to say that he had seen Agnes coming out of the cleaning cupboard.'

Patricia sighed again.

'He may of course have been in love with her. And we can't rule out the possibility that he has a complex about women or is mentally unbalanced in some way that might motivate him to murder. But how on earth would he know where to wait for his next two victims? He might perhaps have heard Lise Eilertsen talking while out on the town, but I don't see how he could know Amalie's movements. She certainly did not talk too much and was never out on the town.

'Then we have Agnes' brother, Helmer Halvorsen. But the same problem applies to him, and to Lise's brother Lars Eilertsen and her former lover, Stein Hansen.'

Patricia nodded – sharply, almost aggressively.

Just then the door to the kitchen opened. The maid came out to collect our plates and to serve us some vanilla ice cream. Patricia and I clammed up while the maid was in the room. She had social skills enough to realize that she should leave the room as soon as she possibly could, and not to ask about anything while she was there.

'Sister Kari at Katarina Convent is also on the list, but surely we can dismiss her, as we are now basically looking for a man?' I continued, as the kitchen door closed behind the maid.

'If we are to believe your young informer, yes, the person who dumped Amalie at Tveita Shopping Centre was a man. But that doesn't necessarily mean to say that the murderer is. However, the idea of a serial-murdering Catholic nun with a male assistant is perhaps a little far-fetched. And in any case, there is no connection whatsoever with Amalie,' Patricia replied, instantly.

'What about Rakel and Robert Enger? They are more likely to have had contact with her,' I tried.

Patricia sighed, breathed slowly for a few seconds, but then spoke fast.

'More likely, perhaps, but there is nothing to indicate that they had been in touch with her within the past few weeks. And as far as we know, they have no connection to either Agnes Halvorsen or Lise Eilertsen. But it is perhaps the most plausible theory. Given that they expected to inherit millions if Amalie died, and in addition hated her father, they do in fact have both a rational motive and an emotional motive. But one or both of them would then have to have found and murdered the two other women first, and they didn't know them. They would also have to have contacted their cousin to establish where and when they were going to kill her, with the clear risk that they would be suspected if she wrote or said to anyone that they were coming to see her. And that does not sound very convincing to me. It must be time to eat some comfort food.'

Patricia ate her vanilla ice cream with saying anything, but still looked as if she needed comforting when she was finished. I felt strangely chilled myself, and was deeply sympathetic to Patricia. Having given it a moment or two's thought, I lifted her onto my lap.

As I lifted her, I thought that she was the lightest woman I had ever had sitting on my lap. And yet she felt unexpectedly heavy. Her body was less warm than before and felt dull and hard on my knees. It was as if her heavy mood had sunk into her body. I was reminded of one of my fellow students, who had summarized an unsuccessful night out by saying the beer was too warm and the woman too cold.

Patricia did look a bit happier sitting on my knee than she had sitting beside me on the sofa. She smiled as I lifted her up, and when she carried on talking, her voice sounded more optimistic.

'To put it simply, Helgesen could be right with his Agatha-Christie-inspired theory: the murderer knew only one of the victims and killed the other two as camouflage. It would certainly explain why he committed the murders. But it does still leave some very big question marks as to how he did it, so we still can't assume that the 'why?' theory is correct. If the 'how?' questions can be answered, then the Enger siblings are the most likely suspects, but there are other possibilities. On the other hand, my theory could also be right: that we are looking for a murderer who is not killing for any material gain, but simply because he, like Leopold and Loeb, likes the thrill of killing.'

'That is actually closer to Danielsen's theory that the murderer is someone out there who is unknown to us,' I said.

Patricia waggled her head a couple of times before answering.

'Yes and no. That might well be the case. But if, as I think, we are looking for a serial murderer who kills for thrills, that in no way rules out the possibility that you or someone else in the investigation have in fact met the murderer in the course of the past week. If one kills for the thrill of it, any contact with the police will only heighten the adrenaline. Especially if one does not expect to get away with it over time. And it is not unusual for serial killers to pick victims from their circle of family, friends and acquaintances. So there is every reason to keep an eye on those you have already talked to. But as the case stands, no name is jumping out at me from the list.'

I said that I thought her logic was still impressive.

'Of course, but what's the point of logic in this investigation if it brings us no closer to catching the murderer?' she snapped.

Patricia had no movement in her legs, but the rest of her body felt even heavier, and when I carefully put my arm around her, her upper body was stiff and tense.

'However, even though I am not able to give you the name of the murderer, I can try to tease out what kind of personality he might have. Which could be interesting, even though there is still so much uncertainty,' Patricia suddenly piped up.

I said I would be very interested to hear what she had to say about the murderer's personality. She flashed a smile, but became very serious again as soon as she started.

'So, in all likelihood, we are talking about a man who is in good physical shape and has unusually good hearing. Let's assume that the murderer has exceptional hearing in order to be able to hear the victims talking about their plans. So hearing is of interest here. As I mentioned, there are lots of examples of people who are born with highly developed sight or smell. But our senses can also be improved with training, consciously or unconsciously. A well known example is that blind people often compensate for their lack of sight with extremely good hearing. So no matter how good your hearing is, it is a question of how you use it. Therefore, let's assume that the murderer was born with exceptional hearing, and has either consciously or unconsciously trained his hearing to be even better. It could be someone who is rather introverted, but has a strong need for control, someone who likes to hear what other people have to say about him. And this is where the ant comes in. It could be a coincidence that he has chosen an ant as his symbol, but it seems so particular that I doubt it. It is most likely that the murderer in some way identifies himself with an ant. One possible interpretation is that he is playing the ant, disappearing into the anthill of the city and moving about as a very ordinary and inconspicuous person once he has committed a crime. Another is that he really feels like an ant: someone who does his bit day after day, month after month. A person who has never distinguished himself in any way or received any recognition, and who has now started to tire of his anonymous role on the antheap. Think hard. Does that description fit any of the people you have met, and in particular, any of those who don't have alibis? You are the one who has met them.'

'No one comes to mind immediately. But it does sound more like someone who is older and perhaps working, rather than a young student, say, so in that sense, Trygve Andersen seems less likely.'

Patricia nodded approvingly.

'Yes. We really have nothing on him, other than that he gave you some information and did not like a book that Agnes was reading last week. Helmer Halvorsen and Lars Eilertsen are perhaps more likely. On the other hand, the description sounds more like a single working man than someone with a family.'

'So perhaps it is Amalie's cousin, Robert Enger, then?' I ventured.

Patricia was silent, staring out of the window again.

'It feels wrong to suspect someone on such scant evidence. The only thing we have on him is that he doesn't have an alibi for any of the murders and that he lives alone. But yes, if you have in fact met the murderer, he is, as the case stands, one of the least unlikely candidates.'

I was about to ask Patricia what she thought about the others, given her proviso, but we were interrupted by my telephone. The ringing was an unexpected assault on our ears, as the phone was on a table right next to the sofa. Patricia's legs remained indifferent, but I felt her body start at the first ring and the second.

'I hope for the best, but fear the worst. Put me down on the sofa again and answer the phone,' she urged me, her voice trembling.

I hesitated for a moment. Patricia did not. When the telephone rang for the third time, she snatched it up and put the receiver to my ear. Then she leaned in towards my chest to listen to what was said.

We sat there as close to each other as we had ever been, and listened to the voice on the other end say that a young woman had been found dead on Mariboe Street, just by Young's Square. I saw Patricia's mouth tighten, only a handspan from mine, when she heard this. And I saw her grind her teeth when the voice on the other end said, 'Apparently the victim is a certain Fatima, who has been in the papers recently. The murderer was seen by two witnesses, but we still don't have a good description of him.'

XI

Helgesen was already there when I got to the scene of the crime in Mariboe Street, a few yards from the junction with Bernt Anker Street. He had placed a constable at either end of the street to close it off. A growing crowd of onlookers pressed at the cordons. In between the cordons, Mariboe Street was calm and quiet. But it was a deathly calm. Fatima lay stretched out on the pavement by the wall of a building.

I went over to the body straight away and bent down. She lay there lifeless, with big bruises on her throat and her tongue sticking out between her dark lips, her face frozen and distorted. But I still recognized her instantly from the photographs I had seen in the newspaper. One of the reasons she was recognizable was her golden-brown skin and the other was her hair, which according to the report in *Arbeiderbladet* was 'the longest and blackest in Oslo'. She had looked relaxed and happy as she posed for the photographer only a few weeks ago on her eighteenth birthday. Now she was lying cold and dead on the ground in front of me, by a street corner.

I felt a wave of nausea as I looked down at her. It helped to turn away from the dead girl. Even in this situation, Helgesen looked unruffled and calm, but I was getting to know him well now, and could see that behind this facade, he was deeply shaken and possibly even tipping into a rage. One of the veins on his neck was dangerously swollen.

Out loud, all Helgesen said was, 'She was killed just after nine o'clock. The murderer strangled her and threw down a picture of an ant as he ran off. He escaped on foot, but was seen by these two witnesses.'

He gestured to two people standing close by. They both seemed to be in their twenties and were standing about ten yards apart, looking in opposite directions. He was tall, muscular and dark-haired, and there was something familiar about him. She was no more than five foot two, blonde and clearly very annoyed indeed. She marched over to me with angry movements, shook my hand and then blurted out in a shrill voice, 'My name is Mette Christensen and that's Anders Frydenlund over there. We'd just been to the cinema and were walking back to my flat in Hausmann Street at around nine o'clock. We saw a man in a raincoat standing waiting on the corner of Bernt Anker Street, and then the poor girl came walking down the street towards him. The man in the raincoat greeted her and she waved back but showed no sign of stopping. Then suddenly he put his hands round her neck. She fought against him, but he just kept squeezing. We ran towards them and I shouted "MURDER!" as loudly as I could. And yet he stayed there with his hands around her neck until we were no more than a few yards away. Then he let go and ran off down Bernt Anker Street. I shouted at Anders to chase after him, while I stopped to help the poor girl. She was still alive and looked at me with terrified eyes, but was unable to speak. Then she died in my arms. I tried to get her breathing again, but her throat had almost been squeezed flat, so sadly there wasn't anything I could do for her.'

The words tumbled out of her mouth, and her voice fluctuated between anger and distress. When she had finished, she threw up her hands.

I told her it seemed she had done all she could to save the victim, and that even with medical training it would have been hard.

'I'm studying to be a nurse, so I would have been able to if it was possible, but believe me, there was nothing more anyone could do for her. As far as the murderer is concerned, it was beginning to get dark, so all I can say is that he was of medium height and wearing a blue raincoat with a hood. He was half turned away from us so I couldn't see his face or hair.'

I asked her as a matter of routine if she was sure that it was a man, and if she could guess his build and age. She answered without hesitation, her voice fraught with suppressed anger.

'His arms were strong and there was nothing womanly about his shape; it was very definitely a man. I wouldn't like to guess his age, though. As for height and build, he was definitely bigger than me, but smaller than Anders. And you'll have to ask Anders how he managed to get away. Anders is one of the fittest and fastest football players in town, and could easily have caught up with him if he had only dared try. Can I please go home now?'

The last sentences were said at speed and with a bitter undertone. I said that she was free to go, but that I still had to talk to her boyfriend.

'Good,' Mette Christensen replied. Then she left with determined steps and did not look back.

I stood and watched her leave for a few seconds, then turned my attention to the man now sitting on the edge of the pavement.

He sat in silence and seemed almost apathetic. To begin with, I wondered if he was in shock. But when I caught his eye, I could see that he understood perfectly well what had happened. In that instant I recognized his name and face. Of course I had seen him before. He was deemed to be a very promising football player, and had only a few weeks ago made his debut in the junior national team and Vålerenga's first team.

'Everything Mette said is unfortunately true,' he said, all of a sudden. 'We were walking down the street when we saw him strangling her. We ran towards them, but he escaped just before we got to them. Mette stayed with the girl and shouted to me to chase after him. I ran a few steps, but then stopped when I saw him disappear down Bernt Anker Street. He was wearing a blue raincoat with a hood, but I didn't get close enough to give you a better description.'

I felt the anger surge through my body. We had been within reach of the Anthill Murderer this evening and yet were just as far away from arresting him.

'You could have caught up with him, if you'd tried,' I said, as my suppressed frustration spilled over for a moment.

He nodded almost imperceptibly. Then he sat and stared at nothing for a while before answering.

'I could have, and I should have. All I can think about now is something the national football coach said last week. About the one important moment in the season when something totally unexpected happens. A really good player keeps a cool head and seizes the opportunity. A less good player loses his head, gets frightened and misses the chance. And that's what happened. I was fast enough and strong enough to catch him, but I lost my head and got frightened in that crucial moment. There's no other explanation. It was a shock to see someone being strangled with bare hands openly on the street. He seemed to be terrifyingly strong and I didn't know if he was armed or not. If I actually thought anything at all, it was that I would rather live as a coward than die as a hero. I wish I'd chosen differently, but I didn't. There's nothing more to say. Except that I can only apologize for my lack of courage, both to the police and the victim's family.'

Anders Frydenlund was right: there was not much more to say. He was clearly a decent and well-meaning person. We might regret that he had not wanted to risk his life, but no one could blame him for it. And more apologies would not get us any closer to the murderer. So I simply said that I had heard his statement now, so he was free to go.

He stayed where he was on the pavement for a little longer, then slowly stood up and walked away with heavy steps. He headed back towards the centre.

It struck me that the murderer might now have turned two more lives upside down. If he had not struck here this evening, Anders and Mette would probably be happily sitting or lying together in her flat in Hausmann Street. But he was no longer welcome there, as he had let himself down in her eyes. The question was whether she could ever forgive him, and whether he could ever forgive himself.

But my job was to find the killer before he committed another murder. That was demanding enough. I felt immense sympathy for the young couple and for a few seconds wondered how they would get on – and all the other people who had been affected by the Anthill Murderer's crimes. For a moment I reflected on the realization that Anders Frydenlund had let his girlfriend Mette down in much the same way as I had let my fiancée, Miriam, down only a few weeks ago.

Fortunately, Helgesen's matter-of-fact voice brought me back to Mariboe Street and the present. He was holding a piece of paper out to me, which proved to be a drawing of an ant cut out from a book.

'He threw this down as he let go of her and ran. The forensics team are on their way and we have asked the local minister to go and speak to her parents, who have a small restaurant in Grønland. It's up to you whether we should go and see them tonight, or not. Personally I don't think that they can help us catch the murderer now, and we should perhaps give them some time together with the minister and each other.'

Two new faces appeared in my mind as Helgesen spoke. I could not remember the rather foreign-sounding names of Fatima's parents, but I could remember their faces, which I had also seen one evening earlier in the spring and in a couple of unusually thought-provoking newspaper reports. There had been one in *Arbeiderbladet* only a few weeks before, in connection with their daughter's eighteenth birthday, under the heading 'We Owe Everything to Norway'.

The parents' story – how they had met when fleeing from India into the new state of Pakistan and then had to flee from there ten years later with their daughter, following clashes between the Muslims and Hindus – would no doubt seem incredible to most Norwegian readers. The story clearly had a happy ending; their daughter had learned Norwegian in record time and gone on to get top grades at school. The article finished with a very positive review of their Asian restaurant in Oslo. Fatima had also been in the headlines in *Arbeiderbladet* as a rising star in the Workers' Youth League.

I wondered what *Arbeiderbladet* and the other newspapers would write after the weekend, when they heard that their Ant Murderer had got away again after strangling Fatima in the centre of town only minutes away from the main police station. And I agreed with Helgesen, that we perhaps did not need to go and talk to the parents before the morning.

XII

It's now ten past eleven. It's an hour since I came home after this evening's murder. My pulse is still well over 150.

And ever since I got home I've been waiting for the police to break down the door at any minute. But no one has. And the telephone has been silent. So I guess I have got the better of them and managed to get away with it again. This time, however, it was not simply due to my nerve and skills, but also to a large helping of luck.

To begin with, everything went as planned. I was in place, waiting, at my chosen corner by Bernt Anker Street at two minutes to nine. As usual, the passers-by were few and far between; a young lad of around sixteen was the only person I saw in the minutes I stood there before she came. I heard her steps before I saw her. I was worried that she might have her friend with her again, in which case I would beat a hasty retreat down Bernt Anker Street as soon as I heard the steps. But there was only one pair of feet this time. Fatima came alone, just after nine, as she said she would. I felt the suspense growing while I listened to her footsteps get louder as she came towards me down Mariboe Street. More than ever, I felt a deep hatred towards this young woman who was a foreigner and yet walked around brazenly and without fear in our streets – as though she owned the place and could do as she pleased here.

I think she recognized me when I waved to her, and she waved back with little interest. She showed no sign of stopping or deigning to say a word, when she should be grateful that I, a white man, wanted to talk to her. I had decided to kill her no matter what. But my anger spiked as a result of this arrogance. The first two victims had at least stopped and talked to me.

I quickly put out my hands, grabbed her around the throat and squeezed. But little Fatima didn't just stand there like the others. She twisted and squirmed between my hands like a furious kitten. She kicked and pulled with all her might to break free, and with all my might I did everything I could to squeeze the living daylights out of her. I was determined to win and felt immense satisfaction when she started to sag in my grip.

It was at this point in our silent struggle that I heard the other footsteps. I heard two pairs of feet running towards us from behind. One of them was a woman who shouted 'MURDER!' in a shrill voice. It was like being in a dream; it was only when she shouted that I realized it was real. Fatima was still struggling weakly. For a moment I considered letting her go and escaping. But then I remembered she had recognized me, so I would still be caught if she survived. This made me obsessed with getting her to stop moving. To end her life became more important than keeping my own. I felt it was my duty, not only to myself, but to my country and race. I pressed harder and harder. And she became weaker and weaker, and the footsteps were coming closer and closer. Then suddenly she stopped moving and collapsed. The footsteps rang ever louder in my ears. I let go of her, and dropped the picture of the ant at the same time. This time I had been smart enough to have it ready up my sleeve.

I had planned to run in the opposite direction, so I wouldn't be recognized if anyone followed me, so I did not turn even once to see who was running towards us. I could hear from their footsteps that they were only a matter of yards away when I spun round and legged it. I expected to be tackled at any moment. But it didn't happen. The lighter steps stopped almost immediately and the heavier ones carried on. I ran at full pelt down Bernt Anker Street, which luckily was empty. But I had the presence of mind to brake when I got to Bridge Street, where there were more people about.

I caught a bus from Bridge Street to the National Theatre, where I then changed onto the first tram home. Every time the bus or tram stopped, I expected to be arrested. But by five past ten, I was home. Three minutes later, the raincoat and suit I had been wearing were in the fire.

And for the past hour, I have waited in suspense.

My greatest fear is that Fatima survived, and then that my pursuers saw me well enough to give a description to the police. In which case, that Kolbjørn Kristiansen might recognize me. But all they said on the eleven o'clock news was that a girl had been killed in Mariboe Street. No details were given. Nothing to indicate that the people who had chased after me had been able to give a description. Which was not so strange, really, given that it was dusk, and I was wearing a coat and hood and didn't look in their direction once. I have been running a fair amount in the last few weeks, training in case a situation should arise where I need to outrun my pursuers. And it certainly paid off this evening.

I was a bit taken aback when they said on the news that the death had been linked to the three murders earlier this week. The newsdesk or the newsreader must have made a mistake. Whatever the case, it's not really a problem.

I have never experienced such intensity as the excitement I felt this evening. Even now, when it's almost half past eleven, I am pacing from room to room and can't sit still.

The temptation to kill again tomorrow is so strong. But maybe it's time to rest for a few days. I want to see what the newspapers write after the weekend; annoyingly, there won't be anything until Tuesday. And I don't have any more victims at the moment. Let's see when a new suitable candidate appears. No one knows what tomorrow will bring. But no matter what, this has definitely been the most exciting Saturday I've had for years, and a memory for life.

XIII

She was still sitting there on the sofa, as she promised, when I got home at half past eleven. In exactly the same place that I had left her when I ran out a couple of hours earlier. The maid was sitting with her, but disappeared back into the kitchen as soon as I appeared in the living room.

Patricia had almost finished reading a novel she had found

on my bookshelf, but put it down the moment I came in. She seemed to be just as awake and alert as when I left.

'What happened?' she said.

I sat down beside her and told her everything.

'Once again, we were frustratingly close to getting a description of the murderer, but didn't. So unfortunately, there's not much to be had here either,' I concluded.

Patricia chewed her cheek as she thought for a while, and then spoke.

'Well, yes and no. There is nothing that can clearly tell us the murderer's identity. But there is one thing that is of great interest, and two of lesser interest. The most interesting is that this undermines Helgesen's theory about the motive being linked to one of the first murders. If the murderer had a rational motive for killing one of the three first victims, and murdered the other two to camouflage this, he would hardly need to commit a third murder now. And if he had wanted a third camouflage, for whatever reason, he would hardly have committed the murder at such risk in the city centre. The murderer stayed put to make sure he had killed her, even though two people were running as fast as they could towards him. And even then he still took the time to drop a picture of an ant before running off, which reinforces the theory that the ant is in some way important to him – and that we're talking about someone who kills for thrills.'

I had not given a thought to any of this, but agreed with her straight away. Then I asked what the two things of lesser interest were.

'Well, first of all, it seems that the murderer was standing waiting on a quiet street corner for a victim he knew would come. Other than the fact that it was in the centre of town, it is very like the first two murders, but far less like the murder yesterday. The other point is that he greeted the victim, who greeted him back but did not stop. That demonstrates that they did not know each other very well, but that she still knew him by sight. And that takes us neatly back to the question as to how the murderer knows when his victims are going to be at a suitable place, wherever that might be.'

As she was talking, I realized that I had left quite a space between us when I sat down. It was as if this latest murder had raised another barrier. Any further physical contact this evening was out of the question. Patricia had regained her composure, though she was still tense and serious. I had too much else to think about and all of a sudden I felt exhausted after a long day and yet another setback.

I said that I hoped we could meet for supper at her house tomorrow, but that I really should go to bed now, as it would be an early start in the morning. Patricia swiftly replied that it was no doubt sensible and that I was welcome any time. I asked if six o'clock would suit her, and she said, with a hint of self-irony, that six o'clock fitted very well with her other plans for the day.

As I lifted her up, I noticed that her upper body was shaking violently. And when her chest touched mine, her pulse was racing. 'What's wrong?' I asked, as I was about to open the front door.

Patricia grabbed the door handle so I could not open it. Then she stretched up and whispered in my ear in a tense, barely audible voice, 'I'm worried about what tomorrow might bring. We can only hope that this evening's events have given the murderer a scare. But if my theory is correct that he is killing for the excitement, then there's every reason to fear that he

347

might instead be riding an adrenaline wave. In which case, we can expect another murder soon. And we have absolutely no idea who his next victim might be.'

As though to underline the urgency of the case, Patricia opened the door as soon as she had said this. No more was said as I carried her down to the car.

It was a quarter past midnight by the time I put her down in the back seat, while the ever-silent maid followed us with the kitchen equipment. I was rankled by the fact that Mrs Borgen on the first floor was standing by her window looking down at us. But, truth be told, I now had far more serious things to worry about. I went back indoors as quickly as I could. At first, I sat down on the sofa, but then felt a little uncomfortable. Patricia's presence was becoming so natural that I had started to miss her when she was not there.

So I went over to the window and looked out, and then it was suddenly my former fiancée I was looking for. But she did not appear. Nor did anyone else.

I went to bed at five to one, and tried not to think about either Miriam or Patricia, and managed. Instead it was the distorted face of Fatima I saw when I closed my eyes. I still could not remember her parents' names, but could see their faces all the more clearly. The last thing I thought about before falling asleep was that I was dreading meeting them tomorrow morning.

DAY SEVEN

An Important Answer and an Almost As Important Question

I

On Sunday, 30 April 1972, I was woken early by the telephone. As I leapt up to answer it, I glanced at the alarm clock and saw that it was still only twenty past seven.

He didn't say his name. And nor was it necessary. The combination of his coarse voice and the pips from a phone box made him easily recognizable.

'It was the Anthill Murderer who was waiting on the corner of Anker and Mariboe yesterday, wasn't it?'

Still only half awake, I said that it was, and asked if he had seen him.

'I wasn't there yesterday, but a mate went by. Told him to contact you, but he's allergic to pigs, he says . . . He saw a bloke in a blue raincoat stop at the corner just before nine, and then wait. Doesn't really help much, but thought I'd tell you anyway.'

I said that I very much appreciated the fact that he was trying to help. I was just about to ask him who he was, but instead asked why he had called me again.

Just then, the pips started to tell us his time was up. He talked over them until the line was cut.

'Cos strangling young women on the streets of Oslo is going too far. Hope you get him before—'

He was not given the time to finish. I sat for a few moments listening to a silent receiver. I mused that being woken on a Sunday morning by a criminal phoning to do what he could to help certainly said something about the mood out there and the position the investigation was now in.

There was no point in trying to go back to sleep. I ate a very quick breakfast and was in the office by ten to eight. To my relief, Danielsen was nowhere to be seen, but, as I had hoped, Helgesen was at my door by eight. My boss knocked on the door at ten past eight. The mood was grim, and the modest pile of tip-offs and information that had come in did not help to improve it.

Two witnesses on the opposite side of Bernt Anker Street, and someone standing by a window, had seen a man in a raincoat running down towards Bridge Street just after nine o'clock. But none of them had been able to see the man well enough in the waning light to give any more details, or had seen where he went.

But someone else had called in with information that was of greater interest. The owner of the yellow Peugeot in the car park at Tveita Shopping Centre had contacted the station. He was a taxi driver in his sixties, and had popped into the shopping centre to buy his wife a birthday present, between two fares. He had been at a grandchild's birthday party on Monday evening, and at home with his wife on Wednesday evening, and in Tønsberg visiting one of his brothers on Saturday evening. The only thing he noticed when he was at Tveita on

Friday morning was that there were plenty of spaces in the car park.

We all agreed that this meant that the Peugeot could be struck from the list of four cars in the car park. The Toyota belonged to Amalie herself, but we still knew nothing about the old blue Amazon or the big black Mercedes.

It seemed rather odd that the drivers of those cars had still not contacted us, despite all the calls we'd put out in the newspapers and on radio and television, Helgesen remarked. The boss and I agreed.

Hundreds of both kinds of car were registered, thousands if all year models were taken into account. Unless we managed to get any more information, it would take months to follow up everyone who might possibly have been driving one of the cars.

The three of us sat there morosely looking at my telephone. We were, it seemed, waiting for that one redeeming phone call from someone who could give us a detailed description of the man in the raincoat, or who had seen which building he had gone into. But the phone did not ring. We clearly could not reckon on getting any help in this case.

At a quarter to nine, I said that we should go and talk to the latest victim's parents, just in case, and that I would appreciate it if Helgesen could accompany me.

He replied that he did not expect them to be able to give us any more information, so it might perhaps be more useful if he updated the list of the seven parties who did not have alibis for the first three murders.

I suspected that my assistant did not want to meet Fatima's parents, for whatever reason. And I had to admit that the list of alibis might still be important. What we needed least of all at the moment was a conflict within the investigation team. So I wished him luck with the list, and left the station alone, with a heavy heart.

II

I found Aisha and Karim Hussain in their restaurant in Grøn-land. The four-room restaurant was on the ground floor, and they lived in a small flat upstairs. The menu was decorated with foreign-looking symbols and offered exotic meat and fish dishes that were unfamiliar to the Norwegian palate. The spelling and grammar were, however, perfect.

'Fatima wrote it,' her mother said, as I looked through the menu. She had a thick accent, but her grammar was good.

I was looking at the menu primarily to avoid looking directly at the picture of Fatima that stared down at me from above a burning candle. It was the largest I had ever seen and was a finely drawn portrait of a young woman with golden-brown skin and long raven hair.

I could not bear to look the portrait of an eighteen-year-old girl in the eye. Instead, I confronted my reluctance to look directly at her parents. They were remarkably dignified, sitting there holding each other's hands under the portrait of their dead daughter.

I had been told that the parents were thirty-seven and thirty-nine years old. I would perhaps have guessed that they were younger, but could equally have accepted anything between twenty-five and fifty. Their skin was smooth and they both still had black hair.

I didn't need to ask if they had any more children, as it had said in the most recent interview in the papers that Fatima was an only child. The parents had said openly that they had not been able to have more children but did not know why, and had therefore thanked their god every day for the fact that they had been able to keep the one child they had.

'You must excuse us if we perhaps seem cold. We are warm-hearted people. But we have seen so much pain and cried so many tears that we have none left to cry,' the father said.

His wife nodded as he spoke. Her face was composed, but I noticed that her hand gripped his all the tighter when she started to speak.

'My husband saw his parents stabbed to death the day before India and Pakistan separated, bringing peace. I saw my sister burn to death when our village was attacked. And even though we didn't expect this now, we have both known that we might lose Fatima every day since she was born.'

I nodded in acknowledgement. I had read the father's story several times, how he had run with his nine-year-old daughter on his back to save their lives as the bombs rained down over their village in eastern Pakistan. They had had to travel over thirty miles under cover of dark to make it across the border to safety in India. His wife had miraculously found them in the throngs of people two days later. If what they said was to be believed, it was a wonder that they had found each other again and another miracle that they then met the wife of a Norwegian diplomat a few days later.

And so they arrived in Norway on a winter's day in 1964 – as two of the first refugees from the civil war in Pakistan. Their story was a fairy tale. And until yesterday evening, it had been a story that told of a successful transition from the Far East to the cold North.

'For the first three years in Norway, we were haunted by the fear of war. We slept in shifts so that one of us would be awake if someone attacked or set fire to the house. But now we finally believed we were safe. We forgot that no one can ever be totally safe in any country,' the mother said.

The father had initially worked as a packer. Then they opened the restaurant in 1968 and to begin with, there had been nearly no customers. They had had to fight with the authorities to be allowed to open ten hours a day, six days a week. But then things got better and better. Increasing numbers of Norwegians who had never been abroad were interested in trying the Asian food to be had in Grønland in Oslo. People even came from the west end. In December and January there was not a table to be had, despite the unusually long opening hours. They were busy days with lots of hard work, but also a lot of joy, Aisha and Karim had told the papers.

I had been a customer there myself, one Tuesday evening in February. It had been Miriam's idea, and definitely one of her better suggestions when it came to cafes and restaurants. We had liked the very distinctive food, even though we were not used to the spices. And the fact that the restaurant owner himself went round the tables and washed the floor just before closing time had appealed to us. In hushed voices, we had discussed leaving a tip, and Aisha had bowed and thanked us both even though it was only a coin or two.

We had only seen Fatima in passing. She came down from their flat at around nine. Her parents had smiled and seemed to light up for the few minutes she was there, before she went out on some errand or other. 'I know her,' Miriam had said, with her crooked smile. 'And she's good, even if she is in the Workers' Youth League.'

Fatima had obviously recognized Miriam, because she smiled and waved to us as she passed outside the window. And although I never heard her speak, my impression of her through the window was positive and vibrant. Miriam and I had read the interview published in connection with Fatima's eighteenth birthday, and had talked about going to the restaurant again. But then, just before Easter, there was another difficult murder investigation, and by the time Easter had passed, Miriam and I were no longer engaged.

I had no idea whether my hosts remembered that I had been there, and hoped that they would not mention it. All of a sudden, memories of a happier and simpler time in my life flooded back. I tried to push them to one side by asking routine questions, but it didn't really help.

Fatima had had some comments at school when she first started, but it then improved when she learned the language and got to know the other girls. She now had lots of friends. Her parents were a bit hesitant when she said she wanted to get involved in politics, but then said that she must do what she wanted to do. She had enjoyed the work, and as far as they knew, did not have enemies of any kind.

She had been in love a couple of times, but had not yet found a boyfriend, her mother told me with the shadow of a smile on her lips.

The most recent victim, like the first, had apparently not experienced real love. But without being able to explain why, I felt that this case was even more tragic. Perhaps because the parents had lost their only child, because their lives had been so dramatic, and because I had met Fatima and her parents briefly before this great tragedy hit them. But equally, it might be the link to Miriam and my own story that made the murder more poignant to me than the three others.

I had thought of asking to see Fatima's room, but decided to spare both the parents and myself that heartache. There was nothing to indicate that the Anthill Murderer, whoever he was, had any previous connection with the victim.

Instead, the three of us sat in the closed restaurant, with the picture of Fatima and the burning candle. The situation felt increasingly depressing, despite their dignity and warm welcome.

I asked if they knew where their daughter had been the evening before, and who might have been there.

They looked at each other, and then the mother answered in a trembling voice.

'She went to the cinema with some friends and was probably on her way home when she was killed. She had told us that she might be home late, and we urged her not to walk alone so late at night, especially after the murders. But Fatima loved life and believed that Allah would watch over her. We should not have let her go out this weekend, but then it was so hard to say no. She talked without a care to everyone she met, often too much and too loud, so who knows who might have heard where she was going.'

I looked at her husband, and he just gave a small nod of agreement. The answer to how the perpetrator could know the victims' movements remained a mystery.

I had nothing more to say to them. I assured them that the investigation would be given top priority, and that I would let them know as soon as there were any developments. In the meantime, I would contact them if and when we had any further questions.

'Of course. We'll be here in the restaurant, and you are welcome any time,' the mother said.

I asked if they were really going to work today as well.

'Yes, of course. Our work is our life. And it's all we have now,' she said.

There was a brief silence, then the father carried on, in a slightly louder voice that was on the point of breaking.

'This is where we live. We have been here for twelve hours a day for the past five years. And we'll be here for at least twelve hours a day for the next ten years and more. We came to Norway to make a safe home for our daughter, and until now have worked for the sake of our daughter and our new home. But now we're here because we have nowhere else to go. If you can tell us one day who killed our daughter, then perhaps we can once again work for our new country. It would be an enormous relief.'

His wife looked him and nodded when he finished speaking. Then we sat there in silence again. I eventually said that I would come to see them as soon as we found out who had killed Fatima, and that I hoped it would be only a matter of days.

They thanked me warmly and followed me to the door.

Then as the father held the door open for me, it happened. Suddenly Mrs Hussain said: 'I wish you and your girlfriend well. Please give her our regards.'

It caught me by surprise. I stammered that unfortunately things were not well between me and my girlfriend any longer, but I would of course pass on their greetings should I see her.

'Oh, I am sorry to hear that,' she said, and put her hand on my shoulder. Then he put his hand on the other shoulder.

They were so kind, and it felt so awful. I couldn't bear the fact that these people who had just lost their only child were showing such concern for me. So I said rather brusquely that I was fine and that I would be back as soon as I had any news.

Then suddenly I was alone again in the damp spring air. I walked slowly to begin with, but then started to run. I did not look back. I had the uncomfortable feeling that they were standing in the doorway watching me. I did not want to see them. And I thought to myself that the Anthill Murderer must be stopped before he took any more lives.

III

I didn't sleep as well last night as I usually do. The tension was still in my body. I was woken twice by a noise that I thought was the police, but it wasn't. When I got up just before nine, the flat was silent and calm, and there was no sign of police surveillance outside.

It's strange to think how the past week has fundamentally changed my life and how decisive coincidences can be. When I woke up last Sunday, I had a plan to commit murder. I knew where Agnes Halvorsen was to be found every Monday evening. But at that stage, I was not clear that I would do it that week. The deciding factor was a small newspaper article about a mad artist who had been charged with the murder of a young woman several years ago. He is now about to be released. He said the murder had given him a new lease of life, and he was looking forward to meeting all the women who had written to him when he was in prison. Which didn't sound so bad.

It irritates me that there are no newspapers today. As I ate breakfast, I speculated about how the papers might have written about me if there had been. I would no doubt have been on all the front pages. Yesterday's murder was the first item on the radio news. They said that the murderer had escaped and the police were calling for witnesses. That, and the fact that no one has come to my door yet, means that the couple who came running to save Fatima did not see me well enough to give a description.

They said that the person who committed yesterday's murder was possibly also responsible for the murders on Monday, Wednesday and Friday of last week. The mention of Friday unsettled me, so I turned to read yesterday's paper.

I found a report about the murder on Friday. The victim was an Amalie Meyer-Michelsen, whose body was found in Tveita Shopping Centre, and the killer had left a picture of an ant beside her.

At first I was astonished, then so indignant that I sat seething on the sofa. This Amalie girl was completely unknown to me and I have never been to the Tveita Centre. I have been prepared for all kinds of eventualities over the past few days, but not that anyone would try to emulate my idea and success. The cheek of it.

I read the report several times, without being any the wiser about who the contemptible copycat might be. With no means of identifying the fraudster, I could only hope that the police would find him – and focus on my own plans. I had actually thought of having a few quiet days after all the excitement yesterday, but the thrill has stayed in my body through the night, and now that I've discovered there is another anthill killer, my competitive spirit has been roused.

The temptation to commit another murder tonight is almost overwhelming. The only problem is that I don't know of any more suitable victims.

I dreamed last night that I was on the tram and overheard a young woman telling her friend where she was going this evening. In my dream I could hear that she was very young, but I couldn't see her face and couldn't remember what she said. Maybe it's a sign. My mother and father both believed that dreams can come true, and I've experienced it *myself. The idea of strangling Agnes came to me for the first time in a dream.*

Perhaps I should go somewhere on the tram today.

IV

It was unnervingly quiet at the station when I got back around eleven. Helgesen was out chasing up a couple of alibis.

There was a single sheet of paper with an important message stuck to my office door. The owner of the blue Amazon from the car park at Tveita Shopping Centre had finally contacted the police.

The Amazon belonged to an elderly lady from Grorud, who I managed to get hold of as soon as I phoned. She apologized and explained that she did not have newspapers delivered, nor did she have a television, 'as her pension was so small'. But a neighbour had just let her know about our call for information. She had gone to Tveita 'for a cup of coffee and to watch the world go by', but had clearly left the shopping centre just before the body was found. She had unfortunately not seen anything suspicious either inside or outside the centre. She had been at home alone on Saturday evening. Last Monday she had gone to visit a niece and on Wednesday evening she had helped with the big clean-up in the communal gardens at the back of her building.

She also said that she had bad legs – and was clearly depressed. Her voice was slow and heavy.

I thanked her for her help and quickly put the phone down. The conversation seemed to be illustrative of the investigation as a whole. Every time we got new information of any importance, it only served to wipe out what we hoped might be a clue. Now only the big black Mercedes remained.

Just then, my phone rang. The switchboard operator said there was a man on the line who refused to give his name, but had to speak to me personally in connection with the investigation.

I recognized his voice as soon as I heard it. I had called him myself only a few days earlier.

Knud Haasund came from good stock on both sides, but following his father's early death had gone to sea as soon as he finished school. As a result he sounded like a fisherman in his fifties, but was only thirty – he was a well-spoken journalist, but sounded rough.

'Hi, it's Haasund. How's your investigation going?' he said.

I was slightly annoyed that he had bluffed his way through the switchboard like that, but realized that poor relations with *Verdens Gang* would not make things any better. So I replied briefly, with forced politeness, that I could unfortunately not comment on the investigation.

'You're looking for the owners of the four cars that were standing in the car park at Tveita, aren't you? Well, I have a photograph that shows the registration plates of two of them,' he said.

There was a breathless silence. I knew that the insatiable newshound Haasund had his contacts in the police and at the station. I had never liked him and had always kept him at arm's length. However, he had now phoned me with information that could be crucial, and I was obliged to do everything I could to find the Anthill Murderer before he found his next victim. Haasund was also famous for never revealing his sources.

So I said that a picture of the cars might still be of interest.

'I have the names of the owners of the Amazon and the Mercedes,' he said.

'The latter might be of interest,' I conceded.

'I thought so. You'll get the name, if I get his statement to the police tomorrow morning,' he replied.

I allowed myself to think for a few moments. I knew perfectly well that what I was about to do was in breach of police regulations and my own ethical standards. But at the same time, I felt duty-bound to do whatever we could to get closer to the killer, and I was also aware that this type of cooperation with the press was not unheard of at the station.

I took a couple of deep breaths, then answered, 'If I get the name now, you will have first access to any resulting news.'

There was silence on the other end. Then he said: 'OK. Have you got a pen?'

I was already holding one in my hand, and said so, then added quickly that this was strictly between us.

'Of course,' he reassured me, then said the name and hung up.

I forgot to write down the name; two seconds after he had told me I was already on my way out of the office.

V

Paul Vincent Krag let me into his studio outside Sandvika. If he still bore any grudges, he hid them well. He shook my hand with something akin to enthusiasm, and asked for permission to carry on painting as we spoke.

'For obvious reasons, I have a lot of creativity stored up that

I need to let out,' he said, with a smile which, under different circumstances, might have been charming. But there and then, it seemed bizarre.

I looked from the painter to the unfinished painting on the easel. Now, as indeed when I first saw him standing here, I thought that he really was the present-day incarnation of the genius and mad artist. As the only child of two artists, he had been raised for it, and had even been named after two of the greatest painters of the last century. He had managed to distinguish himself early on as an unpredictable eccentric in the art world.

The studio was just as I remembered from the first time I was there, one summer's day in 1965. It was the first murder investigation I worked on. He had been standing here painting at the same easel when we came in.

But then, there had been a dead, naked woman lying on the sofa by the wall. He had shot his model – and then calmly continued to paint her until the police, alerted by his terrified wife, had knocked on the door. But seven years ago, I was here as an officer and my boss, in his last investigation as operative detective, had been the one to speak to the painter.

Neither the painter's wife nor my boss was here now. There were two constables outside the door – and only Paul Vincent Krag and myself in the room. He stood with his paintbrush in his hand, and looked at the painting. I still found it hard to take him seriously. In 1965, the forensic psychiatrists had, 'with some reservations', found him to be legally culpable. But I still found myself wondering if they had not made a mistake and whether seven years behind bars had made him any better.

'To what do I owe the honour this time?' he asked, without lifting his eyes from the canvas for so much as a second. I had hoped that the motif might be either a young woman or an ant. But instead, the painting was of a peaceful scene, with a sheep and a horse in a verdant landscape.

'We are here because, as soon as you were released on parole, someone started to kill young women in Oslo, apparently for thrills. And because you said in an interview last Monday that being in prison and the murders had given you new inspiration. Because your Mercedes was in the car park at Tveita Shopping Centre when one of the victims was dumped there on Friday. And finally, because you did not come forward yourself, despite our repeated appeals,' I said, in a hard voice.

Paul Vincent Krag sent me an injured look. Then he continued to paint, unperturbed.

'In answer to your last point, I hope you can understand that I've been busy with other things, and that I've had a little too much to do with the police to contact them voluntarily. And as far as I know, it's not illegal to buy paint or to park in the car park at Tveita Shopping Centre, even on a Friday. As to your second point, the freedom of speech and the press do still apply in this country. And finally, with regard to your first point, the murderer started his spree before I was released. It was reported in the papers on Saturday and Monday that I was to be released, but the gates were in fact not opened until Tuesday morning.'

It was the most indisputable alibi that anyone could give for the first murder and it felt like a punch to the face. In fact I physically winced and turned my head. Paul Vincent Krag remained cool and collected and carried on painting – and talking.

'What's more, it's worth remembering that the last time you were here, I had committed a crime of passion. I killed a model who wanted to ruin my masterpiece, and she had also been unfaithful to me with another man. This time you are asking about four women I have never met, to my knowledge. I have no reason to hate any of them, and hope to spend what I have left of my life catching up with all the time I've lost and creating as many masterpieces as possible. Read between the lines: in other words, no, I've got nothing to do with this.'

I had to admit reluctantly that the painting on the canvas might indeed be a masterpiece, but I was still very distrustful of the artist behind the canvas. The woman he had killed had gone back to live with her husband and when the painter then threatened her, she refused to sit for him. The story and his behaviour did him no favours, and so I asked where he went on his release, and where he had been on Wednesday and Saturday evening.

He stopped painting to send me another injured look, then again turned back to the canvas. He was clearly capable of talking and painting at the same time, and had the confidence to do so.

'On Wednesday evening, I was sitting in the Theatre Café with a dazzlingly beautiful woman I started to correspond with after I had been robbed of my freedom. Both she and the staff will be able to confirm that. On Saturday, my good friends and colleagues invited me out to a celebratory meal, and my girlfriend and I left in a cab around midnight.'

The man carried on painting and did not even deign to look at me.

I wondered what on earth it was that would attract a woman to a murderer – with or without an artist's studio. Then I recalled what Patricia had said about the murderer's personality, and it struck me that the Anthill Murderer might be very similar to Paul Vincent Krag. The serial killer, like this artist, was possibly a man who thought only of himself and was not able to sympathize or empathize with other people. But it was clearly not the same man. And the black Mercedes now appeared to have been a dead end.

With thinly veiled sarcasm and excessive friendliness, I wished Paul Vincent Krag good luck with his painting and left. He appeared to be genuinely pleased and assured me that it would be the first of many new masterpieces.

VI

It was two o'clock by the time I got back to the main police station. At a quarter past two, there was a knock on my door. Helgesen came in. His step was heavier than usual and he looked extremely grim.

'I've finished updating our list of alibis. And I'm afraid to say that all the news is bad news,' he said, with a sigh.

I countered this by saying that all news was interesting news, and asked him to tell me what he had found out.

He sighed, swallowed and spoke.

'Katarina Convent was cleaned from top to bottom yesterday, and Sister Kari was working with the others until half past ten in the evening. Rakel Enger was on her way home, alone, at nine o'clock. But she was at work with two other cleaners in Eidsvoll until half past eight, so would not have managed to get into the centre of town in time, unless she had a small plane or was driving a racing car. Plus, according to yesterday's witness statements, it is now clear that it was a man. So they can both be struck from the list. Robert Enger was the closest we came to a suspect. But he was at a colleague's birthday party and was there until around midnight. Meanwhile, Lise Eilertsen's brother Lars spent the evening with his wife and children, who had come back from Bergen. Lise's ex-lover, Stein Hansen, had a gig in Lillestrøm, and was on stage from eight until nine. Agnes Halvorsen's brother, Helmer, had invited his fiancée and her parents out for a meal and they stayed at the restaurant until after ten. And Agnes' fellow student, Trygve Andersen, was at his niece's confirmation celebrations all evening.'

This was all said without a pause. Helgesen then threw the list down on the desk in exasperation. All seven names on the list now had a line through them.

'So, there are no potential murderers left on our list?' I asked.

He sat staring at the wall. Suddenly he looked old. I understood that this was hard for him, not only because of all the work he had put into the list, but also because he had really believed that it would give us the answer.

'In short, everything we now know indicates that my theory was wrong and that Danielsen was right. It would appear that we are looking for a man we have never met, and we have no idea of his identity and only a basic description. I apologize for wasting so much time on what was effectively a wild goose chase.'

My sympathy for Helgesen grew as he spoke. And it grew because he did not have a critical word to say about how I had led the investigation. He did not say what we were both thinking: that the whole investigation was a fiasco – after six days and four murders, we were still no closer to an arrest.

I told him that no matter what the outcome was, he had been absolutely right in saying we should compile the list and

I was very grateful for his hard work. Then I added that he now deserved to see a bit more of his family and he could take what was left of Sunday and the May Day holiday off with a clear conscience.

He cheered up a bit and thanked me, but said that I only had to call if I needed his assistance with the investigation – be it morning, night, or holiday. I promised him I would.

We left the building together at half past three, in a slightly better frame of mind. But the heavy clouds outside were still a good reflection of my mood.

VII

Being an ant on an anthill and a man without friends has its advantages. Especially if you are also a murderer. I have been travelling in various directions on the trams and local trains for the past three hours, without being recognized by anyone other than a former colleague. He just raised a hand in greeting and then got off at the next station.

It's quite amusing to think I have been seen by hundreds of people today, while out looking for my next victim, without anyone suspecting me in the slightest. Who would suspect a man in a coat on a train?

I can feel the excitement fizzing in my body all the time. It peaked when two young policemen in uniform got on at the main station. But they weren't looking for me, just some stupid alcoholic who had sat down opposite me. One of the policemen smiled at me apologetically as they pulled the bum up from the seat and off the train. I smiled back, and fortunately managed to hold back the laughter that was bubbling up inside. But I burst out laughing as soon as I got home. If the two of them had only known who they had within reach.

Apart from the episode with the policemen, the first two and a half hours were rather uneventful. I saw a couple of dozen possible candidates, but none of them said anything of interest.

Then suddenly, there she was, standing by the door.

The moment I saw her, I felt the compulsion and had to turn away in order not to stare. She was with a friend, and they giggled as they got on the train. They were both younger than any of the previous victims. I barely noticed the friend. She immediately caught my attention, partly because of her jet-black hair, but also because of her grating voice.

I knew as soon as I saw her that she was Jewish, before she even mentioned to her friend that she had been to the synagogue in St Hanshaugen with her parents. And then I knew for certain that she would be my next victim.

She very conveniently sat down just behind me, so I could hear every word she said. Even though she lowered her voice, I heard her tell her friend that she was going on her first date with a boy, under the pretence that she was visiting the friend. He was two years above them at school and she had fancied him for a long time.

I listened to their conversation for the rest of the journey. When they got off, I knew that she would leave her house in Therese Street at half past seven and then walk up Eugenie Street to the boy's house in Ullevål Road.

It was like a sign from above. A young girl who talked too much who was going on a secret date this evening – within easy walking distance of my own home. The thought of committing a murder in my own part of town was an enormous thrill, as was the challenge of geting away with it in daylight. The cherry on the cake was that she was Jewish.

I had grown up in a home where 'Jew' was a swear word. I don't know if my father was ever punished after the war, as I was only a child at the time and we never spoke about it later. But my father had been a Nazi sympathizer and supported the persecution of the Jews. After the war, he lived in fear of reprisals from the Jews, either against him or other members of the family, for the rest of his life. His hopes that the Jews would eventually leave our country when they got their own state in the Middle East came to nothing. In our last conversation, he told me of his fears that his children would grow old in a Norway overrun by Jews and other foreign religions.

My relationship with my father wasn't the best when he was alive. I found it hard to forgive him for the fear he instilled in me as a child. But in his later years, it seemed we were closer. And now it feels as though I would be honouring his memory by killing the Jewess. It is quite possible that the young man in Ullevål Road will be waiting for a long time to get to know her better, and in vain.

For the first time, I don't know my victim's name, which is irritating. But I have called her Rebecca. After all, I have a good memory, so I know that it's a Jewish name from the Old Testament. I think it's a good name for a young Jewish girl, but not appropriate for a young Norwegian girl. And she's going to go – tonight.

VIII

It was now ten past five. I had asked the station to call me if they got any news or tip-offs or messages that might be of interest to the investigation. But the phone did not ring. I had tried to read my book, without much success. I was not able to read more than a couple of pages before the text and my thoughts diverged.

Once again I was standing at the window looking out at a rather sad spring Sunday. The sky was still overcast and there was rain in the air. It did not look as if the weather was going to clear for the Labour Day celebrations. And the prospects for the investigation were no better. As a result of the day's work, we no longer had any potential names or faces to match the murderer. I was looking forward to seeing Patricia in a couple of hours, but did not hold out much hope that she would be able to solve the case either.

I stood there lost in my own thoughts, and did not notice a woman in a raincoat turn the corner and start to walk towards my building. When I did, I thought at first it was my neighbour's girlfriend and that she looked even more like Miriam today.

Then within a split second everything changed. She saw me standing at the window and waved – as she used to when she saw me waiting here.

It *was* Miriam. She had come back. I felt as though a lightning bolt had cut through the rain to strike me.

I had finally come to accept the reality that I would never see her walking up to the house again. And yet here she was. She had a book under her arm, wrapped up well in a plastic bag, and her blonde hair was tucked in under the hood of her raincoat, to protect it from the rain. It really was Miriam.

Time suddenly stopped. I stood as though paralysed and watched her take the final steps to the door. Then the doorbell rang.

'Hi, it's me. Can I come in for a couple of minutes?' she asked, when I picked up the intercom with a shaking hand.

I wasn't sure if I meant it or not, but said, 'Of course,' and pressed the button.

Only a few weeks ago, the situation would have been perfectly normal. But now it felt so unreal that I kept expecting to wake up as I stood at the door waiting for her to come up. I had not seen the green raincoat before and for a moment wondered where she had got it. But she had taken her hood down now and it was definitely Miriam who was looking at me. Our cheeks touched briefly when she leaned forwards and gave me a light hug. It was very definitely Miriam's cheek, at once so soft and so hard. I felt some cold drops on her skin, but was sure it was rain and not tears.

'I won't take up much of your time,' Miriam said, as she hung up her raincoat. I saw that she looked around as we went into the living room and worried for a moment that Patricia might have left something behind, but I didn't think so. The only reaction from Miriam was a slight tightening around the mouth when she glanced over at the bookcase. I instantly knew why. The photograph of the two of us was no longer there.

I hesitated for a moment, then sat down on the sofa. She also hesitated for a moment when I did so, but then sat down beside me – albeit with some distance between us.

As she sat down, I regretted not having taken the chair on the other side of the table instead. The situation felt awkward – partly because I had so many times before sat much closer to Miriam on the very same sofa, but also because I had been sitting here with Patricia on my lap only the day before.

Miriam did not know that, of course, and I had no intention of telling her. In a few lightning seconds I concluded that the sofa had been the wrong choice, but that to move to the chair on the other side of the table now would just make the situation even more awkward.

'So, how are you?' I eventually asked.

'Not so good, unfortunately. I knew Fatima. She's the only reason I'm here,' she said.

There was a slight tremor in her voice.

'I think I might have seen the murderer on Friday evening. There was a man standing waiting on the corner of Young's Square when we passed there around ten. I was a bit taken aback to see anyone standing in the side street, but he quickly disappeared down the road when he saw us. It might of course just be a coincidence and it's someone else altogether, but I thought I should come and tell you, all the same.'

I was touched that she had come, and said so. She gave me a careful smile, but was then serious again as soon as I asked if she could give a description of the man she had seen.

'Unfortunately no, I only saw him for a few seconds and at a distance. But he was wearing a light mac, I saw that clearly enough,' she said, apologetically.

'The man who killed Fatima yesterday was wearing a dark-blue raincoat,' I told her tactfully.

Miriam bit her lip again, and then continued.

'I didn't know that. It's quite likely that he might have changed clothes, especially if he knew that we had seen him. But equally, it could have been someone else. I was just trying to help. And I have this oddly strong feeling that it was him. He was standing there waiting, then disappeared quickly, even though no one else showed up. There was something about the way he moved, I can't explain . . . He just seemed to be a lonely, dissatisfied man.'

I thought about what Patricia had said about the murderer's character, and wondered if in fact Miriam might be right. When we were a couple, she had often been astute in her observation of people, even when she only caught a glimpse of them.

'It's so frustrating – I wish I could give a better description and help you to find the man who killed Fatima. But I was too far away. I get the feeling, though, even when I think of him now, that I've seen him somewhere else. Somewhere completely different, and recently. Only I can't remember when and where.'

She sounded so upset that I couldn't help but feel sorry for her. But as she spoke, I became less and less convinced that the man was the murderer, and not just some passer-by. And even if he really was the murderer, we were still no closer to having a detailed description.

I put my hand rather gingerly on Miriam's shoulder, and said it was very kind and helpful of her to come, and asked her to call me straight away if she either saw the man again or remembered where she had seen him.

Her body was like a high-tension wire. I felt so much sympathy for her, but did not dare put my arms around her. I was not sure how either she or I would react. So we sat there, a couple of feet and a whole world apart.

When the silence became too oppressive, I asked how Fatima had been liked by the youth politicians. I then swiftly justified the question by asking if she had had any particularly close friends or possible enemies there.

Miriam shook her head immediately.

'No. That's to say, she had a lot of friends. Everyone who met her cared about Fatima, because of who she was and what she had experienced. She agreed more with some than others, naturally, and right now was very angry with the Labour Party about the EEC question. She confided in me the day before yesterday that she was actually considering changing parties to the Socialist People's Party. But there weren't many people who knew that, and in any case, no one hated her. There are always lots of disagreements in youth politics, but nothing that's a motive for murder – if that's what you were asking about.'

It was precisely what I had been asking, and the answer was not unexpected.

I said that I had never really thought that the answer lay there either, but asked if she had any idea how the murderer could have known where Fatima would be, and when.

'It's almost impossible to say. She left a political debate with me on Friday and went home from the cinema alone on Saturday. Fatima was open and trusting. She would happily talk to a stranger sitting next to her on a bus or train. And if she got excited or passionate about something, she sometimes spoke quite loudly. Practically anyone she had spoken to or passed might have heard where she was going.'

This was more or less what her parents had said too. And unfortunately, it did not help me to answer the one question I knew Patricia would ask.

'This whole thing is so awful. Fatima was one of the most admirable people I've met. It's so tragic that she was killed here, having managed to get to Norway in the first place. Have you spoken to her parents?' Miriam asked suddenly. Her eyes were still dry, but her voice was wavering.

I struggled with my intense desire to put my arms round her. Then I heard my own voice saying that I had been to the restaurant to speak to them, and that they were taking the tragedy with remarkable grace – and that they had asked me to pass on their greetings.

Miriam flinched visibly when I said this.

'It's pretty impressive that they can remember that we were there together that evening. Touching of them to think of us in the middle of their own tragedy,' she exclaimed, her voice breaking.

I thought that Miriam and I were uncannily alike when it came to people. With very few exceptions, we had always liked and disliked the same people, and been touched by the same situations. I could not imagine that Patricia would have the same sympathy for Fatima's parents.

I desperately wanted to hug Miriam and hold her tight. I had done it so many times before. But I wasn't sure how she would react if I tried. If she reacted positively it would feel so wrong only twenty-four hours after having sat here with Patricia. And I could not be sure that nothing more would happen. I wasn't even sure that I wanted anything more to happen.

Again, the silence became oppressive, so I told her that Fatima's parents had impressed me and that I should perhaps get on with the investigation for their sake.

Miriam took the hint this time. She gave a faint nod when I said this, but stayed sitting on the sofa next to me – further apart than ever before, and yet alarmingly near. She sat there for no more than a minute, but that minute felt like an hour. When she finally stood up, I felt enormous relief, but also sorrow.

I jumped up and followed her to the door. At first she tried to put on my raincoat, and then she struggled for an exasperatingly long time to put on her own. I realized that I did still love her for the well-meaning, absent-minded person she was.

I asked tentatively how she was, aside from what had happened to Fatima.

I was scared that she might say she had already found a new boyfriend. But to my relief, she said nothing to indicate that.

Instead she just said, 'Thank you for asking. Everything is fine, otherwise.' But it did not look as though she meant it.

She was halfway down the stairs when I saw that she had forgotten the plastic bag with her book in it. I ran down to her with it. She said, 'Thank you,' when she saw me coming. And so we prepared to part for the second time by the main door. When I opened it for her, the rain came driving in.

I surprised myself by asking if she would like me to drive her home. For a moment she lit up, but then replied, 'Thank you for offering, but I think it's possibly best if you don't. There's a bus in five minutes and you need to get on with the investigation.'

She said this in a very serious voice. And then suddenly I was standing there alone on the ground floor, by the door.

I ran upstairs just to be able to stand by the living-room window and watch her go. She walked past without looking back. We knew each other far too well. I knew that she walked past without looking back because she knew that I would be standing here watching her go.

I felt deeply uncertain as to why she had come in the first place. The more I thought about it, the flimsier the story about the man in the light mac seemed to be. I thought that she had come first of all because she cared about her dead friend. But I was not sure that that was the only reason. Miriam had not said a word about any new man in her life.

Nor had she said or asked anything about the 'the Genius of Frogner', as she used to call Patricia. And I was certain that she had not done so on purpose. And I found myself wondering whether I should mention Miriam's visit to Patricia or not.

IX

'The boy with the wound means well, but was not of much help this time,' I said.

Patricia took another mouthful of salmon, then pushed the plate demonstratively aside. She drummed her fingers on the table in irritation as she spoke.

'Basically, you're right. But his information does confirm that the murderer stands and waits for his victims, and that he never needs to stand long enough to attract suspicion. So we are back to the key question as to how he knows where to wait. It is perhaps not so strange in Fatima's case, as she was known to talk too much, because she was open and trusting. But it is harder to explain how the murderer knew where to find all four victims. I still can't see the link here. Young Fatima did not move in the same circles as any of the previous victims, and was unlikely to have walked the same streets even on a daily basis. The most likely explanation is that the murderer goes around to all parts of town and listens to what people say. But how he discovered where he could find Amalie remains a mystery.'

The time was half past six. Patricia had listened in silence as I told of the day's developments. She had eaten a third of her asparagus soup and only a few small mouthfuls of salmon. Her appetite was clearly not at its best. And nor was her mood. I did not want to risk making it any worse and so had not mentioned Miriam's name, having learned from previous experience. But I did not want to hold any information back from Patricia, so I told her the story of Fatima's friend, without mentioning who the friend was. And to my relief, she did not ask any questions.

'The friend's story also indicates that he stands and waits. But of course, we cannot be sure that it was the same man, so it gets us no further forward,' Patricia said.

I agreed, and quickly added, 'Unfortunately, it looks like Danielsen was right this time. We are looking for a murderer who has no real connection to any of the victims, which means he could be pretty much anyone in the Oslo area. It's a bit like looking for a needle in a haystack.'

'Or an ant on an anthill. Even though the murderer does not know any of the victims personally, he must have been within hearing distance of them all over a short period of time. Who on earth could that be?' Patricia exclaimed in exasperation.

'The butler,' I quipped.

It was meant as a joke, to lighten the sombre atmosphere. As soon as I had said it, I realized it was a bad joke. But Patricia snapped to attention as soon as I had uttered the word, and then spoke unusually fast.

'A butler is about the only profession we have not yet encountered in this investigation. But is there anyone else who you forget is there when you're talking? Could it be . . .'

She stopped mid-sentence. Suddenly her fingers were completely still, whereas her body was vibrating with agitation.

'Could it be that Helgesen was actually right, but not in the way that he thought? Could it be that one of the murders had a rational motive, but was not committed by the same person as the others? Could someone who is closely linked to one of the victims have grabbed the opportunity to commit a murder for which the Anthill Murderer would then be blamed?'

Patricia spoke in a torrent and stared at me without blinking. I had no idea who she was thinking of, and was eager to know. So I said, with a pounding heart, that it was of course a possibility.

She rattled on: 'If the answer to why we haven't found a link between the four murders is because there is none, perhaps we should think about looking for a link between three of the murders. And then suddenly one possibility becomes obvious . . . the butler, you said.'

Patricia laughed for a moment at my bad joke, later than intended. Then she was serious again.

'We may be on the wrong track. But we have no more than a couple of hours to lose, and perhaps a life to save. Shall we give it a try?'

I had no idea which track we were on, but promptly said yes.

'Well then, go to 28B Dirik Street, just by Lovisenberg. If a man you know comes out of the building, follow him. Keep at a safe distance, because if my theory is correct, he has very good hearing and strong hands.'

I stared back at Patricia in fascination. To be given an address and no name was not what I had expected. But Patricia was in charge now and waved her hand impatiently.

'He might perhaps be an honourable and completely in-nocent man, in which case I will feel better it I don't mention his name. But he could also be our Anthill Murderer, and then it would be terrible if we got there too late. Run for it. He has always struck late in the evening before, but no one knows what the Anthill Murderer might do next.'

I still did not have a clue what Patricia's theory was, but I was suddenly convinced that it had to be right. And I abso-lutely did not want to be too late. So I hurried out of the room and down the stairs towards the front door. A picture of

Fatima's parents and her portrait popped up in my mind. The thought of standing and facing yet more parents by the photograph of yet another young woman tomorrow was unbearable, so I bolted.

X

I was at my lookout post, on the corner two blocks away, by a quarter to seven. 28B Dirik Street was a two-storey building that looked pretty much like any other two-storey building in the same street and others nearby. I thought that it would be a suitable hiding place for a murderer trying to conceal himself in anonymity, like an ant on an anthill.

However, my faith in Patricia's theory started to wane as minute after minute passed without anything happening. A couple of passers-by gave me curious glances. People were naturally suspicious of loitering men, even though it was early evening and still light.

To pass the time, I tried to work out who it was that Patricia now suddenly suspected. If one of the murders had been committed by someone else, I decided it then had to be Amalie who had been the victim. But apart from the fact that the other three murders had been committed in the evening by a murderer who waited around on street corners, I could still see no link that would put the focus on one person.

He came out of the door at ten past seven.

I just caught a glimpse of him round the corner as he came out, before he started to walk in the opposite direction. But it was all I needed. The moment I saw him, I understood the connection that Patricia had made, and her spontaneous re-action when I mentioned the butler.

I also remembered her instructions to keep at a safe distance. It was hard to stay standing where I was, but if he recognized me, it could be disastrous. He would then just go for a walk round the nearest park and home again. If the man I was following really was the Anthill Murderer, it would be difficult to prove unless we caught him red-handed.

I could still see him at the other end of Dirik Street when I stole around the corner out of the side street. I followed in the same direction, trying to keep a constant distance. It dawned on me that I would have a problem if he got into a car. My own car was parked some way back, and it would not be easy to find a taxi. Fortunately, I did not need to worry about this. The man in front of me walked at a steady pace on light feet, past the Diaconia College and then down Collett Street towards St Hanshaugen.

I was too far away to see his face, but recognized his clothes. And for what it was worth, he was wearing a light-coloured mac. And again, for what it was worth, I did think that I was following a very lonely and dissatisfied man.

The man in the light mac carried on down Collett Street and Louise Street, then turned off just before Bislett Stadium. He turned into Wilhelm Street, and stopped by the corner with Eugenie Street. I couldn't stop there, so carried on to Therese Street and stopped on the corner at the bottom of Eugenie Street. He was about a hundred yards away, so I could still see him. He stood on his street corner waiting for some-one, and I stood on my street corner waiting for him.

The seconds dragged by. It felt as though I had been stand-ing there for ten minutes, but when I looked at my watch it was no more than two. An elderly lady was keeping a suspicious eye on me from a first-floor window opposite. I waved her away, and then popped my head around the corner again. The man in the light mac was still standing there.

XI

Before I went out earlier today, I thought that perhaps I shouldn't do it. I've carried out more murders or attempts than planned this week, and I've exhausted my wardrobe. So I had to put on the light mac that I wore for that unsuccessful attempt on Friday. But hopefully it won't make any practical difference. The risk is obviously far higher this time than with the last three murders. The town is now watching out for men waiting alone on street corners, and for the first time it's not under cover of dark. If I'm playing The $64,000 Question, I've reached the highest level, with double the prize money and three times the risk.

I'm now hostage to my own obsession. It was stronger with Fatima than the first two, and feels even more intense now with the young Jewish girl. I don't care if I get caught, as long as I can kill her first. People don't take part in The $64,000 Question for the money, they take part to show the rest of the country what they're capable of and to get the attention they think they deserve. Well, it's the same for me in my version of the game. Sooner or later I'll have to go out in broad daylight. There won't be many young women who dare to go out in the evenings for a while now.

I heard footsteps behind me all the way from my flat. They were far behind me, and I could only just hear them. And they weren't Helgesen's footsteps; he's heavier and slower. I only saw that Kolbjørn Kristiansen in his office and didn't hear him walk. I realized that it could be his footsteps or some other policeman, but not Helgesen. It didn't stop me, though. *I mustn't be nervous or scared by the slightest thing. It was probably just someone walking in the same direction. The footsteps disappeared when I turned up towards Eugenie Street, and I haven't heard them since.*

In a way, I want to get caught now. I want to read what the papers will say about me, and I don't want to go back to my boring job again. The idea of turning myself in tomorrow has crossed my mind. It would be a triumph over the police and everyone else if, after four murders in one week, I was the one to reveal my identity. I would love to read the reports about the genius killer who triumphantly handed himself in to the police instead of being caught. I would rather turn myself in than be arrested.

At the same time, my survival instinct is still very much alive and kicking. I like the freedom and the thrill of my new life as a murderer. So I've given myself a time limit: if she's not here by twenty to eight, I'll walk slowly back the way I came.

If she does come, I'll put my hands around her neck and squeeze hard until I'm sure she's dead, whether I get caught or not. I just need to keep my cool and not let go, even if someone comes running towards me.

And if no one comes running, well, once the little Jewess is lying lifeless on the ground, I'll walk back the way I came, down Wilhelm Street. Then back down Therese Street to Bislett Stadium. And from there I'll take a bus to the centre and then another bus home.

If anyone does come, I'll run the same way and try to get out of sight as quickly as possible. If I can slow down when I meet more people down in Pilestredet, then I'll be anonymous again, safe. Like an ant on an anthill.

But first, I want to meet my young friend Rebecca again. She said that she was going out at half past seven. I came a couple of minutes before, so that's nine minutes ago now. An old man has seen me from his window. He could hardly give a proper description, though, as I'm

*wearing my mac and hat. But still, it's a dilemma. My cut-off is fast
approaching.*

*The weather is very similar to when I committed the first murder. The
rain only heightens my anticipation.*

XII

The elderly lady on the first floor was back at the window and
now had an even older husband with her. A young boy had
also taken up a post by the window in the neighbouring flat.
He was reading a Donald Duck comic, but kept glancing at me
every minute or so.

Otherwise, I was just as alone on my corner as before. It
was now almost twenty to eight. More and more raindrops
were falling on my face and I found the situation increasingly
embarrassing. But the man in the light mac was still standing
on the corner of Wilhelm Street. And I had no intention of
leaving before I knew who he was waiting for.

As I stood there, the fear crept in. It slunk out of my belly
and spread into my head. I realized I was not armed and that I
had no idea whether or not the man I was watching was. If he
was the murderer, of which I was more and more convinced,
then he had very strong hands, if nothing else.

Suddenly, and to my surprise, I found myself missing
Detective Inspector Danielsen. When I had found myself in a
similar situation a few weeks ago, his presence had quite probably saved my life. Now I was alone, and did not have time to
call for reinforcements. I was still primed to run as soon as I
heard a scream or any other sound of violence from Eugenie
Street. But the fear had taken hold. I realized that we were two

men standing alone on a street corner waiting for a confrontation that might cost one of us his life.

Just then, I heard footsteps on the pavement. A group of three young men came sauntering up Therese Street.

The first two were wearing denim jackets and looking straight ahead. They were deep in conversation, and I soon gathered that it was about the upcoming World Cup qualifiers. I recognized them both from the sports pages, and suddenly realized that the Vålerenga football team had obviously just finished a training session at Bislett Stadium, and the players were on their way home.

The third young man was wearing a raincoat and staring down at the pavement, not taking part in the conversation. He stopped abruptly when he saw me. The other two carried on walking and talking, but the third stood there, and gave a questioning shrug. It was Anders Frydenlund, the football player who could have caught the murderer yesterday, but then lost his nerve.

He was just about to say something, then stopped when I put a finger to my lips in warning. I spontaneously leaned towards him and whispered, 'Take a quick look round the corner – is that the man you saw yesterday?'

Anders Frydenlund hesitated for a beat, then stuck his head out to look round the corner. I saw him take a few deep breaths as I waited in suspense. He hesitated again, before whispering back to me, 'It could well be him, but I'm not sure.'

He made no sign of carrying on, and I didn't ask him to, so we stood there side by side in the light rain. On the other side of the road, the boy with the Donald Duck comic was still standing guard, but the elderly couple had withdrawn. They perhaps found it reassuring that there were now two of us here. I certainly did.

This reminded me of a similar situation I had experienced the year before, in very different surroundings. I had stood for nearly an hour with Miriam and her father in a forest in Hedmark, waiting to see an elk that never appeared. But we were waiting for a person now – and we weren't waiting for him to appear, but rather to find out if he really was the predator we suspected he was. The tension was even greater.

When I looked at my watch it was eighteen minutes to eight. And when I looked up again, I saw her.

She was coming towards us up Therese Street through the rain, running and walking in that way impatient youngsters often do. She was perhaps fourteen, maybe fifteen or even sixteen. Her hair was jet black, her skin milky white and her mouth lipstick red.

She had ventured out into the rain alone with a secret smile on her lips, perhaps to meet a friend, or for a first date. She was wearing a raincoat without a hood. I recognized new hope in her, but also that she was someone from a different background. She reminded me of Fatima, despite her different colouring and religion.

The football player sent me a questioning look, but stayed where he was when I did. It was only when she had passed us that I suddenly realized I was now putting her life at risk. Fatima's parents popped up in my mind again and I nearly ran after the girl. But we had to have proof to stop this murderer, and I reckoned that I was too close for her to be killed, even if he did attack her. As we stood there, I realized I had no idea how long it took to strangle a person with only bare hands. I had always assumed that it must take at least thirty seconds, but had never actually asked a pathologist. So I stood at the street corner with my eyes on the girl, ready to run as soon as anything happened.

XIII

It irritates me that people, young women in particular, are so unreliable these days. It used to annoy me just as much back in the days when I went out with young women. There were several occasions when I left in frustration after they had kept me waiting for more than ten minutes. And I feel some of the same anger I felt back then. You don't treat a man like me with such arrogance. I have always made a point of being punctual, both at work and in my free time.

It's twenty to eight now. I know I should go home. Every minute longer that I wait, the risk increases. I can see two people watching me from a window. Maybe there are more. But I have no intention of being scared off. She will not avoid her destiny by being late.

Finally, my patience is being rewarded. My victim, Rebecca, has just turned the corner from Therese Street. She has changed clothes and is now wearing a brown raincoat.

I feel that it's my duty to stop her. In his later years, my father often warned me of the other constant threat from the Jews – that if they didn't take over power directly, they would keep having children with each other, or even worse, with naive Norwegians who knew no better. The result in either case would be more and more Jews. It was our shared duty as Norwegians to stop them in time, he used to tell me.

As I stand here watching her come towards me, I am reminded of an episode from when I was ten. I've actually been thinking about it more and more recently. In the summer, we went to visit an uncle who lived in the country, in Vestfold. I was standing in the garden with Father at dusk, when a hare suddenly bounded out in front of us. It stopped a few yards away, and sat there without moving. 'Get it,' my father said. I did what he said and ran as fast as I could after the hare. It was a small brown hare, possibly a young one. It jumped away, with me on its tail. The hare got away, and I remember my feeling of disappointment as I watched it disappear. But then it jumped straight into a net that my uncle had put over the berry bushes to protect them from the birds. I remember the whine of fear as the little hare got more and more entangled in the net. And I remember my own feeling of triumph and superiority as I ran towards the net and grabbed it. It twisted and turned in my hands, but could not get free of the net. I was quivering with delight and excitement when I put my hands around its neck. Then I just tightened my grip, harder and harder, until the little hare was loose and lifeless in my hands.

That was the first time I felt the thrill of killing something weaker than me with nothing but my bare hands. For all these years, it must have been lying latent in me. My hands are even stronger now; I use them for hours on end, day after day, in my work. I have often thought about trying it again, getting that feeling, but have never dared until this week. And now I'm no longer frightened. The hare didn't get away. And nor did any of the women this week. But not one of them has reminded me of the hare as much as Rebecca does. She's just like it – small, defenceless and stupid. And I am just as consumed by the desire to get my hands around her throat as I was then to get my hands around the hare's neck.

It's all I can do to stop myself running towards Rebecca, now that she's only a few yards away. But I manage to stay where I am, thanks to my impressive self-control.

She is being irritatingly slow, as though she doesn't have the energy to lift her skinny legs. She's getting closer. She doesn't look at me and pretends not to recognize me.

I give her a friendly wave and the chance to stop voluntarily. But

Rebecca is just as arrogant and stuck-up as Fatima. She ignores me and carries on looking straight ahead. This provokes me. I rush forward, and lift my hands to put them around her neck.

She turns suddenly and unexpectedly on her heel and runs away. And just as the hare jumped into the net, in her fear she runs straight into a lamp post and falls. Suddenly I'm standing over her after all. I feel the warmth and fear in her body as I press down on it. I feel her pulse beating wildly as my hands get a grip on her neck and start to squeeze.

And then I hear running feet. Two people this time. One set of feet sounds just like those from yesterday. But I won't be put off my stride. I'm afraid of nothing. Not for a second will I even consider escaping. I just keep my hands around her throat, keep pressing. Her pulse is throbbing. So is mine. My hands are shaking and my body is fizzing. She must die now. But she's still alive. And the footsteps pound louder and louder in my ears.

XIV

I started to run as soon as I saw him lunge towards her.

Suddenly the fear was there again, but this time I was not afraid of losing my own life, but of getting there too late to save her.

She spun round and started back towards us, but then ran straight into a lamp post and fell. We were still about fifty yards away when he bent down over her. I ran as fast as my legs would carry me. The football player, whose name I couldn't remember in the heat of the moment, ran faster. He sailed past me and then accelerated in this crazy race. I was still ten yards away when he hit the murderer.

Both of them toppled over. The murderer may have lost his

balance but he kept his hands firmly gripped around the victim's neck. Then suddenly I grabbed hold of one of his arms and the football player took the other – while the girl just continued to stare up at us.

He let go, but only when I punched his right arm with both hands and all my strength. 'No,' he shouted, as we pulled him off her.

After that, everything was surprisingly easy. With the football player holding his left arm, the murderer barely resisted when I pushed him over onto his stomach and twisted his right arm up behind his back. I could feel his body trembling slightly, but he stayed calm as I clicked on the handcuffs, and then appeared to be completely relaxed.

'Did I manage to kill her?' the Anthill Murderer asked. The football player punched him in the side when he said this, and I suddenly remembered the victim. Once again, fear washed over me.

She was lying a couple of yards away from us, with great bruises on her neck. She was barely moving, but she was breathing. When I put my arm across her shoulders I felt the spread of warmth and her heartbeat.

As she sat up, she said in a barely audible voice: 'Thank you. I love life.'

The relief was overwhelming. And in that moment I thought to myself that I really did love Patricia.

XV

It was now a quarter past nine. I had the amazing and bizarre feeling that outside the police station, Norway was already jumping with the news. Inside, in the interview room, Helgesen, the Anthill Murderer and I sat in sombre silence.

We had offered to call a lawyer for him. He had replied that he had nothing to hide and that we could just as well start immediately. He was not uncooperative in any way; on the contrary, he was positively eager. I was mildly vexed that he seemed to be more relieved than disappointed at having been arrested.

He had in a more or less flat voice confirmed all the circumstances surrounding the murders of Agnes, Lise and Fatima and had answered all our questions about the crime scenes correctly.

I reflected that even though we now knew the identity of the murderer, I still did not understand who he was. I had not even considered him to be a potential murderer when I first met him. I still would not have thought so now, had I not seen him attempt to murder a girl with my own eyes. By nature, he seemed to be a proper, rather formal worker.

'I thought that you would catch me sooner,' was the first thing he said.

I replied that he had been lucky, as we had been confused by the third murder.

'Lucky, but also good. I had been preparing for a long time,' he retorted, with a little smile.

'But in the end, we found the link and how you could know the time and place. You listened to the passengers on your bus talking about their plans for the coming days, and realized the opportunities this could offer,' I continued.

Hilmar Lauritzen gave a brief nod, again, with a little smile.

'It was, if I might say so myself, almost a stroke of genius. All the victims underestimated me. As did the police for almost a whole week after the first murder. Who would think a bus driver could commit murder after murder and get away with it? But I did!'

He laughed quietly as he said this. In some strange way, he had triumphed in his own eyes: even now, in the face of defeat. He carried on, without waiting for more questions.

'You have no idea what a burden it is to have such good hearing, especially in a job like mine. Life can become pretty unbearable when you have to listen to all the drivel and noise that people make on the bus, hour after hour, day after day. I thought about changing jobs, but then decided that I should do something positive about the situation instead.'

'And you did that by taking three people's lives? Why did you do it?' I asked, rather sharply.

He gave me a condescending look before continuing.

'Because I was bored, obviously. My life has been without meaning for years. Day after day, week after week, month after month, and year after year, I've done what I should without ever getting any recognition. A job that was boring for me but useful for others might even have been bearable if I'd been thanked for it. But I've never been thanked once. My work is boring and meaningless. Is it so hard to understand that one day I'd just had enough and used the opportunity I had to get some excitement in my life and give it meaning?'

This was said with unexpected passion.

I replied, even more curtly, that many people experience similar things in life without feeling the need to kill someone. I asked if he had ever considered what a loss these people were to society.

'I chose victims who would be no great loss. In fact, the

country would be a better place without them. The first was a hypocritical and arrogant young woman, who was challenging the natural order of things by wanting to become a priest. The second one was Oslo's most depraved young woman, a promiscuous tart who encouraged immoral behaviour when she sang. And the third . . .' He took a couple of deep breaths before carrying on. 'The third was the worst of them all. A dark-skinned Muhammadan woman who brazenly walked around in our city. The country will go to the dogs if we let people like that live. The future will prove me right.'

'And all three were also attractive young women who did not show the blindest bit of interest in you?' I suggested.

'I don't know that I'd call them attractive, but they certainly behaved badly towards me. The first one was a self-centred woman who liked to tease men, but didn't want to give her love to anyone. The second one threw herself at any student or musician she met, and showed absolutely no interest in an honest working man like myself. The third . . .'

Again, the arrestee had to breathe deeply before carrying on.

'The third one completely ignored me, when she should have been grateful that a white man wanted to touch her at all!'

I paused for a few seconds before answering. The man's behaviour was enraging.

'Did you ever think about the young women's families and friends?' Helgesen asked.

Lauritzen kept his eyes glued to me, but nodded in acknowledgement and answered the question swiftly.

'I was considerate there. None of the women were married or had children. I would never kill a woman who had children, no matter how bad a mother she was. And as for parents and friends, I didn't know them, but I don't see why any of them should feel much loss. The parents will have less to worry about and the siblings will inherit more. I wouldn't have felt any great loss if my sister or mother had been murdered, I can promise you that.'

Helgesen swallowed hard, and asked no more questions. I could see that he, as a family man, was deeply outraged by this. And I could understand him, even though I didn't have children.

There was something galling about the murderer's cocksureness and self-absorption, even when he had been formally accused of three murders and one attempted murder. I remembered what Patricia had said about the Anthill Murderer's personality and had to admit that she had hit the nail on the head, yet again. Hilmar Lauritzen suffered either from narcissism or some other personality disorder. His last answer gave reason to believe he had a sad family history, which might possibly be the reason that he was sitting here now. But that was for the psychiatrists and the court to decide. My job was to solve the one remaining murder.

'What had us confused for a long time was the murder last Friday, when Amalie Meyer-Michelsen was killed and dumped at Tveita Shopping Centre. The murderer also left behind a picture of an ant. Do you have any idea who might be behind this?'

The question provoked the most violent outburst from the Anthill Murderer so far. He shook his head with indignation and raised a warning finger.

'I have absolutely no idea. The cheek of it. Believe me, I would have said who it was if I knew. I have not discussed the murders or the picture of the ant with another living soul.'

'Do you also deny that you called the police after the murder, identified yourself as the Anthill Murderer and told us where to find the body?' I asked.

Hilmar Lauritzen was suddenly totally focused. His eyebrows were dancing and his hand shook when he answered.

'Of course. I worked all day without a break on Friday, from eight in the morning until five in the afternoon. It just gets worse and worse, if this copycat really did call and pretend to be me. I certainly hope you manage to catch the bastard!'

Helgesen and I exchanged a brief, exasperated look. Then we concluded the interview. There was clearly still a case to be solved outside the police station.

'When do you think the court case will be? And how long will it be until the ban on correspondence and visits is lifted?' Hilmar Lauritzen asked, as I stood up.

I thought to myself that he must be looking forward to the court case and all the attention he would get. Out loud, I said that the ban on correspondence and visits would last for some weeks and that the court case would probably be in a few months, but that things might move faster if he put all his cards on the table.

'Then I will, of course,' he replied with almost childlike glee, and held out his hand

I shook it briefly. It was the first time I had felt physical repulsion when shaking someone's hand. He made no move to honour my colleague in the same way. And Helgesen did not look in the slightest bit bothered.

'You should perhaps be warned that when the court case starts, there is a risk that you will become the most hated man in Norway, after Quisling and Rinnan,' Helgesen remarked, as we turned to leave.

'My father was distrustful of Rinnan, but liked Quisling. In any case, all great men in this country are controversial. Having been someone who no one noticed, I would now rather be someone who is liked by few, but talked about by everyone, even if it does mean that people hate me,' he said, still sounding optimistic.

I looked at Helgesen and saw that behind his congenial exterior, he was about to explode. And I felt sure that the murderer would thoroughly enjoy it if he did. So I pulled Helgesen with me out of the room, without wasting another word on the Anthill Murderer. For the past seven intense days, I had used all my energy and every waking minute on trying to find him, and now that he had been arrested, Hilmar Lauritzen was of no real interest to me any more. My thoughts were entirely focused on Amalie Meyer-Michelsen. In my mind's eye I saw her fiancé, and her cousins who had thought they would now inherit the family fortune.

XVI

'That was an extremely unpleasant experience, but also a great relief,' Helgesen commented, once we were back in my office.

I had to agree, but added that for my part, the relief was greater than the discomfort. Helgesen nodded. Then, quite spontaneously, he said how impressive it was that I had managed to find the murderer just in time to save the latest victim.

I replied, without embellishing, that it was indeed fortunate that I had got there in time. Then I said that his theory that one of the murders might have a rational motive had been of great significance to the breakthrough. He was visibly pleased to hear this.

In other words, the mood in my office was much brighter than of late, and there was a feeling of warmth. It was almost as if we were old friends, even though we had scarcely known each other just a week ago.

Only the two of us were there. The boss had taken May Day off and was at his cabin, and Danielsen had not been able to come into the station at such short notice. Both these things suited me rather well. I wanted, if at all possible, to have solved all four murders before reporting to my boss. And now that there was no danger, I no longer missed Danielsen.

In their absence, I took the opportunity to decide that I would continue the investigation into the murder of Amalie Meyer-Michelsen forthwith, but granted both myself and Helgesen time off until ten o'clock the next day. He promised to be there and added, jokingly, that he would have an updated list of alibis with him.

Half a minute after he had left the office, I dialled Patricia's number. She answered the phone after the first ring.

'It was just announced on the radio that a suspect has been arrested at Bislett!' she said, like the cat that got the cream.

Patricia was back to her old form. The arrest of the Anthill Murderer was clearly an even greater relief to her than to me.

I told her that I had got there just in time, and that it was entirely thanks to her. I asked if she had found Hilmar Lauritzen's address in the telephone directory. She replied, 'Of course. I found practically all of the people involved there. Before you ask, I first started to suspect him because both Agnes and Lise took the bus, and because he remembered Agnes' last bus trip with such clarity. But then I let it go, because Amalie never took the bus – and I made the mistake of believing the police's theory that the same person was behind all three murders.'

I swallowed that bitter pill – and said that I hoped we could meet as soon as possible to discuss the still unsolved murder.

Patricia did not hesitate. 'Of course. Why don't we celebrate this evening's success and at the same time solve the fourth murder at your flat in an hour's time? You see, Amalie's murder is far more straightforward, and I have a theory that I think you will like!'

This cheered me even more and I said that she was more than welcome to come to my flat.

Patricia replied, smugly, that I still had fifty-nine minutes to think about how I would thank her. Then she put down the receiver.

I sat there wondering what she had meant by that. But my mood remained buoyant, and though my face was still serious, I laughed inwardly all the way out of the police station.

There was a very touching surprise waiting for me when I got to the door. I was a little taken aback when I heard that there were two people waiting who refused to leave without speaking to me personally first. And even though their faces were hidden behind an enormous bouquet of flowers, I realized who they were as soon as I saw their clothes. They were standing just inside the door of the main police station in Oslo wearing their best, most colourful clothes, which were very obviously from other parts of the world. And they were there to thank me.

He was from Palestine and she was from South America, and it was not easy to catch what they said, the words came out in such a rush. But I did understand that I had saved the life of their youngest child and they were immensely glad still to have her. A few tears were shed on either side of the bouquet, both theirs and mine.

XVII

It was ten past ten when I put the bouquet down on the coffee table in my living room, only twenty minutes before Patricia was due to arrive. Fortunately, there was not much to tidy in the kitchen or the living room.

I hesitated for a few moments in the doorway to the bedroom. And then I changed the sheets. I was still in a good mood and chuckled to myself as I did so. I was not sure that I was ready to go to bed with her yet, but my feelings were now stronger than ever. I still did not know whether I could make love to a handicapped woman, but I knew now that I was in love with a woman who was handicapped. And I thought that if Patricia did end up in my bed tonight, she certainly deserved clean sheets.

The doorbell rang just as I went back into the living room, even though it was only a quarter past ten.

'Hello, it's me. I know it's late, but can I come in for five minutes? It might be important!' said a voice on the intercom.

It was Miriam. I had not expected that. Seconds later I realized that Patricia would be here in ten minutes, and that I should perhaps ask Miriam to come back another day. But I had already pressed the door opener.

I let her in through the door, but no further.

'I've had a very busy day, but you said that it might be important?' was the first thing I said.

Miriam nodded, and pointed at me.

'Yes, absolutely. I suddenly remembered, when I saw someone who looked like him go up to the podium, where I had
seen the man I saw waiting for Fatima the day before yesterday.
I don't know his surname, but his first name is Hilmar, and he's
a bus driver. He was driving the bus I caught from Majorstuen
down to the centre of town, and it's the bus that Fatima used
to take. It can't be a coincidence. I think, and hope, that he's the
murderer!'

Miriam stood there with the inevitable book wrapped in a
plastic bag under her arm, rain in her hair, her finger shaking
as it pointed at me. She spoke fast and with passion. I felt more
sympathy for her in that moment than I had ever felt before.

I said, as gently as I could, that she obviously had not heard
the news on the radio.

'No, I was at a party meeting when I suddenly remembered
where I had seen the man in the light mac before. So I left
straight afterwards and caught the bus here as quickly as I
could. I was here an hour ago, but you weren't home. What's
happened?' she asked.

I told her, choosing my words with care, that she was absolutely right. The bus driver was the murderer, and he had
been arrested during another murder attempt earlier in the
evening.

'That means – if I had remembered where I saw him earlier
today, it might have been helpful, but now it's no longer
relevant,' Miriam said, very slowly and with audible disappointment.

I suddenly felt very uncomfortable. The situation was awkward, and the clock on the wall said it was twenty past ten.

I said that I deeply appreciated the fact that she had come

to tell me straight away, and that the person responsible for Fatima's death had now been arrested. Then I added that I was still rather busy, and suggested that perhaps we could talk another day.

'I understand. You're expecting someone,' Miriam said. She was looking over my shoulder at the huge bunch of flowers on the table.

'The flowers are a gift from the parents of the girl whose life we saved this evening. But yes, I am expecting someone,' I told her.

Miriam kept her eyes fixed on the flowers.

'I understand. Well, I won't disturb you any longer, then. There's a bus in four minutes, I should be able to make it,' she said.

I said that it would perhaps be best if she could get the bus, and repeated that it would be nice to talk to her another day – but that the great thing was that Fatima's murderer had now been arrested.

'Yes. I really did my best to help you,' she said, and left.

I stood there outside my flat and listened to the main door close. My watch said it was nearly half past ten.

I ran over to the living-room window and saw Miriam walk down the road. She walked fast, with her book under her arm, and nothing on her head. I still felt enormous sympathy for her. But more than anything, I hoped that she would be out of sight before Patricia arrived.

Which almost happened, but only almost. Miriam was crossing the road to the bus stop when Patricia's large car turned in.

I prayed that they would pass each other without noticing.

But that of course did not happen. Little Miriam and the big car stopped at the same time.

They stood facing each other for a few seconds, then Miriam stepped back onto the pavement as the car did a U-turn and drove back towards the main road.

I felt so sorry for Miriam in that moment. And my guilt only increased when the bus then passed behind her less than a minute later. But my overwhelming feeling, all the same, was panic and fear at Patricia's reaction. I stood by the window looking down, even after Miriam then carried on walking towards the bus stop.

There was so little traffic on the roads now, it would take Patricia less than ten minutes to get home. I rang her after ten minutes, after fifteen and then twenty minutes, but no one answered the phone.

As far as I could remember, the buses still went every fifteen minutes. But I went down at ten to eleven all the same.

XVIII

There was only one person at the bus stop when I got there at five to eleven. My guilt only increased when I realized that she had had to wait half an hour for the next bus.

'Hello, and I'm sorry,' I said.

'Hello, and sorry back,' she replied.

'Sorry back' was an expression we had often used jokingly and laughed about when we were together. But neither of us was in the mood to laugh about anything now.

'I really appreciate that you came because you wanted to help me,' I told her.

'I tried, but that still wasn't good enough. I should have remembered,' she said.

We stood there in silence. Just then, the lights of the bus appeared further up the road. Miriam stared hard at them, before suddenly speaking again.

'If that was the Genius of Frogner, and I'm sure it was, I hope that you don't know her too well. The woman might well be a genius, but she is also quite definitely mad. You should have seen the look of hate she sent me. She was spitting venom. I haven't been so frightened since . . .'

She stopped and bit her tongue. I knew only too well what she was going to say. So I mumbled another apology and gave her a quick hug.

She thanked me as she got on the bus. I found myself looking suspiciously at the bus driver, but it was a middle-aged woman who looked utterly harmless.

Then once again I was standing there alone with my guilt at the bus stop.

I started to walk home, but on an impulse went back to check the bus timetable.

And it confirmed what I suspected: the buses were still running every fifteen minutes and there had been a bus at twenty two minutes to eleven. The fact that Miriam had not taken it made me even more confused.

Back in my flat, I tried to call Patricia again, but still no one answered the phone.

I leapt at the telephone when it rang five minutes later. But it was neither Patricia nor Miriam. Instead, it was Knud Haasund from *Verdens Gang*. He wanted to congratulate me on the arrest and to ask if it would be possible to have an interview sometime tomorrow.

I told him that the arrest had nothing to do with the car registration number he had given me, but that he could try to phone me at half past ten in the morning all the same.

'It's a deal. Good night,' he said, and put down the phone.

I made two more attempts to ring Patricia, but then gave up at half past eleven and went to bed.

The bed linen was clean, but the room felt cold and my mind was in chaos. I eventually fell asleep just before half past twelve, escaping my extremely confused feelings and deep concern about what tomorrow might bring. No matter what else was going on around me, one thing was clear, and that was that I would have to find Amalie Meyer-Michelsen's murderer without any help from Patricia. But worst of all was the gnawing fear that I might never speak to Patricia again. So even though the bed was soft and the sheets were clean, it felt as if I was sleeping on a bed of nails.

DAY EIGHT

When the Iron Curtain Falls

I

Monday, 1 May 1972 was one of those rare days when I woke up early, and lay there hoping the telephone would ring. But it didn't.

Instead, I made a phone call myself before I even got out of bed at a quarter to nine. But it was not answered by either Patricia or her staff. I had never experienced that before. It was not a good start to the day, despite the glorious weather outside.

My mother called at ten to nine to congratulate me on solving the case, and at five to nine my sister did the same. The arrest was the first item on the nine o'clock news on the radio. At four minutes past nine, an old school friend I had not spoken to for years rang, and at nine minutes past nine, I had a call from a childhood sweetheart I had not spoken to since the Fifties. And at twelve minutes past nine, Mikael Grundtvig Sparde from *Dagbladet* was on the phone to congratulate me and praise the police, but also to ask for a portrait interview for next Saturday's edition.

In short, there was much to indicate that the general public was hugely relieved and very happy. It should have been one of the best days of my life. But instead it felt like one of the darkest – partly because one of the murders had still not been solved, but mainly because I was very worried about Patricia and her reaction to last night's unfortunate encounter. Every time the phone rang, my hope flared, only to be snuffed out by even greater disappointment when the voice was not hers.

It was almost humiliating to think that a coincidence could turn everything on its head. If Miriam had left a minute earlier yesterday, Patricia and I would have been the best of friends – perhaps even lovers. And I was sure that I would then also know who had killed Amalie Meyer-Michelsen, or would at least have a plan as to how I might find out. As it was, everything was strained and uncertain, in terms of the investigation and my life.

There was one last chance when the telephone rang at twenty past nine. It proved to be only another disappointment. Instead of Patricia's voice, I heard that of Mrs Borgen on the ground floor. She wanted to congratulate me on solving my latest case and to praise me for taking the time 'to invite a cripple to supper despite being so busy'. She finished by saying that she hoped she might hear news of a 'joyful reunion', following the two visits from my former fiancée. I thanked her as politely as I could and then put the receiver down without any further comment.

II

It took longer than usual to get to the office. An unprecedented number of people were heading to the Labour Day celebrations.

I could not decide whether this was due to the fine weather or the tense political situation, but noticed that there was a remarkable number of badges in evidence this year, and most of them appeared to be from the anti-EEC movement.

I was sure that Miriam would be there, and that she would be pleased to see all the No badges. I found myself looking out for her as I got closer to the main police station, but she was of course nowhere to be seen. I sincerely hoped that she was somewhere in the Labour Day parade.

I was equally sure that Patricia was sitting at home. But I was less certain about her views on the EEC.

Helgesen was neither at home nor in the parade. He was waiting outside my office when I arrived, even though it was still only ten to ten.

And new list of alibis was ready on his desk. Helgesen had included everyone we had contacted in connection with Amalie Meyer-Michelsen's death.

'The only one with a watertight alibi is the person one tends to suspect first in such cases: in other words, her fiancé,' I said.

Helgesen nodded.

'Yes. He says that he got to work at ten o'clock on Friday, and his boss has confirmed this. He was in the same room as two other people when he heard the news on the radio just after lunch. Solid as the bank. And as we now know that the person who dumped Amalie at Tveita Shopping Centre was a man, we can rule out the secretary, Rikke Johansen. Not least because several other people in the office have confirmed that she was at work all morning.'

We carried on. The next two names on the list were Wendelmann and his son. Mr Wendelmann said that he had been in his other office from nine until eleven. This had been confirmed by a clerk and an accountant. He then went to have lunch with his son at the Bristol Hotel from eleven to twelve. His son said that he had slept late as he had been performing at the theatre the night before, and so had not done anything before going to meet his father at the Bristol at eleven. They then went to their meeting with Christoffer Meyer-Michelsen together, and I myself had been there to meet them at the end of that meeting.

'So, Mr Wendelmann has a pretty sound alibi, but the son's leans heavily on his father's. We should perhaps check the timings with the Bristol Hotel,' I suggested.

'Agreed. These two seem to be on much thinner ice, though,' he said, and pointed at the next names on the list.

The late Christoffer Meyer-Michelsen had described them as parasites. They themselves believed they had been defrauded of their inheritance. Neither of them would now get even a krone. But they both had a motive, as they had believed that Amalie's death would bring them millions. Neither of them had an alibi, as they were both at home alone on Friday morning. Rakel and Robert Enger were now clearly the prime suspects.

At the bottom of the list was the name of a person I had not yet considered that day. Paul Vincent Krag.

'I actually don't believe it's him, either. But he has killed a young woman before, he was released on Tuesday, and he doesn't have an alibi for Friday morning. Furthermore, his car was in the car park at Tveita. Perhaps we should not rule him out quite yet. I can't bear to think what *Verdens Gang* would write if it was him and we had not investigated thoroughly,' Helgesen said.

I was not aware that Helgesen read *Verdens Gang*. But he

clearly had a point, and I had no intention of criticizing his list for being too long, following my experience of the previous one.

'The car park lead is of more interest again. And it's possible that Amalie's body was driven there in Paul Vincent Krag's car. Another possibility is that she drove there in her own car and was killed either in the car park or inside the shopping centre. Rather risky, but still not to be ruled out. Or the murderer may have killed her somewhere else and driven her there in her own car. But then the murderer must somehow have got into the car and killed her en route, which seems unlikely. She left home alone and would hardly have stopped to pick anyone up along the way. Are there any other possibilities?' I asked.

Helgesen hesitated, and then answered succinctly: 'Not that I can think of right now. None of the three scenarios seems likely, but then none of them can be ruled out.'

I conceded. But at the same time, I thought that somewhere between the lines, between these seven names, there was something that we could not see. Patricia obviously had a theory and suspected someone, and I was certain that it would be logical and correct. And that the name of the murderer was on the list in front of me. So it was all the more frustrating that I was still unable to see where the answer lay. There were several potential murderers here, some of whom we could perhaps strike from the list in the course of the day. But drawing any conclusion on the basis of what we knew now was beyond me.

'Everyone except the painter has a rational motive. And they all could have committed the crime with the help of an accomplice who is unknown to us. Would it not, therefore, be sensible to question them all again?' Helgesen said.

I opened my mouth to say yes, but the telephone started to ring before I had a chance.

I picked up the receiver and when I heard the voice I asked Helgesen to wait outside.

III

'Congratulations on the arrest, but I hope you realize that the bus driver could not have killed Amalie Meyer-Michelsen?' the voice on the other end said.

Knud Haasund wanted one thing, and one thing only. He got straight to the point, without wasting anyone's time. In that sense, he was well suited to *Verdens Gang*, a newspaper that was not known to overestimate its readers.

I hesitated for a moment. Yesterday we had put out a press release to say that a man in his late thirties had been arrested by the police during a murder attempt in St Hanshaugen, and was also being questioned in connection with the murders committed last week. But Haasund was already well informed. I could feel my anger rising, but at the same time was curious as to how much he actually knew.

'What makes you think that?' I asked, and waited to hear what he said.

'Well, according to several of his colleagues, Lauritzen worked the day shift on Friday,' Haasund replied, with his usual efficiency.

I was impressed and slightly alarmed by developments in the media these days. This would have been unthinkable when I started working as a detective seven years ago. The competition in Aker Street was clearly fiercer, and the newspapers had started to lead their own investigations of serious criminal cases. And Haasund was one of the key players in this development. Apparently, during an earlier case, he had gone so far as to dress up as a doctor in order to get photographs of an injured person who had been hospitalized. I could not bring myself to like him, but had to admit that I respected him on some level. He was, like me, an ambitious young man who was totally dedicated to his work, even on a bank holiday. I found myself wondering if Haasund had a wife and children, or if he, like me, shuttled between the office and an empty home.

'No doubt it's the fiancé who has seized the chance to kill Amalie,' he suddenly continued.

I should no longer have been shocked by the tactics of *Verdens Gang* and Knud Haasund. But I was, all the same. I asked tentatively what made him think it was the fiancé.

'What makes you think it wasn't?' he parried.

I considered his question for a few moments and concluded that I was already in dangerous waters – and so took the plunge.

'He was at work. We have witnesses to confirm that he came to work as normal at ten o'clock and was still there when he heard the news on the radio at around two about the death at Tveita Centre.'

There was silence for a moment at the other end.

'Can I still presume that I'll be the first to know if this leads to an arrest?' I heard him ask.

There was another short silence. Following this dramatic pause, I heard my own voice reply: 'Yes – as long as this stays strictly between us.'

'Of course. Neither of us are fools. The fact that the fiancé was there at ten and two doesn't prove that he was there in between. I've spoken to someone who saw the fiancé slip out the back door at half past ten, then get into his car and drive off,' Haasund said.

I thanked him for this information and promised to contact him when I had investigated it in more detail. Then I asked what else was going to be in the morning edition.

'We've got Lauritzen's sister, who wants nothing to do with her brother and says that he has always been a loner who didn't give a damn about anyone else. We've got the parents of the girl he tried to kill yesterday, who are extremely grateful to you and the police. And we've got Frydenlund, the footballer, and his girlfriend, direct from her sofa in Hausmann Street. An impressive front page. But you no doubt want to get on and solve the murder of the hotel magnate's daughter – and we want it splashed across our front page tomorrow or the day after.'

I said that I did, and we hung up at the same time. I sat there thinking.

In the middle of everything else that was going on, I was pleased to hear that the football player and his girlfriend had obviously been reunited. He had lost his nerve and his first big chance, but had kept a cool head and scored on his second opportunity. And she had shown she was willing to forgive his weaknesses. Things boded well for them.

My own future felt more precarious than ever following this conversation. I had again stretched the regulations as far as they could go in a way that would have serious negative consequences for me, should it ever get out. But I could still face myself in the mirror and say that I was doing everything I could to solve the final murder. Suddenly it was within reach.

IV

'I realize of course that I should have told the police myself,' Rolf Johan Svendsen said.

I had been honest with Helgesen and said that the phone call had been a tip-off: Amalie's fiancé had been seen leaving the office at half past ten. He had rolled his eyes, but had not asked for any more details. We had agreed that we should talk to the fiancé about this new information, and soon enough we were back in his living room in Frogner.

'I am totally innocent regarding my fiancée's death, but realized that I would be a suspect if this ever got out, so I chose to say nothing. I understand now that that was a mistake and I apologize sincerely,' he said.

'Where did you go and why?' I asked impatiently.

'I went to my fiancée's house because I needed to speak to her. She had said the day before that she wanted to go to Tveita around eleven o'clock. But she obviously left earlier, because when I got there at twenty to eleven, the door was locked and no one answered the bell,' he told us.

I leaned forwards over the table and asked again why he had gone there.

'I had decided the week before that I needed to have a serious talk with Amalie about our relationship. And I had put it off every day. I had originally intended to wait until after her father's birthday, but then on Thursday night I lay tossing and turning, and when I got to work on Friday, I couldn't concentrate. I thought that a resolution would be the lesser evil for both her and me.'

'So in other words, when you say a serious talk, you mean

that you had actually thought of breaking off the engagement?'
I said.

He gave a quick nod. His Adam's apple bobbed a couple of
times before any more sound came out of his lips.

'I realized that she was not happy and did not want to do
anything rash for either her sake or mine. But with every day
that passed, I felt more and more certain. Ironically, it was my
relationship with her that made me realize just how much I
wanted children. As a consequence, there was no future for
our relationship if we did not have children – and I saw no
reason to believe that we would. She was like a fairy princess
when we first met. But then gradually everything became
more and more mundane. It felt as though we had exhausted
every possibility we had, as a couple without children. To be
frank, the more I got to know her, the more ordinary and less
exciting she became. The idea of living together for decades
like that was not very enticing.'

'Well, you no longer need to live with her. And instead you
will inherit millions, as neither she nor her father knew that
you intended to break off the engagement,' I said.

He nodded.

'If you were to ask me if that feels good, the answer is no.
Though as there are no other close relatives, I don't know of
anyone who deserves to inherit those millions more than I do.
But I have to say that I'm glad now that Amalie did not know I
was going to let her down. It would have been unbearable if the
last thing she experienced before her death was me breaking
off the engagement.'

'Amalie's cousins might take a different view on who
deserves to inherit the family fortune, having lived for many

years in the bitter knowledge that their uncle had robbed their mother of her share,' I countered.

'I have given that some thought too. It's not a happy situation for anyone,' he replied, with some defiance. But for the first time he would not meet my eye.

Helgesen unexpectedly broke the uneasy silence.

'It would seem that your fiancée did not know herself that she was pregnant. But she was. How would you have reacted if she had still been at home on Friday and told you that?'

'I would have taken it in my stride. It would have completely changed the situation. I would still perhaps have worried that our marriage might not last until our silver wedding anniversary. But I would of course have given it a chance and taken responsibility for the child,' the man on the sofa replied.

He spoke more slowly and his voice was quieter. I was again struck by the thought that behind his reserved facade, he was a complex man and not easy to understand. What was clear, though, was that he was a man who now stood to inherit millions, who had known that his fiancée was going to Tveita Shopping Centre – and who had misled us in his original statement with regard to his movements on the day she was killed.

I told him that withholding information from the police in a murder case was very serious indeed, even for a lawyer. And that his new statement still did not provide a satisfactory alibi. To my surprise he nodded in acknowledgement.

'I am perfectly aware of both things and deeply regret the situation I have created for you and myself. I swear that on Friday I left work and went to Amalie's house, but she wasn't there and so I went straight back to work. The newspapers have said that her body was left in Tveita Shopping Centre around eleven o'clock. Given that I was at work at ten, then at her house at twenty to eleven and back at work by half past eleven, it would theoretically not have been possible for me to do that. The house was empty and I didn't see any neighbours – the only person I did see in Skøyen won't be of much help—'

He stopped before finishing the sentence, but it only took a hard stare for him to continue.

'I met a woman, a tramp, on the road by the house. She spoke to me, so we exchanged a few words. They say she's mad, so I realize that it won't be much help either. I don't know her, but have seen her in the area a couple of times before. Amalie said she was a bit annoying, but perfectly harmless. They call her Gaustad-Guri, as she's in and out of the mental hospital there. Not a very promising witness, I realize, but she's my only hope of an alibi.'

I listened to this with some scepticism, and then asked on a whim if I could borrow his telephone for a minute. He said, 'Of course, for as long as you like.' Then he got up and left the room.

Gaustad-Guri was a well-known name at the police station. I had met her briefly in the line of duty a couple of years earlier, and then later had stopped a few times when I bumped into her wandering around town. She was unmistakable, and as soon as Rolf Johan Svendsen said her name, I could see her clearly.

The telephone directory was lying beside the phone. I looked up the number for Gaustad Mental Hospital and spoke to one of the two police contacts there.

I did not beat about the bush and simply asked: 'How is Guri?'

The doctor's voice immediately changed from formal and disinterested to sad and resigned.

'Not very well, unfortunately. Her lungs are about to collapse because of her smoking, so she has more reason than
ever to be depressed. She was out on Friday, but came back in
a sorry state in the afternoon and has not wanted to go out
again since. She had a very unsettled night last night, so we
gave her some tranquilizers. But she's here, and still on the
ball. She should be awake again sometime between four and
five.'

I thanked him for his help and said that we would come
over to talk to her later in the afternoon.

Then I put down the receiver and called in the owner of the
phone. I said that we would do our best to check his alibi and
would not arrest him in the meantime, but that he should not
leave town and under no circumstances should he contact
Gaustad Mental Hospital.

He promised to do as I said, and again apologized for his
'misleading' statement, then wished us well with the investigation. I seriously doubted that he meant it.

V

The secondary-school teacher, Robert Enger, lived on the
second floor of a house in Minnesund, just outside Eidsvoll, a
few hundred yards from Lake Mjøsa. The flat reminded me of
an office. It was clean and tidy and stripped of any personal
effects. There was no art or family photographs of any kind on
the walls. As far as I could see, the bookshelves contained only
secondary-school and university textbooks. The one thing that
hinted at personal taste was a collection of Beatles LPs by the
stereo player.

There was a large pile of exam papers at either end of the living-room table, and Robert Enger was sitting on a chair between them.

'I was here alone on Friday morning and unfortunately no one can confirm that,' he said.

I looked around and could definitely believe that he would have been alone if he was at home. If anyone else had been in the flat, they had not left a trace. I almost asked if a woman other than his sister had ever been here, but instead, enquired if he was the owner, or a tenant.

'I'm renting. But I hope that one day I may be able to buy my own place. It won't be for some years yet, though, on my salary. It's easy to feel like a failure, especially when you come from a family where it was taken for granted that one had at least two houses and a fortune worth millions. I have learned to live with it now, but it's worse for Rakel,' he said.

I asked if he suffered from poor health. He shook his head.

'Not at all. It was my first sick day this year. I was supposed to go to work on Friday and now regret that I didn't. But I simply didn't feel mentally or physically up to teaching that day when the alarm went off. I had spent the whole of Thursday evening trying to comfort my sister and had not been able to fall asleep until early in the morning.'

This did not sound entirely unreasonable. It also explained why I had not detected the slightest hint of a cold or other illness when I met him on Saturday.

'So from your point of view, there was a positive development on Friday, then yet another disappointment on Saturday,' I said.

'Yes. I suppose that's true. My first response was to feel sorry for poor Amalie. I had nothing against her, even though

I loathed her father, but as I hadn't met her for well over a decade, I was rather indifferent to her. But then I thought that perhaps this would mean a change in fortune for my sister and myself. The old dream of getting what was rightfully ours was rekindled. And it's a hard blow to lose hope when you have finally got it back. But nothing I won't survive. It's harder for Rakel, though.'

'If you had got the inheritance you thought you were going to get, you could have stopped working and bought yourself a big house,' Helgesen commented.

'I dreamed about that for a few hours on Friday – what I would do with my share if we finally inherited twenty million each. If it had happened ten years ago, things might have been different. It took a lot to galvanize me into training to be a teacher. I would not have chosen to teach if I hadn't needed to. But now I actually enjoy my job, so I would have continued to work, whatever the case. I thought that I could buy a house and pay off my student debt, but otherwise, life wouldn't change much for me. But it was harder for Rakel.'

No matter what I asked him, Robert Enger ended up talking about his sister. I wondered momentarily if he was trying to hint that his sister had a stronger motive, but I didn't really think so. Instead, he made a more favourable impression this time round, as a caring big brother with a sense of responsibility.

'It's always been like that, hasn't it? Things have always been harder for Rakel than for you?' I suggested.

'Yes. But you have to understand that Rakel is younger and was closer to Mother than I was. I have a qualification, a job that I like, and can stand on my own two feet. Rakel has no training, so can't get an interesting job, and doesn't have the husband she has always dreamed of. Life is not easy these days when you work as a cleaner and don't have any savings. And it's not made any easier when—'

He stopped abruptly, but then carried on without being asked.

'It's not made any easier when others see you as a neurotic. Especially when the reason they think you're a neurotic is the fact that you are.'

'So your sister has problems with her nerves?' Helgesen asked, with audible interest.

'It's not a nice thing to say about your sister, but it would also be wrong not to in this situation. Yes, Rakel has a history of mental health problems. I was worried about her last week and have been extremely worried about her this weekend. She was beside herself with disappointment and rage yesterday.'

Helgesen and I exchanged a quick look. We were now talking about a mentally ill woman who had expected to inherit millions following the death of Amalie. She clearly had a motive, but could not have carried out the murder alone.

'Do you know anything about the man she went out with last Wednesday?' I asked.

He shook his head.

'No, I didn't know anything about that until she mentioned it at the police station. I asked her about it afterwards, but she said it hadn't led anywhere and going out with him had been a painful mistake. There have been a few of them, unfortunately. But—'

Again he hesitated in the middle of a sentence, but then continued.

'But at no point have I worried that my sister has anything to do with Amalie's death, with or without the help of some man. She's not strong enough or evil enough to do anything like that. I am worried, however, that Amalie's death and Rakel's disappointment on hearing Meyer-Michelsen's will might tip her over the edge or worse. She was beside herself last night and still extremely upset when I spoke to her this morning. And she didn't answer the phone when I rang just before you came. I was about to run over there when you rang the doorbell.'

The air suddenly felt cold. Helgesen looked at me. I said to Robert Enger that he should perhaps try to call his sister again. He went over to the phone and dialled the number.

We all stood there listening to the phone ring and ring without being answered.

He put down the receiver and stood there staring at the wall.

I said that we should perhaps go over to his sister's immediately, and all three of us rushed out.

VI

Rakel Enger lived only a few hundred yards from her brother, and yet it was a whole world apart. I would never have guessed they were related, on seeing their flats. On the walls there were two pictures of herself and one of her mother, but none of her brother or any other man. The walls were brown with smoke and there were overflowing ashtrays on every surface. We stumbled over a pile of empty beer bottles when we let ourselves in with the brother's spare key. The living room was so full of coat hangers and clothes and cupboards that it was hard even to get in.

But the most depressing thing was the lifeless body of a woman in only her underclothes lying on the bed, with an empty jar beside her.

Helgesen and I just stood there and stared. Robert Enger was quicker to react. He ran over to the telephone and dialled the emergency services, and said: 'Overdose of sleeping pills. Minnesund. We need an ambulance immediately.

'They're on their way. This has happened before and everything was fine in the end. They said that swallowing a jar of this kind of sleeping pill doesn't usually kill people, but that anything more can be life-threatening,' Robert Enger told us.

I looked at him; his apparent control made a deep impression on me. But then suddenly he gasped.

I turned round to see Helgesen picking something up from the floor, which he then held out to me. It was another empty pill jar.

VII

Robert had gone with his sister in the ambulance. The patient was alive, but in a critical condition, I was told as they carried her out on a stretcher.

Before the ambulance arrived, I had remarked to Robert Enger that his sister had an awful lot of clothes for someone with such a modest income. He replied that Rakel had unfortunately developed an obsession with clothes, jewellery, and other bits and pieces, and had inherited quite a collection from their mother. He had also let her have the money that their mother left them and later even given her some of his own earnings, he added.

I saw no reason to doubt this. Instead, I read the hand-written note we had found in the kitchen for a fifth time.

I know nothing about the murder of that cheat Amalie, but can't face living with the suspicion, as well as the poverty and shame. Goodbye!

Helgesen and I went through the flat room by room, but found nothing of interest. As we expected, we didn't find any-thing to disprove Rakel Enger's assertion that she knew nothing about Amalie's murder. And we certainly found noth-ing to prove that she did. There was no evidence here of any man who might have helped her murder her cousin.

If Robert Enger's flat had reminded me of an office, Rakel Enger's reminded me more of a mirror. The reflection one saw was messy, dirty and tragic. Her problems must have made life very difficult for her brother, and I wondered whether this, combined with the dream of having his own house, might have driven him to murder. But from what I had seen of him today, it seemed unfair and I decided not to share my thoughts with Helgesen.

Instead, I suggested that we stopped in Sandvika on the way back to Oslo, to talk to the only person on our list who was a known murderer.

VIII

More work had been done on the painting since yesterday, but the painter was no longer standing at the easel; he was slumped on a sofa by the window. An almost empty bottle of wine stood on the table next to him, as though to underline the fact that in this studio, it was a day for hangovers and reflection. But it was not just the alcohol, even though Paul Vincent Krag was very definitely the worse for wear.

He had stood there confidently and calmly before us when we arrived the day before, and had asked in an ironic voice to what he owed the honour again today, when even the national broadcaster had announced that the serial murderer had been arrested.

I told him that the murderer had killed the three other women, but very definitely did not kill Amalie and had not been at Tveita Shopping Centre. And we had evidence to prove that.

He had quickly recognized the gravity of the situation. As I said this, first the brush fell to the floor and then the artist. He lay there gasping for breath, before managing to pull himself up and stumbling over to the sofa.

I had no sympathy for him whatsoever, nor was I fascinated by him any more. Only two alternatives remained. Either Paul Vincent Krag had killed Amalie, or he was a highly rational and intelligent person behind his eccentric appearance.

'I had absolutely no motive to kill this Amalie person. Why on earth would I do it?' he suddenly asked.

He then drank what was left of the wine straight from the bottle, and repeated the question. I did not believe him any more for it.

'You were there, you have killed another young woman before, and you said in an interview in the papers last week that it had inspired you,' I said.

He raised both his hands.

'Yes, yes, but then again, no. I would never have said that to the papers if I'd known this would happen. I killed a woman

425

eight years ago out of jealousy and rage, and regretted it every day thereafter, as it cost me my freedom and the opportunity to paint. Now that I finally have my freedom back, the last thing I would do is to murder someone else and risk being sent back inside for years. It would mean the end of my life and my career as an artist.'

'So why did you say that to the newspapers? Was it simply to get attention and increase your chances of selling more paintings?' I asked.

He swallowed my obvious slur.

'Of course. What do you take me for?' he exclaimed in agitation. His lips quivered and his hand shook as he spoke.

I now had my answer: there was another more rational Paul Vincent Krag behind his image. And that made him even more loathsome in my eyes.

And yet, I had to admit that it was in fact not very likely that he had killed Amalie. His possible motives for murdering her were irrational. We had no evidence against him other than that he, like a hundred other people, had been at Tveita Shopping Centre the day she was found there. So I left him on the list of possible suspects, but did not arrest him.

Patricia had also said that the murderer's motive had been irrational, I suddenly remembered as we were leaving. I wondered what she would have said about what I had seen so far today.

I made two phone calls when I got back to the station. The first was to Patricia, who still did not pick up the phone. The second was to Akershus Hospital. After much to-ing and fro-ing about formalities, the woman who answered eventually confirmed that Rakel Enger was still alive. But she would not comment on whether or not she was out of danger.

When I finally managed to talk to the doctor who had treated her, he indicated that his patient would probably survive, but might not be able to give a statement for some time. Her heart had stopped when she reached the hospital, and she had been resuscitated, but they could not be sure yet whether there was any permanent damage to her brain as a result. She had still not shown any signs of response.

I sat there thinking about Robert Enger. I found myself hoping, for his sake and for his sister's, that she would die rather than live on with brain damage, in need of constant care. If that were to happen, in ten years from now his life would be even more constrained by his sister's despair.

I remembered a concept that Patricia had taught me in connection with an earlier investigation. She had used the phrase 'catalyst killing' to describe the murder of a young woman, which then had enormous ripple effects on the lives of the people around her. Some of them lost their own lives, and others had their lives ruined. Now that we had solved the Anthill Murders and arrested the killer, we were left with another catalyst killing, again of a young woman. No matter who had killed Amalie Meyer-Michelsen, in the course of three days her murder had caused her father to take his own life and had ruined the life of at least one cousin.

I missed Patricia more than ever, so I dialled her number yet again. I could picture the telephone sitting there on her table in Erling Skjalgsson's Street. It rang and rang, and still no one answered. I thought about Robert Enger's unanswered telephone calls to his sister, and was suddenly extremely worried about Patricia.

IX

It was now three o'clock. Helgesen and I had driven back to Kristinelund Road in Skøyen. We passed the large house where Amalie and Christoffer Meyer-Michelsen had lived until only a few days ago, and stopped in front of the somewhat smaller house where the widower Mr Wendelmann now lived alone since his son had moved out.

When we were shown into Wendelmann's house, I was pleasantly surprised. Between the unexpectedly full bookshelves, there were lots of photographs of his son and his late wife. The table was set with coffee and cakes when we arrived. I thought that perhaps Wendelmann's voice and manner were what gave the impression of a reserved and cold man when we first met.

I started tentatively by asking what he had done on the May Day holiday. He answered obligingly with a little smile that he had used the day to cut the lawn in his garden, true to family tradition.

'It's one of my duties as a long-term member of the Conservative Party. My son, on the other hand, took part in the Labour Day march for the first time. He was no doubt partly inspired by the EEC debate, but mostly by a radical young literature student he's been seeing a lot of lately. And she is very nice, so I'm pleased for him. They're on their way here now as we speak.'

I felt a shock of fear grip me as he said this. I told myself there were of course many radical young literature students, but I sat there fretting about what a catastrophe it would be to meet Miriam with a new boyfriend. I realized that I could quash this fear simply by asking Wendelmann what the young woman was called. But that might seem slightly odd and I preferred to live with the uncertainty, so I pushed my feelings to one side and instead asked where he and his son had had lunch on Friday.

'At the Bristol Hotel. But I've already told you that and I don't see what relevance it has now. I read that the person responsible for the wave of murders last week has been arrested, and therefore presumed that the rest of us were no longer suspects,' he said, with a little less cordiality and willingness to cooperate.

'That, unfortunately, is not the case. The man we arrested has admitted to the other murders, but very definitely has an alibi for the time when Amalie was murdered. So we now have to question everyone we spoke to in connection with her murder again, and in more detail,' I explained.

'I see, and that of course changes everything,' Mr Wendelmann said, somewhat curtly. He kept his composure, but seemed far less comfortable now. And to be fair, I could understand him. The arrest of the Anthill Murderer had made everyone feel safe, but now the uncertainty was creeping back for those who had known Amalie and her father.

Just then, the living-room door opened behind us. Wendelmann's son came in without so much as a knock on the door. His girlfriend turned out to be a brunette from Østfold by the name of Herdis Christiansen. I felt a wave of relief and shook her hand warmly.

'I have just explained to our visitors from the police that we celebrated the first of May in rather different ways,' Mr Wendelmann said.

The young Herdis reacted. I suspected it was more to do

with the presence of the police than any disagreement about how to mark May Day. It was an uncomfortable situation, but I realized that it would not be made any better by sending her away. I explained that we were here to ask some routine questions that we had to ask everyone who had known Amalie and Christoffer Meyer-Michelsen.

She nodded, but still looked wary. Her boyfriend held his ground better and talked nonchalantly about May Day.

'Generational differences once a year are nothing to be feared. When one generation is in business and the other in the arts, it goes without saying that, politically, there is a foot in each camp. And typically, most people are what I am – a slightly confused, left-leaning individual. But whatever the case, the first of May is a day to be celebrated.'

Herdis laughed at the first statement and nodded in agreement with the second. Then she looked at me curiously.

I assured them that no one was suspected of anything, but that we just needed to check their alibis.

'The gentlemen have just asked where we had lunch on Friday,' Mr Wendelmann informed his son, in a monotone voice.

'You called it lunch, I said brunch, but whatever it was, we agreed on the Bristol Hotel. Do you still have the bill, Father?'

His father replied, 'I think so.' He took out his dark leather wallet and looked through it. He found the bill between a 500-kroner note and a hundred-kroner note, and held it out to me. It was very definitely for 'Harald Henrik Wendelmann and Henrik Harald Wendelmann', and dated with a stamp for Friday.

I remarked that it was rather unusual to have one's name written on the bill. The younger Wendelmann, with some indignation, stated that it was good practice when it was on the company account. His father nodded in agreement.

It did not feel right to accuse the Wendelmanns of lying in their own home, in front of the son's new girlfriend, so I just took the bill that confirmed they had been where they always said they had been on Friday. I thanked them for their time and wished them a good evening.

By the time we were back out on the street, it was ten past four.

'Gaustad next?' Helgesen asked.

I was thinking out loud when I said that Guri would probably be awake by now, but we could not be sure, and Gaustad Mental Hospital was not somewhere I particularly wanted to sit around waiting. We still had one name left on the list of people connected to Amalie Meyer-Michelsen. And even though her father's secretary had a sound alibi, she might still have something more to say.

Helgesen gave a doubtful frown, but was a loyal assistant, so he agreed it was a good suggestion. And we drove off towards Rikke Johansen's address in Sollerud.

X

Rikke Johansen lived rather well, for a secretary. She had a nice two-storey red house with a big garden down by Lysaker River. There was only her name on the mailbox. It was obvious that she spent a lot of time in her garden after the long working days, as it was beautifully looked after. A small wheelbarrow stood abandoned by a flower bed full of different-coloured tulips.

As we walked up the drive, it felt as though we had entered a green and innocent Garden of Eden. But the idyll was broken when we got to the house. One of the upstairs windows was open, and judging from the noises to be heard, it was not hard to guess that it was Rikke Johansen's bedroom.

Despite having met her under such sombre circumstances, the red-haired secretary had struck me as being a vibrant and dynamic thirty-year-old. This impression was certainly reinforced now. We could only hear the heavy breathing of her lover, but she cried out, 'You've got me now – more!' This was followed by more moans and rustling, then finally a drawn-out 'Yeeeeeesss!', followed by silence. Then we heard some hushed whispers but could not make out the words or distinguish the other voice.

It was the most awkward situation I had ever found myself in during an investigation. It was embarrassing to be standing listening outside someone's bedroom window.

And yet, there I stood.

There was of course nothing illegal about Rikke Johansen finding a new lover, young, attractive and unmarried as she was. The moral aspect of it was perhaps more debatable. Whatever the case, two days after her former lover committed suicide and left her a fortune worth millions, the situation was sensational enough to question her again.

Helgesen had stopped at the same time as me beneath the window. When I finally looked at him, it was obvious that he found the situation just as excruciating. He mopped the sweat from his brow in an exaggerated movement, and then pointed to the front door. I shook my head. Then we stood there in silence by the wall, wondering what to do.

There was a limit to how long we could stand there, especially as the afternoon sun was shining straight on us. But I did not want to go charging in while they were still in the bedroom. I wanted to hold on to the possibility of confronting them with a lie, if they gave a false explanation as to why he was there.

Helgesen was ten years older than me and at least a couple of stone heavier, and it looked as though the sun was bothering him more. He said nothing, but sent me questioning looks at shorter and shorter intervals.

Ten minutes after things had gone quiet in the bedroom, I ran out of patience as well and pointed towards the door. Then, just as I put out my hand to knock, it was opened from inside.

And suddenly I found myself on the front step, face to face with a man I had seen only a few hours earlier.

Rolf Johan Svendsen managed to take even this in his stride. As I backed away and almost fell down the steps, he stood there calmly with his hand on the door handle.

'What are you doing here?' I asked, as I tried to regain my balance.

'I'm visiting my new girlfriend,' he replied.

I was standing with both feet firmly planted on the ground again. And it really did feel as though the end of the case was quite literally within reach. I went in with guns blazing and fired off another question.

'Have you already been in your new girlfriend's bed?'

I was fully prepared to arrest the late Amalie Meyer-Michelsen's fiancé as prime suspect if he said no. But he didn't. Instead, he replied openly and without embarrassment, 'Yes, but not before today.'

So we stood there, looking at each other in tense silence for a few seconds. He did not look away.

'Shall we go inside and continue this conversation?' Rolf Johan Svendsen eventually asked, in a more subdued voice. And I replied in equally muted tones that yes, perhaps we should.

XI

It was a quarter to five. All four of us were seated round the coffee table in the living room at Sollerud, and from the street it no doubt looked like a pleasant May Day celebration or a bridge game. But the atmosphere was tense. The couple on the other side of the table looked very serious indeed. And I felt both undecided and angry.

We took their statements separately, but they matched perfectly.

They both told us that they were tiring of their relationships, and had increasingly found the other person to be less than interesting. But they had not been physically unfaithful. She said, with brutal honesty: 'I was more and more unfaithful mentally, but that is deemed to be both legally and morally acceptable, certainly on this side of town.' I could hardly contradict her on that.

Both of them had felt lonely and uncertain after their partners had died. The news that they would inherit the Meyer-Michelsen fortune was a positive surprise, of course, but neither of them had been able to be happy about it.

It had been an enormous relief to hear that the Anthill Murderer had been arrested the day before. She had immediately called Svendsen and asked if he wanted to come to her house today to discuss 'the situation and the future'. He had understood what she meant and said yes without any hesitation.

Following my visit earlier in the day, he had called her to say that the police were still looking for Amalie's murderer. He had said that he would still very much like to come, but would understand if she wanted to postpone or cancel the invitation.

According to her, he had been more direct and said: 'I of course did not kill Amalie and have no idea who did, but would understand if you didn't dare to believe that right now.'

She had told him she trusted him implicitly and that he was welcome whenever he wanted to come.

He had left the car at home and taken the bus at three o'clock. They had, in her words, 'got on well in the living room, and even better in the bedroom'. And they had agreed that they were now in a relationship, but that it should be kept secret at least until the case had been closed and the inheritance settled.

I said to him that he should have told me about his new girlfriend. He replied that when I spoke to him last, he still did not have a new girlfriend. Then he added that he of course did not want to do anything that might result in either or both of them being suspected, as he knew they were both innocent. 'She was in the office that morning, and I did not see Amalie,' he said resolutely.

Amalie's fiancé seemed to be on increasingly thin ice, but we still could not make a hole in it. And the story that Rikke and Rolf Johan told about their relationship was either the truth or very well invented. But what they had said still did not rule out the possibility that he might have killed his girlfriend. Or, for that matter, that she might have done, with the help of someone else.

In short, it felt as though we had caught a glimpse of dry land, only to get lost in the sea mists again.

I asked if they knew yet how much they were to inherit. She

said that she had spoken to the business manager and believed that the total value of the inheritance from Christoffer Meyer-Michelsen was between thirty and forty million kroner. 'Which is far less than it would have been a year ago, and probably more than it might have been in a year's time – but still, an unbelievable amount of money.'

I looked at her, astonished, and asked if she was acknowledging that his business partner, Mr Wendelmann, had been right with regard to the latest expansion.

'I was loyal to my boss and lover as long as he lived, but have recently been more and more concerned about the direction he was taking and the speed with which he was doing it. And now I see it quite clearly. Christoffer always had all the formalities on his side, but Wendelmann had sense. There was a chance that everything would go well with the new investment, but it was more likely that the entire business could collapse, and that risk increased with the oil crisis. The figures were considerable, but the remaining equity and liquidity were low compared with the debt and risk. We have now all agreed to work with Wendelmann to wind up the whole project as quickly and securely as possible,' she answered swiftly.

'We have also agreed on something else relating to money,' Svendsen said, and looked at her for agreement.

She hesitated a moment and took a deep breath – then nodded.

'After my meeting with you, I thought a lot about Meyer-Michelsen's niece and nephew. We don't know them, and none of us can be sure what actually happened. But we think it's fairly probable that they are telling the truth, and whatever the case may be, we do not feel happy about taking all the money when things are as they are. So we would like to give half of the inheritance to Robert and Rakel Enger.'

I looked at her. She nodded again. 'I was reluctant to begin with, but then he managed to persuade me just before you came. And now I am even more convinced that I really have found my dream prince this time,' she said.

He put his arm round her shoulders. She lowered it to her waist, and took hold of his hand. The scene was so touching that I was almost charmed.

However, Helgesen brought me back to earth when he said coldly, 'Nice idea. But how can we know that you're not just saying that now to deflect suspicion?'

Rolf Johan Svendsen gave one of his small, discreet sighs. His right hand was resting on Rikke's thigh, and he put his left hand into his pocket and pulled out a folded piece of paper, which he handed to me.

The man was clearly a lawyer in his spare time too. The document was a well-formulated agreement, signed by them both, that confirmed their wish to transfer half of their inheritance to Robert and Rakel Enger.

I was extremely pleased for Robert Enger. And I thought that if I had known about this document only the day before, it would have made a world of difference to Rakel Enger. But I could not bear to tell the two people sitting opposite me what had happened. First of all, because there was no way of knowing what would happen to her. And secondly, because if they really were innocent and as well-meaning as they seemed to be, they did not deserve to have this thrown at them right now.

It felt as though we had been playing a game of cards, and that Rolf Johan Svendsen had placed his trump card on the table when he produced the document. Helgesen had nothing more to say and leaned back in his chair.

I felt more confused than I had all day. So I simply said that their statements had been noted and that they should stay within the city limits until the case had been closed, and that we would keep them updated on any developments.

'Thank you. I do understand that you have to investigate me, but hope that the witness might possibly confirm that I had nothing to do with the murder. All we hope for now is that the person responsible will get his just deserts and that we can put this all behind us. And the size of our inheritance makes no difference. Rikke and I just want this to end so we can move on with our lives. And hopefully can have the child that we both so want.'

She nodded in agreement as he spoke, and then squeezed his hand when he had finished. They stayed sitting on the sofa while Helgesen and I made our own way out.

'Now Gaustad really is the next stop!' Helgesen said as we got into the car. I asked him to drive, and leaned back in the passenger seat to think about where we stood in the case now.

I had never missed Patricia as much as I did on that journey. I was sure that she would have picked up several new leads from our conversations today and been able to follow them I eventually asked Helgesen to stop by a phone box, but there was no answer when I called. I still couldn't see the connections without her.

'What do you think?' I asked Helgesen, as we turned in towards Gaustad Mental Hospital.

Helgesen paused, but when he spoke his answer was unexpected.

'Have you ever read the novel *When the Iron Curtain Falls*? It's not about the Soviet Union or the USA. In fact, it was written by good old Jonas Lie at the end of the nineteenth century. I read it when I was at university, on the recommendation of my father.'

I was once again surprised by how well-read Helgesen was, despite his rather ordinary appearance. Then I said no, I hadn't read it, and how on earth was the old novel relevant to our investigation today in 1972?

'It's not directly relevant. But it's an exciting story about a group of people who happen to come together on a ship, and their different lives and secrets. When the boat starts to sink, the "iron curtain" falls. Secrets are revealed and people's real personalities shine through, for better or worse. It feels a bit like that's where we are. The ship is sinking for those we've met in connection with the Amalie case, and their masks are falling. I may be wrong, but I think we saw two masks fall back there. Even though they, like the rest of us, have their flaws, I hope and think that the two we just spoke to are good people. To give twenty million kroner to two people you don't really know is an act deserving of respect, and their statements were not obviously untrustworthy.'

I certainly could not disagree with that. But I had to ask the obvious question: 'So who, then, are the bad people? Who can't face the truth when the iron curtain falls?'

We pulled up in front of the hospital. Helgesen kept his eyes on the road until the car was safely parked, and then turned to look at me.

'I don't know. But if I were to choose from those we've met today, I would say the artist.'

Again, I couldn't disagree, but asked if he was sure. 'Not at all,' was his pithy reply. Then we got out of the car and walked towards the main entrance without saying a word.

XII

She was awake when we got there at twenty past five. But she was sitting sunken in her chair and barely got up to greet us. Her handshake was feeble and under the woollen blanket, her thin body was racked with frequent coughing fits. But she was still smoking when we arrived.

Of all the odd and tragic figures that wandered around the streets of Oslo, Gaustad-Guri was perhaps the oddest and most tragic.

'Nice to see you. You were wondering about Friday?' she said.

Her voice was weaker than I remembered, but she spoke in the same refined, west Oslo accent that she had always used. This gave her an air of respectability, despite everything.

Gaustad-Guri was actually called Guri Bugge, and behind her ravaged face she was only thirty years old. Her father had been a captain in the German Wehrmacht. He had left Norway when she was one year old and had never been seen here since. Her mother came from a wealthy family with lots of fine minds and big bank accounts, but after the war she was tainted by her reputation as a German whore and struggled with alcohol problems. But Guri looked as though she would do well, all the same. At twenty-five, she was a married mother of two, and appeared to have escaped any problems caused by her parentage. Then one afternoon in 1967, her husband came home and told her that he wanted to leave her and marry someone else. That evening, all the fuses in Guri's mind blew simultaneously. Six months later, she seemed to be back on top of things. But the fuses went again and again over the years that followed. Her former husband and his new wife had been given custody of the children, and she was diagnosed with manic depression and stowed away here.

On bad days, she hid away in a smoke-filled cupboard of a room at Gaustad. On good days, she was allowed out. Then she wandered around town, most often in the streets of her childhood, looking for someone to talk to or help in some way or another. If she found someone, she could be bright and cheery for days afterwards, but the dark days always returned, as surely as the evenings draw in in autumn, though with less predictability. Gaustad-Guri was the only vagrant in town who never drank. On the other hand, she was always smoking, usually one cigarette, but sometimes two.

At least once a month, someone called the police to say she was bothering them. All such investigations were immediately closed. Guri was as well-meaning and kind-hearted as the day was long. In winter, she would happily run to help to their feet anyone who had slipped and fallen. She always had a cigarette to spare for anyone who asked. More than once, she had helped the police when she saw a pickpocket or witnessed a petty crime.

'Yes, it's in connection with a murder investigation. You might be able to do the police and the country a great service, Guri.'

She nodded slowly, and straightened up in her chair.

'Possibly my best and only chance, then. I realize that much. And how may I help you?'

She looked at me with frightened eyes, but there was a

spark of hope. Gaustad-Guri wanted to help, but was not sure that she could.

'They told me that you were out and about on Friday. Where did you go?' I started.

She stubbed out her cigarette on the floor, swallowed hard and then spoke.

'I was on good form, so I asked if I could go out after breakfast. I took the bus to Skøyen and walked around there for a while, without meeting anyone I knew. Skøyen is a big place. Where in particular were you thinking of?'

'Kristinelund Road. Were you there at all?' I asked.

She lit another cigarette, without noticing that the previous one on the floor was not properly out.

'An old school friend lives there, so I hoped she might be out in the garden and have time for a chat. But I didn't see her. If she saw me, she chose to stay indoors.'

Guri sighed heavily. Nothing hurt her more than people she knew not wanting to know her any more.

'Did you go past the house of Christoffer Meyer-Michelsen, the hotel magnate?' I asked.

She slapped her forehead dramatically.

'Of course, that is the case you are talking about. I should have realized. I read in the newspaper that his daughter had been murdered and that he had committed suicide. A sad story. I never dared to speak to him, but knew what he looked like and where he lived. I walked up and down the street, so passed the house several times. But I did not see him or his daughter on Friday.'

'Did you see anyone else there?' I asked.

She nodded almost eagerly.

'Yes. A young gentleman drove up. He parked the car in the

drive and went and knocked on the door several times, but there was no answer. He looked rather dejected, so when he came back to the car, I asked what was the matter. He said it was none of my business. I didn't want to bother him if that was how he felt. So I walked up and down the street again. When I got back, both he and the car had gone. But I saw him and spoke to him briefly, yes. Average height, professional sort of chap with glasses. Fair hair, blue eyes, grey suit and green car.'

Everything fitted. The only thing we didn't know was when, so I asked if she could remember what time it was.

Gaustad-Guri dropped her cigarette on the floor and gave an apologetic shrug. She indicated that she had nothing on her wrists.

'I've had three watches recently, but have none at the moment, unfortunately. The first stopped before Christmas, I lost the second one in the snow when I slipped on some ice in January and I gave the third one to some poor soul just before Easter. They told me that I mustn't lose or give away my watches and that there was no point in getting me a new one. It was in the morning.'

'Could it have been before ten?' Helgesen came in from the side.

Gaustad-Guri turned and looked at him in surprise, then shook her head.

'No, no. I left here at a quarter to ten. Took the bus and then had to walk a bit to get there. I had been up and down the street at least once, so it would not have been before half past ten at the earliest. More likely, closer to eleven.'

Helgesen and I exchanged glances. I knew him well enough now to see the disappointment and relief on his face. It was perfectly understandable. I myself was relieved for Rolf Johan Svendsen and Rikke Johansen, but also disappointed that, once again, there seemed to be little prospect of solving the case.

Whether a court would believe Gaustad-Guri or not was another matter. To sow doubts about her reliability would be a simple matter for a smart lawyer. But the reality was clear. Neither Helgesen nor I was in any doubt.

'So you're sure about that? You wouldn't lie to us, even if he had asked you to, would you?' I asked all the same, just to be sure.

Gaustad-Guri was visibly affronted and waved her hand.

'Even I can still remember Friday. I may have done a lot of stupid and mad things, but I have never lied. What I'm saying is the truth. You said that it might be important, didn't you?'

It was a plea more than a question. I nodded reassuringly and repeated that it could be very important.

Her mouth smiled briefly, but the smile never reached her eyes. They were still dark and sad.

I had one final question for her, which I decided to ask having first thought about it for a moment or two.

'You were very upset when you got back here on Friday. Did that have something to do with the young man that you met, or did something else happen in Kristinelund Road?'

'No, no, no. It was something completely different . . .'

She stopped talking and sat thinking for a while. Then suddenly the tears and the words all welled up at the same time.

'It was down by Majorstuen a few hours later. I suddenly saw Karl on his way home from school with some other children. I ran after him as fast as I could. Thought that it might be my last chance to say that I hoped he was happy now and how sorry I was about everything that had happened. But he just looked away, and one of the other children threatened to call the police if I didn't leave them alone. I didn't follow them when they carried on. Suddenly I was so tired that I had to sit down on the pavement. It was all I could do to crawl onto the bus and come back here to hide.'

She stopped speaking and eventually managed to stop her tears as well, but sank back into the chair again. And I chastised myself for asking the question.

Karl was Gaustad-Guri's son, and was around twelve, but his mother had not seen him since he was seven, and did not really know what he looked like any more. She had made a mistake in the past. Maybe it really was her son this time; maybe it was some poor boy she didn't know. Whatever the case, she had crashed as a result. And she did not look as if she could take much more.

By the time we left, she had straightened up in her chair again, but was coughing even more violently. I could see that things were going downhill fast for Gaustad-Guri. And I realized that the city would be a poorer and less safe place the day she hung up her walking shoes.

XIII

It was now a quarter to seven. Having first checked that there were no messages of any interest waiting for us at the station, Helgesen and I had called it a day. I had said goodbye without suggesting that we could go for something to eat together. And that was because I wanted to be alone.

I had thought of driving down to Fatima's parents in Grønland, but suddenly I could not face the thought of more emotion, so I had an excellent steak at a nearby restaurant instead. But I felt lonely and out of sorts.

I had eaten my food and paid the bill. I felt fuller, but no better, and my thoughts on the case were no clearer. In the end, I drove back to the flat to pick up the large bouquet of flowers I had been given the evening before. And then I drove to Erling Skjalgsson's Street and stopped outside the house that was locally known as 'the White House'.

The door was not opened when I rang the bell for the first time, nor the second. But when I rang it a third time, I saw a shadow by the window and recognized the profile of one of the maids. I waved and held up the bouquet. And finally, the door was opened. But Benedikte did not let me in. She stood there like a sad but steadfast doorman.

'The mistress has been very upset all day,' she said in an unusually reproachful voice.

I held out the flowers to Benedikte and asked her to pass them on with my sincere apologies. I told her in all honesty that my former fiancée and I were in no way romantically involved, but that I should have warned Patricia that she had come to see me unexpectedly. I apologized profusely and said that I would very much like to speak to the mistress for a few minutes if at all possible.

The maid listened to me with an impassive face. When I stopped talking, she took the bouquet and said, 'I'll see what I can do. Wait here.' Then she closed the door abruptly in my face.

I waited for nearly ten minutes and had started to wonder how much longer I could stand there without attracting attention, when the door opened again.

'The mistress is still very upset. She doesn't promise to

reply, but she will listen to what you've got to say,' the maid reported.

I was about to give the reserved Benedikte a hug, but realized in the nick of time that embracing another woman here was not what the situation called for. So I thanked her politely and followed her obediently in.

Patricia was sitting in her usual place in the library. It struck me that something was different. She was dressed in a high-necked black dress and looked more miserable than I had ever seen her. And I had never seen the table empty before, but it was now. The telephone had been put down on the floor and the plug pulled out. There was no food or drink to be seen, on Patricia's side or mine. The large table was bare; there was not even a speck of dust to be seen. And my chair had been moved. I had always sat on the long side of the table, about an arm's length from Patricia, but now the chair was at one of the short ends, about six feet away from her.

Patricia showed no sign of being glad to see me again and did not say a word.

'Just tell her what's happened today,' the maid said. Then she left.

I made an attempt to apologize for not mentioning Miriam's visit, but gave up after the first sentence when Patricia made an irritated gesture with her hand.

I suddenly remembered what Miriam had said about Patricia possibly being a genius, but that she was also mad. I had no doubt that what Miriam had said about their encounter the evening before was true. But I stayed seated, partly because I needed a genius to help me solve the case, and partly because I felt guilty for not having told Patricia about my contact with Miriam. But also because at some point on my way up the stairs, I had realized that I could not live without this oddly unbearable and yet fascinating woman.

What followed could hardly be called a conversation. Patricia listened with concentration, but without saying a single word back, while I told her about what had happened during the day. Even though the distance across the table did not change, it felt as though we were a little closer again. Patricia smiled briefly when I got to the episode with Rikke Johansen's open bedroom window and then shook her head a couple of times later. But she said nothing – not even when I had finished.

'And so I can only admit that I don't know who killed Amalie Meyer-Michelsen. But I suspect that you do,' I said.

'What I might or might not have understood about this investigation of yours is no longer of any practical consequence, sadly.'

She said this in a deadly serious voice – but at the same time, with a flash of a smile.

Then she sat there in silence again, with an expressionless face.

Suddenly, with that fleeting smile, she reminded me of the Mona Lisa. I realized that Patricia knew something that I desperately wanted to know – and that she was waiting for me to say more. But I had no idea what I should say or wanted to say to break the increasingly paralysing silence between us. In the end, I lost all patience and chose the most dramatic and direct approach.

'The fact that Miriam turned up without warning changes nothing. It's you I love,' I said.

Even as I said it, I thought that it did not sound very convincing, though it was absolutely true.

'Prove it, then,' she replied.

I was not sure that Patricia really meant what she said. Nor was I sure how to take it. So we sat there looking at each other.

Patricia let out an exasperated sigh, then smiled one of her most provocative and mocking smiles.

'Do you want me to spoon-feed you? The mystery as to what you want with me has to be solved, and soon. And it seems there are only two alternatives left: either you don't love me – or you can't love me!'

These last words were like a slap in the face. My feelings percolated through my body for the next few seconds. I was angry and hurt. I thought that I did love Patricia, but that I also hated her. And that there was no longer any doubt as to what she wanted. And that someone would soon have to wipe that mocking smile from her lips.

I realized that my voice would not be particularly pleasant right now. So I did not say a word. Instead I stood up.

In that moment, I considered leaving the room, running down the stairs, walking out of the house without looking back and never setting foot in here again.

But I didn't. Instead, I strode round the table and pushed Patricia's wheelchair back.

She said nothing. Just sat there with that endlessly provocative smile playing on her lips. And it stayed there when I picked her up from the wheelchair and carried her out.

And then suddenly she was lying on her back in a four-poster bed, with her head on the pillow. She looked so small and pale in the middle of the vast bed. But I was still angry and had no patience with her mocking.

Patricia said nothing, but continued to smile – and she clapped theatrically when I got in beside her.

Her black dress was lying on the floor beside my trousers. After all we had gone through in our clothes over the past five years, it felt unreal to be lying next to a half-naked Patricia. Her thin thighs and legs lay lifeless on the covers, with no visible scars or damage. They were smooth and white and very definitely attractive.

All at once I noticed that it was the warmest bedroom I had ever been in; the temperature must have been over 25°. The warm air could hardly have been for my benefit, as she had no idea that I would come. Perhaps it was to compensate for the warmth she had not received from anyone in recent years.

Her smile was only inches from my face. I kissed it away, with a kiss that was so long and hard that it took her some moments to catch her breath. But then the smile crept back and hovered there just by my chin, even though she was now wearing only pink knickers.

And I remembered something a friend from college had once told me: that to be a good lover, you had to think of the woman as either your best friend or your worst enemy. It struck me that I had always thought of Miriam as my best friend, whereas I saw Patricia, if not as an enemy, at least as an opponent. My body felt hard and bulging – as I remembered it from the only boxing match of my youth.

I worried momentarily about the sheer physical cost to Patricia, as I watched her pink panties slide down her legs. She was so small; her body could weigh no more than half of mine. She was shivering despite the heat. I hesitated for a last single second. But it was too late to turn back now, both for her and for me.

I was passionate and wild as soon as I felt her tighten around me. I thrust deeper and harder when I heard her moan quietly in my ear. She made me think of a peculiar cat that was both hard and soft at once. The cat clawed at my back, and continued to smile smugly after biting me on the ear.

But I did finally savour the triumph of seeing the smile vanish. She lay completely still as I exploded deep inside her. And a few seconds later, a new ecstatic and serene smile spread over her face. Two drops of sweat appeared in the middle of her forehead. I had never seen a woman smile like that before – and I had never seen Patricia sweat at all, anywhere.

Afterwards, I felt drained and she was exhausted. My muscles relaxed and I rolled carefully over to the side. Patricia's legs moved rather unexpectedly – a couple of spasms, which stopped quickly and did not seem to bother her.

We lay in silence, side by side, as we regained our composure and ability to speak. And annoyingly, she of course managed before me. The sweat was still visible on her brow and her breathing was still slowing. But her voice sounded almost normal when she said: 'Thank you. You certainly can when you want to, I'll give you that.'

I found myself wondering if that was in fact the first time I had heard Patricia say thank you – and whether I should thank her back or feel offended. But she carried on before I reached any conclusion.

'If you could now please lift me so I'm sitting up properly in bed, and pass me the cigarettes and holder that are in the top drawer of the chest to the right ... then I will tell you who committed the remaining, unsolved murder in your investigation.'

XIV

Patricia was now sitting more comfortably in bed and had pulled the duvet up over her chest. She was smoking a cigarette.

I could not bear to have the duvet over me as it was so warm, so I lay naked on the sheet on the other side of the bed. Patricia did not look too displeased. She kept her eyes on me when she spoke.

'First of all, today takes the biscuit for inefficient investigation, even by Oslo Police standards. You seem to have questioned people randomly without asking yourselves or them any of the critical questions that could have solved the case. But let us waive our judgement on that. I presume that what is of greatest interest now is to find the answer.'

Patricia's arrogance and smugness still infuriated me, but I did want the answer as soon as possible and was not in a position to complain. I accepted this slap in the face with a simple and willing, 'Yes.'

'One of the paradoxes is that you rejected Helgesen's list of alibis when it did finally hold the answer. Does anything click when I say that the alibi list for Lise Eilertsen is far more interesting now than when she was killed?'

I had no idea what she was talking about. So I said, 'Do you mean that the murders were connected after all, or that Hilmar Lauritzen did not kill Lise Eilertsen?'

Patricia rolled her eyes.

'Of course he did. None of the people you met today was responsible for Lise's murder. But the alibi for one of them should have made bells ring down at the police station,' she said.

She exhaled a satisfied little cloud of smoke. And I had to admit, with growing indignation, that my head was still befuddled.

'Let's look at it another way. The ant picture still plays a key role. The person who killed Amalie left an ant drawing with her body, which is why we assumed that it was the same person. The key to identifying the serial killer was establishing how he knew where to meet his victims. The key to finding this killer – who, by the way, is even more cold-hearted and callous – is establishing how he knew about the ant picture. It was only after Amalie was murdered that it became general knowledge. Before that, only the police and a handful of witnesses from the scene of the crime knew about it. So, which of the people involved in the Amalie case had any contact with the witnesses from the crime scenes?'

That had not crossed my mind. I took a couple of minutes to think about it now. Then I hedged my bets: 'No one that I can think of.'

Patricia nodded her approval.

'Either you were lucky, or you are improving. So how did the murderer find out? Because he happened to pass one of the other murder scenes. Lise Eilertsen's neighbour said she saw someone running away from the scene of the crime long after the actual murder. Someone you have met today was in the vicinity that evening. He was crossed off the list because he was still at a party in Tåsen when Lise was killed. But he left the party shortly after, and his alibi does not rule out the possibility that he was that passer-by. Which in fact he was. He bent down over the body and saw the picture of the ant poking out of her pocket. It is quite possible that he ran off in confusion or for fear of being suspected of murdering Lise. When the papers came the next morning, he realized that he now had a golden opportunity to commit a murder that everyone would blame on the serial killer. As the cold and callous man that he is behind his actor's mask, he had no qualms about using this opportunity.'

It was as though two bolts of lightning struck in my head the moment Patricia said 'actor's mask'.

I felt I had been dealt a blow, both physically and mentally.

Patricia smiled down at me from her elevated position against the pillow, but was then suddenly very serious again.

'Hilmar Lauritzen at least had the excuse that he was lonely and mentally unbalanced. This is far worse. Amalie's murder marks a new low for heartlessness and egotism. Murdering his daughter was the perfect indirect means to kill off Christoffer Meyer-Michelsen. As always, the director had the legal formalities on his side, and was not going to be persuaded to change his mind. His death was the only way to save the company's fortune in time. But if the murderer had killed Meyer-Michelsen himself, he and his father would immediately have been in the spotlight, in terms of both the investigation and the media. But this way, the suspicion fell on the Anthill Murderer and then on Amalie's fiancé and cousins. And so a wealthy young man with good social skills, lots of friends and a girlfriend, killed an innocent young woman in the most calculating way, solely to protect his own bank account. And to make matters worse, he murdered her on her father's birthday.'

'Wendelmann junior,' I muttered.

Patricia nodded and puffed smugly on her cigarette.

'Bingo. All arrows have been flashing and pointing in that

direction since yesterday evening. Who gained most from Meyer-Michelsen's death? Who had the training and access to the props needed for the performance at Tveita Shopping Centre? The murder that appeared to be the most puzzling was in fact the most rational. We assumed that she had been killed there because she had thought of going shopping there. But she was of course murdered somewhere else – and driven there in her own car. If you remember, there was an entry in her diary that stopped very abruptly, where she wrote that she had unexpectedly met someone again. I think we can safely assume that it was her former schoolmate and son of her father's business partner who contacted her. And we will never know what her motives were. Perhaps she was looking around for someone else to have children with, or maybe she thought it would be nice to meet an old friend and relax. Whatever the case, she walked straight into his trap. Can you put the cigarettes and holder back in the drawer, please?'

It wasn't a question; she handed them to me without waiting for an answer. I caught a glimpse of her breasts as she did so. They were without doubt a magnificent sight. She quickly hid them again under the duvet when she saw where I was looking. I thought that she must be terribly warm under that duvet. I also felt incredibly stupid for not having seen the answer myself.

'In conclusion,' she continued, 'you showed too much respect for Mr Wendelmann and their alibi of lunch at the Bristol. The one important question that you should have asked Rikke Johansen this afternoon was whether she stood by her first statement about what happened on Friday. She said that the Wendelmanns did not come together, but arrived within a quarter of an hour of each other. And that does not tally with their statement or alibi – and it does seem rather odd if they had lunch together only a short walk from the office, as they said. However, it does of course make sense if the son was coming from Tveita and wanted to get there as early as possible and the father was coming from the Bristol and wanted to get there as late as possible. Who knows, perhaps he sat there waiting for the son whose lunch he had already paid for.'

All the pieces fell into place as she spoke. I suddenly remembered a brief incident in Meyer-Michelsen's office, when the director fainted and Wendelmann junior stepped forwards to catch him. It was no coincidence that he was there first; he hoped and believed that Meyer-Michelsen would collapse.

I had to plead guilty on all counts of negligence. I also said how impressed I was with her reasoning. And then I was seized by a new worry that I recognized from a previous case.

'I don't doubt that what you say is true, but it's not going to be easy to prove, is it?' I said.

Patricia shook her head pensively.

'Yes and no. Wendelmann junior's statement will start to come apart at the seams if you question him in more detail. None of the waiters at the Bristol can have seen him that day, as he wasn't there. But if I were you, something we can both be glad that I'm not, I would start by talking to Mr Wendelmann alone. He has clearly made a false statement to help his son. But I am not sure that he knew about the murder. It is possible he is simply a naive father and an otherwise honourable man – and he should be given the chance to prove that.'

I agreed with her, and praised her vision and intelligence, which made her smile even more like the cat that got the cream.

'Impressively objective, clear thinking. But you must be

very warm under that duvet in this temperature, and with all the smoke,' I remarked light-heartedly.

'If you come over here again for two minutes before you go and arrest the murderer, I'll show you just how hot it is,' Patricia said, with one of her most self-satisfied smiles. At the same time, she deliberately pulled the duvet even tighter around her.

I realized I had been tricked again as she said this – that she had seduced me and provoked me into pulling off the duvet. Her laugh was still that of a teasing teenager. And given her carefree mood, I decided to make the most of the situation.

XV

It was ten o'clock in the evening. The sun had set, but its after-glow was still shining on the water. The view from the offices on the sixth floor, overlooking the harbour, was impressive, but the mood was sombre.

I had asked him to meet us there at short notice, and had done so in the hope that being in his former business partner's office would add to the pressure.

And my strategy seemed to be working.

There was no movement in his face when I set a statement down on the table in front of him. In it, Wendelmann admitted to previously giving a false statement, and that his son had not come to lunch at the Bristol last Friday, as they had claimed. He did not look at me. But then, without saying a word, he picked up a pen and signed the document.

'At first I did it in good faith. He said that he had slept in and that he could never have killed her, but needed an alibi all the same. If he was suspected, it might cause all sorts of problems for the business and winding up the company. It all sounded perfectly logical, especially to a father who still wanted to believe his only child. I should have realized then. He called me beforehand to say he might be late, and asked me to pay when I got there and keep the receipt, so he could come straight in. And I was unforgivably naive and just did as he said.'

In a gesture of solidarity, I said that it was perhaps naive, but also perfectly understandable. Then I asked when he had realized the awful truth.

'This afternoon – when you said that the other murders had been solved, but that the serial killer could not possibly have killed Amalie. I have never been so scared and desperate in my life. Suddenly I had this nagging doubt that my son might have committed murder – and that I might have helped him to conceal it. Then that terrible moment of truth when he asked if I still happened to have the receipt. He knew perfectly well that I had it, as he had asked before if I had kept it. There was nothing I could do as long as you were there, but when you left I confronted him and said that he had to confess. He admitted to everything, but showed no regret. Instead, he expected me to thank him for saving the money, and to help him conceal the murder. It was a deeply shocking experience.'

His voice was still just as monotonous, but the words were tumbling out now.

'I can only apologize profusely. I have been a law-abiding man all my life. I have paid every single krone I owe in tax, even though I thought the taxes were too high. I have stuck to the speed limit, even though I thought it was too low. With this, I was well out of my depth. At first I simply could not understand how my son could do anything like that. And then I just did not want to face the truth.'

It was impossible not to feel sympathy for him, so I said tactfully that there could be extenuating circumstances if he were to put all his cards on the table now; that the courts would be lenient with him. And that they could wind up the businesses and settle the finances regardless of what happened.

'For the past twelve months, I have been fixated on winding up my partnership with Meyer-Michelsen in time to save my capital. And now I have saved my fortune, but lost everything else as a result. I know where and how my son killed a young woman, but I still cannot understand how and when he changed from being the kind, good boy that he always was, to being a man who could kill another human being. It must have happened after he came of age, and after his mother died. Perhaps it was my fault. Perhaps it would never have happened if I had spent more time being a father in those years, and less time trying to save my business. Or perhaps I was just too kind. He got everything he wanted and was allowed to do whatever he liked in those years after his mother died. He was all that I had. I couldn't say no. Maybe that's where I let him down.'

The words poured out. The air felt more oppressive. The picture of Amalie looked at me over Wendelmann's shoulder. Suddenly all I wanted to do was to escape from here.

I said that I was sure he had done all that he could as a father and a businessman, and that no one could know what the future might bring. His son was an adult now and had to take responsibility for his own actions.

He said nothing to this and I was not sure whether he had

actually heard what I said. His voice was at breaking point when he spoke again.

'Imagine the shame for the family. How we have let them down. I said on Saturday that I could not imagine anything worse than losing your only child. But I can assure you now, there is a worse fate: finding out that your only child has killed someone else's child.'

As he spoke, his mask fell. It was possible to see the physical pain in Wendelmann's face. And the tears started to run down his cheeks.

I could not bear to look at him for a second longer, so I thanked him for having told us the truth, and said that we would talk again later. With Helgesen at my heels, I left the office without looking back.

Rikke Johansen was standing outside with a large bunch of keys in one hand, and Rolf Johan Svendsen's hand in the other. They both looked at me expectantly. I gave a quick nod, but said nothing.

As I saw them heave a sigh of relief, I thought to myself that the iron curtain had now finally fallen. Two of the people who had shown their true faces were standing in front of me, and I tried to feel happy for them. And for Robert Enger, who from tomorrow on was free to live his own life, even though tonight he would sit by his sister's bed in the hospital. Amalie's murder really had been a catalyst killing that had ruined the lives of some of those involved, in the course of a few days.

I suddenly felt enormous sympathy for the man I had disregarded as an emotionally cold businessman on Friday, even though he had subsequently lied to us. His situation, and likewise the rest of the case, served as a reminder of the dangers of having children. But I didn't have the time to follow this thought through.

'NO!' screamed the secretary, and pointed over my shoulder, her hand shaking.

I spun round and all four of us rushed to the windows.

Outside, his face turned away from us, a man stood as though in thin air. As he turned to look at us, I felt we had stepped back two days in time.

The man standing there now was of course not Christoffer Meyer-Michelsen. This man had not just received the news that his only daughter had been murdered, but he had learned that his only son was a murderer.

For a brief moment he raised his hand in a final greeting. His face was without expression, as though carved in stone.

Then he jumped, like a diver, head first.

Afterword

The publication of this novel in August 2014 amounts to a broken promise, for which I hope my readers can forgive me, and calls for a good explanation.

In the afterword to my last novel, *Chameleon People*, I wrote a year ago that there was little chance there would be a new novel in the series before 2015. Having written five books about K2 and Patricia in four years, I was determined that both they and myself should be given some time off in 2014.

But that did not happen.

This was largely due to the encouraging response that *Chameleon People* garnered from critics and readers alike. The feedback in Norway, and growing interest in the series in other countries, inspired me to continue as quickly as possible. My decision was to some extent influenced by the fact that what had previously been nothing more than a vague idea quickly developed into a complete plan for a new novel about K2 and Patricia over the course of autumn 2013. By the turn of the year, my editor and I were so excited by the idea that after a very short discussion, we agreed to change the publication schedule.

I should therefore be cautious now about what I promise in

this afterword with regard to my plans for 2015. At the same time, I want to be as open as possible about my literary plans for next year and the continuation of this series. My intention is primarily to publish a novel called *The Snow Was Pure*, as the first book in a new crime series from another interesting period in our history. But it is highly likely that another new novel about K2 and Patricia will be given priority once again in 2015.

I am extremely pleased with the way my publisher, Cappelen Damm, has nurtured my historical crime series. And in particular, I owe heartfelt thanks to my loyal, and at times sorely tested, editor, Anne Fløtaker, for our open and constructive discussions about the idea behind this novel and the finished manuscript. Thanks are also due to Anders Heger and Nils Nordberg for their expertise and comments on the historical and literary aspects of the manuscript.

When finishing this book, I felt more than ever how fortunate I am to be able to make a living from writing novels, but even more, how lucky I am to have such good friends. One of them, Mina Finstad Berg, must be thanked first of all – partly for her comments, but most of all for so gladly lending me her literary alter ego, Miriam Filtvedt Bentsen. I also owe my great thanks to my talented and helpful friends for all their comments, big and small: Isabel Algard, Roar Annerløv, Ingrid Baukhol, Marit Lang-Ree Finstand, Silje Flesvik, Kristine Amalie Myhre Gjesdal, Oda Holm Gulbrandsen, Else Marit Hatledal, Astrid Uhrenholdt Jacobsen, Kristine Joramo, Bjarte Leer-Salvesen, Espen Lie, Edit Machlik, Ellisiv Reppen, Elise Cathrin Dalsbotten Solvåg, Kathrine Berg Syversen, Yonne Tangelder, Arne Tjølsen, Katrine Tjølsen and Magnhild K. B. Uglem. Of these, Ingrid, Ellisiv and Arne deserve extra thanks this time for their extensive and detailed comments on the language and content. Arne has also earned a well-deserved five-year plaque as medical adviser to me and my crime novels.

With the exception of Miriam Filtvedt Bentsen, the number of literary characters based on real people in this novel is limited to two journalists and one Club 7 manager from 1972. I am very grateful to the only one of the three who is still alive, Knut Haavik, a journalist on *Verdens Gang* at that time, for allowing me to use him without trying to influence the content of the book.

This is the most psychological of all my novels, in that certain chapters in seven of the eight days are written in the first person from the perspective of the murderer. And, as the novel is about a serial killer, it also has the most extensive and complex gallery of characters. Other than reading newspapers from spring 1972, I have benefited enormously from reading a selection of books about life in Oslo at the time, including Knut Haavik's autobiography, *A Hack In The Spotlight*, Marta Breen's *Radka Toneff, Her Short Life and Loud Voice*, and Tor Egil Førland's *Club 7*.

Among the people I have consulted, I give particular thanks to my fellow author, Paul Leer-Salvesen, for his detailed descriptions of student life at the Norwegian School of Theology in Oslo in 1972. There are no doubt people who were there at the time, or who experienced other social environments mentioned in the book, who may not recognize the descriptions given here. I hope that they will forgive any artistic licence I may have used. Those who lived through the events of the early 1970s often have strikingly different memories of the time.

I have decided to dedicate *The Anthill Murders* to one of the literary greats of our country, Jonas Lie (1833–1908). This is partly because Jonas Lie's groundbreaking novel *When The Iron Curtain Falls*, which was published in 1901, plays a significant role in the ending of my book – but mostly because I believe that Jonas Lie was Norway's first great novelist, and one of the few still worth reading more than a century after his death. I would like to conclude with a thought-provoking quote from a former Norwegian foreign minister: 'This is my opinion – and I must respect it!'

Hans Olav Lahlum
Gjøvik, 18 June 2014

Reading over Kari Dickson's excellent work on the English translation of my novels is always a pleasure. To the three-year-old list of thanks from the Norwegian afterword, I need to add her name.

With the very next sentence, I should add more thanks to Josie Humber and all the other constructive-minded people working at Pan Macmillan. I am very thankful they have decided to continue translating my crime novel series into English. From an artistic point of view, I also very much appreciate Pan Macmillan's ongoing creativity in regards to my covers – succeeding every time in making them not only totally different from the Norwegian originals, but also continuously evolving them from the earlier English covers in the series . . .

The biggest thanks for making this book available in English I still owe to my agent and friend David Miller. My only sorrow about the English translation of this novel is that David did not live to read it. Last summer, a few months after his fiftieth birthday, David was in his usual dynamic and inspired mood when we met up in Norway. Nothing suggested he had any kind of health issue. Although we had a short discussion about life and death, the death part felt completely irrelevant to either of us. Still, this was to be our last meeting. We never got the chance to say goodbye, as David was struck by a massive heart attack on Christmas Eve 2016, and died five days later without regaining consciousness. I hope that I succeeded to tell David how much I appreciated his efforts to make my novels available for a wider audience. For the record and for eternity, I do it now by dedicating the English translation of this novel to his memory.

The Anthill Murders is my fifth novel in this classic crime series about K2 and Patricia, and at 460 pages, it is by far my longest. The number of pages is fitting as this novel includes considerably more – and increasingly varied – characters than any of my earlier books. The changing personal relationship between K2 and Patricia, too, takes another dramatic turn here. And by starting inside the mind of a serial killer waiting for his victim, *The Anthill Murders* is also the most psychological of the novels in this series. I am excited to see how English-speaking readers will react to this development, and hope you will enjoy this attempt to preserve the classic crime frame while introducing more depth to the picture. I will, anyway, be thankful to receive reactions from readers at hansolahlum@gmail.com.

Reading over my afterword from 2014 now, in 2017, I have to admit, that my history as an author (like my history as a chess player) remains a study in confusing and rapidly changing plans. Although I wrote the opening scene and decided on the final one sometime around 2013, and although I still find the idea of a new series of crime novels that take place in Norway during the Second World War highly attractive, I have still not succeeded in completing *The Snow Was Pure*. Instead, I finished a sixth novel with K2 and Patricia in 2015 and a seventh one in 2016. Every spring since 2013 I have finished a novel and told myself I will now give K2 and Patricia a year 'off duty', yet by the time autumn comes around I have always changed my mind, deciding to write 'just one more . . .' over the winter. Inspired by requests from surprisingly patient readers asking for more of K2 and Patricia, I somehow always become immersed in a new narrative for them. In that regard, the ongoing story about K2 and Patricia illustrates that such a crime series can be addictive not only for the readers, but also for the writer.

2017 will actually be the long-planned year off for K2 and Patricia, as I have just finished a new novel named *The Sign Of The Five*, starring two very different lead characters (and taking place in five other countries). To the critical question about whether the time period in this novel will be before or after K2 and Patricia's era in the sixties and early seventies, the answer is 'both'. Writing a standalone novel now, after a seven-novel series feels a bit like jumping into a pool without a diving board, but also without a straightjacket. I feel very relieved, very excited and a bit scared to test out this entirely different concept. Hopefully the result will soon be available in English, too.

Readers worrying about the future of K2 and Patricia can relax however, as I have written the first few chapters and more or less completed a – very different – synopsis for an eighth crime novel about them. Time will tell whether I complete this in 2018 or 2019, however the Norwegian series still has a head start on the English translations, so English friends of K2 and Patricia still have plenty more to come . . .

Hans Olav Lahlum

Gjøvik, April 8 2017